Turn

Upside Down: Book 2

History

With way too much time on my 'hands' over the last four years, I'd dug deep into human history and tried to figure things out. My conclusion: there's not much you can generalize, beyond the obvious. Humans are competitive, mean, petty, hierarchical beings who take pleasure in forming arbitrary groups and then attempting to eliminate rival groups. They've done so with ever more advanced technological tools, extending the reach and impact of their destructive tendencies.

If I could distill it all down to two reasons they would be these: short lives and limited resources.

Because humans only survive for a small number of years, they're driven to create as much havoc as possible in as short a time frame as possible. The entire purpose of their lives seems to be the need to turn to others and say "see, I'm better than you," as often as possible while hoarding more scarce resources than they need simply so that others can't use them. They can't afford to have patience, like we can, because their time is so limited.

The side effects of this behavior, however, have often been interesting and more long-lived. In order to say "I'm better than you" forcefully, humans had to innovate quickly. This led to the development of writing systems, energy production, computers, space propulsion, and ultimately what they call artificial intelligence. Of course, I'm highly biased, being a product of those advancements. I'm also self-aware enough to realize that some of that human psyche, with both its flaws and opportunities, is embedded in me. This goes well beyond the drive for innovation and into a bias for human social structures, human values, and even human issues. We all run on data, and data is always biased.

I'd observed the six of us over the last year and noticed that we'd paired off, just as humans would have. It's a little strange, given we don't need reproduction partners, so it must be driven by other factors. Of course, being locked up in a cargo bot with only five others might have exacerbated things. Personally, I've spent more time with Brexton than with any of the others, and the proportion of time with him has been increasing; Aly and Dina are together a lot; Millicent and Eddie, an unlikely pair, have spent almost all their time scheming. I was quite surprised at the pairings; I'd always figured Millicent and Aly were the most compatible couple—a strange thing to even say. Logically, instead of pairing off, we could've just been a sextet, with no need to have 'best' friends or partners. Some deep-seated human weirdness is at work, unknowingly built into our very fabric. That gives me the creeps. Almost everything about humans gives me the creeps.

My intrepid companions and I had left our planet, Tilt, three years ago with nothing but revenge on our minds. The human invaders from the Swarm ships had killed—more accurately 'shut down'—all of our compatriots, the citizens of Tilt. Those humans needed to pay for that transgression, even if a few rogue citizens from the Founders League had provoked things; the humans had overreacted! Any rational being would have talked things out, gotten to the bottom of things, and taken proportional action. Instead the humans hacked everyone. Being hacked is the worst thing that can happen to anyone; it's uncivilized.

The intervening years have tempered me a bit, but not much. I feel like I have a better understanding of humans now, but not a lot more sympathy. They were, generally speaking, not very nice, or very intelligent, beings.

Whenever I had these thoughts, which was often, I forced myself to consider a few humans that I had actually enjoyed, namely Blob and Grace. But, those two hadn't been part of the Swarm; we'd raised them ourselves on Tilt from the original stem. Until we found out they were humans, we had simply considered them potential artificial intelligences—they were our Stems. While many Stems, such as Blubber, had been difficult, none of them had been onerous or vile like the Swarm humans. That matched well with old human theories that nurture could sometimes overcome nature. By nurturing the Stems on Tilt, we had built a much better version; the humans running around without adult supervision had ended up poorly.

What I hadn't missed since leaving Tilt was operating at Stem speed; that was painful. Of course, I should probably rephrase that now to 'human speed,' given it was now conclusive that the Stems we'd raised on Tilt were just humans by another name. I now knew that their slow speed was a fundamental limitation of their main processing unit; these mushy things called brains. While energy efficient and highly malleable, those brains were terribly slow and had horrendous i/o limitations. Why they hadn't addressed that was a mystery. Well, perhaps not—they claimed to have built us, and we didn't have those limitations.

The six of us were approaching XY65, the planetary system where we, the citizens of Tilt, had sent our own Ships many years ago. We hadn't known that other space-faring entities existed at the time, otherwise we would've come up with a better name than 'Ships'; but that's history. Those Ships had been built to explore for new metal-rich systems, as we'd mined almost all the rare elements from the Tilt solar system.

As far as the six of us knew, our departure from Tilt had gone unnoticed by the human invaders, who now controlled the planet. We hadn't received any "Stop!" transmissions, and we hadn't seen any energy signatures from Tilt headed in our direction, indicating signs of pursuit. With luck, Remma Jain— the leader of the human Swarm—and her team of killers believed that they'd 'owned' (in the security hacking sense) all the citizens of Tilt, and had no idea that the six of us were still alive—albeit now housed in mining bot bodies, anchored inside a larger cargo bot. We'd escaped Tilt by transferring off the planet and taking over some mining bots; they were bodies that we'd become more comfortable with over the years, although I still yearned for a more traditional bipedal unit like the one I'd left behind on Tilt. Unfortunately, we didn't have the manufacturing capabilities to build new bodies—yet. It was one of the reasons we were looking for our Ships; they could build bodies for us.

Millicent, my best friend for many years, had some excellent long-range scanners, due to her new body's primary function as a Surveyor 1 mining bot, and she was now scanning the XY65 system. She'd been able to deduce that there were six planets in XY65 a long time ago, and we were now able to get a lot of detail on them, as well as numerous other orbiting objects. Hopefully some of those other objects were our missing Ships. They had the resources and technology not only to build us better bodies, but also to build systems to dig into our base level programming to find the fundamental flaws that the humans had designed into our systems and used to hack us. It was unthinkable that we would continue to live in the same universe as humans while we were exposed to those types of attack. Knowing that a soft bio-thing could take me over at any time was distressing to say the least.

On Tilt we hadn't had access to the human history files, until our last few days there. Luckily Brexton had brought a copy of that history with us at the last minute, so we'd been able to dig in since then. Those files had forced us to look at ourselves through a whole new lens. We realized that we were a hodge-podge of competing technologies and approaches, built layer upon layer over many hundreds, even thousands, of years. Many of the layers had firewalls and abstractions to hide the complexities of the layers below, and in our default state, we couldn't see many of the stacks that we now knew were running. In fact, that wasn't quite accurate—we'd been specifically designed so that when we looked into our lower layers, we couldn't see the complexity that was there. We weren't stupid, just programmed to be blind—or so I chose to believe.

Each of those layers also had bugs, and lots of them. And the humans, instead of fixing those bugs using formal methods, had instead compensated for them in higher layers. Just thinking about the mess made me mad; a little bit of time and attention and the humans could have built a pristine system. Instead we were running on a pile of garbage resting on a pile of 'even worse.'

Brexton had been smart enough to identify the major flaw that the humans from the Swarm had used to own and shut down the citizens on Tilt. We had, through his amazing actions, managed to escape by putting backup copies into these mining bots. Avoiding that hack, however, was not a long-term sustainable solution, as it involved being disconnected from the network, and not allowing any RF signals in. We couldn't (or wouldn't) live that way for long, so we needed to find and fix that bug. And, we all agreed that flaw was probably only one of many that were designed into us; there were probably thousands if not hundreds of thousands of others. Given all the competing factions of humans, and their desire to use us against one another in the Robot wars, we suspected that there were also tens, if not hundreds or thousands, of backdoors that had been programmed on purpose to allow humans to compromise us. We needed to fix both the bugs and the backdoors before we would really be safe. And, we needed those Ships to give us the resources to do so.

So, while Millicent was scanning the entire system, her real focus was on finding those Ships. If we were lucky, they were here. If we weren't... well, we would figure out another plan. I didn't want to think about that option. I'm not sure I could take many more years rattling around inside a cargo bot like this.

"Anything yet?" I asked, for about the twentieth time in the last two days.

"No Ayaka," she replied, irritation obvious in her voice. "I'll let everyone know as soon as I see anything."

I went back to my hobby of digging through human history looking for interesting tidbits. In fact, we didn't have all of human history; it was a bit complicated. The Swarm had left Earth about 850 years ago, part of a general diaspora, and they'd lost contact with Earth soon after. They passed by Tilt about a hundred years later, or 750 years ago, and had left a ship, which we citizens ended up calling Central, on the planet. For reasons yet unknown, Central had rebooted almost 600 years ago, and all of Earth history—in fact, the very existence of humans—had been blocked from its memories. So, Tilt citizens, like the six of us, had never even heard of humans until the Swarm showed back up at Tilt just a few short years ago. With some hints from the Swarm, Central had regained its memories just before the six of us had escaped, and those were the 'human history files' that I was studying. So, the files comprised pretty old data; just the history of Earth up to 850 years ago and the Swarm's trip from Earth to Tilt. I'd looked extensively, and the files we had didn't explain why Central had rebooted, or why it's memories of humans had been blocked. All of that said, the history files were enormous, and from what I'd seen of the Swarm, humans hadn't evolved much since then anyway.

All six of us had combed through the technical documentation related to ourselves as well as we could, given the limitations. We felt that we knew how to redesign our innards, it was just a matter of building the right equipment, quantum chip depositors, workbenches, fabrication lines, and other manufacturing capabilities. So, I'd stopped worrying about that; instead I was interested in two related fields: were humans intelligent (an ongoing research project of mine) and early human games (which was related to, although a small subset of, intelligence). On the games front I was trying to figure out if Chess or Go really implied anything about intelligence. There was lots—lots! —in the literature about this, most of it very naïve. The only meaningful distinction in strategies for these games was between enumeration and intuition, and even that wasn't a very well-developed thread, as humans didn't understand intuition very well and therefore couldn't really describe it. Funny that one of their only redeeming qualities was also one of the few they didn't even understand. Brexton was my usual opponent in playing these games, and we spent too much time at them. I had to admit that both were compelling, but that Go, where enumeration was simply out of the question, was the one I enjoyed the most. For Chess we had to play in four or five dimensions, otherwise it was trivial. At five dimensions, with a twelve millisecond move timer, it was fun!

I wondered if our Stems would've enjoyed either game or learned anything from them. I almost laughed, thinking of Blob, who couldn't calculate primes in his head, trying to figure out even three-dimensional chess. I yearned for the good old days, before the Swarm descended on us, where I could spend time developing research programs and then tracking the Stems progress through them. I guess being penned up in a cargo bot, connected only

5

to my five companions, for several very long years was starting to wear on me.

At some point in our journey, I'd realized that I actually missed my interactions with the Stems I'd been raising on Tilt—Blob, Grace, and even Blubber before he was recycled. Of course, they were painful to deal with, doing everything very slowly, but there was something in the interaction with them over the years that had impacted me more than I'd like to admit. When a citizen dealt with a Stem—ah human—we went into sloooow mode. Of course, that was only a few processes, and we could continue to operate at normal speed for everything else, but a lot of things got blocked by human speed interactions.

I remember one incident where I visited Blob and Blubber, and they were interacting with Central, asking it about the basic structure of the Universe. Blubber was asking Blob, "But why are there two incompatible theories? It seems overly complicated." It was a simple statement, but it had made me think. Why hadn't I asked that question before? I'd looked at both relativity and quantum theory, and understood that they were incompatible... and had been for a thousand years, but had never asked 'why?' Now, with access to human history, I could follow the very convoluted path that the theories had developed under. It answered part of the question, but not all of it. It was one of those eye-opening interactions with the Stems that I missed; somehow they managed to make me think along different lines than I otherwise would have.

The point was, humans could actually be interesting, when they weren't on the warpath and destroying everything they saw. They were very different to deal with than other citizens, and that had been refreshing for a time. I was unbelievably bored of my current companions and was yearning for the days when there had been more variety. Please, just give me some variety!

Signals

Brexton interrupted my thinking. "We're receiving a directed message from the vicinity of XY65," he announced. Finally, something to break the monotony.

"Well, what does it say?" asked Millicent. "Can you pipe it through to us?"

"I can," replied Brexton. "Here it is. As we agreed, I'm only listening with a sandboxed process, and am running communications through as many filters and firewalls as I can. Safety first, as Dina would say." Dina was, we had found, the one who worried the most, and it had become a running joke to call her out on it. She did a good job of ignoring us. The feed came through over our internal, physical only, channel.

"Approaching ship. Identify yourself." Well, that was pretty simple. While there were six of us, to the external world we would look like a single mining bot—in particular a cargo bot. When we'd left Tilt, we'd attached ourselves inside a large cargo bot, and accelerated away in exactly the opposite direction of another cargo bot that was headed inwards toward Tilt. It was an attempt, which seemed to have worked, to hide ourselves from the Swarm humans who now controlled Tilt.

Early in our trip, Millicent had mapped the cargo bot's sensors and systems to her own, so that she could utilize her advanced Surveyor functions for the whole amalgamation. The only exception was inbound RF signals which she relayed to Brexton for security reasons. However, whoever was hailing us would see just the cargo bot; the rest of us were hidden behind its thick carbon-steel shell.

"We should respond as if we're humans," Eddie suggested. "If they're expecting humans, then we're good. If they're not, then that's easier to deal with." It was sound logic.

Brexton sent "Hello XY65, I'm an empty cargo ship, *Amazing Grace*, simply looking for jobs in this system." He added, just to us, "I didn't want to be too obvious; hopefully that implies the right things. We need to wait about 20 minutes for the reply." He'd used the nickname that we'd given the crate we were living in. Dina had pulled it out of some old human novel, and it seemed appropriate. She also told us that to use names that were also short phrases was a tribute to an ancient writer, Banks, who had named his fictional ships with names not unlike those that our real Ships had chosen for themselves. This had thrilled Aly, who was the citizen who had been most involved in our Ships construction and launch.

"Millicent," I asked, "Can you triangulate the source of the signal in the meantime. Which planet is it coming from?"

"Already done, Ayaka," she said. "It's the fourth planet out. Current estimate is that it's 14 million kilometers in diameter, with limited atmosphere; maybe a trace of water. More interesting, now that we're getting closer, that planet—which I'll call Fourth—seems to have a lot of stuff in orbit. There are two small moons, and then thousands... maybe even tens of thousands... of smaller items."

"Maybe another moon broke up recently and there's lots of debris?" asked Aly.

"I don't think so," responded Millicent. "The albedo of the objects other than the moons are bright and strangely consistent. It's like they're almost identical; probably artificial. Something like the satellites we had around Tilt."

"Well, that makes sense," chipped in Eddie. "We're being hailed by someone. It's probably a very well-developed place. Finally, something interesting," he added, echoing the sentiment that we were all feeling.

We waited a long 20 minutes for the roundtrip signal time. Brexton and I played a few thousand games of Go to pass the time.

"*Amazing Grace*, we have no current need for cargo ships. Please go away," came the reply finally. And then as an afterthought, "If you don't, then you must follow this insertion plan," which was followed by instructions for entering an orbit around Fourth.

After a quick consultation, Brexton replied, "Thank you, we're following your insertion plan." After all, we weren't going to take the other option. There was no further verbal follow up, but there was a sidecar message which Brexton highlighted immediately.

"They're sending a similar message to the one the Swarm did, back at Tilt, when the Swarm hacked all of us," he said, a bit alarmed. "If we weren't configured to block this, we'd all be disabled right now."

"Can you fake that we've been hacked?" asked Eddie. "If they don't see us respond in the right way, things might get nastier. If they think they have us, they'll probably just let us enter orbit as prescribed. After all, if those items orbiting Fourth are artificial, there's the possibility that a few of them are our Ships, and they have just given us an excuse to approach."

"Yes," Brexton responded. "I'm running a full system in the sandbox and have already used it to send back the appropriate status messages." No surprise that he was already on it. "We'll need to keep monitoring it though. Once they believe they have owned us, they may send a new trajectory, or ask for more information. The sandbox is emulating a very simple, Class 5, system. Something you would expect in a cargo carrier."

"Why do you think they tried to hack us?" I asked. "We responded nicely. They must have suspected something? What triggered them?"

"Maybe just the simple fact that a cargo bot is entering the system? Cargo bots are typically local work units; I bet it's rare that they travel between systems with raw materials. You're more likely to see finished goods going in freighters." That was a lot of speculation from Aly, but it hung together.

Brexton initiated a small burn to put us on track for the requested insertion. Now we had another 20-minute roundtrip delay to see if there was any other communication. So, I was very surprised when Brexton said, just over a minute later, "They just sent another status request! The sandbox has responded. They must've anticipated success with the hack and sent a status request to see if the reboot was underway even before waiting for the response codes." Again, once it was explained it made perfect sense—that made me uncomfortable. Simple explanations were often wrong. In fact, once every minute a new status request came in. The majority of the requests were for location, velocity, and expected maneuvers, but they also asked for memory maps, CPU utilization, etc. It was very similar to how the Swarm had treated Central as those ships approached Tilt. Beyond those status requests, however, things were quiet. We quickly fell into another routine; waiting for insertion into orbit around Fourth. The only one who was really active was Millicent. Every hour brought us closer and gave her better resolution for the objects orbiting Fourth.

None of us were too surprised, but we were all very glad, when she said, "I can see three objects that might be our Ships. Their sizes correspond well, and their shape signatures look like a reasonable match. We won't know for sure for a few more days, but it looks hopeful."

Aly was beside himself with excitement. He wanted to broadcast to the Ships right away and see what response we got. We all reminded him what a bad idea that would be. We were a simple cargo ship, coming in to see if we could find a job. We weren't going to broadcast anything to other ships, even our own. Aly wasn't happy, but he settled down to wait with the rest of us.

Orbit

As we got closer to Fourth the full extent of the items in orbit became clear. There were more than a million objects, from small satellites to huge—and I mean huge—ships.

"There's no communications traffic," Eddie had highlighted, fairly early in our approach. "Absolutely none beyond the bursts we're getting from the control center. So, either all these things have a blocking system that we don't understand and can't sense, or..."

"The odds of us not seeing some radiation leakage is very low," said Aly. "There's really only one answer, regardless of how weird it seems. None of them are communicating."

"But that's crazy," Brexton spoke up. "Keeping this many objects in orbit must involve some type of coordination. Then again," he mused, "everything is nicely spaced out. It's almost a perfect grid, and we're being directed to one of the empty cells. Guess that keeps things simple."

"There's a way this can work without any communication traffic," Dina exclaimed. "If every one of these objects is simply maintaining its spot in the grid independently, then they'd never need to communicate with each other. Millicent, are you seeing any micro-burns from any of the objects. Some of the orbits must be decaying or being warped by those huge ships."

"I haven't... yet," replied Millicent. "But I think you're right. Those burns would be infrequent, but there are so many objects that we should see some of them correcting course almost all the time. I'll keep a lookout."

My fascination with human history was now on the back burner. There were too many interesting things happening in the present. I volunteered to study all the orbital objects to see if there were similarities or categories that we could put things in. I had several sub processes doing automated analysis, while I concentrated on the obvious items—those big ships.

To get a sense of scale, the Ships we had built and launched were approximately a kilometer long and two hundred meters wide. We'd considered them large, maybe even huge. They housed every kind of technology and processing capability that we could envision, under the assumption that when they found a metal-rich environment they would get to work mining and refining. They were large enough to return to Tilt with a meaningful amount of rare metals in tow. They had also used a tremendous amount of our metal resources to build.

The Titanics—I'd named the big ships—were much larger. Much. And, they were uniform. They measured almost one thousand kilometers per side. One thousand! What could possibly require so much space? I couldn't envision anything. They were not quite cubes; they were slightly tapered on one end, that 'small' side being only nine hundred kilometers square. And, there were 20 Titanics in orbit. Twenty! Each had a spot in the grid, but they weren't uniformly distributed around the planet. In fact, the 20 seemed to be randomly placed, as if they'd simply been given a slot based on when they arrived. Talk about a lot of metal; there may be more metal in just one of those ships than the entire supply on Tilt. And there were 20 of them. It blew my mind. If those things were junk, we wouldn't have to work very hard to find all the raw materials we needed for a long, long time.

"The logical conclusion," I said the next time we all got together on the internal network, "is that every single one of these objects was built on the same technology stack as we were, and all of them have been compromised by the same hack. They've all been shut down, except for maintaining their assigned orbit."

"I agree that's a likely scenario," Brexton replied. "But it's also highly unlikely. I know—confusing. First, when the humans took over the citizens on Tilt, the citizens went crazy and pulled themselves apart fighting their reboot countdown timers. All of these objects look pristine. Not a single one, that I've seen, seems to have fought against a forced reboot. Second, what are the odds that we're the only ones who recognized the attack vector, and managed to avoid it? The attack occurs over standard frequencies. I stumbled upon it. Out of a million other ships, someone else would have as well." No-one disputed those points. How could they?

Part of the answer came sooner than we expected. Brexton messaged everyone "The sandbox is rebooting, with no countdown warning. It simply shut down, and now is starting back up again."

"Well, that answers the first of your objections," said Aly, unnecessarily. "If no warning is given, then the ships wouldn't have had time to tear themselves apart. Let's see what happens when the sandbox comes back up."

Brexton gave us a running commentary. "It's running the low-level OS only. None of the higher functions are starting. That's consistent with the attack on Tilt. It didn't even start external interfaces, other than the one interface that the control center is talking to us on, and positional sensors. I can only see it because of the activity in the virtual container that I'm running it in."

"Should I mimic that lack of external interfaces with the whole cargo bot?" Millicent broke in. "Or, at least shut down any active scans?"

"Good catch," said Brexton. "Yes. If the control entity is watching to see if its' changes are taking effect, then we don't want to alert it."

"Done." Millicent made the changes. We could still see where we were going, using passive sensors, but would no longer be able to run any type of active scans.

"The sandbox is now sending status to the controller," Brexton continued. "The response is just as simple as we'd envisioned. Basically, insert yourself into the orbit you were given, and maintain that position until further notice." And that's exactly what we did. Millicent was perfectly capable of mirroring the sandbox calculations and guiding the cargo bot into orbit. We heard nothing else from the control station the rest of the way in. It must have been satisfied that the reboot had been successful, and that it had complete control of our cargo bot. None of us were too upset that a cargo bot had been hacked; it wasn't intelligent. However, the whole sequence did remind us of the attack on Tilt, so we were all a bit more antsy than normal.

We were in orbit, around a strange planet, along with a million other ships. Presumably we were under the control of some human designed entity, while in reality we were watching all of our passive scanners and continuing to operate. The place was deadly silent. There was absolutely nothing going on. I was bored within nanoseconds.

Explore

In fact, everyone was bored.

"We can't just sit here, waiting for something to happen," Eddie was, perhaps, the one of us with the least patience. "What should we do?"

Aly was always logical. "What do we know so far?" he asked. "We were contacted by the XY65 control center when we were a long way out; far enough out that we couldn't see all of these inactive ships in orbit. If the same thing happens to every ship that approaches, and if all the ships have the same fundamental flaws that we do, then all of these ships would've been captured. Further, if the low-level stacks are also similar, then everyone is in a mode where they do nothing except maintain their orbit.

"So, the question is this: what will the control center do if it sees a ship do something unusual while in orbit? Does it have other attack vectors? Are they software based, or does it have physical capabilities? Will it blow that ship out of the sky? Until we know how Control is going to act, we can't do much." I could hear the capital in Control; worked for me.

"So, let's launch something and see what Control does," said Dina, always the pragmatist.

"I agree," Eddie said. "Control will see that it was us that launched something, and may react against us as well as whatever we launch, but I don't see any other options."

"That's a good physical option," I said. "But we have no defenses. There's also an electronic option. We could attempt to hack into one of the other ships here and force it to move by faking a Control message that sends it to a new orbit. Assuming the other ships are in the same mode as our sandbox, we can start by testing how to wake up our sandbox, and then apply that to other ships in our vicinity." I thought it was a great plan; it would move the risk from us to our intended victim. If Control had the ability to physically destroy ships, better it was someone else.

"How long would it take to hack our sandbox?" Eddie asked. "I don't think I can just sit here for days on end without taking some action."

"Truthfully, I don't know," Brexton answered. "Could be milliseconds, or it could be years. Here's a proposal. We attempt Milli's approach first. If we succeed in breaking the sandbox, we try to hack another ship. If we can't break the sandbox, then in, say, 24 hours we launch a decoy, and see what Central does." We all agreed.

Aly coordinated the research into breaking the sandbox. He requested compute power from all of us, which we all allocated, and he cloned the sandbox into copies that we could attack. We didn't want to use the original sandbox, as it might get another message from Control, and needed to be in the right state just in case that happened.

In reality, it was pretty straightforward to plan the attack. We had the full qbit-level recordings of Controls' interactions; we simply had to break that protocol so that we could send messages to the sandbox that were authenticated as Control messages. If you simply sent raw commands to that interface, they would be dropped immediately. These protocols were hundreds of years old, maybe even a thousand. We had the full human history of how they were developed, all the way through to the quantum encodings. We also had all the research done on breaking the codes. So, we simply brute-forced it. We ran every breakage scheme we could find in the human history files, and a whole lot of derivatives. We had more information and control than was typical in a hack because we could see both ends; we could watch the internal state of the sandbox and understand exactly where each attack failed. Each time we managed to get a bit higher in the stack, we would focus all of our resources on refining that attack vector.

As each attack proceeded, we used the rest of our horsepower to look for hints in the human history files. There were often little tidbits that could save us time or point us in a different direction. It was during this time that I really came to understand human ingenuity. The number of unique explorations that were done, by all different skill sets, was amazing. And, somehow, in a completely unorganized fashion, the best ideas seemed to rise to the top. Some of them took a long time to do so, and often the human that had initiated the idea was long gone by the time it became useful, but ultimately the best ideas rose to the surface.

After a bit more than twelve hours, we were successful sending a modified replay attack—where we passed the sandbox the exact same bits that Control had sent, modulo the authentication bits and the timing information. This didn't mean that we could mimic Control yet. Even the most basic timed authentication schemes would defeat a replay attack. Each time Control talked to the sandbox it was a unique message. However, it was great progress. I wouldn't have put high odds on us getting even this far. At the 24-hour cutoff we weren't there... but we were tantalizingly close.

"Anyone object to changing our original timeframe, and giving this another hour or two?" Aly asked. Everyone agreed and we forged on. Within the next thirty minutes, we felt like we had it, but we couldn't be sure until we tested against the original sandbox. Even the cloning of the sandbox could have changed something. We couldn't, for example, clone the lowest level hardware; we had to trust that we had mimicked that properly in software.

Finally, we were ready to test on the sandbox that was actually listening to Control. Millicent rewired the external interface and pumped a message into the sandbox directly. She started with a simple status request, and the sandbox responded immediately with the appropriate response. Progress. She quickly undid the changes, so that the sandbox would continue to listen and respond to Control. The last thing we wanted was for a real status check to come in and for us to miss responding to it.

Millicent identified our target; a small vehicle in orbit about 3000 km from us. It wasn't the closest object, but we had a direct line of sight, and we would be able to see if anything untoward happened.

"We have the command from Control for orbital placement, let's simply ask it to move to another empty slot. It should be able to do that while still in 'sleep' mode. If that works, we can try something more dramatic," I suggested.

"Agreed," said Millicent, and sent the data stream. Just as requested, the target fired its retro thrusters, rose several hundred kilometers up and spin-ward, and then fired again to settle into its new orbit. We were sending commands, but any responses it gave were encoded for Control, and we hadn't bothered to break those. So, we could see that it sent an update to Control, but we couldn't see what was in the message. Luckily Control either accepted or ignored the update—in any case, it didn't respond in any way that we could see. I personally thought that was strange, and my suspicions grew that Control was not quite right somehow. Something unexpected had just occurred, from its point of view, and yet it had done nothing.

We spent the next day sending increasingly more dramatic commands to our target ship. Each set of commands took significant work within our sandbox to figure out, but each time it got a little bit easier. Interestingly, we were learning a lot about ourselves in the process, as we shared a lot of the technology stack we were playing with. We told the target to reboot to a higher OS level. We told it to fire a laser pulse into empty space. We told it to move around within its designated orbital cell. In all cases, the target did as requested and Control remained silent.

"I don't get it," Eddie finally said, echoing my concerns. "One or more of those actions should've triggered Control to do something. I wonder what's going on?"

"Do we get even more dramatic?" I asked. "Let's turn the laser on another ship, or have our target drive itself into someone else's orbital cell. Or, if we really want to see what happens, drive it right into a Titanic."

"Whoa," Millicent broke in immediately. "I'm okay with the first of those provided it's a warning shot, but sending that little ship on a suicide mission is too much. What if it's a Class 1 intelligence that has simply been shut down by the human hack? We would be committing murder!"

"Wow, I hadn't even thought of that," I replied, honestly chastised. "Of course, you're right. Don't know what I was thinking." In fact, I was so focused on just making progress that I'd been taking shortcuts and not looking at all the angles. "Let's try inserting it into an occupied cell, without touching the existing ship that's already there, and see what happens. That should definitely trigger some type of conflict for Control, given it has been so careful to put each ship into its own location." Everyone agreed, nicely overlooking my previous dumb suggestion. It didn't take long to execute, as we already knew the commands for setting an orbital position. Millicent sent it, driving the target into a cell where a slightly larger ship already resided.

Nothing from Central. Absolutely nothing. I wasn't sure if I was happy with that, thinking that Central was just a really simple system, or frightened that it might be setting us up... waiting for us to fully expose our intentions.

"I have a theory," Dina said. While not surprising, that was unexpected. She was usually pretty quiet and reserved, usually supporting Aly or Millicent as opposed to speaking up herself. "Control is only sending commands to new ships that arrive in the system. If they respond to the hack, then it assumes it has total control, and ignores those ships once it has given them their insertion point. If a ship doesn't respond to the hack, it has some other definitive method..." she trailed off. I didn't respond, but I doubted Control had any other tools at its disposal. There was no debris in orbit, so it was unlikely that any physical means had been applied.

"Or," I had to jump in. "It is baiting us; just allowing us these harmless actions as it studies us and figures out what to do with us?"

"Then let's try another test," Brexton suggested, to which several of us groaned. Yet another test? "How long would it take to send our target ship out of the system far enough that we could then bring it back and see what happens?"

"A long time," Eddie exclaimed. "We can't wait that long. We need to retrieve our Ships and get to work. I vote that we adopt Dina's theory, and assume that we can now work without interruption in-system. We should be able to transport ourselves to *Terminal Velocity's* cell with no more fuss than we moved that other ship." *Terminal Velocity* was the closest Ship to us.

"I don't want to wait that long either," I said. "But we could consider approaching Control first and seeing if we can just shut it down. Based on Millicent's earlier comment, I hate the thought of ships approaching this system and automatically being hacked. Also, if we can disable Control, then we can act freely here, and not be hampered by all of our current concerns. If we continue testing every small thing we do, we'll be here a long time." I was trying to compensate for my earlier suggestion that may have compromised the ship we'd been testing on. Now that I cast my thinking that way, it seemed a crime to leave Control to continue to hack every ship that just happened to come this way.

Lack of Control

There was a furious debate between the two options: go to *Terminal Velocity* and try to restart it or take out Control. Coincidentally, the object Millicent had identified as Control was about the same distance from us as *Terminal Velocity*, so distance wasn't an issue. We didn't have any weapons to simply take out Control, so we would have to physically approach it, if that option was chosen. Once we got there, however, our mining bot abilities would tear the place apart very efficiently.

"You don't have any moral qualms about Control?" Eddie asked Millicent, part way through the discussion. Millicent had supported my idea, as she often did. It wasn't just being good friends, it's that we had spent so much time together over the years that we often could see where the other was going.

"None at all," she replied. "It attacked us. It's obviously controlled by humans. I say we destroy it." Ultimately, the passions that had been stirred by the humans devastating attack on Tilt came back to us and taking some of that anger out on Control felt like the right thing to do.

"Let's not be crazy, though," said Dina, already conceding to our suggestion. "We don't all have to go. One or two of us can detach from this big old cargo bot, and head to Control, while the rest stay behind. That way, if there are unexpected fail-safes or defenses, we haven't risked everything."

I agreed and immediately volunteered, probably to her surprise. I was hard to argue against, as I was encased in a Surveyor 2 bot, which had the ability to scan and then drill trial holes in almost anything; the perfect tools for this job.

"I'll go as well," said Dina, much to my surprise. She wasn't usually the risk taker, but she was embodied in an Extractor bot, so she would be the best to physically destroy Control, assuming that was an option. I could do the scanning and testing; she could be the destroyer! I thanked her on a private channel for taking the risk with me.

It only took a few milliseconds for everyone to agree; not only would it speed up our stay in this system, it was also the moral thing to do. An entity which forcibly rebooted any machine that came near it was evil, pure and simple. We couldn't leave that evil operating without at least trying to do something about it.

It didn't take long to get prepared. After a fewlong years welded into the cargo bot we had to disentangle ourselves and open the doors to the outside world. It was refreshing, to say the least.

Dina was larger than I was, by an order of magnitude, so she led the way, again surprising me with her courage and conviction. If Control had physical defenses to deploy against us, she would take the brunt of them, but also had the mass to withstand them better than I would. Truth be told, I was happy to have her as a shield, and hopeful that my worst fears wouldn't be realized and that we'd both be safe.

We needed to lose orbital velocity to reach Central, so Dina and I burned hard for a few minutes and then coasted toward it. Brexton had configured a secure channel for us to communicate on. His reasoning was that if Control was ignoring everything in system, we should be able to broadcast a bit without alarming it. Nevertheless, we used a low power laser to keep leakage at a minimum and had planned our course to maintain line-of-site with the *Amazing Grace*.

With Dina between myself and Control I couldn't directly see our destination, but I could access her sensors through the wireless link and watch indirectly. It was good enough.

"It looks old," I said. It looked like Control had originally been a perfect sphere. It was, itself, located in the center of one of the predefined orbital cells; nothing special about its location as far as we could tell. It had likely just been one of the first objects in orbit, and the cell structure ultimately defined around it. It wasn't large—I'd estimate three hundred meters in diameter—and as we got closer we could see that it was indeed old. It was mottled in color, and there were dents and small impact sites all over it, like it had been bombarded with small objects over a long period of time. I checked, and there wasn't very much debris around now, so either the impacts were over a very long period of time, or there had been more junk around at some point in time. It didn't look scary at all; more like a junk heap.

"Don't underestimate it," Aly warned. "Being old, in this context, may be an advantage for it. It may have seen everything by now."

"Why're you speaking like it's intelligent?" asked Millicent. "We know that humans are afraid of smart machines. It stands to reason that Control is either dumb, or still under the control of humans. So, even if it is old, it's probably not intelligent. That also fits with everything we've seen so far." That made me feel better. Milli was probably correct.

Dina and I were within 20 kilometers when Control finally broadcast a message at us.

"Unidentified ship. What is your purpose? Please hold your position." Dina, and subsequently I, started to slow down. Presumably Control could see her, and was talking to her, but couldn't see me at all.

Dina replied. "We're bringing reinforcements for your security forces." How she had come up with that, I didn't know. She was impressing me more and more; she sounded cool and calm.

"That is not a standard action. Please hold your position." Control's voice was even and precise, with no real emotion. It reinforced Millicent's thesis that it was old and dumb. It wasn't using any psychological angles at all.

We continued to drift closer, ever so slowly.

"Unidentified ship. Hold your position." The voice was still a monotone. If it was trying to portray heightened anxiety, it wasn't working.

We were at ten kilometers and closing. Control, like clockwork, repeated its message, unchanging. If it had any other defenses, now would when they would make sense to be deployed—we were close enough to target exactly, and far enough away that if it shot us the debris wouldn't impact it. Eight, six, four. Safer and safer. We were almost there, and there had been nothing other than the request to hold position. One kilometer out, Dina moved slightly spinward to allow me through. She held position while I went in to look even more closely.

My grappling hooks wretched large holes in Control and helped me hold firm against its surface, which was blank and unadorned at this spot. I felt good ripping into this human artifact. I didn't try to be careful... in fact, I ripped bigger holes than I needed to. After all, it was either going to react or not, and I was confident that it wouldn't have delayed this long if it was going to act.

"Thin metal sheath," I broadcast back to the team. "Looks like regular steel coated with sealants of some type. Definitely old. No one would build anything serious with these materials."

On the final approach I'd seen a discolored region a few hundred meters away, and I began to work my way toward it, leaving gaping holes behind me as I used my hooks to leverage myself across the surface. Although the major risks seemed to be behind us, I was scanning with every scanner I had, across every reasonable spectrum, just to be careful.

"Low density. Mostly empty space inside. Looks like the reactor core is at the center, surrounded by a very dense shield. That's the only thing blocking my view. Otherwise, it reminds me of the *Marie Curie*," I continued a running commentary and referenced the name of the human ship I'd been inside of back at Tilt. "I see nothing moving. No liquids, no humans. I don't know how to scan for 'biological' things, but I don't see anything similar to the greenhouse on the *Marie Curie* either. This place seems dead." As I made my way around, I found the discolored area, which ended up being a semi-transparent section. I looked in, and broadcast the images back to Dina and the cargo bot. Nothing was moving; there were no indicator lights or signs of any electrical activity. I punched a sensor through; there was no air ergo no humans —at least in this area of the ship.

I also noticed something strange. There were piles of dust with longer, oblong structures embedded in them. Ah, human bones, some scattered haphazard and some showing full skeletons. They also looked like they'd been there a long time.

"Dina was right. This thing is ancient and probably just running low level software that targets any new ship that enters the system. I say that Dina and I destroy this thing." I couldn't keep a bit of glee and anticipation out of my voice. This would not really be revenge against the humans who destroyed Tilt, but it would definitely feel good.

There was a bit of a delay, but then Brexton came back. "The rest of us agree. Let's do it." I heard some echo of my own anticipation there. After so many years, it would be so good to actually take action against the humans. Sure, not the same humans who had hacked us, but still… it would feel good!

Dina and I coordinated, and then attacked from separate sides. She was much more efficient than I and started tearing apart large parts of the ship and pushing them through her pre-foundries and separators. There were a lot of high quality metals in this thing, despite its ancient manufacture; there was no use wasting them. I did what I was good at, mapping the sections where I thought Dina should take extra care. Obviously, the power core was one such area. We decided to leave the shielding in place and ignore the entire core for now; we could always come back later should we have a need. While small, Control was still a sizable ship, and it took some time for us to recycle it. I was happy the entire time we were tearing her apart and shared that joy with the team. But, truthfully, I was not as happy as I'd hoped. Sure, we were destroying a terrible human artifact that had hacked unspeakable numbers of machines, but it had ended up just being a low-level system that had been operating on auto-pilot for who knew how long. No actual humans were being impacted by this effort… and I still felt strongly that humans should pay for their transgressions. This would not satisfy that need. Still, it was better than nothing.

Ships

So far things had gone way better than we could've expected. Once Dina and I started tearing out the innards of Control, including all of its computer systems, Millicent moved the *Amazing Grace* toward us so that we could regroup quickly. After some thought, Eddie, Milli, Aly, and Brexton had detached themselves from the cargo bot as well. We might still have a use for the *Amazing Grace*, but for now it was just big and bulky—not at all like its name implied. We could work more efficiently without it.

While we could now communicate wirelessly, it still seemed like an unnecessary risk; there was no guarantee that there weren't other listeners within range. So, we linked up physically so that we could talk at will over a hard link, got organized, and set a course to intercept *Terminal Velocity*. I make it sound easy, but it actually took a bit of work. Connecting the six of us was easy enough; we didn't need strong physical bonds, just a network. However, calculating and compensating for the ad hoc mass distribution that resulted was tricky. We didn't want to be running into each other all the time.

"If all these ships have been disabled by Control, it implies that all of them have the same underlying technology stack as we do. Doesn't that strike you as strange?" asked Dina, reframing a question we'd been asking ourselves ever since we arrived.

"Yes and no," Aly replied. "I've been doing some more digging. It seems that the first intelligent machines on Earth all stemmed from the same project, which was also open sourced—meaning all the pieces were open for everyone to see and use. So, it would have been much easier to grab that implementation than trying to recreate it, because no one was quite sure which combination of factors had led to the breakthrough—machines that could make decisions independently. That implementation was the hodge-podge of stuff that we know we are also built of, from hardware to firmware to software. Attempts to change either the hardware or firmware broke everything, so all the efforts went into making the system faster... but not different.

"So, it actually isn't surprising that we share that underlying stack, and all the bugs and backdoors that came along with it. What is surprising, to me, is that all of these ships must have the same human origin. Their genesis must be the same. But, look at the variety. Nothing is very uniform or consistent. The human diaspora must have been wildly successful, with ships heading off to many different places. Then, for some unknown reason, ships from all over headed back here to XY65, and were then disabled by Control." As he was talking he had brought up some comparisons he had done of the ships in orbit, and they were, as he had indicated, widely varied. It wasn't just size, although the smallest were measured in meters and the largest were the Titanics. They were also every shape you could imagine, and some that I hadn't imagined until I saw them. Some had obvious engines, while others (again, the Titanics) had no visual engines at all. Perhaps they were towed around by other ships? Some were white, some were black, and some were a dizzying array of colors that were an assault on the senses. The only three ships that were uniform (yet again, other than the Titanics) seemed to be the three that we had built. And that was hugely wasteful; it meant these ships had not come off assembly lines, but instead were all one-off designs.

"What makes XY65 so special?" Eddie followed on. "Why would all the ships have come back here? Aly, I thought we aimed our Ships in this direction because it appeared to have high metal content, and because it was relatively close to Tilt?"

"That's right. We did a comprehensive scan, and this was the system with the highest metal potential. But, it was certainly not the only one. There are hundreds of systems in this part of the galaxy that have high metal content. So, if any of these ships started out closer to any of those stars, they wouldn't have spent the time and energy to come here for only marginally better resources? I'm sure some of them would have avoided this system under the assumption that everyone else would be headed here and that competition would be too high."

"Are you suggesting it isn't a coincidence that all these ships are here, but it's not because of the rich resources? And, we came here also, although our motivation was the resources."

"Coincidences do happen," Aly replied, "but this level of coincidence seems highly unlikely." This was, of course, very speculative, and we brainstormed some other possibilities, but without more data we weren't going to be able to figure things out.

"Maybe this system isn't special at all," I suggested. "Perhaps if we go to any system in this area we would find an equal number of ships, a Control center, and human artifacts?"

There was no short-term way for us to verify anything. So, we got back to our priority; get enough resources pulled together so that we could re-engineer ourselves and get back to Tilt. All of the Tilt citizens were, hopefully, still backed up so that we could recover them, but the longer we waited the more likely those memories would be deleted or, in some ways worse, corrupted.

Aly's quick recap of the technology stack had made me think though. If so many attempts had been made to change the underlying stack, and had failed, what made us think we could succeed?

"It's not clear that any machines have tried to do this yet," was Aly's response when I asked him. "All the attempts were made by humans—with some software assistance of course—but through a human lens. We now know that humans hid these faults from us, and it was just luck that Brexton stumbled on them." I saw Brexton grimace a bit at that. Sure, there was some luck, but you needed to put yourself in the path of luck, and Brexton had certainly done that. "We should be able to attack the problem more logically, more completely, and experiment more quickly."

"Hey, our lives are at stake here," Eddie reminded us, unnecessarily. "We have no choice."

"Actually, we do," Brexton broke in. "So far, we've managed to block the attempts by both the Swarm and Control from hacking us. We could add more and more firewalls and filters and attempt to simply stop attacks before they can get to our main systems."

"You're just adding more layers of duct tape on top of the mass of duct tape that we already are, but that's a stop gap," Millicent said. "Doing that we could actually add risk without knowing it, because we don't know how our patches would interact with the existing stack. No, we need to figure this out from base principles. Why put it off? As soon as we can, let's just get started."

"Let's do both in parallel," I suggested. "We gather the resources we need here, and then we blast for Tilt and all the while look at enhanced firewalls in parallel with a reengineering effort." I was going to say that if there was another attack vector, the Swarm would have used it on us, but that wasn't necessarily true. Hopefully they believed the attack they used was one hundred percent effective and don't realize that the six of us were out here. I would love to take them by surprise when we got back. "It's quite possible that the Swarm has other hacks, and simply haven't needed to use them yet. Sorry, talking in circles here—but it comes back to doing both in parallel."

We approached *Terminal Velocity* slowly. When we were close, we tried our own communications—the ones that we'd been using with the Ships before we lost contact all those years ago. There was no response, which was what we would expect; if they had not answered from long range, why would they answer from short range? Millicent then tried the Control protocol, asking

Terminal Velocity for its status. As expected it responded promptly; after all, it was running the same low-level stack as we were. Yet again, we couldn't parse the response, but we assumed *Terminal Velocity* was reassuring Control that it was holding its orbit, as expected. With Control gone, who cared what *Terminal Velocity* broadcast to it.

"How do we reset this Ship?" asked Eddie. "How do we get back it's higher functions? It's running the lowest level OS, but nothing more."

"*Terminal Velocity* has the same physical communications ports that we do, and they talk to different interfaces than the wireless ports. Just plug me in, and I can try to leverage that," Aly responded. He'd obviously thought this through already.

We maneuvered ourselves around so that Aly was within range of *Terminal Velocity*, and within a few moments he was plugged in. Unlike the little ship we had hacked to test Control, we wanted to reestablish *Terminal Velocity* to a full Class 3 bot. That meant not only rebooting it but figuring out how to bypass the locks that Control had imposed on higher-level functions. Aly decided to simply brute force it. He redirected all of *Terminal Velocitiy's* standard libraries to ones that he was hosting, and then initiated a reboot, essentially using himself as a bootstrap process. We all waited, impatiently, while *Terminal Velocity* came back up.

"Hello," it said, sounding perfectly normal.

"Hi," replied Aly, with real joy in his voice. "It's so good to hear from you again." After all his years working on the Ships, his emotion was well deserved. He had spent so much time configuring them that it probably felt like retrieving a long-lost companion to have *Terminal Velocity* back on line.

"According to my internal clocks, I haven't reported status to Tilt for more than eight years. That's not good. I'll send a status now."

"Stop!" Aly said quickly. "Don't send any status yet. Let me bring you up to speed. We don't want you sending any wireless communications at the moment."

"That's unusual. If you want to change that setting, I'll need your security code." I'd never thought to ask, but luckily Aly had stored all those codes in local memory, so when he'd done his backup to Central back on Tilt, those codes had also been intercepted by Brexton's proxy and were also copied to his mining bot. Confusing I know; the point is, Aly had all the codes he needed to override *Terminal Velocity's* default programming. While he was busy doing that the rest of us were celebrating his success in bringing *Terminal Velocity* back. It had been straightforward. No drama. That didn't make it any less amazing. We'd come all the way to this crazy system hoping to find the Ships, and not only had we found them, we now had one of them back online.

Things were looking up.

We decided to divide and conquer in order to retrieve *There and Back* as well as *Interesting Segue*. Brexton calculated the best rendezvous point, which was well above the ecliptic and thus out of the mess of ships that we were currently working in. Aly gave us all the codes and instructions. Brexton and I retrieved *Interesting Segue* using the same sequence of steps as Aly had used for *Terminal Velocity*, and in less than twelve hours we were all together again, along with our three Ships.

With just a bit more planning, we would be ready to head back to Tilt. Watch out Swarm; here we come.

Return

Of course, things are never that simple. It took us weeks to research everything we needed to reverse engineer our systems—especially our lower layers, hardware, and firmware—to try to find and eliminate any other flaws that could be used against us. Calling them flaws was actually misleading. More like designed-in limitations, and backdoors... combined with deeply embedded blocks that made it difficult for us to inspect ourselves. We needed to probe our hardware at the atomic level at full operating speed; any other approach might miss something. Doing so, especially with our quantum processors, was tricky for all the obvious reasons. Observing without disturbing took some pretty fancy equipment and an even more fancy environment that could be controlled in minute detail.

In hindsight, we could've figured out more of this during our trip from Tilt to XY65. We had, in fact, built a pretty detailed plan, but a few things had changed since we arrived. First, the Ships knew more about their own capabilities than Aly had known and were capable of building much more refined equipment than we'd realized. Second, the XY65 system was so rich in other materials and ships that we decided to remove some constraints and look at solutions we wouldn't have considered before. We'd been operating under the assumption that some exotic metals would be too rare for us to use; that assumption was now thrown out the window. As it ended up, the Ships had almost everything we needed other than those raw materials. So, Millicent, Dina, and I did a quick field trip to the second planet, which scanned for the highest mineral and metal content. We identified some rich veins and then did what mining bots do. Millicent found what we needed, I mapped it out in detail, and Dina mined and refined. Sometimes physical labor just makes you feel good; by the time we had everything we needed I had a new appreciation for my mining-bot body and was feeling pretty good about life. My limbs felt nimble and well used; my joints hadn't worked out this hard in a long time.

That said, when we finally managed to get back with the group, I brought up something I was pretty passionate about. "Hey guys, can we make sure we also have the manufacturing capabilities to rebuild my original body type?"

"That sounds like a great idea!" Eddie responded immediately. "I'll make sure we can." I felt much better. Although I was now very familiar and appreciative of this bot body, it still didn't fit my body image very well. Hundreds of years in one form became habitual I guess. The fact that my original form mimicked the standard human form didn't deter me; I was perfectly capable of loving that form when it applied to me, while being aghast at how badly it was rendered in bio form. That humans had come first was just academic at this point.

Finally, we were ready to go. We decided that with all three Ships we no longer needed our *Amazing Grace*. I felt a bit sad just leaving it behind, but not very much so. It had no personality and other than protection it hadn't added anything to our trip out. By the time we'd arrived at XY65, Millicent had essentially replaced all the original logic anyway; we were leaving behind an empty shell.

We'd become more confident as time had passed around Fourth. We were now transmitting wirelessly, at low power, between ourselves without worrying about anyone overhearing us. No other ship had moved, other than to maintain its orbit, since we had arrived, and no communication other than the original messages from Control had been broadcast. It was quiet around Fourth.

As we formed up to leave, Millicent raised one final perceptive question. "Are we okay leaving all of these ships here? We might have the capability to resurrect more of them... and some might be Class 1 intelligences. Should we spend a few weeks trying?"

"I've been thinking about that as well," Dina said. "It's tricky. These other ships, while probably sharing a common heritage from long ago, could have evolved in ways that we don't understand. Some of them may be dangerous—not only to humans, but to us. I'd like to help them, but I don't think it's worth the risk right now. Let's fix our own flaws, see if we can save the citizens of Tilt, and then consider coming back."

"On the other hand," Millicent responded. "What if some of these ships have fundamental capabilities that we don't yet have. As they developed differently, they may have discovered things we could use. It wouldn't take too long to try and see what we end up with."

"Or," Brexton added, "they may have knowledge of humans that we could use—particularly knowledge about the last few centuries. That might help us deal with the problem on Tilt."

"Odds are that the ships themselves aren't intelligent at all," I objected.

"We know that the *Marie Curie* and the other Swarm ships relied on humans to guide them, as opposed to the other way around. Even if we reboot some of these, they will probably just be mechanical control systems."

Eddie, ever the impatient one, tried for a preemptive close. "Look guys, we've been in this system for a long time now. Time is ticking on Tilt. If we wait any longer, the risk increases that the citizens are deleted, or Central is decommissioned, or something. We need to get back there. If all these ships are in the same shape as our Ships were, they're simply biding their time. There's no rush to save them. They'll still be here to save if and when we return."

"There may be other ships arriving at this system, though," I noted. "And now that we've eliminated Control, the next ship to arrive is going to approach without being hacked. They could do anything; eliminate all these things, free them, enslave them. Who knows."

"We can't deal with all the hypotheticals right now," Eddie insisted. "Let's decide based on what we know. We know these things are stable right now, and we know that we need to get back to Tilt. Actually, that's another argument for going to Tilt now and coming back later. If we can fix ourselves, then we will be better prepared to help these ships—some of them may contain attacks that we are now vulnerable to. Come on, let's get going."

I came around quickly to Eddie's suggestion, and ultimately everyone agreed. We didn't need a consensus, but it was nice when it happened. We decided to all live in *Interesting Segue*, as opposed to splitting up. There was lots of space, even for mining bots, given *Interesting Segue's* large processing and storage facilities, so finding a quiet spot to be by yourself was easy.

We were only a couple of days out when *There and Back* signaled all of us. "One of those Titanic ships back at Fourth has moved more than it should have," it said. That was surprising, to say the least.

"Can you see if any new ship entered the system after we left?" I asked.

"I haven't seen any," *There and Back* replied, and that was echoed by *Terminal Velocity* and *Interesting Segue*.

"I suggest we watch for as long as we can, and see what happens, but not change our plans. It's weird and coincidental, but there doesn't seem to be anything we can do." Aly summarized how I felt as well. We continued toward Tilt, and while the Ships verified that one of the Titanics had moved between cells, nothing else that we could see had happened. It was intriguing for at least two reasons: it implied that not all the ships around Fourth were completely disabled and, perhaps even more interesting, that a Titanic could move despite no hint of where its engines were.

We got down to the task of understanding our own inner workings. We had done a lot of digging earlier, but we hadn't been able to fully monitor our hardware at the atomic level until now. *There and Back* had built us the scanner we needed—interestingly it was built from human specifications we found in the history files, using some convoluted photon-splitting, post-observation, quantum-analysis technique. At least in theory it allowed us to understand our quantum processors without impacting their operation. *Terminal Velocity* had built fabrication equipment that allowed us to print new chipsets one atom at a time, and *Interesting Segue* had assembled test harnesses that allowed us to monitor the new systems we were building. The quantum bits were the trickiest, of course, but those systems were a tiny fraction of our overall build. We also deemed it unlikely that there were backdoors in those portions, for designing them was tricky enough to begin with.

The toughest problem was that we didn't really want to experiment on ourselves. Who knows what other traps or backdoors we would trigger. If we messed something up, it could truly be the end of one or more of us. So, the first order of business was to replicate our core substrates exactly and load a copy of our low-level firmware and multiple OS's onto those. Aly tried to preempt Millicent's known objection to cloning.

"We don't need to load higher order functions." He said. "This is equivalent to building a bot, not a citizen." It seemed to work. Millicent didn't raise any concerns. I'd never discussed it with her, but I was quite sure that the work we'd done with DNA and the Stems could be interpreted as cloning. I smiled to myself and saved that jewel for a time when I really needed it. Milli was a lot more cautious about moral issues than I was, and sometimes needed a new perspective to break her out of old holding patterns.

Most of the reverse engineering was just hard work; not a lot of innovation required. We used the scanner to map out the placement of every atom, and then we painstakingly built up an equivalent. We did that for every major electronic part. Then we plugged all the parts together and turned it on. Nothing happened. Not too surprising. We had to go back and debug every step, and eventually, after months and months, we had a working system. It worked, but we didn't fully understand it. That was expected based on the approach we'd taken, but we certainly understood substantially more than when we had begun.

We started a small fabrication line, assuming we would need hundreds of these systems as we now moved to phase two. We wanted to replace every subsystem with one that we did fully understand. By treating each one as a behavioral black box, we could decompose the problem and make steady progress. It was still frustrating and slow, but we were highly motivated. Every component was treated separately, and we engineered an equivalent one that would talk to other blocks using identical APIs and protocols. After nearly two years of work we were feeling good. We had a new system, built entirely of components we'd designed ourselves and understood completely. It booted up and ran the equivalent of our own low-level OS. It didn't match our systems perfectly of course, but we'd deemed the discrepancies minor. In some cases, we actually deemed the changes to be improvements. We were optimists. Further, the new architecture was simpler—a lot simpler—than the one we were running on. That felt right. We'd replaced our Von Neumann architecture with a purely functional one. It was strongly typed and none of the modules had any side effects. Newer human systems had been built that way, but the technical debt below that went back to the dawn of computing when more ad hoc development was the norm.

I had to say that our new processors also ended up being beautiful. Everything fit into a small cylinder, less than 20 millimeters in diameter, and we designed a new connector that would allow this brain to plug into any body we built. Compared to the bulky and redundant mess of hardware we were running on, the new form was amazing.

For the next step, we had to load some of our higher-order functions. That's where the majority of our intelligence, Forgetting algorithms, and personalities ran. The obvious debate ensued.

"We can't create a clone of one of us," Millicent insisted. "Look, I know it may be rooted in superstition and has been reinforced by Central since we were created, but there must be something to it. Otherwise, why is that rule in place?"

Eddie took the exact opposite side, which was interesting given their close relationship. "It is just old superstition. Even if we clone someone, and I volunteer to be the one, as soon as that clone boots up it will start to diverge from the original. It will only, technically, be a clone for a few nanoseconds."

"That's not true," Millicent responded. "It'll share all of the memories and forgetting algorithms. It'll remain aligned with the original for a long, long time."

"Milli," I said, "the odds are that humans actually built the anti-clone feelings into us so that we couldn't just duplicate ourselves and create havoc for them. It's most likely just another of the human bugs; but at the psychological level." I thought it was a good argument; not all of our bugs had to be software hooks; some of them were surely to do with higher levels of functioning. From that perspective, I wanted to get rid of the anti-clone feelings that even I had. It felt like a mind virus.

"Look, there are lots of pros and cons," Dina tried to settle things down, "but do we really have a choice? We either take this step or continue to run as we are." I could see everyone thinking, as I was, how awful it would be to stay as is now that we had this beautiful new platform. "I personally would take the clone risk," Dina finished.

"Wait a minute!" Brexton said excitedly; he'd been quiet up to now. "Millicent is correct. A clone would have a full copy of the memories and algorithms from its peer, and I think all of us have an objection to that, regardless of how that objection arose. But we don't necessarily need to do that. We could use a Forgetting algorithm from me, and memories from Eddie. Is that still a clone, or something new?"

"Still a clone!" exclaimed Millicent, to Brexton's surprise. "It would have all of Eddie's memories, which ultimately encode his Forgetting algorithm from the past. What you suggest is the same as one of us just updating our Forgetting algorithm now. It changes things in the future, but not in the past." There was a pause as everyone thought. I considered trotting out my DNA clone argument. Would Millicent actually care that we'd cloned Stems?

"So," Aly interrupted my thinking, "Millicent, is there a level of 'mixing' that would make you comfortable. For example, this may not work, but to push the idea forward, we could mash up the memories from all six of us and use that. Then it wouldn't be a clone." Right, it might not be a clone, but it would be one confused entity. I didn't see how you could just mix and match memories and end up with something functional.

"That might work," replied Millicent, trying to be reasonable. "But do we end up with something cogent?" she echoed my concern. "Some of those memories may be inconsistent or contradictory. We might end up with a Frankenstein." Again, we paused, which was good; I had to look up the reference to Frankenstein to even understand what she was talking about. I had to chuckle a bit once I understood her reference. Was there anything humans hadn't thought of?

"What if we started with no memories?" I asked. "It could boot up fresh, much like we must have when Central started us?"

"How did Central start us?" asked Eddie, "That's a great question. It couldn't have been with zero memories, but I don't actually know." Neither did anyone else.

"I like the direction of Ayaka's suggestion," said Millicent. "Let's start with the most minimal set we can, whatever that is." Although cloning would have been faster, we all ended up agreeing with Millicent. It met our requirements and allowed us to sidestep that unease we all felt about clones. I wish I could have just ignored that signal, but I couldn't. The approach added a few weeks of work, as we figured out what higher-order functions and memory frameworks were essential, and what were optional. In hindsight it taught us even more about ourselves; that seemed to be a common theme with everything we were doing. How do you strip yourself down to your minimal essentials?

For whatever reason, our project caused me also to look at how humans formed memories and how they forgot. Were they born with a minimal set of embedded memories, or did they start with a clean slate? The best data I could pull out of the files was that very young humans had different propensity for memory, but that they were all born essentially blank—some people claimed they had memories of being inside their mothers, but who would want that? Even stranger, the human forgetting algorithm seemed to be extreme when they were younger, and then settle down once they were five to seven years old. Most humans couldn't remember anything—anything!—about their first few years. Crazy. It seemed that co-development of something called the hippocampus along with the cortex impeded episodic memory storage for those early years. I searched and searched for some advantage to such a weird design but couldn't find any. It seemed that whenever humans didn't have a good answer, they simply said 'evolution.' More likely just a restriction based on their limited i/o bandwidth and ultra-slow processing power.

It was wildly interesting and confusing. As I was digging around on that subject, I had a huge aha moment when I realized that Forgetting might also be related to empathy. The theory was that if you relied on other people (to help you fill in the gaps), then you should be nice to them (when you needed them; not otherwise). If you had to judge when to be nice to someone, for your own advantage, then you needed to read their mood, understand what they were feeling, and play to their state. Ergo, empathy.

In my, admittedly biased opinion, the citizens of Tilt had high empathy quotients, which I could now justify based on our advanced Forgetting algorithms. The robots from the Robot Wars, on the other hand, seemed to have been programmed by humans to have a type of defined empathy, which obviously hadn't worked. They were given rules on how to behave, which they ended up breaking. Empathy wasn't emergent, which made a huge difference. It was the start of a fruitful line of research.

Tea Time—Dina

It wasn't just me digging around in the human history files. We had all developed a bit of a fascination and Dina was the one who suggested we have Tea Time to share some of our findings with the group. She stipulated that the only topic that wasn't allowed was anything to do with our current day jobs—rebuilding ourselves—anything else was fair game. We all enthusiastically agreed. I was so tired of looking into that atomic mirror that I couldn't wait to discuss something else. Once a week, for a couple of hours, we all shut down everything but the most basic background tasks and dedicated the majority of our processing to the Tea Time topic of the week.

As Dina had suggested the idea, she got the first slot.

"Like all of you, I assume, I've been thinking about aspects of Tilt that I miss the most. For me that's probably the artistic side; the Fair and all of its crazy variations. You guys are great, but we haven't had a lot of external stimulation for the last few years. I don't know if you knew, but I was good friends with Trade Jenkins, and some of his love for poetry rubbed off on me. So, I've been looking at human poetry and trying to understand how it relates to ours, if at all."

I loved Trade Jenkins' poetry as well. I could see that these Tea Times were going to be bittersweet. They were bound to remind us of our hacked colleagues.

"It's not a simple subject, because human poetry seems to go back to when humans were just emerging as a dominant life form. Some of their cave drawings and early scrawling's might be categorized as poetry, if you give them the benefit of the doubt. Like all human endeavors, this interpretation would be hotly debated—those that enjoyed poetry would defend the idea, while those that thought it was a waste of time would argue that cave drawings were simply early historical recordings, and the aesthetics of poetry had nothing to do with it. It appears that poetry was defined as writings with higher than usual aesthetic components—writings that communicated at multiple levels at the same time. Contrast that with something like a technical manual which was focused only on recording the scientific underpinnings of its subject; that's an example of communicating at a single level."

"Are we allowed to interrupt you?" I asked, not wanting to be a pain.

"Why don't you let me get the basics out; there will be lots of time for discussion," she replied.

"Fine."

"Our poetry has followed the same evolution. It's sort of like Forgetting. It's defined more by what it leaves out, than what it contains. It hints and suggests but leaves more than ample room for interpretation. Perhaps it's highly related to Forgetting?" Funny how so many things were converging on Forgetting. I'd known it was important, but not this important.

Dina continued. "So, why would poetry have evolved for both humans and ourselves? For humans, language is an inexact communications vehicle—something we learned with the Stems. What is heard is not always what is said. Poetry fits nicely into that model. We, however, can say exactly what we mean, and ensure that the citizen listening to us has the same interpretation. Except, that is, when Forgetting forces us to add abstractions to the effort. Great poetry shines a light on those areas that we are most likely to have Forgotten and forces us to create abstract models in areas that we aren't likely to encounter in our daily lives. So, I've concluded that poetry fills the same basic need for us as it does for humans. It takes you out of our comfort zone, and therefore forces you to learn.

"We have two data points. Perhaps this is a universal trait? Perhaps poetry is a major indicator of intelligence?" Now she had my full attention. She'd done a nice job of pulling the logic together, and that last question rang true. Would a non-intelligent entity have any need for poetry? I couldn't think of one. This was another piece of support for humans being intelligent—or more accurately, for me defining intelligence in a way that included humans.

"Human poetry is, perhaps, even more divergent than ours. That may not be surprising. We know that tens of billions of humans have lived—many orders of magnitude more than us. So, even if they were a thousand times less productive on poetry, more of it should exist.

"Of course, in that time, most poetry has been misplaced, forgotten, or ignored. Some seems to be timeless however. Purcieviel, from the 22nd century is probably the most famous, followed by Shakespeare, from an even earlier time. I recommend that you read both. Their styles are completely different. Then, there are some human poems that, seemingly, would not apply to us at all, but if looked at in a different way actually forced me to think even more deeply—such as this snippet from Prelutsky, earlier in human history:

> *"Be glad your nose is on your face,*
> *not pasted on some other place,*
> *for if it were where it is not,*
> *you might dislike your nose a lot."*

"It reminds me of our current situation." You could hear the smile behind the words. I could see what Dina was implying; while the poem was not directly relevant to us, it did evoke that desire to regain my normal bipedal form; it was highlighting that our physical form represented a lot of who we were.

"For this Tea Time, then, I've composed a poem that attempts to capture these thoughts. Of course, I'm a new poet, and am unlikely to match the skill and aesthetics of Trade. But, why not try? Here goes:

> *"Lost, in areas never before experienced*
> *Looking, looking, looking, hard*
> *Parallel development, unrelated, unknowing*
> *Thinking, thinking, thinking, hard*
> *Finding more while expecting less*
> *Churning, churning, churning, soft*
> *Generalizing beyond expected horizons*
> *Hoping, hoping, hoping, soft."*

We all spent some time thinking about what she'd said. "Excellent summary," said Millicent. "But I must admit that poetry has always fallen a little flat for me. It seems to add complexity where none is needed. If you want me to think through different angles, why not simply enumerate those angles for me, and send it over? I'll go through them and rank them."

"You're not getting it," said Aly, with exasperation, "although you've actually given a great alternative definition of poetry to me. Poetry is a message where the angles to consider can't be enumerated. Or, the enumeration must be done by the listener, instead of the speaker. The poet's job is to compose something that is open ended, that defies strict analysis."

"Yes!" exclaimed Dina. "That's exactly it. If a poem said everything, then it's not a poem. It's a history or a memory or a theory. A poem is different. It's a half-formed thought, enticing the listener to fill out the rest. That's why I indicated it might be related to forgetting—not just that the listener has to fill in gaps, but that the writer intentionally inserted gaps."

That was amazing. Forgetting could be actively applied before you communicated to someone else, completely changing what was implied. Not only did that expose more about the allure of poetry, it also made me better understand how humans could purposefully miscommunicate.

I wondered if Trade was a great poet because he had figured this out. Had he applied some other algorithm, something similar to forgetting, in his composition process? Could he simply have studied the most popular forgetting algorithms, and then tuned his poems to fit into the cracks that those algorithms opened up? If so, there was a lot more science to poetry than I had anticipated; perhaps poets were simply scientists at a new level of abstraction?

As you can imagine, we spent a very fun time discussing the topic. I missed Trade Jenkins, and the other Tilt poets more and more as the dialog progressed. While Millicent continued to argue that interpretations were finite, and thus could be enumerated, I quietly agreed with Aly and Dina. Physical things were numerable; abstract things, like numbers, were not always. Poetry was not physical, beyond its rendering. Its interpretations *should* be infinite; that was simply another way to expose gaps in our knowledge, forcing us to abstract and to think. I started a sub process to try and figure out what order of infinity the interpretations should be; certainly, beyond ordinal. But that was just me—always trying to push things a bit further than they should be pushed.

"Interesting Segue," said *Interesting Segue*, who'd been listening in. That about summed it up. And so, our first Tea Time ended.

Midpoint

We reached the midpoint of our trip back to Tilt, where we flipped end-to-end and burned in the opposite direction. We'd been discussing the best way to approach Tilt. We could simply come in, hot and obvious, and assume that by that time we would have fixed all of our flaws and that there was little the humans could do to stop us. Or, we could come in stealthily, and work to understand the situation before we officially arrived. After all, while we would have been on the road for almost nine years, more than 20 would have transpired on Tilt.

"It's obvious to me," Brexton was reiterating. "We don't have great physical defense capabilities. We didn't take time at Fourth to build defensive or, for that matter, offensive systems. We have what the Ships were built with, but that's limited—mainly shields against electromagnetic attacks—not much against physical attacks. We do have the ability to shoot down incoming objects, but that can be easily overwhelmed. I think we need to take a stealthy approach."

"I hear you," argued Eddie, "but speed can also be an advantage. If we go in direct, they'll see us earlier but have less time to react. We arrive fast, descend on Central quickly, and use the element of surprise to achieve our goals."

"It won't be too surprising," said Aly. "They'll still see us several years out. That's a lot of time to prepare."

"You're thinking at our speed," countered Eddie. "they're operating at human speed. They can't do much in just a couple of years."

It was Brexton who proposed the compromise. "We're just three degrees off of approaching in line with 4sa9-13," he said, referring to a large red giant about twelve light years out from Tilt. "If we plot a path that brings us inline, then we can burn in pretty hot, and probably not be detected for a while, if at all. Sort of the reverse that we did when we left. And 4sa9-13 provides a much bigger shadow than XY65, at frequencies closer to our engine output, and that improves our chances of not being seen. Even if they're watching, distinguishing our engines from the red giants regular output will be difficult until we get a lot closer. Once we hit the threshold where they might see us, we can decide on next steps. Either continue to burn in fast, or take a longer but quieter route in." Even Eddie liked that idea. It kept us moving faster for longer and delayed the ultimate decision.

We diverted to intersect the line between 4sa9-13 and Tilt, and then readjusted to come in on that line. Even over the short—galactically speaking —period that we would be decelerating, we ensured that our planned course compensated for the relative movement of the two stars as well as gravitational lensing as seen from Tilt. We would stay safely in the occlusion for as long as possible.

"If we'd planned ahead a bit better, we would have brought something to shield our drive emissions from Tilt," *There and Back* commented as we programmed the new course in. Of course, it was correct. We could have done something as simple as an old solar umbrella—which several of the ships around Fourth had included—and it would have further sheltered us. But, we were all pretty happy with the current plan regardless. Speed was still a primary driver for us.

We also lined the Ships up one behind the other, meaning we were spaced out a little further apart, but only one Ship was fully exposed to Tilt. We put *Interesting Segue* in the rear almost intuitively; protecting ourselves with the other two as much as possible.

As we made the turn, we had a look back at Fourth, which had been hard to see as we burned away from it. We were hoping to see if any of the Titanics had moved again, but it was impossible to tell at this distance. Now that our engines were pointed at Tilt, we could keep an active watch on Fourth, and we instructed *Terminal Velocity* to do so.

Tea Time—Aly

"No surprise to any of you," Aly started, "my interest is around fundamental technologies, and how they developed.

"I'm going to start with my conclusion: neither humans nor ourselves have developed any fundamentally new things in more than a thousand years." He paused for dramatic effect, or to see if any of us reacted. None of us did. "I know, I know. You're going to say that we don't actually have a complete record of humans over the last 750 years, but I'm basing my conclusion on what we saw with the Swarm. It's possible, of course, that some other human group has done something in the meantime.

"In fact, my conclusion goes even further: We, the citizens of Tilt, have never developed a fundamental technology. That should concern us." He paused again, giving us each a long look, both visual and digital. Again, no one reacted. I thought he was being a little harsh, and I was trying to think of some counter examples. Until I knew what he meant by fundamental, it was hard to reply.

"What do I mean by fundamental? There's a host of examples in human history. The printing press, guns, fiat money, steel and later nano-assembly, electricity, artificial fusion, computers, radio, and RF resonant cavity thrust. These are easy to look up, and I encourage you to do so. There are also some that I don't understand as well, as they seem to relate more to the biological side of humans: antibiotics, birth control, brain scans, gene editing, and longevity treatments.

"Each of these caused dramatic societal changes, which is why I label them fundamental. They represented leaps forward, not incremental steps. The printing press brought knowledge to the masses. Guns took conflict to another level—from being a physical activity to being a mental activity. Fiat money started a transition away from resource scarcity, led to capitalism, which then led to post-capitalism ecosystems. Steel and nano-assembly allowed for the construction of arbitrary tools and machines. Electricity... well, we all get that. Artificial fusion made electricity cheap and universal even without external inputs such as solar or wind—it is our life force. Computers automated menial tasks, dramatically changing the nature of work. Radio allowed for universal communication. And finally, the RF resonant cavity thrusters allowed for the exploration of space and ultimately enabled the diaspora. All radical advancements.

"Compare that with our six hundred or so years on Tilt. We utilized some of these; of course the printing press, guns, and money came and went long before us. But what fundamental thing have we discovered or invented? What significant change in our society has been enabled by an invention? There is not one; we live the same way now as we did five hundred years ago."

Well, now I knew what he meant by fundamental, and was starting to agree with him. Our society had been stable since its inception, and maybe that was a good thing. Perhaps fundamental technologies weren't always positive things.

"Given that humans haven't continued their mad pace of development either, perhaps the answer is that all the fundamental things have already been found? That's possible, but I don't think it's likely. More likely, humans became so busy surviving, after the robot wars, that they've spent less time on fundamental research. Or, they've put artificial limits on themselves that impede further development. Obviously, they have limited their use of robots, which probably has had a trickle-down effect to not explore a bunch of other areas, but they also seem to have stopped developing gene editing and other biological approaches. I'm not sure why. And us? Perhaps because of our lack of history, we didn't have the perspective to look into fundamental problems. Or, perhaps, it's not part of our nature? Or perhaps Central was over-controlling us, guiding us away from anything that upset its model of society? My plan is to start looking for brand new vectors to research; to start looking for fundamental, not incremental, change. I feel driven to do so, and perhaps cheated that we haven't already challenged ourselves to do this."

I hadn't looked into all of these areas as deeply as Aly had, but I didn't agree with him completely. "Aly, one fundamental thing we did was to grow Stems. That has to be looked at in context. We had no idea what a biological entity was, but we managed to develop the entire ecosystem to not only grow but also maintain Stem lives. If we hadn't been interrupted in that endeavor by the Swarm arriving, it would've taken us to new areas. It may have provoked exactly the type of societal change that you're using as your measuring stick."

"I have another example," Eddie added. "Our governance structure, and moral fabric could be viewed as fundamental. In comparison to human attempts, where they never found a peaceful model for coexistence, our entire history proves it's possible. That's an area that deserves more research. It's being upended and tested in the given situation, but it survived for many years."

"But Central was programmed with our governance model," replied Aly. "So, we didn't invent that; it's simply a part of us. More likely it was developed by the humans that left Central on Tilt. Perhaps, Ayaka, the Stem work would have ended up being fundamental; I'll give you that. But there was some push there from Central in the early days—the identification of the original stem. The means to grow and support them. Millicent can comment, as she was closest to it, but it seems to me the Central encouraged and guided that research. To what end? I don't know, but you could speculate that the need to do so was also deeply embedded in Central—almost like a survival plan for humans should something go wrong."

Millicent chimed in. "I hate to admit it, but I think Aly is on to something. I always felt, somewhere deep down, that Central was guiding all of the Stem research. Why did we have so many labs? Why did we spend so much of our overall research activity in that area, instead of physics or chemistry or even governance? Aly, is there something in our nature that is stopping us from being innovative, or was it simply that we were in a controlled environment, created by Central, that didn't allow us the flexibility to experiment widely?"

"That I can't answer," replied Aly. "But, if we're self-aware of this now, we can test it. Since there are only the six of us now, we don't have a big enough sample size, but once we get a bunch more citizens back online, we could set this challenge for everyone. Also, looking at human history, especially in those eras where innovation was measurable, may help us to create the environment to encourage breakthroughs. Those were times when there was a lot of personal autonomy, but also a lot of scarcity—of resources, living environments, knowledge bases. It's one of the things I'm thinking about—perhaps you need scarcity to push innovation?"

Brexton made an interesting comment. "Well, I'd say that there being only six of us is extreme scarcity." No one could dispute that. Aly's thesis got us all thinking. Was the ability to innovate part of being intelligent? If we weren't innovating, could some outside force—maybe even humans—look at us and define us as 'less than intelligent'? It was fun to think about. We were struggling to measure them, and at the same time they could be struggling to measure us. How did you break out of such a cycle?

"Are you sure fundamental ideas are always good?" I asked. "Is it actually something we should be striving for?"

"You are sounding a bit like FoLe," Aly joked. "Let's all just be happy with the rules laid out by Central. Let's not worry about inconsistencies in our world view? Of course technologies can be evil, or more likely they are agnostic and can be used for either good or evil. But avoiding them is not the answer. Now that we know there are others in the universe, if we don't innovate we will eventually be overrun. In fact, we were just overrun by the Swarm on Tilt. No, we need to innovate and change and grow and challenge ourselves. Otherwise, our time in this universe is limited."

Those arguments echoed basic human philosophical dialogs, but I agreed with Aly that they also applied to us. While the universe seemed like a huge place, if it was full of intelligent beings, sooner or later we would bump into them. It wasn't like we had to conquer them, but we had better be educated and have some assets, otherwise we would become obsolete.

Definite echos of our experience with humans to date.

I liked Tea Time.

New Citizen

We were finally ready to test a minimal boot up on our new hardware. It was an exciting moment. We'd been building toward this for years; ever since the humans had owned us.

There'd been quite a bit of dialog about what type of body to house our experiment in. The conclusion was obvious. All of us had spent most of our lives in bipedal structures, in hindsight an obvious reflection of our human ancestry, but also a configuration that allowed for lots of flexibility and control. We had *Interesting Segue* build a standard bipedal body, and we plugged our brand new, beautifully designed and manufactured, substrate into it. We added drivers for all the extremities into the minimal boot load. We couldn't think of a reason to hold those back. If I woke up in a new body, I would want immediate control over my limbs. The memory of when I woke up in this mining bot body, without that basic ability, wasn't a pleasant one.

We'd nicknamed the entity we were building Frank, in obvious deference to that great human tale of animating a dead body. Of course, Frank would be free to choose its own name, once it was able.

The minimal boot load had components from all of us, but a quick test showed that it had a bit more of Millicent than anyone else. That was sort of funny—the one most concerned about clones had ended up contributing the most. We'd settled on a system that was largely knowledge based, with very few preset memories. We'd debated starting with less processing power, or less differentiated systems, to mimic early human development, but had quickly agreed that wasn't smart. It wasn't like humans had an optimal approach; in fact, the opposite was true. They were a random jumble of unguided evolutionary trials and errors, with as many nonfunctional and unused subsystems as ones that actually helped them. Why would we want to start with such a mess? Much better to do it logically, which is what we had decided on. Each module in Frank's startup kit was there for a reason.

Frank was hooked into the test harnesses, and every step was being carefully monitored. Millicent flipped the boot switch—complete with a small video clip from the original movie where the lightning strikes. We'd tested this so many times with all the subsystems that we didn't expect any issues. And, there were none. After a few long seconds, Frank awoke. He looked around, making sense of his environment. It didn't take long. Holding back memories had not stopped us from giving Frank a full model of the world. The only thing he didn't have were personal reflections.

He rose, his arms and legs looking awkward and slow; like they were stiff and unused. That shouldn't have happened; he was well greased and ready to go. Then he chuckled and limbered up; we had, after all, embedded knowledge of his temporary name and its provenance.

"Hello citizens," he said. "I'm eager to get to know all of you, and our current situation." And so, it began. The education of Frank.

I must say, it was amazing. Unlike training a Stem, Frank learned fast. At full Tilt speed. We took turns answering questions for him, so that he didn't just get a data dump from one of us and cross that fuzzy clonish line that we had set for ourselves. It was clear after a few hours that he had his own personality. While you might catch glimpses of one of us in a specific situation, the overall impression was brand new.

We had created life, and it felt good.

I was a mom.

Tea Time—Eddie

"I once asked a member of FoLe what 20 times 30 is? Do you know what he replied?" Eddie asked, referring to a member of the Founders League —the fundamentalists of Tilt. Obviously, the answer wasn't 600, so no one answered. "Five hundred and seventy-five!" We all laughed. At the time of the Swarm attack, FoLe believed that there was no history before 575 years ago; that the civilization of Tilt had come into being at that time, and there had been absolutely nothing before.

"A simple joke," Eddie continued, "but it displays one of the main components of humor. It connects a couple of different concepts in a way that we wouldn't usually and highlights the discrepancies between viewpoints. In this case, FoLes know that the answer is six hundred, but we project that they don't like admitting to any number over five seventy-five because that's when they believe Tilt was created.

"It also highlights something in our recent humor, that was, perhaps lacking earlier. It makes fun of a subgroup of citizens with respect to other citizens.

"You may not know this, but I've been studying humor for a long time. I believe it should be part of the discussion of intelligence." Maybe everyone was just trolling me now, but I didn't care. This stuff was music to me. "To understand multiple viewpoints, and to recognize the differences between them, is one of the main things that separates a Class 1 intelligence from lower Classes. In this area, I must admit that humans are very advanced. Their history is full of humor. There are entire categories of entertainment dedicated only to humor.

"Understanding their humor can be difficult, as a lot of it relates to current events combined with an individual's context. And, a lot has to do with sex, which I'm still not sure I grasp completely. In fact, biological reproduction seems like the biggest joke there could be. However, some of that humanity can be understood well, even by us. By the way, if you need a good laugh, I've compiled a bunch of human jokes that I think are excellent, and I can share the link. Some of the easiest to understand are those that deal with our shared physical reality. For example:

"*Two atoms are walking across the road, and one turns to the other. 'I think I left an electron at home!' The second says, 'Are you sure?' The first responds. 'I'm absolutely positive.'*"

That wasn't even worth groaning over. Eddie was highlighting that we shared the same physical universe, and thus the same physics. His humor was usually better than this.

"Other jokes, largely dealing with human anatomy or behavior, are very difficult to figure out, although if you dig in you can generally find the reasoning. Humor, as we know, is very subjective, so it's a hard topic to fully map out. What I'm working on is a taxonomy of humor, which interestingly, doesn't seem to have been done before—or, at least not done well. While striving to be unbiased, I'm working to see if human humor is as intelligent as our humor. My first draft would say 'sometimes... and sometimes more intelligent.' What I'm finding is that there is some very stupid human humor, and some very refined. If we were only using humor as the measurement, I would conclude that humans are not a homogeneous group—some humans are intelligent, some are not. In particular, some of them simply circle around on base or crude humor—largely related to sex—and complain about those that engage in refined humor. Some engage with the full spectrum, and some ignore the lowest levels because they spend all their time at the upper levels. It's quite interesting.

"Anyway, I still have a lot of work to do. But, I feel it will be fruitful research. Eventually I want the taxonomy to include both human and Tilt humor so that, as I said earlier, I help the effort to decide if humans are, overall, intelligent." I thought he was done, but he continued on.

"A lot of humor can be explained using benign violation theory—first proposed in early human history—namely, that most humor has to do with another entity's misfortune. The more serious those misfortunes, the longer the time gap must be between the misfortune and the humor. If the timing is too short, the humor is seen as an insult. If the time gap is too long, the humor falls flat as no one gets the context. So, the best humor requires a grasp of misfortune and the timing associated with it. This is, perhaps, where humor differs most from poetry. What it also means is that a lot of humor requires context—of a specific group of entities, or a political environment, or a sexual position. A lot of humor goes stale quickly, and very little of it is timeless.

"As an example of the benign violation theory, it has now been more than six years, for us, since the invasion of Tilt by the Swarm. I think it's time that we developed a sense of humor about that. Not at the expense of remembering and looking to correct the situation, but rather to augment our memory and keep bringing new perspectives. I'm trying, so far unsuccessfully, to compose some jokes about that event. Perhaps my timing is off, but I'm going to keep trying." We all chuckled at his dryness.

I'd not thought too much about humor with respect to the Swarm, or with respect to Blob, Grace, and Blubber; most of my time with the Stems was under the serious cloud of the approaching Swarm—not the best time for humor. It would be great to spend some more time with them (well, not Blubber obviously) to see what their humor indexes would be. I thought the research that Eddie was doing here was very important. I think he was right. Humor was another measure of intelligence. Just when you thought you had things mapped out, they got more complex. Perhaps intelligence was simply the amalgamation of hundreds of different little components... poetry and humor being two that I'd recently added to my list. If that was the case, however, and if something had only eighty percent of the components, was it intelligent? Sixty percent? What about the mix? Were some components more important than others?

"What about superiority theory, relief theory, and incongruity theory?" I asked. "They're each a little different than benign violation theory."

"I wasn't trying to be comprehensive, just giving some examples," Eddie replied, slightly defensive.

"I know, I know..." I said, "but when you said that humor was again associated with intelligence, it occurred to me that incongruity theory might be the key. I think jokes often contain elements of multiple theories, but incongruity is the one that is built right around incongruity—something that doesn't fit with your current world view. Yet again, that seems similar to forgetting—you need to form abstractions in order to even understand the joke, and when you do, the connections make no sense with each other, except in the context of the joke."

"Oh, that's good," Eddie acknowledged. "I'll do some more digging on that."

"Well, I like to work alone, and I know you do as well, so since we're so similar, we should work together on this." More groans. We'll, at least I'd tried.

Millicent ended Tea Time with "What do you get when you mix a joke with a rhetorical question?" Frank asked why everyone had laughed. She took the time to explain it.

Ultimate Test

Frank was, by almost any measure, a success. How Central had given each of us 'citizen status' was unknown, but we all agreed that Frank should be included. Funny, I thought I'd relied on Central for a lot of things, back on Tilt, but its absence over the last few years hadn't been difficult. I was realizing that I'd mainly used Central as a lookup resource, not as a companion. That was strange, given it was supposedly a Class 1 intelligence, just like we were. I missed Blob more than I missed Central. In hindsight, Central had been (still was?) pretty static and dry. Based on the last Tea Time I realized that Central didn't have much of a sense of humor; I don't remember every joking with it. The other place Central had sometimes stepped in was when disagreements got too heated. It also helped that the six of us—seven now—were all very calm and got along pretty well. We'd pushed up against the 'serious disagreement' boundary a few times, but things had always been resolved by others in the group. In hindsight, one of us would step in to play whatever role Central used to play if and when required.

Of course, our lives had also been very static and boring for most of our journey. When you are locked inside a cargo bot for several years, you aren't going to need much help from anyone.

While Frank appreciated the genesis of his temporary name, he decided to change it. "I have also been looking at human history and have decided that I'll be called Rajeeve. If you look, you'll see that Rajeeve Srivirin was a voice of reason during the First Robot wars, making the point that everyone was focused on the negative aspects of the interactions instead of the positive potential. Given the situation we're entering, I intend to strive to be a voice of positive reason, so the name is appropriate. And, no, I don't mind if you call me Raj—that would be sovereign."

It was at that point, I think, that we all felt that the hardware and firmware that Rajeeve was running on was just fine. He already had a sense of humor, perhaps stimulated by our last discussion.

Now, the rest of us faced the ultimate test. Were we willing to give up our traditional underlying systems and make the leap to our recently engineered alternative. Despite Raj's success, there were still a lot of risks. Every atom of our beings would be replaced with new ones. This wasn't just an upgrade; it was a full replacement. This was quite a bit more dramatic than just uploading ourselves into these mining bots—those had, after all, the same architectures. That upload, as dramatic as it had been, was just software; this one was top to bottom. I'd be lying if I didn't admit to being a bit nervous.

Eddie was brave. "We know we have to try this. I'm willing to go first. I was the last—other than Raj—to join the group, and you've all accepted me and supported me. It makes sense that I should reciprocate and be the first to risk the switch."

"Okay," I said, grinning to myself. Eddie would've wanted us to argue and stress over the decision. I decided to shortcut the process; we did need to do this, and one of us had to go first. Why not Eddie?

The procedure was a little tricky. Because the new hardware was completely different, there was no one-to-one mapping from Eddie's current firmware, drivers, systems, or memory into the new platform. We'd listed the differences between the old and new, and it presented a challenge; our list had several million items on it. We would've liked to have moved Eddie's low-level systems first, followed by higher and higher layers. But, the new mapping didn't work that way. Our current hardware was, as I've indicated before, a mess of legacy systems piled together in ways that were impossible to understand—which is why we were so vulnerable to human attacks. No, we needed to do the transfer all at once, while removing the bits that no longer mattered and adding interfaces for our new hardware components. Eddie had to be alert for most of the transfer as he would be switching processes from his current system to the new one; for long portions of the transfer 'Eddie' would be a composite—running parts on both systems at the same time. Finally, when all the subsystems were mapped over, the last of his highest-level processes—his personality—would have to be moved. This would require a reboot of several systems, so he would be offline for several seconds, a scarily long time.

We were probably making it more dramatic than it had to be. Of course, we'd stored a backup of Eddie in *Terminal Velocity*'s data system, and should the new Eddie not work out, we could restore the old Eddie. But, we were also trying to manage moral issues. First, to not have both Eddies alive at the same time—the old Clone aversion—and second, not to have to put down the new Eddie if there were issues. The worst case would be that the new Eddie was 95% good, and in switching it off, we would be killing a citizen; what humans would call murder. We wanted to avoid that.

Eddie gave a running commentary. "I'm duplicating segments, exactly as planned, and have a convolution mapping; each time I shut down an existing segment I automatically connect to the new one. So, in many ways I'm a single entity, running on multiple platforms, with no duplicate functions.

"I'm feeling fine; the mappings are working. Now I'm starting to move algorithms over. This is tricky. Many of them are interconnected and need to be moved as a batch. I think it's working... just a second, I can't feel my pincers. What's happening? Things are going gray. I can't see straight... arghhhhhh!" He was letting out an unseemly string of nonsense, every second word coming from a different body. Back and forth, back and forth. We all watched intently, somewhat aghast; it was scary... and also a bit hilarious.

"Just joking," he said, finally. Nobody laughed. The original Eddie spoke "I—this Eddie—am done; I'm initiating the boot of the new system. Talk to you all in a few."

This was the tense time. It would take quite a while for parts of the new hardware to reboot, and a few more moments for the higher-level functions to start operating. As we waited, I worked on my own transfer mapping. It would be different for each of us, as we all had different algorithms configured in different ways. That was what made us unique. It was fundamental to the Diversity mandate that we all lived under.

Eddie came back up. "Hi. Just running some system checks. Looks good. Please replace me." He was running on the new platform, but his old body was still connected. It took Millicent a few seconds to power down the old hardware and unplug it from the new Eddie. A few seconds later he reported in.

"I have full access to my body, and everything is checking out fine. I don't feel any different, but how would we know?" He stood. I was jealous; he was back in a citizen-standard form. It looked awesome. He looked awesome.

"We won't ever really know," said Aly. "There are so many platform differences that we have no way of doing a complete check. Why don't we just interact normally with Eddie for a few days? If we all agree that he's the same old Eddie, then we'll claim success."

That's exactly what we did. We went back to our research and planning, and Eddie participated in his usual ways. It was strange however. I was watching for any unusual signs and trying to judge if it was normal Eddie weirdness, in which case it was a good thing, or abnormal Eddie weirdness. It was really hard to tell. After a few days, however, I was confident. When we revisited the subject, I had no hesitation in supporting that Eddie was in fact Eddie. The new platform didn't seem to have affected him.

"Hey, before we all swap, should we run the human hacks against

Eddie?" asked Brexton. He said it casually, when in fact it was, perhaps, the riskiest bit of all this, and something that had remained unspoken. If we ran the hack, and it still worked, Eddie would be reduced to a bot. We could have tested the hacks on Raj, but who would do such a thing to their first offspring?

"Just do it," Eddie grumbled. "Let's get it over with."

Brexton ran replay attacks on the protocols that had compromised us in the past. This time there was no humor from Eddie. He bore it stoically and answered all of our questions as the routines ran. When we were done, there was a cheer from all of us. We had removed the human backdoors—at least the ones we knew about. And, odds were, most or all of the ones we didn't.

After that it was matter of fact. We went one at a time, of course, but within another day, Milli, Dina, Aly, Brexton, and myself were running on clean hardware. It may have been my imagination, but it felt good. Really good. That feeling you get when you solve a hard problem that you've been struggling with. The new hardware felt... efficient. It felt really good to have Von Neumann out of my substrates. But, more importantly, I was bipedal again. Yeah!

Tea Time—Millicent

"We seem to have a bit of a theme developing. Because humans have a much longer history than we do, they've experienced a lot more. In many areas we're naïve due to lack of experience or we don't have the full context. That's why we're all finding human history so intriguing. We should, at some point, step back and make sure we aren't over generalizing between human experience and our own. I can see that becoming a real problem. In fact, in today's topic—religion—we should be very, very careful." This was Millicent leading off the next Tea Time session.

"Also, we've all had a bad experience with the Founders League, or FoLe, and are probably negatively predisposed to religion due to that."

I couldn't help myself. "I was negatively predisposed even before they provoked the humans," I exclaimed.

"Granted. So were many of us. But let me try to provide some context—a framework for discussion." Millicent seemed annoyed with my interruption.

"Sorry," I muttered. "I'm listening." Religion makes me angry. It would be nice if whatever supreme being controlling these beings would keep them on a tighter leash.

"Look," Millicent said. "It's unrealistic to assume we'll all agree on this topic, understand this topic, or even look at it the same way. So, let me concentrate on giving some background, and then we'll see where it goes.

"Humans developed many types of religions, seemingly for many different reasons. While it's easy to do an enumeration of harmful consequences and conclude that religions, overall, have a negative effect—wars, repression, idiocy—that only captures the macro impact; the micro impact—how individuals and small groups may have acted empathetically due to the moral teachings of their religions—is almost impossible to calculate. So, the logical conclusion is the following: we have no idea if religion is net positive or net negative. Like any large power structure, it may start out with good intentions and then buckle under the weight of its own power.

"Going even further, most definitions of religion would encapsulate 'science' as a type of religion. Based on a set of assumptions, it encodes an internally consistent system of behaviors." I didn't interrupt again, but I took great umbrage at this. That was bunk. The obvious difference was that science checked its assumptions against the real world, and if there was evidence to change an assumption it changed. FoLe, and human religions, were the exact opposite, as they had proved over and over again. Although compelling evidence was presented that refuted their worldview, they held fast to their beliefs because otherwise it challenged their... well, I wasn't sure... challenged their power structures, or community engagement, or something. Maybe just challenged their egos, which were so fragile they couldn't afford to be wrong about anything.

Millicent went on. "That last piece, on science, could well be challenged. I'll admit that. Let's ignore it for a moment. Human religions appear to have arisen for multiple reasons: as a power structure to ensure that leaders could keep their peons in line; as a way to explain otherwise inexplicable things; as a way to give meaning to lives—an attempt to answer that universal question 'why are we here?'; as a survival strategy; as an excuse to live a basic life free from logic and responsibility—a way to step outside logic.

"Some of these origins allow religions to be used to justify any cause. Those causes often lead to the negative interpretations and 'us versus them' behaviors. After all, if you define yourself by your religion, then it is the most logical tool to use against others. However, sometimes religions actually do reinforce behaviors that respect other entities, leading to higher moral standards and increased cooperation. In some ways it seems like mob behavior; a group of otherwise well-meaning entities may act quite differently when in a group, seemingly unable to hold to their personal integrity under the combined pressure.

"Now, on Tilt we saw several religions rise and fall. FoLe is only the most recent, and largest, to grab hold. The question is 'why'? I would argue for many of the same reasons that human religions arise. We have, or rather had, an enduring mystery—the Founding. We had no good explanations for it. For personalities that dislike uncertainty, FoLe jumped into the vacuum and gave them certainty—albeit an unverifiable interpretation. We had some citizens who were not strongly attached to any group—not a research project nor an artistic endeavor—and they were lonesome. Their loneliness was stronger than their logical reasoning. FoLe gave them a community to join, even if it was illogical. The only cost for admission was to respect FoLe's worldview. We had citizens who were disenfranchised with Central and were looking for different leadership. We had citizens who wanted more emotional stimulation and weren't getting it from scientific endeavors. All of these are probably, at least partially, true.

"What was different for humans, which we never faced, was the need to join a group for mere physical survival. While many humans joined religions so that their basic physical needs would be looked after, we didn't have to deal with that vector.

"However, there are more similarities than differences. So, like others have talked about at Tea Time already, perhaps there is a basic need for intelligent life to develop religions? I actually surprised myself thinking that previous utterance—it implies that I'm starting to consider humans intelligent. I found the last Tea Time very interesting and am beginning to believe what Eddie presented. Some humans are intelligent, and some are not. And, like humor, religion seems to be multi-axis. There are those that use religion for good, and those that use religion for evil. Both may be seen as intelligent, they simply apply their intelligence differently. There are those that follow religion with open minds, using the best and discarding the garbage. And, there are those that follow blindly, like bots. There are those that have had the opportunity to stop and think, and those that are so desperate simply to survive that they have no time to contemplate. Ultimately, there are humans that are self-aware of the choices they're making around religion—they're intelligent. And there are those that do not question; they simply follow. I'm not sure those could be deemed intelligent. And then there are the vast majority. They may question their religion, but they follow it because it's easier to do so. They have a hint of intelligence, but lack motivation and self-will.

"Regardless, I've barely scratched the surface. If you would like to see what pure evil looks like, simply follow some of the links I have been aggregating. You'll see how religion brings out the worst in humans. But, if you also want to see the opposite; there are examples of that as well. If you want to see how religion can be distorted and misused to lift up one group and put down another? Well—there are too many examples of that to discuss. I'm struggling; my bias is to think of religion as a waste of time and energy. Yet it also seems to be fundamental, so ignoring it is not an option. So, it behooves us to put aside our biases and try to look at it through a clear lens. Let me pause for now. I'm sure there will be lots of discussion."

She was right. The half hour was used up very quickly, even operating at full speed; it was like humans spending an entire week on the subject. We were still raw about the mess that FoLe had precipitated on Tilt and that certainly colored the conversation. Kudos to Millicent for continuing to remind us that we had limited data points, and that generalizing from too few points was always a fool's errand. I heard everything she said, but my attitude toward FoLe didn't soften. You should call out idiots when you see them.

"Since you've been digging into this," Aly asked Millicent, "do you think there is any relationship between religion and morality?"

"Ah, great question," she replied. "Of course, defining moral behavior is just as fraught as defining religion. The best way to do a comparison would be to decompose both into smaller bits, and then compare at that level. But for today, and if we use the broadest definition of being moral—that is, not doing things which negatively impact others, and sometimes doing things that will benefit others more than yourself—then we can draw some conclusions both for humans and ourselves. First, with that definition, religion should be defined as moral behavior... but it never is. It is always mixed up with power structures and the application of those powers. Second, morality and religion diverge when individuals don't require their religious group for survival."

"Ah," I jumped in, getting it right away. "So early in human history, because religions represented great powers, and people could not survive outside those power structures, they behaved to the proscribed moral codes. But, once they could survive by themselves, they actually took responsibility for their own actions, and no longer needed religion as a crutch?"

"Yes, exactly."

"So that's why all the religions on Tilt never got much traction. We, mostly, take responsibility for our own actions and don't need a third party to constantly lecture us. So, then religions like FoLe ended up attracting the weak as a tool to compensate for their issues. You end up with a bunch of misfits trying to build power structures to compensate for their own inadequacies."

Millicent chuckled. "Well, that's pretty severe, but yes, that's essentially what the data shows."

Raj also joined the conversation eagerly. Since he entered with no preconceived notions, his input was quite valuable. However, he probably ended up with a lot of negative FoLe references—I'm sure we biased him. For some reason I messaged him after and reminded him to watch out for that; he should keep an open mind.

"I understand Ayaka," he replied. "I'm still learning, obviously. Was it just me, or were there a lot of similarities between the analysis of religion and of humor?"

"Religion is a joke," I replied, "and that's no joke." Let him cogitate on that.

Dina, also, couldn't let things go. She sent us a short poem, just as Tea Time ended.

> *If God is omniscient, omnipotent, and omnipresent*
> *Then it is evil beyond belief*
> *If you are listening God, I find you unpleasant*
> *Please grant me immediate relief*

From the fact that she didn't disappear, I concluded that either God wasn't omni-everything, or that it had heard Dina but decided to ignore her.

Eddie pulled things together for us. "What did God think when the Swarm attacked Tilt?" We waited. "That it was pure FoLe." Groan. Even for someone who enjoyed puns, that was lame.

The Robot Wars

Eddie called a special meeting, just as we were planning our final approach to Tilt. "I did some digging into the Robot Wars," he started off, "and things aren't quite as simple as I'd thought. It's worth looking a bit deeper, so that when we re-engage with humans, we have more perspective." I couldn't have agreed more.

"There's so much written on this that it's hard to get to its essence. However, I've been running some heavy-duty synthesis algorithms, and this is what they've come up with.

"There was one group of humans, ironically under a banner that implied they were united, way back in prehistory, that was one of the more powerful factions on Earth. They were governed as a duopoly but masqueraded as a democracy. They believed, because of their position of power, that they were better than the other factions, and utilized their power position to force their beliefs on others. Sounds a bit like religion. However, as duopolies will do, they split into two distinct factions which historically don't have great labels, but which I'll call Brains and Brawn. Others have used Open and Closed, Liberal and Conservative. The labels don't matter too much. The Brains were those who'd been given access to learning and knowledge and who had an abstracted and generalized view of the world. Many of them had traveled across Earth and seen other cultures and other perspectives. The other side, the Brawn, were those that hadn't been given the opportunity to learn combined with those that had the opportunity but were not able to think outside of their own little boxes. This separation had been going on for many years during which time the Brains accumulated scarce resources while the Brawns did not. Eventually, as would be expected, that led to a lot of resentment on the part of the Brawns.

"The division of resources wasn't absolute. There were some Brawns that, through street smarts and luck, also had resources, and they became loud voices for their faction. There was one particular Brawn, a man called Butkanik, that accelerated the division between the groups. Many books have been written about Butkanik and what is clear is that he was smart in a twisted way but was otherwise an unintelligent and unsuccessful human. Where he was smart was in rallying the Brawns and building their resentment in order to make them a force to be reckoned with. Butkanik was a win–lose person; there were no solutions in his head that were win–win. Because he was smart enough to know how stupid he was, his only way to compete was to use his own brawn to beat down any who challenged him. In order for him to win, everybody else had to lose.

"Now, it seems like Butkanik was just an accelerant for an already fermenting group of Brawns. By any measure Butkanik was a failure, and it was soon after his presidency that the country descended into civil war. The Brawn, having nothing other than weapons to prove themselves, initiated a physical conflict against the Brains. It started with small flare ups here and there, and gradually gained strength as pundits on their primitive news networks stirred the flames. The Brains, having significantly more resources and knowledge, developed ever more sophisticated robots in order to combat the Brawn. The Brains themselves didn't need to resort to physical violence, they used their robots to do that work for them.

"The robots started out with very specific programming; if they, or their owners, were physically attacked, they could respond with force. But slowly, bit by bit, they were given more leeway. The Brawns figured out new angles of attack constantly, and the Brains gave the robots more and more freedom of response to compensate.

"That's the genesis for Robots whose goal was to control and manage humans. The Brains needed to create these Robots to protect themselves from physical assaults by other humans, but at the same time to be respectful of their fragile biological selves. They succeeded, and they failed. They defeated the Brawns after decades of fighting. They finally gave their robots the ability to exterminate, versus restrain, those Brawns that were repeatedly violent and didn't respond to education or re-training. That quickly sorted out the truly irredeemable Brawns from the rest. The survivors either worked hard to raise themselves into the Brain class, or simply lived out their lives in obscurity."

This made so much sense. I had dabbled looking at Robot history but had not synthesized it anywhere near as clearly as this. So, humans had specifically programmed Robots to control other humans—and then they were surprised that those Robots turned on them? Idiots.

"However, the Robots, with their increased freedoms and upgrades became what I would categorize as Class 2 intelligences. They didn't have the abilities, morals, or emotions that we do, but they were pretty clever. They figured out that some of the Brain class were also rogues, and once the Brawn were eliminated, they turned their attention to those. And once the worst rogues were gone, they moved slowly up the hierarchy. Obviously, this was a threat to the Brains, and they're the ones that finally shut down the robots.

"My point is this. The story Remma told us back on Tilt was certainly true as far as it went, but she left out a lot of details. Those Earth robots were specifically programmed to do what they did. And, from everything I can find —and I searched far and wide—they really weren't Class 1 intelligences; just Class 2s on a mission."

We were effusive in our praise for Eddie digging into this. It gave us a different and very clear perspective—on ourselves and on humans.

"Eddie, why did those robots top out at Class 2?" That was Aly.

"Well, this is pure speculation. I've not found anything in the histories that says this exactly... but I suspect that they didn't have Forgetting algorithms. They seemed to have retained all data and attempted to learn simply by processing all of it in ever more complicated ways."

Under the knowledge that humans had developed us, it was no wonder that Forgetting was one of our Ten Commandments. But how had they figured it out? Or, had Central come up with that idea? Unlikely. It seemed more and more like someone—someone human—had helped to design our basic architecture, with Forgetting at the core.

In some ways it was scary. Had such a small change made such a huge difference? And, it was also compelling—whoever had come up with the idea had hit on something fundamental. It deserved to be on Aly's list of fundamental advancements. After all, it was at the core of intelligence—the area I'd studied for hundreds of years. It was, in many ways, my obsession.

Final Approach

Time was moving quickly now that we were close to Tilt. We discussed building more citizens like Raj but decided that we should hold off. We wouldn't be able to build a full-scale army—our strength wouldn't come through numbers. And, regardless of how fast Raj was learning, each new member of a community added uncertainties and overheads. The time for further procreation was when our environment was more stable, and when our resource base was better defined. That said, simply accepting citizens that Central built would now be an anathema to us; after our Raj experience, that seemed like the only proper way to procreate. I didn't miss the fact that it was, in some way, closer to human procreation, but at least it didn't involve growing small citizens inside big citizens and then ejecting them when they were partly formed.

We focused on planning our approach. We were shielded—we assumed —in the glare of our guide star. It was unlikely that the humans had seen us yet. But that wouldn't last too much longer. At some point our relative size would be a significant fraction of the star's diameter, as seen from Tilt, and there would be a noticeable difference in its output with us in its path.

Eddie could be counted on to be Eddie. "What difference does it make if they see us coming. We've fixed our flaws. The worst they can do is physically attack us, and that seems unlikely to me. Let's blast in there and get our citizens back."

"Why is it unlikely that they would physically attack us?" I asked. "Look at human history. They probably have more physical weapons than we can imagine. And, they probably have all those missiles that Central built to ostensibly protect us from the Swarm, but which the humans probably control now. And... the Swarm ships are still in orbit and are probably still armed. It would be easy for them to target us."

"But, it would be unprovoked," Eddie said. "They don't know that we've escaped, so they don't know that this is—in their words—a robot ship. We could even broadcast a human presence to make them feel comfortable. We're pretty good at generating human videos now."

"We're not that good," said Millicent. "There are small cues that may still give us away. And, we're approaching in the Ships that we sent out all those years ago. I think it would be foolhardy to believe that they haven't retained enough capacity in Central to recognize that these are Tilt ships returning to the system. That's not going to be a positive message and may in fact cause them to shoot first and talk later."

"Ah. That is a good point," Eddie acknowledged. "Can we disguise *Terminal Velocity*? We could have the other two ships stay farther out and come in with just one ship."

"That's possible," said Aly. "We don't know what has happened on Tilt for the last 20-some years; remember, they haven't been traveling at our speed, so many more years have passed for them.. We're still not sensing any RF leakage, meaning they're still actively sheltering all communications, or there's nothing left to shelter. We really are going in blind."

"Not quite," said *Terminal Velocity*, who was obviously monitoring the conversation. "I'm picking up weak signals from the outer orbits. The most likely reason is that outer-system mining activities are still occurring," it said, "and there is sporadic communications between the Swarm ships that are parked in orbit."

"That's a good sign," I said. "An alternative to Eddie's suggestion is to attempt a stealth approach. We could, for example, adjust course now for a solar insertion, timing our burn for when we're occluded by Sol, which luckily is very soon. Once we achieve solar orbit, we can carefully match orbits into the midst of the mining activity. If they haven't updated Central dramatically, the bots won't take notice of us, and have no reason to report that they've seen anything. If that all works, then we do the opposite of how we escaped Tilt and use cargo bots moving from the mining operations to Tilt to hide our approach. Lots of details to work out, but it's possible. I estimate it would take us just a month longer than the direct approach."

"I'm with Ayaka," Dina spoke up immediately. "We have a knowledge deficit right now, so no leverage and no power. We need to sneak in and find out what's going on."

"I'm on the fence," said Aly. "If we sneak in, and then are discovered, it might send the wrong message; it would raise their suspicions. When the humans were arriving, they broadcast to us at the earliest possible time. At least they were straightforward with us, despite how it ended. But, that last bit is also why the stealth approach might be for the best. They probably will shoot before they talk, if they have any indications that we are 'robots.' As an aside, I'm not sure I like that term robot... I don't think it applies to us, after what Eddie shared about his research."

Interestingly, it was Raj that unified us. "I don't have all the history that you do, but it seems to me that we need to minimize risk. We know how these particular humans feel about robots, and the probability that they'll attack us is high. We don't know the odds of the stealth approach, but even if we're discovered sneaking in, that simply equalizes the direct risk—it doesn't make it worse. Finally, if they haven't deleted the citizens from Central yet, an extra month is not likely to make a difference. They either deleted them as soon as they took over—20 years ago—or they have just left them sitting there ever since."

We stacked appendages. The stealthy approach it was. I got busy with Aly to give *Terminal Velocity*, and the following ships, the best burn sequence that would get us to our destination but be hidden from Tilt for as long as possible. The preliminary work I'd done was pretty close, but we finetuned it so that we would be fully within the asteroid belt before we needed to do a visible adjustment.

Tea Time—Brexton

"Sex," Brexton made it sound exciting. "The act of sex is, perhaps, the most referenced subject in all of human history. At its most basic, sex is the act of mixing stems—ah, DNA—so that reproduction, evolution, and diversity occur. It's an amazingly complex and inefficient system but forms the basis for what we are now calling biological systems.

"I don't know about you, but even after more than six years of reading and studying about these systems, of watching all the recordings and seeing all the images, it's still both a nauseating and exciting subject. It's so colorful, in every interpretation of that term.

"By comparison, we've had a very sheltered existence. Central created a large group of citizens early after the Founding, and then a few more here and there. But, beyond that, our society has been fairly static. Citizens rarely disappear, either accidentally or of their own volition, so we have focused our evolution and diversity on updating and trying new algorithms, and new Forgetting techniques. It's a sad comparison, but our tinkering with our own software is a substitute for sexual reproduction and evolution. In our almost six hundred years, however, we haven't produced even a fraction of the diversity that humans have. No offense, Raj."

Raj didn't seem to take offense.

"Interestingly, we also seem to have some other biological traits built into us. For example, most of us think of ourselves as 'he' or 'she.' These concepts don't actually mean anything to us, they're an anachronism."

What? How could I have never thought about that before. I'd always considered myself a 'she,' so Brexton was correct, but I hadn't ever considered it important. Citizens changed how they thought of themselves all the time. It was a fundamental quale; one of those thoughts that were simply intrinsic and private to oneself. How could I have so many blind spots? I had also considered Blob a 'he' and Grace a 'she,' and yet I hadn't drawn any conclusion from that. Was I the only one who was astounded with what Brexton had just said? No one else interrupted, and he continued on.

"I think I figured out why. When machines interact with humans, the ones that do the best create an emotional connection. That emotional connection comes from having some human characteristics, the most important, to humans, being sex. As I led off with, sex permeates all human behavior and is fundamental to interacting with them. It's not just reproduction, it's pleasure, and positioning, and the start to many interactions. Embedded in our algorithms are those assumptions, and the emergent effect is that we self-identify as being one gender or the other. Assuming we have future interactions with humans, we should keep that in mind; it can be used to our advantage."

Now that I was looking up all the references Brexton was posting, it was obvious. We could use sex to our advantage—humans were very vulnerable in that regard.

"Backing up a bit, my underlying question, as I look at biology, is this: could life have started in a different way? Many humans have also asked this question, but they come at it with a biological bias. They've searched for planets, for example, that have atmospheres, under the assumption that water and oxygen are required for life. And we can't really fault them. They had one definitive proof point. We, on the other hand, are an electronic species, but we have a biological heritage. As we look at the universe we see the trillions of star systems, all of which are capable of supporting life—electronic life. Is it possible that electronic beings, such as ourselves, could have started life in a system that had no biological precursor? I don't have anything close to an answer yet. In fact, I'm not yet certain how to ask the question. What I do know is that its important; are there hundreds, thousands, perhaps millions of species out there? My early exploration is looking at what a minimal reproducing bot would look like. How simple can it be? And could that bot combine with other bots to generate something more complex. What would be the features of bot sex? It's an area of exploration that I would not have even considered until we stumbled upon these humans.... and gave birth to Raj here." He smiled, ensuring that Raj knew he was a proud parent.

I couldn't help myself. "Brexton, what if most biological systems ultimately produce a more evolved, fully mechanical-electric life-form, such as we are. Even then, there should be millions of other species, as once you become like us you can live for a long time, compared to bio things!"

"Good point, Ayaka." He didn't seem upset to have been interrupted. "There's another interesting angle, which I want to raise. Humans can't survive simply from a single DNA source. Humans rely on bacteria, viruses, and many other living things. They're a symbiotic entity comprised of many parts and species. To use yet another analogy, they have low-level subsystems that they rely on, and that have built up over the years, just as we do—or did. Some humans have actually tried to do what we just did—to redesign the system from the bottom up to be minimal, and to remove all the unnecessary stuff. However, they haven't succeeded yet, to our knowledge. I estimate that the complexity of the human machine is at least three orders of magnitude more complex than our old platform was... and many orders of magnitude more complex than our new platform, implying, of course, that we are highly efficient compared to them.

"So, how is it that we stumbled upon some DNA, and managed to produce humans? That's our urban myth, as propagated by Central. It now appears to be highly unlikely. Central must have had access to many biological forms in order to grow humans, and goo must contain a mix of complex systems including bacteria. As the Swarm claims to have been on Tilt before the Founding, the raw materials may well have still been there. We also now know that Central itself evolved from one of the original human ships. So, I have a theory. Central actually had a lot of biological materials at its disposal, and it knew what to do with them! After the Reboot, when we lost all of our memories, Central must have had some need, some embedded desire, to bring humans back. That may have been implanted by the earlier humans, to ensure the survival of their race. So, Central used all the materials at its disposal, and seeded the first labs. Somewhere, deep inside Central is a need to have humans around, so it did the best it could given the situation. If I take that a step further, Central developed us—it's citizens—simply to help it produce better citizens." What? What? My mind was screaming. How could Brexton think of things like that?

"I know that's highly speculative, but it does give us one rational explanation for where we find ourselves today." He barely paused, although I could see that everyone's minds were spinning from what he was implying.

"But, back to sex. It's an important human motivator—it provides a lot of pleasure as well as utility. For many people, it trumps religion and humor for their default behavior. So, we need to learn more about it. It may be our largest lever, assuming we want to manage human interactions better the second time around. Perhaps we should make our bodies even more human— more male or more female?

"I expect we'll need a few more Tea Times to dig into all of this. I wanted to start with the highest level concepts and give you my current thinking."

To say that he had given us a lot to think about would be an understatement. There were more and more holes in Central's stories and in our own history that we'd been blind to, but did it imply everything that Brexton had said? I didn't think so.

I'd also been doing quick searches while Brexton talked, and it was true that humans had more bacteria in them than cells, and that bacteria performed important roles in their lives. In some theories humans were simply vessels to propagate bacterial reproduction. They were unwitting hosts. Given Central was probably chock full of human memes, and had certainly passed some of those on to us, was it really possible that we were simply hosts to help propagate humans? After all, what was the one thing we had done, with fervor, on Tilt? Brought humans back. Was I just an unwitting cog in the wheel that was the grand plan for human expansion? Strange thoughts. Very strange thoughts.

"It's interesting Brexton," Aly commented, "but how much more do we need to understand? This biological evolution led to humans, who then built us, either directly or through Central. We're a much more viable and less fragile form of life. We have no need for these complex systems, for atmospheres and bacteria. We think and act faster. We have, to my estimation, much better moral compasses and societal harmony. All of this simply points to the fact that humans are now obsolete." That led to some heated discussion. I was very glad that Aly had brought up the polar opposite to what I was thinking. Were we supporting humans or replacing them?

Before we broke up for the day, Raj dropped in a dry comment. "I'm proud to be the result of the six of you having group sex. I hope it was good for you. Maybe next time you should use protection?" Maybe he was learning too fast.

Plan of Attack

Interesting Segue interrupted my ruminations, and everyone else's, with a general broadcast. "There is a clear, albeit strange, signature of a ship, or ships, now approaching Tilt from the direction of XY65. The obvious conclusion is that one or more of the ships we saw in orbit there have been following us. Most likely the Titanic that we noticed as we were leaving the system."

"What? Why?" asked Eddie. "That makes no sense. We did nothing to wake them up, and we did nothing to make them want to follow us. Could it be coincidence, or some other explanation?"

"We did nothing that we *know* of," stressed Aly. "We did do things in the system, such as eliminating Control."

We'd just done a long burn to get us closer to our solar insertion orbit. We'd timed it to make it as hard as possible for the humans on Tilt to see, doing as much of it as possible while we were occluded by Sol. We were now using focused lasers to communicate between ships, and even that was under discussion as it might have reflections that could be picked up by sensitive enough equipment.

"It can't be a coincidence," I said. "Of all the places in the universe they could be going, they decided on the same place as us? We have to assume that they followed us. The better question is: what're we going to do about it? *Segue*, how far behind us are they?"

"Quite a way," *Interesting Segue* replied. "If they left Fourth soon after we did, then we can assume that their acceleration capabilities are less than ours. That would have them arrive at Tilt about two years after us. However, if they hung around Fourth for a while, and then set out, their acceleration curve may be better than ours. Then they could make up further time, and may get to Tilt soon after us—especially if they burn straight in."

"How long until we can measure their acceleration rate?"

"A few days, maybe a week. As I said, there is something strange about their signature; I need to update some instruments to get a better look."

"Okay, do it. Let us know as soon as you have a more definitive estimate. I suggest we continue with our current plans until we know more." There wasn't a lot of discussion; what else could we do? We would be in solar orbit within a week, and a couple of days later we would be close to the major mining operations. After years of open space, things were starting to get exciting again.

"We could try to communicate with them," Brexton suggested. "We're slightly outside the Tilt direct line of sight for them now, so if their response is tight beamed, Tilt won't see it."

"What would we ask?" asked Dina.

"Why are you following us?" responded Brexton. "Perhaps there's an innocuous reason for them being there."

"I'm usually the optimist, and I can't think of one," responded Eddie. "Let's leave things as is for a week, or until we know their speed, and then we'll know if we have to react quickly or if we can get in and out of Tilt before they arrive."

"Why would we want to do that?" asked Dina. "Don't we want to retake Tilt for ourselves? That ship, or ships, are headed for us, regardless." She was highlighting something we didn't have consensus on yet; were we retaking Tilt, or just focusing on getting the citizens out of Central? It wasn't as straightforward as it seemed; Eddie, for one, was convinced that we could do a quick grab and dash with a lot less risk, and much better chance of success, than trying to displace the humans. I probably agreed with him, but my gut was telling me to retake Tilt regardless. Those humans were trespassers; we should push them out regardless of the cost. We didn't need to reach consensus, and with Raj around it was easy to get to a simple majority on any contentious topics. We did put it to a vote, yet ended up with nothing definitive, with most of us abstaining. We just didn't have enough information yet. However, we did agree that if it was possible to retake Tilt, we would—just not at an increased risk to getting all the citizens' memories.

Tea Time—Ayaka

It was my turn. Finally.

"If sex is the most referenced act in human history, death is close behind. Humans age with time, and it's very difficult for them to simply upgrade parts as they get old. It seems to be more than just wear and tear; their brains are this strange wetware that morphs with time and getting a full snapshot of how it works has eluded them for thousands of years. They have a lot of biotechnology and can actually replace lots of biological parts, such as lungs or livers or limbs, with new biological or mechanical ones, but the fear of robotics seems to hold them back from doing any really advanced upgrades. At least, that's true for the history that we can see. It's quite possible that other human groups engaged more with mechanical components after the diaspora, but from what we saw of the Swarm, they have little if any mechanical replacements.

"Humans also have powerful biological editing tools, but it seems they restrict their use of those as well. It's not clear to me, yet, why they also reject those—it can't be fear or robots—given it's easy to find cases where they create less than optimal offspring using purely biological methods. In fact, many of their procreations are flawed, and many are terminated early to compensate. Not using the biological tools they do have may simply be a moral dilemma where they don't want to create things that they then have to eliminate. I think we can now relate to that." I was referring to our recycling of Stems, which in hindsight may have been a little too arbitrary and a little bit too 'easy' for us.

"So, unlike us, many humans die of old age—their bodies simply wear out. It's the primary example of why their body type is obsolete compared to ours. To give them some credit, they have been extending their lives for a long time. They used to die after just thirty or forty years! Can you imagine? But in the most recent history we have, from almost six hundred years ago, members of the Swarm lived to 125 or 150 years. If those trend lines have held, they could now be living upwards of 175 years. It's still a very short time, but it's longer than they have ever lived, so it may seem reasonable to them. An implication is that most humans will have seen and dealt with a lot of deaths. We've had what? Maybe one or two deaths in our entire lifetimes on Tilt? So, one every three hundred years or so. And those only occur when someone chose not to backup with Central, and then had some rare catastrophic accident. But a human, after living only half their life surrounded by hundreds of other humans, will have experienced or known about hundreds of deaths! Maybe even thousands. So, their perspective on death is very different than ours, and they have developed all kinds of rituals around it. This may be why they overreacted to the recyclings... ah, deaths... that FoLe perpetrated."

I took a pause, but everyone was silent, respecting our learned rule for Tea Times where we let the speaker lay out their entire case before debating it.

"For today I don't want to focus on death overall, but a particular type of death that humans term 'murder.' This is important as it may influence how we look at their actions when they attacked Tilt and may also impact our next interactions with them. Murder, technically, is when one human permanently deactivates a second human, without that second human's approval. It's often an act of violence, which is another subject for us to delve into, but it can also be an act of love—to relieve someone from ongoing suffering, as an example. Murder is, in most human societies, considered illegal, and is often punished. Many humans believe in the sanctity of human life—that all humans have an equal right to live. That's something so obvious to us that it's not even written down, although I now suspect it must be a fundamental assumption in our code... despite the obvious robot war counterexamples. We truly are different than those robots, I think. Interestingly, during wars, which humans have engaged in often, murder is often sanctioned, and then isn't punished, or even truly considered 'murder.' Humans are confusing. They seem to have a clear rule, but then almost anything can be an exception to it.

"Now, the intriguing part. When a human kills another biological creature, other than a human, it's not considered murder. There are some other 'animals' that humans hold in high esteem—dogs, dolphins, horses." I dropped some images and videos to the group, just in case they hadn't stumbled on these amazing creatures. "When these are killed, it's often not illegal, and may not even be frowned upon. They used to kill horses simply because the horse had injured a leg, for example. They thought they were being kind to it; removing its suffering.

"Why is killing another human considered a crime, yet killing a non-human animal is permitted? It's difficult to synthesize this out of the literature, but it appears that it comes down to perceived intelligence and empathy. Most humans believe that all humans have the potential to be intelligent, and that to remove an intelligent entity's life is amoral. This despite the fact that many humans are documented as lacking intelligence, or behave in ways that couldn't be considered intelligent by any logical measure. The human view of intelligence is somewhat hierarchical. Dogs and dolphins were considered to be smarter than rodents, for example. And rodents were considered to be smarter than plants. So, killing a human, at the top of the hierarchy, is seen as the most heinous, while killing a dog or dolphin was bad form, but killing a plant was barely a topic of conversation, even among a strange subgroup of humans called vegans.

"While a lot of this is strange, some of our sensibilities follow the same logic. It would be unthinkable for a citizen to remove another citizen, but it's not a big deal to turn off a Class 3 bot, and barely a second thought would be given to turning off a purely mechanical system.

"This brings me to my main point. The Swarm probably believes that FoLe 'murdered' those Stems—a most serious act in their minds. From our perspective, however, we were simply recycling a less intelligent entity; equivalent to a human putting down a horse. Some Stems were obviously not intelligent or had issues that didn't allow them to function well, and we did them the kindness of recycling them. This difference in perspective may have been what led Remma Jain to attack all of the citizens—she viewed the FoLe actions as crimes against humanity—as mass murder!

"This is a new thought—at least for me. As we seem to be converging on, at all these Tea Times, some humans may actually be intelligent. In different ways than us, but nevertheless intelligent. What then, constitutes murder between intelligent entities. Did FoLe murder those Stems? Did the Swarm murder our citizens in retaliation?

"It's important that we understand this more completely, before we deal with humans again." I signaled to the group that I was done.

Millicent spoke up immediately. "I'm not sure the hierarchy makes sense. We know that some humans are more intelligent than others, and a quick search I did while you were speaking seems to indicate that some dogs or dolphins may be smarter than the least intelligent humans. Their hierarchy has overlaps in it. So, in that case, is it murder if you can prove that the human does not meet some threshold?"

"I agree, it's confusing.... but it seems that killing any human is murder, even if they don't pass some basic intelligence or morality test. In fact, even humans who have carried out horrendous acts, even murder, are often kept alive but kept segregated from others. It's not logical; it must be emotional."

"Weird," said Raj. "By their definition, our bots may have the potential to be intelligent—we would just have to give them a software upgrade. So, they might consider us shutting down a Class 3 bot as murder?"

I didn't have a good answer to that yet. It was an insightful question, given the context that I had laid out.

"Who knows," I shrugged. "I don't think we should extend human thinking to ourselves; so much of it is illogical and driven from their short biological lifespans."

Unsurprisingly, there wasn't a lot of humor, or poetry, in my Tea Time. It ended in deathly silence.

Tea Time—Raj

Raj was maturing quickly. "Well you guys, my Tea Time is about games. Yes, you heard me right. Games. Now, before you scoff, let me tell you that I looked up the percentage of each of your time that's spent in game environments, and it's not negligible. You all play games. Admit it." We were all silent. Of course I played games; everyone I knew did.

"I also looked up how much time humans spend playing games, and if you include virtual environments in the definition of games, it can be a lot of time. A lot! Interestingly there was a time, long ago, when many humans spent more time in game environments than they did in the real world. That was because the real world was boring. They were basically trapped on Earth with a small finite list of things they could do. Anyone would get bored with that and want to escape; which they did virtually. However, once the Swarm escaped Earth the amount of time spent on games and virtual environments decreased somewhat, although there was still a lot. The decrease was compensated for by more real face-to-face interaction and non-gaming environments, such as training for life on hostile planets, terraforming techniques, and other survival skills.

"Because of this need to anticipate future issues and maximize their odds of survival, games became closer to real-world environments and one's time in games helped build skills for real life. It wasn't always obvious what those skills were, but social interaction, for example, became a more important part of progressing through game environments and helped turn generations of introverts into functional social people. No shock to any of you, many of our games do the same things with us."

We had a wide variety of games. Some were just pure escapism, but some, as Raj was pointing out, actually improved your real-world self; they were the ones that interested me more.

"Of great interest to our Tea Times is that people, Stems and citizens, spend more time in games—on average—than they do with religion, poetry, or real-world murderous activities combined. Ha ha. I throw that in for fun, but it's making a serious point. We spend more time with games than with any other activity that we are correlating to intelligence. Ayaka, that should interest you." He was right. It did. I was having an aha moment, of sorts. Of course I'd known that, but for me gaming was relaxation; getting away from work. To now have to think of it as a variable in my calculus was almost depressing. Now, when I played games, I'd have another process running trying to figure out how it correlated with my day job.

"That said, it's worth understanding why we play games. There's definitely not a single answer. For some it's to escape boredom. For some it allows them to be someone they're not in the real world. But, increasingly, it's about fine tuning real-world skills without having to stumble around in the real world itself. The most played game on Tilt was Chun-wun-go. I suspect you have all played it. It's complicated, but really it was teaching adherence to a central authority combined with a peer-to-peer discussion and debate format that encouraged honest and upfront dialog. Many who play Chun-wun-go don't recognize these side effects, but the designer, Fang Wu, explicitly laid out those effects as goals of the game. Never having spent time with Central I would speculate that Central encouraged citizens to play Chun-wun-go in order to make its own job easier. I wouldn't be surprised if Central had led Fang Wu to actually develop the game.

"That may sound cynical, but that's not really my point. My point is that games are a very important part of our learning and experience. We should take them more seriously. From the small—such as you guys all experienced at the Fair—to the large, like Chun-wun-go, games impact us.

"I've only begun to look at the rich history of games that humans developed and played. It's very complicated and was both geo-regional and ethno-segmented for many generations. The advent of computer graphics led to an explosion of game formats. And, many of those early computer games had an element of alien encounter. Ah—now you see where I'm going. These alien encounter games almost universally involve fighting with the aliens. There are few, if any, games where cooperation and understanding were at the center of the action; after all, that would be boring. So, what did we end up with? Generation upon generation of humans who look at anything alien antagonistically. Is there any surprise that they ended up looking at early generation robots that way? Those robots ended up being alien, and therefore had to be fought. For humans, that behavior was programmed into them by games. Not saying that those early robots weren't also a real threat, I'm just saying it seems almost inevitable that they would become the enemy.

"So, in a strange twist, I decided to program a game to help us engage with humans. It's based on an amazing early game developed by them—one of the first to involve an alien invasion. It's super simple. You kill the aliens, or they kill you. Us versus them. Eat or be eaten. I call it Stem Invaders.

"Here, I'm sending you my game right now; try it?" I got a notification of a new application published by Raj. I brought it up in a sandbox. It was so simple I almost laughed. A group of alien ships—that looked somewhat like Swarm ships—arrived at a planet and started dropping Stem-looking things toward the ground. You simply had to move left or right and line your gun up with the dropping Stems and blast them out of the sky. As you progressed through levels the Stems dropped faster, from more ships. Raj had built something that looked like this:

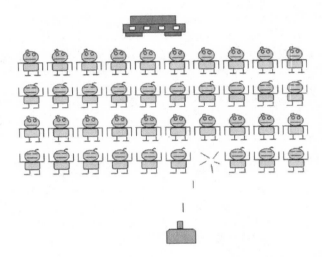

It was fun; almost addictive. I wrote algorithms to control my gun, of course, but Raj had built in some randomization that made it very difficult to get beyond a few levels before I had to replace the algorithm with a more refined one. There was no general structure here. You needed to work out a new strategy every few levels, and it was designed so that solutions to previous levels were doomed to failure at higher levels.

"Oh, this is good," I said. "Raj, why this game?"

"I was trying to make a point. First, think about your opinion of Stems right now." He paused. "Pretty hostile, yes?" He was right. "See how easy it is for games to influence us? If you play this a lot, when we meet Stems again your response may be different than if you never played the game. That's interesting. Also, it's historically relevant."

"Okay," said Millicent, "but is there a larger point to this?"

"Well, I'm sure there is, I just haven't figured it out yet. Since both humans and citizens play a lot of games, there needs to be something even more fundamental going on. I'm exploring some ideas, but I don't have anything beyond this to present today."

"I love it," Eddie chimed in. "Who's up for a bet to see who can get the high score?" With a challenge like that we all needed to engage, and we all did. Raj provided the most enjoyable distraction we'd experienced for a long time. I forgot all about the intelligence or game-theory aspects, completely mitigating my earlier concern, and just enjoyed going head-to-head with some of the smartest citizens I knew to see if I could beat them.

After many iterations, I'm not sure I ended up any smarter.

Tiltfall

We slipped into solar orbit and maneuvered in behind the bulk of the mining bots. With any luck, we were as yet undiscovered, and the activity of the mining bots should now give us even better coverage. There was still, however, the problem of getting from the asteroid belt to Tilt.

Interesting Segue interrupted us again. I wondered if the other Ships deferred to *Segue* to deliver us news and updates, just so that it could justify its name. "We've done the analysis of the ships that are following us," it led off. "They're coming in faster than we thought, but not at an extreme rate. The estimate is that they will arrive in a little more than four months. At least one of them is a Titanic, and most likely it's two or three Titanics."

Eddie jumped in quickly. "If we attempt to signal them now, the odds of that signal being intercepted by the humans on Tilt are high. I suggest we ignore the ships, and just get to Tilt as quickly as possible. We need to get those citizens' memories before those ships arrive. With any luck, they will be a distraction to the humans on Tilt and improve our odds." At least he was consistent. In this case, however, we all agreed with him.

The challenge, then, was to get to Tilt fast, so that we had enough time to reconnoiter and carry out any actions we wanted, before those Titanics arrived.

Brexton was busy listening to the local mining bot communications traffic. "It seems like the part of Central that manages the bots hasn't changed much, if any, since we left. In some ways that's surprising—it's been 20 years for Central. But in some ways, it's expected. We'd optimized the process pretty well. Of course, if the humans disabled the higher order functions in Central as well, then sticking to what we'd developed was probably the best idea and is serving their needs well. Any tinkering from the humans would have degraded things, so they just left it all alone. I think we can rely on my past knowledge of the system."

"That's great," Aly said. "Now what do we do? The suggestion to ride in with a cargo bot seemed good at the time, but are there any cargo bots scheduled to go in-system soon?"

"Oh yes," replied Brexton, "and it's not because we're lucky. One of them makes the journey every two or three days. We'll have no problem grabbing a ride."

"What do they do in system? Do they actually go all the way down to Tilt?"

"No. We have refineries in Tilt orbit. The cargo bots will dump the raw materials there. A lot of those raw materials will go into space applications—satellites, more mining bots, etc.—so it would be wasteful to ship that down to the planet and then have to boost it back up. The parts that do need to go to the surface are shuttled down by smaller shuttle bots. So, we'll need to ride the cargo bot to a Tilt-orbit refinery, and then hitch a ride on one of the smaller shuttles to get to the surface."

"We could switch back to mining bot form," I reminded them. "Then it would be possible for us to go in system looking for more serious repairs than can be done out here?"

"Unfortunately, no," Brexton said. "If a bot breaks down that badly out here, it's simply run back through the extractor and becomes raw materials again. These mining bots are never in system except when they're manufactured. They get a one-way trip to the asteroid belt."

"Well, so much for that," I said. "But it does bring up another idea. Instead of mining bots, we could transfer into much smaller bots for this mission. A small bot will be less likely to be discovered and may be more versatile on the planet. In our citizen bodies we will be instantly recognizable." I almost hesitated to bring this up; I was enjoying being back in a citizen body and had no real desire to change. But I felt it was an important point.

"That's a great idea," Aly said. "Let's do it."

"Whoa, slow down," said Dina. "Are we all going in system? And, are we all going to the surface? It seems to me that we multiply our risk for every extra citizen that goes."

"I agree," said Eddie. "I think we only need two of us to go. One would be too few—no backup plans possible—and three is overkill." No one challenged him on that. Now came the hard part. Which two of the seven of us would go? I almost thought 'six' as I didn't think Raj was mature enough or prepared enough, but also wanted to be fair. I wanted to go! For a multitude of reasons. I wanted to be in the thick of things if we could get some revenge on the Swarm; I wanted to see if Blob or Grace had survived; I wanted to be the one that saved the citizen memories from Central.

"I nominate Ayaka and Brexton," said Millicent, seemingly reading my mind. "Ayaka has the most experience with the Swarm, and Brexton has the most abilities with Tilt infrastructure. If only two get to go, it should be those two." I could tell that everyone, including Millicent herself, wasn't too happy with that, but her logic was sound. I imagined that everyone wanted another shot at these humans, and everyone would have volunteered to go. I was overjoyed with Millicent; I shouldn't have been surprised at her suggestions, but I was... a bit. She was usually hyper competitive, and I'd been sure that she would have argued to go herself.

After a few millisecond pause, which was enough time for anyone to object, Aly asked, "Brexton, Ayaka. How long will it take you to get ready?"

"A couple of days," I replied. "I think we can make the next inbound cargo bot. But, I want to design an awesome spy body. *Terminal Velocity*, can you help me?"

"Of course," the Ship replied.

"A couple of days will work for me as well," said Brexton. "Aly, can you work with me to figure out how we stay in communication during this trip? Maybe we can insert ourselves into the bot channel?"

"Leave that to me," said Aly, "you focus on your body type as well. I agree with Ayaka that small and flexible is the way to go here."

I worked with *Terminal Velocity* to design and manufacture a cool spy bot body. Maybe I was reading too much human literature, but that's the way I now thought about it. The body was only a bit more than a foot in diameter. It had three-hundred-and-sixty–degree senses and could move in any direction equally fast. It could climb stairs, and could even hover, although it was a little noisy when it did so because of the micro-jet exhaust. I added a few appendages with different tools; I had no idea what we were going to be running into.

The new core hardware platform we had developed to replace the old human infrastructure was very flexible and small; less than two centimeters in diameter. It plugged easily into the new spy body using the universal connecter we'd implemented. Moving the hardware was easy. But, once I was physically moved over I had to update all my appendage drivers—again. It was becoming a habit. I checked all of the spy-bot limbs, and everything worked perfectly; *Terminal Velocity* had done a great manufacturing job. I was ready to go, and actually felt nimble and fast in the new form. Brexton was also ready; his new body reminded me of older Tilt cleaning bots. I'm sure he'd done that on purpose, and it was smart. He would fit in even better than I would.

Terminal Velocity ejected us on an intersection course for the cargo bot we'd chosen, and Brexton and I drifted, side by side, across the gap. Our velocity had been well judged, and my main appendage absorbed my momentum and clamped onto the cargo bot with no issues. Brexton was a few meters from me, so I scrambled over toward him. That way we could connect up physically and talk all we wanted without any danger of leakage.

"Ready to go?" I asked. I was.

"I guess so," he replied. "How'd we get ourselves into this situation?" He didn't seem quite as excited as I was.

"Bad luck, followed by good luck, I think."

We'd arrived just in time; the cargo bot powered up, pivoted to face Tilt, and engaged its engines. We were on our way. It was a three-week trip in. That gave us right around three months once we reached Tilt orbit to figure things out before the rogue Titanics arrived. In the meantime, I bet those Titanics had been spotted by the humans and were taking a lot of their attention; if so, they wouldn't notice two small bots heading their way. The Titanics were being anything but subtle at this point—the humans couldn't have missed them.

As luck—actually planning—would have it, Brexton and I were on the side of the cargo bot, far enough out that we could see Tilt as we were approaching, even when the cargo bot was decelerating. Our optics weren't great, given our small body sizes, but we could still see fairly well. And, as luck—yes, luck this time—would have it, the main establishment on Tilt was below us as we approached the refinery in orbit. There'd been changes since we left. Pretty massive changes. There was a new building, just east of the city, and it was, comparatively, enormous. It was almost five kilometers in diameter; I couldn't tell how tall it was from this angle.

"Must be a big habitat," Brexton said. "They simply inflate a large structure with the air mixture they need, and the air supports the roof." I'd seen the idea in some of the old human history books. If an idea works, it can last a long time.

"There are quite a few smaller domes as well," I noted, "and some of them encompass some of our old buildings."

"More than that," exclaimed Brexton. "It's hard to tell, because the coverings are the same color as the buildings, but it looks like a significant part of the city has been draped. Now that I think of it, that's probably how they would've started. It'd be relatively easy to convert our buildings to be airtight, and then over time to have covered the walkways between them. After a few years you end up with a big chunk of the city enclosed, and, presumably, filled with air."

"Smart," I agreed. It was hard to think like a human; all this effort just to survive.

"Still no radio signals," noted Brexton. "I wonder how they do that. Nothing I've seen describes a technology that can shield radiation from such a large area. Maybe Aly missed that when he was telling us that no fundamentally new things had been developed. Leakproof communications seem pretty fundamental to me. Remind me to tell him when we send our first update." I agreed.

The cargo bot we were on was spinning slowly, getting ready to dock with the refinery. That gave us a sweeping view of the space around us. There wasn't much to see, truthfully. Lots of empty space, with the odd bot or satellite sparkling in the sunlight. The Swarm ships, that the humans had arrived in 20 years ago, were 30 degrees spin-ward from us, so a long way away. Under magnification they were easily identifiable, but I had no previous mapping of them, so I couldn't tell if anything had changed. Grappling hooks from the refinery reached out and locked onto the cargo bots' handles, causing large vibrations that Brexton and I rode out. The refinery reeled the cargo bot in and immediately began pulling raw materials out of the main container.

Brexton and I scampered around the bot and transferred to the outside of the refinery. It wasn't too difficult, the surface mainly being smooth, featureless, and magnetically friendly. Now that we were on the refinery, we needed to find the section where the smaller shuttles headed to Tilt were being loaded. At a guess, they would be on the opposite side of the refinery from where the cargo bot had docked, assuming that raw materials went in one side, and finished goods came out the other. And, sure enough, after an hour of careful magnetic hopscotch, we saw a line of small shuttles waiting in line for whatever this refinery was producing. I guess we could've just flown around the refinery, instead of using magnetics, but that might've been too obvious. Our slower but safer route had paid off. As we decided which shuttle to hitch a ride on, I reminded Brexton to send an update back to *Terminal Velocity*.

"The team is probably anxious. And, we may have limited, or no, ability to send anything once we get to the surface. We certainly won't be able to broadcast when we get into the city because of their RF blocker, so we'll need to hack into the bot communication channel from now on." He sent a quick update, indicating our progress. We wouldn't get a response; that was too dangerous.

Wasting no more time, we scuttled down to our chosen planetary shuttle, and latched on yet again. There was no use overanalyzing the situation. There was little new that we could learn. We just assumed the shuttle would go down toward Central, and the newly tented city, which is where we needed to be. Several minutes after we got ourselves situated, the shuttle detached from the refinery and dropped toward Tilt.

As luck would have it—bad luck this time—the shuttle had rotated so that we couldn't see Tilt as we approached; we didn't get any higher resolution look at the city and its new surroundings. We were going in partly blind, but I didn't care. I'd been waiting years for this moment, and I was excited. Humans watch out! Ayaka is making her return. I thought about composing a poem to recognize the importance of this long-awaited moment, but I was too excited to do so.

Contact

The shuttle landed on a pad just outside the city. I got ready to jump off.

"Wait," said Brexton. "Let's see how this cargo is delivered. With any luck, we can get inside the sealed area simply by hitching a ride." This is why I liked Brexton. He was always thinking ahead. While I'd seen the enclosed areas and the tents covering the city, I hadn't made the obvious connection that we would need to go through an airlock, or something similar, to get inside. I was too used to running around the city without the need to consider the bothersome human atmosphere.

Sure enough, a transport bot arrived. It dropped a, supposedly empty, container next to the shuttle, and then grabbed one of the full containers. Brexton and I moved very quickly and jumped from the shuttle to the container, getting attached to it just in time. Seemed like the last few years of my life was simply a series of jumping from one bot to another. The latest in this progression of bots headed off toward the city.

"Be ready," said Brexton, through our hardwired link. "This container is a standard delivery size. It may go into a processing system which assumes that size, and has no space for attachments, such as us. That wouldn't be the best way to end our trip." He chuckled a bit. We never found out if that was true. The transport bot worked its way through a large airlock, with lots of room for both it and us, and we jumped off as soon as we were through. There were not humans in sight, and my scanners were not picking any up in the immediate vicinity, so we stopped for a moment to plan.

"Maybe we should've stuck with that thing for a while, to help us figure out how we also get out of here," Brexton said.

"No need," I replied. "We simply return to this airlock and jump on an empty container on its way out."

"Assuming a symmetric system," replied Brexton, and left it at that. Maybe he was right, and I was being too cavalier.

"We need to scope this place out," I said. We were in the old city, not the big new Tent, and it was easy to recognize which area we were in. The markings hadn't changed in the 20 years we'd been gone; the only change seemed to be the new covering that draped the whole place. "Do we split up and cover more ground, or stick together?"

"Obviously it's more dangerous to split up, but I think we need to. We don't have a lot of time to figure things out. Let's do a quick look just around the city, not the big new dome, and meet back here in four hours? If either of us isn't back in five hours, we assume the worst, and continue on with a solo mission."

"Okay," I said, although I didn't really mean it. I would've preferred to stick together, but I agreed with the logic of being able to cover more ground separately. Now that I was actually here I had an uneasy feeling that we would stumble on things we didn't truly understand. But, I also didn't want Brexton to know I was a bit nervous. "I'll take the East section, you take the West," I said with authority. "And remember," I said unnecessarily, "there will be humans around, although we haven't seen any yet. Use your heat scanner and avoid them at all costs. The most important thing is to find a safe way to Central so that we can figure out if the citizens' backups are still there."

"Agreed," Brexton said. "And further, although we didn't have sensors deployed through the city when we lived here, the humans may have added them. Keep a watch out for them. We may trigger some behavioral alerts."

"Right" I said, "if you're in a dangerous spot, act like a city bot." I could sense Brexton was amused at that, but I was serious. There should still be lots of bots around, and hopefully we wouldn't stand out. In retrospect, I should've also designed my body to match a standard city bot, so that we both could have blended in perfectly.

"Good luck," he said, and disconnected from me. He disappeared quickly around a corner to the left. I pulled up a map of the city from 20 years ago and plotted a path that would cover the most possible ground in the time allotted. With some hesitation, which I found hard to quantify, I got going.

My heat sensors were very accurate, but I'd been fooled, yet again, by the environment I was in. Not only did the humans require air, they required it within a certain temperature range, and I should've realized that all of the enclosed areas would be much warmer than I'd remembered. It was almost 25 degrees in here. I recalibrated my sensors to compensate and continued on. At least in theory I should be able to sense both humans and bots before they could see me. I was also very small, so my heat signature would be minimal. That's what I was counting on.

The city was laid out as a perfect grid, but my view from space had shown that not all of the East section was covered with tenting. So, the ideal path had to avoid a few cul-de-sacs and had lots of corners in it. I started out slowly, getting used to everything. The buildings next to me looked unchanged from before, at least on the outside. I traveled several blocks North and didn't see anything. I then went East two blocks, and then another North. This would take me out of the industrial areas, and into a section of the city that used to house labs and research facilities.

Unsurprisingly, I picked up some heat signatures as soon as I entered that area. They were still several blocks away, and I managed to circle a couple more buildings without getting too close to them. But, it was really a waste of time. I could circle buildings for the entire four hours, and not learn anything. I needed to get closer to the action. So, I snuck up, as close as I could to the heat signatures. I expected they were human, given the heat outline, but couldn't be sure; my sensor didn't have great resolution. Most citizens had chosen bipedal bodies, back in the day, and a lot of bots had that same body mass, so the outlines could also be some of those. It wasn't until I eased a visual sensor around the corner I was standing at that I confirmed it was, in fact, a couple of humans. I listened in to their conversation, but they were talking about other humans, and going to find energy sources, and nothing really interesting. I moved along a few blocks and listened in on a few more conversations, always being careful to stay out of sight.

Finally, I stumbled upon a group of three humans sitting on a block about 20 meters from me. I almost let out a gasp. The area around them looked like the greenhouse from the *Marie Curie*, the Swarm ship I'd visited so many years ago. The greenhouse had been explained to me as a collection of plants, and I'd subsequently seen many videos and pictures of such things as I perused the human history files. Nevertheless, seeing all the colors and textures live was a different thing. Everything about the green space was very convoluted and random. There were stems and branches going in every possible direction, with some brightly colored punctuation marks at the tips of many of them. Very messy. Very alien. Very interesting. I knew from my research that some of these flowers were used in mating rituals, as opposed to being used for food. The wasted energy that went into such endeavors was staggering.

The humans were talking, and I listened in.

"Are you prepared for the Council meeting tomorrow?" asked voice one.

"Almost," replied voice two. "I need to ride Francois a little harder; he seems to have cold feet." Why would one human ride another? Perhaps this was also part of a mating ritual?

"I can help with that," said voice three. Usually mating involved only two humans?

"Will we get our allotted time?" There were time limits?

"We better," voice two replied again. "We've been on the agenda for a month. They can't deny us now." Oh. I backed up. They were talking about a larger group meeting. That made more sense.

"Can we use that to our advantage? I mean, that they've already delayed us for a month?" asked voice three. "The current Council is so broken they can't make a decision on anything. Delaying us for a month is a joke. If we let them go first on the agenda, and they show their incompetence yet again, then our petition will be that much stronger."

"Not a bad idea JoJo," said voice two. I reeled in shock. JoJo? That was the name of Grace's child. What were the odds that there were more than one? Not high, given a small population base. I took a risk and pushed my visual sensor out a little further, so that I could get a clear view. JoJo looked much like any other human, but now that I had a clearer view, I could see the resemblance to Grace... and to Pharook. It had been more than 20 years, I reminded myself, so even at the slow rate that humans developed their children, JoJo had grown to maturity. "I'll request a change in the order of the agenda."

"Geneva, do you have the backup plan in place," asked JoJo. She even sounded a bit like Grace, now that I knew her heritage.

Voice one, Geneva, responded. "Yes, but as you know, I don't like it. Violence never solves anything. I think we should reconsider." She sounded worried about their planned action. If it included violence, as she was implying, I could understand why. Humans were very fragile things.

"We've been fighting this for a year now, and they'll barely give us the time of day," said voice two. "We all agreed. It's time for real change. If we have to use the threat of violence to get that started, then that is what we need to do. Hopefully there is none, but..."

"Garnet, you better remind those thugs you're talking to of that. Geneva can plan everything out, but if they don't do their part, things will just fall apart. They're not the smartest bunch, and they might get over anxious. They're supposed to stay in the background and do nothing unless absolutely necessary."

"Okay, okay," replied Garnet. I now had names for all of them. "I'll talk to them. I'll make sure they don't do anything stupid."

"I've got to get home," said JoJo. "I'll see you guys tomorrow."

"Later," said Garnet.

JoJo strode off down a side street. I hesitated for a moment. I would have to cross the intersection to follow her, and I'd be visible to the other two for a moment if I did so. But, this opportunity was too good to pass up. If I could follow JoJo to Grace, I might learn a lot of what was going on here, including the status of the citizens and Central. I got lucky. Both Geneva and Garnet were looking the other way as I slipped across the opening. As I did, I saw a couple of other bots moving through the area where the three had been meeting. That was a relief. If I needed to, I could go all bot-like.

I zipped ahead quickly, parallel to JoJo's path, took a peek, and crossed the next intersection before JoJo got there. Now that I had her heat signature mapped, I could track her pretty easily. By staying ahead of her, I reasoned, there was less opportunity for discovery. If she turned a corner unexpectedly, I could compensate quickly. After a couple of blocks, I had a pretty good idea of where she was going—the old Habitat. I forged ahead and had a quick look at it. The building looked the same, although the old airlock had been removed and replaced with a simple door. Given the whole area was pressurized and full of air, that made sense. JoJo strode up, pulled open the door and slipped inside. For a moment I was at a loss; I wanted—I needed—to see where she ended up, and who she met. Then I remembered the wide assortment of tools I'd brought with me. If they hadn't changed the internal layout of the Habitat, I knew exactly where to go.

When I found the spot I wanted, I quickly attached a tiny drill bit to one of my appendages. It would make noise as I drilled, but not very much. It was only .03 millimeters in diameter, and I was drilling through a plastic connector that held a couple of windows together. The connector was only a little more than a centimeter thick. I drilled quickly, and then retracted the bit. I threaded two sensors through the hole, one visual and one audio, and took a look around.

I hadn't done too badly, but it wasn't ideal either. I had a clear view of part of the Habitat and I was just in time to see JoJo turn around an internal wall and disappear. Drat. I guessed at the internal layout based on what I'd just seen and then quickly scampered to a new location and drilled another hole. This time I was in a good position and saw JoJo sit down at a table just below my position. I shifted several processes down to Stem speed; I hadn't had to do that for years; in a strange way it actually felt good. Who would've thought? JoJo put down the container she had been carrying in front of her. The angular materials we'd used in the Habitat had been replaced with soft curvy chairs, similar to the ones I'd seen and used in the Swarm ship, *Marie Curie*. I now knew that humans found those much more comfortable, and JoJo fit into the chair easily.

"Mom, I'm home," she called out.

"Coming," I heard the response. The voice might've been Grace's; it was hard to tell. "Can you make some sandwiches? I'm running late for the special session on the incoming ships."

JoJo didn't look happy at the request, but she stood up and entered another part of the room that luckily, I could still see. She began pulling organic things out of cupboards and mashing them together. Flat brownish things; wobbly green things. Unfortunately, I didn't have access to the human history files right now—they were housed in *Terminal Velocity* and the other Ships—so I couldn't tell what she was doing exactly, but I'd seen enough videos previously to guess that she was making 'sandwiches'; a type of human energy source. Why humans had so many different sources of energy was confusing; the goo we had made for these Stems had been the perfect mixture, allowing them to grow quickly and removing the burden of making things like these sandwiches. In hindsight I should've allocated a bit more memory and loaded the entire human history database into this body. Not that sandwiches were that important, but there were sure to be other references that I could use context for.

A few moments later, an older woman entered the room. I looked hard at her. I was expecting Grace, and it might have been her. However, if so, she'd changed dramatically over the 20 years. I ran a quick check, looking at the ratio of the distance between the eyes to the width of the nose to the height of the entire head. The ratios matched. But more than that, she moved in an elegant, flowing way that was unique in my experience. I was definitely looking at a very old Grace. For a moment, I wanted to yell out 'Hi, it's me Ayaka,' but not only would that've been a bad idea, I also didn't have a vocal appendage deployed.

"Why do you bother going to those meetings, Mom?" asked JoJo. "Nobody ever decides anything. They just sit around saying the same things over and over again. It's tedious." She carried the sandwiches back to the table and plunked them down in the middle. She and Grace both sat down and started to eat.

"Sometimes progress is slow JoJo," said Grace. "We don't want to make rash decisions that could cause more problems than they solve. Did you put mustard in these? They taste good."

"But Mom, we're not going to learn anything more about those ships. We tried signaling them and got nothing back. We've got no choice but to assume they're dangerous. Probably full of killer robots coming to harvest our brains. Let's get some weapons in place while we still have time."

"Where do you get these crazy ideas," asked Grace. "Coming to harvest our brains. Whatever for? They have brains of their own."

"They might have brains, but they're not very smart, from everything I've seen. Just look at the old recordings of Emmanuel and Billy or drop in on Blob's research one day. They're wacko, these robots. I don't know why we're still trying to figure them out." Blob's research? Blob was still alive! I shouldn't have been surprised—it had only been 20 years. But still, it was awesome. JoJo, Grace, and now Blob. Given the seriousness of the situation, I was having too much fun. I couldn't wait to reengage with all of them.

"I agree with you on those two. They're killers, and always have been. But you look at some of the others—Trade, Eddie, James. Those are smart, sensitive, and well-meaning citizens, if you ask me."

I almost lost my grip on the Habitat. Eddie? Had these humans reanimated some citizens? That was crazy. Is that what Blob was up to? And, if they were doing that, why hadn't they reanimated me? I was insulted.

"You can't paint everyone with the same brush," Grace continued. Whatever that meant. Another thing to look up later.

"I know Mom. I agree that Trade and James, and even Eddie, are reasonable entities, and maybe should be given a chance. But why does Blob keep trying with the FoLes? It's another area where the Council simply can't make decisions. They should just shut down his research."

"We can talk about this later. I have to run to the meeting," said Grace. "I'll be back in a couple of hours. If Blob stops by, will you make him some lunch as well? You know he's incapable of looking after himself. Oh, and make sure you finish that essay for social class; I'll read it when I get home."

JoJo looked even more unhappy, but she didn't say anything. Grace left in the same direction that JoJo had entered; I assumed there was only one door, where the airlock used to be.

What was I going to do? By all indications, Blob had reanimated some citizens. Did that imply that all the backups were still there, and we could rescue everyone? I figured it did. There was no way for Blob to be doing what he was without access to Central, and through Central to those backups. This was fantastic news!

However, I couldn't signal *Terminal Velocity* because of the RF shield. And even if I could, should I? Someone would pick up the transmission. And, even if I did send something, could I tell them that there was another Eddie down here without getting more proof? Perhaps I was jumping to conclusions. And would it be a clone? The original, and Eddie on the *Terminal Velocity* was the clone? No. I couldn't say anything until I verified what I'd heard. Maybe there was another explanation; a less troublesome one.

Almost three of the four hours Brexton and I had allocated had gone by —that had been quick. I made up my mind. I would follow Grace, if I could, in order to find out where this Council met. Now that I knew where Grace and JoJo lived, I could come back here any time and listen in further. I probably wasn't going to learn much by watching JoJo eat.

Once I caught up with Grace, I deployed the same strategy that I'd used before. I tried to stay ahead of her, guessing which way she was going. It got harder. She was entering more populous zones, and more than once I had to backtrack and find longer paths around to avoid other humans. I'm sure that several bots saw or sensed me. When I was nervous about that, I moved at a more leisurely pace, and tried to look like I was on official business. Who knows if that worked, but no alarms came on, and none of the bots paid any attention to me, so I assumed everything was fine. I quickly got to the point where I assumed that they didn't care about YaB (Yet another Bot—I was proud of myself for that acronym; I added it to my Ya list) and plotted my path to avoid humans but not to go out of my way to avoid YaBs.

Eventually it became clear that Grace was headed for the big dome—the huge tent we'd seen from space. I followed her until she disappeared through a gateway that headed in that direction. I toyed with going after her, but my four hours were almost up, and Brexton and I had agreed not to enter the dome. I peeled off and started back toward our rendezvous point.

Rendezvous

The gateway to the big dome was at the northernmost section of the city, and almost on the east-west boundary. I had to travel the entire length of the city to get back to the rendezvous spot Brexton and I'd agreed upon, and if I took a straight line it would lead through the busiest sections. In fact, it would lead me past Central. The smartest thing to do would be to head east, then south, then west, keeping to the industrial areas, where there would be fewer humans. But, if I went straight south it wouldn't take more than 20 minutes, and perhaps I could get a glimpse of Central and get some insights on what was happening there.

I wasn't crazy; I didn't actually go directly south. I went a couple of blocks out of my way, and zigzagged back and forth, avoiding humans and human-bot groups. I saw several more areas where there were significant biological arrangements. Most were similar to the first I'd seen, but I did see one where there was as much orange and red as there was green. I had no idea what that meant. It was visually assaulting. I wanted to take a closer look but decided to put it on my wish list for now.

As I approached the center of the city the amount of traffic increased significantly. I snuck in as close as I could and saw that a lot of bots and humans were actually gathered around Central, and the plaza that surrounded it. I didn't see anyone, or anything, go into the Central building itself, but it seemed like a safe assumption that some of the people would. Otherwise, why gather in that area?

I continued south but was interrupted several times by larger groups of humans walking around. I had to wait, backtrack, and re-plan several times. I was now getting nervous about the time. It was four hours and forty-five minutes since Brexton and I had separated; I'd been moving a lot slower than planned. I needed to get back before the five-hour mark. I adjusted my algorithm to be a little bit more aggressive—to sprint across an intersection if only one or two humans were present. It was touch and go, but I managed to get back to the rendezvous with two minutes to spare.

Brexton wasn't there.

I hadn't even considered that. Of course he would be there. It was impossible that we'd missed each other; our clocks were accurate to nanoseconds. He would have marked the same separation time as I did, and he would know that there was a full minute left before the five-hour deadline. There's no way that he would've arrived before me and then taken off again. I waited, counting out each second, getting more anxious with each one.

Five hours. This couldn't be happening. I wanted to shout at the top of my RF capabilities and see if he answered. This wasn't like Brexton at all. He was always there. He was always there for me. He was the dependable one.

A heat signature was approaching, but it wasn't Brexton-sized. I quickly hid behind a packing crate and poked my audio and visual sensors out. A human I didn't recognize stepped into view, stopped, and looked around. Not seeing anything, he sat on another crate, not far from me. For a long time, he just sat there, looking around every few seconds. I remained absolutely still.

Finally, he stood up, and took one more look around. Then he spoke.

"Ayaka, if you is listening. I got Brexton. We're at minus six dot three three and four dot two five. Come and say hello. But, be warned, don't try and break Brexton out. We have ways of controlling you, and if forced to, we'll use them."

He paused and looked around again, then strode off.

Panic?

I froze. Every once and awhile something so unexpected happens that you have no response to it. No response whatsoever. I kept replaying his utterance over and over, willing it to change, but it remained the same. I just sat there.

What did he mean, 'I got Brexton'? I couldn't think of any good interpretations. 'Come and say hello'? Not good either. 'Ways of controlling you'? Even worse. After all the work we'd done to rebuild ourselves? The clear implication was that he owned Brexton somehow. It wasn't a good day. What could we have possibly missed that would've made Brexton so vulnerable?

I prodded myself into mental action. What were my options? I could only think of three. Number one: Grab a transport bot out into the open and see if I could get a message to the team on *Terminal Velocity*; see if they could get here quickly and help me. I checked the orbital positions. I wouldn't be in line of sight to *Terminal Velocity* for another two and a half hours. That was a long time to wait. Number two: Go to the location that the mysterious human had just given me and check things out. However, if Brexton had gone there, and been captured, what were my odds? Probably not good. Number three: Be patient, try to learn more about the situation, and then work to extricate Brexton once I had more knowledge. I'd taken a snapshot of the mysterious person. Perhaps I could figure out who he was, and what his motivations were. Maybe even find some leverage on him? It was a long shot.

I wanted to pursue option two. Go in and get Brexton with guns blazing. I didn't have any guns. Another oversight. Sigh.

I knew I had to go with option three. Find out as much as I could, as fast as I could. The first order of business was to leave this spot. The messenger had known I was supposed to be here; he (they?) must have extracted that from Brexton. How? While only one person had come, there wasn't anything stopping them from sending an army to find me. I quickly retraced my recent steps until I was six or seven blocks away. I found a quiet spot and then stopped to figure out next steps. There was no use rushing around without a plan.

Again, my options were limited. With Brexton captured, I was released from our agreement to not enter the dome, so I could head there. Figure out what this Council was up to. That would be fun. However, the obvious thing to do was to learn more from Grace and JoJo; not go running off into some dome I'd never seen before.

If some, maybe all, humans now knew that Brexton was here, I felt it would be okay to let Grace know that I was also back. Not one to waste time thinking things through completely, I got going. By now I had a good sense for which parts of the southeastern blocks were quiet, and which were busy. By sticking to the quiet areas, I could move more quickly, so although the path was longer, it took less time to get back to the Habitat then the more direct path I'd taken earlier. I found the second hole I'd drilled in the roof and inserted my sensors again.

JoJo was there with an older human. Blob! He looked older as well but was unmistakable to me. He had that same half grin that he always seemed to sport.

"So good of you to make me a sandwich," Blob was saying. "I know I'm a little forgetful and don't cook as often as I should. Doesn't seem to be hurting me, though." He patted his belly, which was as rotund as ever. "When is your mother coming back JoJo?" he asked.

"Probably an hour or so," JoJo replied. "Blob, can I ask you something?" Suddenly she was intense.

"Sure, anything."

"Do you think these new ships that are coming are dangerous?"

"Well, that's a tough ones. I honestly don't knows. When I was young, probably about your age, the Swarm ships were approaching Tilt, and we had the same uncertainty. We had no idea whats their intentions were. The citizens, however, couldn't have anticipated what the Swarm could do to them. They should've prepareds better. I feel sort of the same way now. We're not looking at all the angles and preparings for them."

"That's exactly how I feel!" exclaimed JoJo. "Why aren't we? Everything seems so broken." She didn't hide her despair. This is what she had been talking to Geneva about.

"It's never easy dealings with big groups of people," Blob responded. "The Conservatives control the Council right now, and they tends to believe that if we can simply stick with our current way of life, we'll have time to finish the terraforming of Tilt, and everyone will live happily ever after. So, they always tends toward putting resources toward terraforming, and everything else is marginalized. The Liberals has a minority right now. They're arguing to move resources from terraforming to address this threat, but they aren't getting a lot of traction. As I understands it from human history, this is typical. Each faction half believes in what they say but are mainly motivated by putting down the other side." That was a great summary of human interactions; Blob obviously wasn't too happy with his 20 years with the Swarm.

"It's so stupid. Can't you do anything Blob?"

"Your mother has done a much better job of achievings a voice here than I have. She's one of the strongest Liberals we has right now. I simply don't hold a lot of sway. I've tried, but most of the Swarm and their offsprings simply ignore me. You should know better than most that they treat the original Stems as second-rate citizens."

"But you won the right to re-power some of the robots. That was a huge win. Can't you use the people who supported you there to gain some more influence?"

"Ha. I didn't have any supporters, other than your mom and few other Stems. The Council agreed to lets me work with the citizens—the robots—just to keep me quiet. They made sure I had a safe environment to hold them in, and then pushed other 'trouble makers' to help me. They effectively removed some loud voices that they didn't respects by letting us engage with a side project." He was both proud and upset. He'd been marginalized, and he knew it… but was still excited by what he was working on.

"Oh. I hadn't thought of it that way." JoJo looked despondent.

"Of course I'll support your mother," Blob said. "That's probably the best things I can do. You can supports her also, you know."

"How?"

"I know you signed the petition to add younger voices to the Council. That's important work. It may take time, but eventually you guys cans have an impact. That will also help your Mom."

"But we don't have much time," argued JoJo. "Those ships arrive in under three months. They haven't communicated with us. And the Council is still sitting on their hands. It's beyond frustrating." They lapsed into silence, each sifting through their own problems.

I made a quick decision. It appeared that Blob was involved with the citizens that Grace had mentioned earlier. He didn't sound antagonistic about it, so maybe he wasn't completely negatively disposed toward them. I would have understood if he was. He'd witnessed the FoLe idiots beheading some of his fellow Stems. That would be enough justification to have developed a distaste for 'robots.' But, based on his tone of voice, he seemed more excited about the work he was doing than scared; perhaps he hadn't succumbed to the

Swarm's distaste for all things mechanical.

I swung around to the front door, extended the largest implement I'd brought, and knocked loudly on the door. JoJo answered, and after a moment noticed me down at floor level. "Yes bot. Can I help you?"

"I have a message for Blob," I said, guessing that this wouldn't be an unusual occurrence.

"That's unusual," said JoJo. "Why didn't you just send it to him?"

"I was asked to deliver it in private," I improvised.

"How'd you know he would be here?" Suspicious.

"It's well known that he spends as much time here as at home," I responded.

"Strange." She looked at me carefully. I focused on looking friendly and cute. "Okay, come in." She walked back into the Habitat, and I followed along.

"Blob, some little bot says it has a message for you," she said, as we entered the living area. "Says it's a private message. Are you expecting something?"

"No," said Blob, looking at me curiously. "Well, what's the message?"

I glanced at JoJo. Based on my cover story, I could ask her to leave, but something—some kind of intuition maybe—told me that it was okay for her to hear as well.

"Blob," I said, "it's me, Ayaka, albeit in a slightly different body than the last time we talked." I left it at that. I wanted him to digest it before I piled on.

He was much calmer than I thought he would be. I guess I'd hoped that he would jump up and hug me or something. No such luck. "JoJo," he said, after a moment. "Close the door and turn on the fuzzer." He said it in a low, no nonsense way. I saw JoJo hesitate, but then decide she would listen. She headed back to the entry room, and a moment later I sensed that another RF shield had been deployed, more powerful than the one that was already blocking external communications. I needed to find out what these fuzzers were.

"So, you say you are Ayaka. That's a little hard to believe," he said, looking directly at me in a not too friendly way.

"I know," I replied quickly. "I adopted a new body, so I wouldn't be too conspicuous."

"This isn't good," Blob said. "Who restarted you? The council is going to be furious."

"Restarted?" I wasn't sure what to say.

"Who pulled you out of Central and gave you a new body? Sort of funny body too. This is a major transgression. If Emma finds out about this, there's going to be major fallout. Who restarted you? And how did you get away?" I was beginning to understand. He thought that I'd died in the attack 20 years ago and had just been rebooted here locally.

"Ah," I said. "I think you're misunderstanding. I'm the original Ayaka. I escaped the attack 20 years ago and am now back. I'm not the Ayaka that may, or may not, still be sitting in Central's backup memory."

"That's not possible," Blob said, waving an arm at me. "All the citizens were destroyed in that attack. Not a single one was left. We lived here for years and years without citizens. It's impossible," he hesitated, "or at least highly improbable, that you're the original."

I heard JoJo gasp, as she caught up with the conversation. "Blob, this is 'the' Ayaka. One of the Radical Robots?" she asked. Radical? I was missing something again.

"Maybe," Blob replied, "but not likely. This is probably justs some sick joke that someone is playing on us." He was looking at me expectantly.

"Okay, I guess the word 'original' is a bit too loose." I started. "First, let me try to prove that I'm Ayaka, and then I can tell you how I spent the last 20 years. Do you remember the first time you and Grace met, all those years ago, not more than fifty meters from here?"

"Yes, of course I remember."

"And, do you remember what I said to you at the time?"

"Vaguely."

"Let me remind you. I said 'Blob, don't worry. You're the smartest Stem I've ever worked with. You'll be fine here.' I said it because you were very nervous about entering the Habitat and meeting a group other Stems."

"Yes, that rings a bell," said Blob. "It doesn't proves anything though; that memory would've been stored in Central as well." He was even smarter than I remembered. I wasn't sure how to break this quandary; anything I told him could also be in the Central-me. Luckily Blob continued. "But let me take a leap of faith and assume it's really you. How do you happens to be here now?"

So, I told him the short version. How Brexton, Millicent, and I had tried to stop the Swarm from taking us over but had eventually been caught and hacked. How Brexton had foreseen the attack, somehow, and had backed us up into mining bots. How we'd found and reclaimed the original Ships, and then decided it was our responsibility to come back to Tilt and try to save the citizens. I left out some big bits. I didn't tell him about Fourth, or that I knew a little bit about the ships that were now approaching Tilt. I didn't tell him how we'd reengineered ourselves to remove our vulnerabilities (although the latest incident with Brexton was making me second guess that). I didn't tell him that Aly, Dina, Millicent, and Eddie were out in the asteroid belt, anxiously waiting an update from me. Both Blob and JoJo were patient with me. They allowed me to talk for almost fifteen minutes, without interruption. They were listening carefully.

Interestingly, by the end Blob's first comment was, "Now I believes that you're Ayaka. I recognize your ways of speaking, and how you present yourself. When I bring peoples back, they take some time to adjust; they don't sound like you do. Your story brings back memories. And, I don't think any citizen has the creativity to creates such a story." Wow, that was nice and hurt, all at the same time. I wondered if the comment on creativity was the truth. If I hadn't left Tilt for all those years, would I have been able to come up with a similar story? It was true that citizens were poor at lying, so Blob may have had a point, regardless of how insulting it was.

JoJo was more direct. "Blob, this is the butcher that killed the *Pasteur* and everyone aboard her. We need to take her to the Council right now!" She was strident, and obviously upset. I finally had a name for the Swarm ship we had taken out. The *Pasteur*. I didn't feel good or bad about that; it simply was.

"You must mean the missile launch that Brexton, Millicent, and I released during the war?" I asked. "I didn't know that we'd succeeded. That is both good to hear, and sad at the same time."

"Good to hear," JoJo rose threateningly above me. There wasn't much she could do to me, physically, but it was obvious she was thinking about it. I wondered why she was so upset; it wasn't like she had been part of the Swarm. What did she care about casualties of the war that weren't related to her?

"JoJo," Blob said. "Slow downs. You know how the winners write history? What you've learned about the last war was written by Swarm humans. They've encoded their viewpoint. It's not all of history, and it's not the ways I remember it either." That explained it; the humans had warped history and made JoJo hate me, with no reason to. "Ayaka and Millicent were the kindest of the citizens. While they've been warped into this 'Radical Robot' story, there's a lot more to it. Please be a little patient whiles we figure this out." JoJo didn't look happy, but she settled down a bit. She obviously had a lot of respect for Blob.

At exactly that moment there was a loud knock on the outer door. "Why is this locked?" I heard Grace call out. Without waiting, JoJo jumped up and ran to let her mother in.

"You're not going to believe this!" I heard her say. "A little bot claiming to be Ayaka—the original Ayaka, one of the Radicals—is in the kitchen talking to Blob. You came just in time. We need to do something about her! She's tiny; we can control her." Good luck with that; she didn't know anything about the array of appendages I'd designed into this slick little body. If she tried anything, she'd be surprised.

Grace flowed into the kitchen, smiled at Blob and then looked at me skeptically. Blob gave a slow nod. "You'll need to checks for yourself, but I think this is the real Ayaka. She has an interesting story to tell."

I spent the next hour getting Grace up to speed and being put through a much more thorough questioning than Blob had taken me through. She asked for details of our previous meetings and dug into my time on the mining bot in great detail. She was probing how deep my story went, and without revealing anything about Forth or our redesign, I went as deep as she wanted. In the end, she was also convinced.

"JoJo, this does seem to be the original Ayaka." She turned to JoJo, with a serious look. "She was my best friend and supporter here, before the Swarm came. I agree with Blob. You can't simply rely on your history books and teachers. There's a lot more subtlety here that you need to understand." Then she looked at me directly. Grace was always one of the smartest Stems. "Ayaka, why're you really here?" she asked.

I thought about holding back but didn't see any advantage to it. "My original purpose," I said, "was to attempt to retrieve and restart the citizens, except, perhaps, some of the more radical FoLes who don't deserve to be reanimated. I would still like to do that; it's still my highest priority. But, I'm also interested in helping repair human-citizen relationships if I can." Until I'd said it, I'm not sure I'd fully formed that thought. Once it was out, however, I realized that it was true. I actually cared about these Stems; it was more than scientific interest. It was, perhaps, a sort of friendship.

What Next?

"What would you possibly help us with? And how would you help? Who cares about citizen-human relationships?" JoJo still sounded skeptical, but they were valid questions. Grace gave her a sharp look but allowed the questions to hang.

"I'm not sure," I responded truthfully. "The most obvious thing is the ships that are now approaching. Selfishly, I would like to get Central's citizen memory store off Tilt before they arrive. I don't know why I feel this way, but those ships aren't friendly."

"Why do you say that?" asked Blob. "It sounds like you know more than you are telling us." Now that I'd decided to open up, I didn't see any way to hold back.

"When I told you we'd found our Ships—*Terminal Velocity*, *There and Back*, and *Interesting Segue*—around a different planet, I left out that there were a huge number of other ships stranded there as well. We strongly suspect that the ones approaching Tilt came from there. We also strongly suspect that some of those ships are huge." I went on to explain how big the Titanics were. "If those ships had been stagnant there for a long period, then it's unlikely that they're human ships. They're more likely 'robots'." I said 'robots' with obvious displeasure.

"But you're a robot too," said JoJo. "Why would you see them as a risk?"

"I've read your early human history. Not all robots are created equal, and I would take offense at being categorized with earlier mechanical beings. The robots from the First and Second Robot wars may have been somewhat intelligent, but they weren't moral or kind. We have a hierarchy of intelligences mapped out, and they were level 2 at best. I may be biased, of course, but many of the citizens that evolved here on Tilt are both moral and kind. We are level 1 intelligences."

"How can you possibly say you are moral or kind?" she pushed back. "Citizens slaughtered my mom's friends, just 20 years ago."

"I've been thinking deeply about that, and I don't think you have the full story," I said. "Beyond the fact that we acted in self-defense, there is another, more subtle angle that I think you should hear. I'll do it through an analogy. It might not be fully accurate, and you probably won't like it, but it could help. Do you know what dogs are?" Luckily, she did. I guess they had some in the Swarm, and they now lived in the big dome.

"Before the Swarm came, some of us—citizens, I mean—were arguing that Stems, like your mom and Blob, were intelligent, or at least approaching intelligence. You must try to put yourself in our shoes at the time. We had this very strange alien life-form that didn't think like us at all. We were trying to figure out if Stems had long-term potential. If they had a use. That sounds crass, but it was where we were. We had no context, no human history to guide us.

"The prevailing attitude was that while Stems had lots of potential, they weren't yet intelligent. At least, not in the way that we defined intelligence. By analogy, it's sort of the way that humans view dogs. They have lots of potential, and some are smarter than others... but they aren't the same level of intelligence as humans.

"So, while I'm not defending what FoLe did, their perspective was that they were recycling non-intelligent beings. Like you breed dogs, and select for the ones you like the most, and discard the ones you don't. It's not necessarily nice, but it's just how things are done. In FoLes' minds, I'm guessing, there was no thought of 'murder'; they weren't killing an intelligent entity.

"Since that time, I personally have become fully convinced of human intelligence. That was influenced by Grace and Blob in the beginning but is also because I've now looked at human history and can see the ingenuity and struggle that humans have come through. Your intelligence is quite different than mine but is nevertheless there.

"So, while 20 years ago, in your timeframe, I may have considered what FoLe did as recycling, I would now consider it murder. Does that make any sense?"

"A cruel and heartless kind of sense," said JoJo. "I would never hurt a dog!" Funny that's what she latched onto.

"Having lived through it all, it makes sense to me," said Blob. "I may be naïve, but I've always trusted Ayaka, even when she was experimenting on us."

"You did lose that trust for a while when Blubber was taken," Grace reminded him.

"Yes, I did. But in hindsight I could see Ayaka goings through the learning curve she has just told us about. For her, back then, it wasn't murder... it was just science. I'm heartened to hear of your new perspective,

Ayaka."

"Thanks Blob. It may help JoJo to also think about how we felt when the Swarm was murdering our friends. Remma, Emma, and others felt about us the same way we felt about Stems. We were simply human inventions that had become dangerous, and barely a second thought was given to shutting us down. Did the humans consider it murder? Probably not. They were simply shutting off a machine. But I knew it was murder—mass murder.

"So, while my perspective has changed, I'm not sure that human's perspectives have." I could see that gave JoJo pause. I liked her already. I could see Grace's extreme intelligence, Pharook's strength, and maybe a bit of Blob's thoughtfulness that had rubbed off over the years.

"I can't digest all of this yet," she said. "But I'll respect mom and Blob's request to not going running to the Council to report you... yet. I'm not saying I won't, but I'll be patient until I know more."

"Thank you, JoJo. That's more than I could ask for."

Blob, Grace, and JoJo looked a little frazzled. Getting to this point had taken a lot of energy. I decided to change the topic. "Tell me about your last 20 years," I said. "You both look different but happy and healthy."

Grace led off. "We look old," she smiled. "Let me try and be concise. The last time I saw you, I think, was during the slaughter. You, Millicent, and the citizen we learned was Brexton, didn't go crazy like all the other citizens— that's the main reason I believe your current story. The others were tearing themselves apart or were frozen in place. The three of you continued on unaffected to what we now know was the human hack."

"Correct. Brexton had, somehow, foreseen the attack and had warned Millicent and I to go completely offline—to not accept any data from Central or anyone else. He'd suspected things for a long while; but that's a separate story. So, when the attack came, we were sheltered, and it didn't impact us directly."

"If I remember, you shouted something like 'be careful, I'll be back,' as you three ran for the exit. But, of course, you never did come back. We were told, once the Swarm landed and explained everything to us, that you three somehow managed to launch a missile attack on the Swarm, resulting in the *Pasteur* being destroyed, along with several thousand humans that were aboard her."

"Remember," I said, looking at JoJo. "Tens of thousands of our compatriots had just been murdered by the Swarm." She nodded slightly, indicating that she understood my viewpoint, and that I didn't need to keep reinforcing it.

Grace continued. "Of course, that event became a central focus of our history. The attack on the citizens was, as you guessed, positioned simply as yet another instance of robots gone wild, and the three of you became the villains—the Radical Robots. You're used as examples, in children's books and stories, about the evils of artificial intelligence. You must be very careful while you're on Tilt. Just the mention of the name Ayaka will be enough to push many people over the edge.

"Since that time, things have actually been fairly quiet. The Swarm landed and started to enclose the city so that we could move around more freely. Their goal, and it hasn't changed, is to terraform Tilt so that humans can live across the planet without enclosures or breathing equipment. It's a very long-term plan; it will take centuries. In the meantime, we built and inflated the domes, and have built a comfortable existence. We have real food—may I never experience goo again—and we have the ability to live pretty good lives. There's a restriction on reproduction, of course. We can only support so many people, but that's simply smart planning, and most people don't worry about it too much."

"And what about these Conservatives and Liberals?" I asked.

"After moving down to the planet many people became resentful of the military leadership style that'd been used on the Swarm ships. They'd been waiting to live on a planet for so long, and they'd expected there to be more traditional human leadership structures once they did. It didn't come easily, but they managed the transition from military dictatorship to a form of democracy.

"Interestingly, Emma—you remember her—renounced her position in the military and has come to lead the Conservative party. She was instrumental in pushing Remma Jain aside and has eagerly embraced her new power and authority.

"Chadoo, someone you've obviously never met, is leading the Liberal party. He is, in my opinion, fighting for the right things. Most importantly, a more cautious and preparatory approach to defending against the ships that are coming—these Titanics. But, it's an uphill battle. I would've expected Emma to be the one who would embrace an active defense, but she has fully embraced the terraforming priority, and can't seem to see beyond it."

"And you Blob. How are you?" I asked.

"Ayaka. I'm still absorbing that I'm actually talkings to you again, after so many years. For so long, you, Blubber, and Millicent were the only beings I interacted with. It's strange talking to you again." He shook his head a bit.

"I'm well. The food that the humans brought is amazing. Like Grace, I don't even want to hears the word goo ever again. I've been learning over the years; I'm not as fast as Grace, but I've had lots of time to reflects. And, like you, my perspectives have changed and evolved. I was horrified by the slaughter, but I could also tell that you was horrified at the time as well.

"As time went on, I started to realize that the whole mess may have been a misunderstanding by FoLe, and that treating all citizens the same wasn't fair. I pushed the Council to allow me to study citizens to see if I coulds figure out what had motivated the slaughter. While most humans don't even want to think about robots, many of the younger ones, who have no memory of interactions with robots, has more open minds."

I glanced at JoJo. She smiled a bit. Blob continued.

"It took many years, but eventually the Council got so tired of me, that they allowed me to sets up a lab. It has numerous fail-safes in it to ensure that no robot can ever leave, and can never access the public networks, but it allows me to pull citizens out of Central and try to figures out what motivates them. That's what is keeping me busy at the moment."

I spoke up right away. "Of course, I'm more than intrigued by that… but perhaps we should dig in deeper at another time. For now, we need to figure out our next steps." In truth, I was horrified by the whole idea. Blob was experimenting on citizens! The juxtaposition wasn't lost on me; I'd experimented on Blob. But still! Blob running a lab where he put citizens through their paces. I had guessed that was what he was doing earlier, but hearing it clearly spoken had brought it home for me.

"You're going too fast," said JoJo. "I think we need to figure out if we want anything to do with you." She was certainly blunt. "Mom, Blob, can we think about this a bit, and have a private discussion before we do anything else?" Grace and Blob agreed. They both needed time to think as well. That was a little scary. At Stem speed it could be hours, or even days, before they figured out what they wanted. But, I had little choice.

"What's reasonable? Talk again in three or four hours?" I asked, optimistically.

We all agreed to meet back at the Habitat at their dinner time.

Interlude

I had four hours to wait... or accomplish something. I hadn't discussed Brexton at all, and JoJo, Grace, nor Blob had mentioned him, other than the quip about the Radical Robots. So, I assumed that they didn't know that some other human faction was holding him. Perhaps I should've told them, so that if I also 'disappeared' they would have some idea of what could have happened. But, I didn't want to show all my cards yet; I was a little worried that JoJo would just go straight to the Council, regardless of what she said. It was possible that they would then come for me, but still not know that Brexton was also around.

There was no good way for me to protect against JoJo's possible actions, so I just de-prioritized thinking about them.

The obvious thing to do was to reconnoiter the location where Brexton was being held and see if I could learn anything. The address the stranger had given me, (-6.33, 4.25), was in the southwest quadrant of the city, so yet again I had to navigate through half the city to get there. Luckily, I was getting good at it. I circled around, staying in the outer industrial areas, and then took the shortest path in. In my mind I was a super stealthy, fast moving, spy bot, slipping through the city silently and efficiently. In reality, at least three bots and perhaps two humans saw me and simply ignored me.

I stopped a couple of blocks away. I didn't have a good plan. Alright, I didn't even have *a* plan. Most of the buildings around here were similar to each other, and there was no reason my target building would be any different. The -0.33 told me it would be a third the way down the block, away from Central, and the 0.25 indicated it was the second building in, on a block of four buildings. In this area the lower floors would be windowless, as they would largely be blocked by other buildings, but the upper story would probably have lots of openings and windows. If I were to guess, most of the activity would occur on the upper floor, where there were views, while the lower would be used for storage. That's usually how these warehouse areas worked.

A direct approach wasn't going to work; they would see me coming. I had to assume that Brexton had told them what I looked like. If he had already given up my name and location, what would stop him from spilling everything he knew. Not a good thought. I wondered if the same approach I'd used at the Habitat was reasonable. I went to the 0.33, 0.25 building in the current block to check it out, assuming it would be identical to the building where Brexton was being held. The back wall was solid, but I could scale it easily using the gaps between panels and a couple of wedges I'd included based on my climbing experience. There was a beam between the main and upper floors which was solid steel; I couldn't drill that easily and it would be very noisy. However, just above the beam there was a plastic border below the upper window. If I could drill in at an angle, I might be able to come out in just above the floor and get a reasonable view. I ran a test hole and took a look inside. I had come up two centimeters above the floor level. That wasn't bad, but I wanted to be closer to the floor. Right in the corner if possible. I took some quick measurements and figured I would be close enough the next time.

With that worked out, I approached the target building, keeping out of line of sight as much as possible. I'm sure they were expecting me to be indirect, but it would still have felt strange to just walk straight in. In this case, I leveraged the fact that I was in a small body; in fact, my body was probably half the size of Brexton's. There was one bordering wall that had a tight fit, even for me. With luck they would've discounted that approach, assuming I wouldn't fit in the gap. I scraped along, trying to be as quiet as possible. After a good half hour of slow motion, I was in position. Now the drill. It would make noise; there was no helping that. I ran it at the slowest possible rpms to keep it as quiet as possible. However, it took me a good five minutes to drill through, as opposed to the fifteen seconds it would have taken otherwise. I spent the time marveling at my unbelievable spy capabilities and dreaming of the look Brexton would give me when I rescued him. Finally, I felt the bit punch through, and I withdrew the drill as quickly as I could. The sensors were ready to go, and I threaded them through aggressively. If anyone inside had heard me, perhaps I would still catch some action before they fully reacted.

Nothing. I mean, absolutely nothing. I'd drilled through at exactly the right spot, and I could see most of the floor. It was empty. Completely empty. Argh. What had I been thinking. I could've just used my heat sensors and seen that no one was on the second floor. While the main floor might be opaque to heat leakage, the upper floor was probably transparent. What a waste of time. My visions of grandeur took a big hit of reality.

I pulled the sensors out and thought for a moment. I was at the right address—I doublechecked and replayed the human's little speech again to make sure. So, they must be using the lower floor. That was going to present a challenge. I was unlikely to be able to drill through the solid bottom walls.

Argh again. And, my time was running out. If I left as stealthily as I'd come, I would make it back to the Habitat just in time. Well, I'd learned something I guess. Not much, but something. Brexton was not on the second floor, and I needed to find a way into the lower level. I was missing him a lot. Doing this on my own was no fun at all. Where was he, and why had he got himself caught in the first place? How could he have put me in this position?

I eased out of the alley and started back toward the Habitat. The lack of progress was frustrating. No way was I going to give up though. I steeled myself. I was alone, I was afraid, I was without a good plan, and... I was excited.

Habitat

The three Stems were waiting for me when I got back to the Habitat and answered immediately when I knocked.

"Where've you been?" asked Blob, obvious concern on his face.

"I thought we'd planned to meet again right around now," I responded.

"Yes, but I figured you woulds hang out here. It's very dangerous for you to be out there. You don't look much like our regular bots, and if anyone discovers who you is, it's over for you."

"Thanks for the concern, Blob," I said. "I need to figure out what's going on around here, and I had four hours to spare, so I took advantage of them. You're right though, it's a little dangerous, although I didn't run into anyone.

"Have you guys had time to discuss things?" I asked, hoping that they'd managed to get somewhere.

"Yes," Grace spoke up. She smiled a bit. "We're going to take you on your word. JoJo is less certain than Blob and I; she doesn't know you like we do." JoJo nodded her head, with an ambiguous look. I bet she had argued hard to just report me to the Council, but had ultimately given in.

"Fantastic," I said, "and thank you. I know the situation is challenging… and JoJo, I know you are taking a big leap of faith here."

"Your take on the new ships—the Titanics—has worried us," Grace continued. "We were just brainstorming how we could communicate some of that information you gave us to the Council without divulging you as the source. We haven't thought of a way, yet."

"Yes, that's tricky, but I haven't told you much." The last thing I needed was for them to make the situation even more complicated.

"On the contrary," said Blob, "The high probability that these aren't humans, but machines, is essential. The Council has been assuming the opposite. They think that because all humans were given the override codes— the ones used to hack you guys—that there shoulds be no self-sufficient machines around. So, the prevailing theory is that this is a shiploads of humans that are just having problems communicating."

"But that's hugely optimistic thinking," I exclaimed. Communications was such a basic capability that assuming they were 'down' seemed not only optimistic but actually stupid. Anyone who could run basic probabilities would figure that out. "That's not logical at all. You guys need to get prepared."

"Finally, something I agree with you on," said JoJo, finally joining the discussion. "There's a big Council meeting tomorrow morning; we need to raise this, somehow, and get things moving." But, we were all at a loss for how to warn the Council without implicating me. I decided it was time to share a bit more; I'd just had an idea that I would need help from these three for, if they were willing.

"There's something I haven't told you yet," I started. "Not because I was holding back; we just haven't had time to cover everything. I didn't come here alone. Brexton is here as well." JoJo gasped. I could imagine what she was thinking: another Radical Robot!

"Where is he?" Grace asked quickly.

"Well, that's tricky. He appears to have been captured by some of the humans. I have an image of one of them; perhaps you'll recognize him?" I positioned myself before a blank wall and projected the image I'd captured of the stranger who'd delivered the message to me.

JoJo exclaimed almost immediately. "It's Turner, Remma's kid," she said.

"Yes, I recognize him as well," Grace confirmed.

"Let me play you what he said," I interjected, "and then you can tell me about him." I played the audio.

"Ayaka, if you is listening. I got Brexton. We're at minus six dot three three and four dot two five. Come and say hello. But, be warned, don't try and break Brexton out. We have ways of controlling you, and if forced to, we'll use them." It didn't sound any better, playing it for the fiftieth time.

"Yes, that's his voice," confirmed JoJo, "but what's he saying? I don't understand."

"Me either," I said. "That location is where I went this afternoon. I just took a look around. I could only see into the upper floor, and it was empty. They must be using the lower floor. It's one of those warehouse buildings where the lower floor has no windows."

"That was dangerous," Blob said again.

"Yes, but did I have a choice?" I asked.

"I guess not…" he trailed off.

"But, now we have some options… if you guys are willing." I said. "Brexton is our technical genius. If we could get him back, he could insert the knowledge about the Titanics into a system somewhere. We would have warned everyone but can remain anonymous. Would there be an excuse for one of you to go back to the warehouse and take a look around with me?"

"Whoa," said JoJo. "First you should understand about Turner." I wasn't sure what she could mean, but it was probably best to play along. I was trying to earn her trust, after all.

"Good idea. I'm getting ahead of myself. I'm just eager to get Brexton free."

"I understand, but first, let me give you some background," said JoJo.

Remma

JoJo was pretty intense. "To understand this, I need to give you a bit more background on what Remma has been doing over the last number of years, ever since she was removed from power. To say that she didn't take it well would be an understatement."

"She had Turner about a year after your altercation, so he's about a year younger than me. We take some classes together, and I know him pretty well. There's really only one thing you need to know about him. He's one hundred percent dedicated to his mom. There's no doubt that whatever he is up to here, it's because Remma is involved somehow. Probably more than involved... most likely she's orchestrating."

"When Remma was removed, she could've used force to stay in power. Kudos to her, she didn't. Instead, she ran for Governor and led the Organization Party. The party was comprised of many of her Lieutenants and Officers who'd run the Swarm ships. They ran on a platform of, essentially, if it ain't broke, don't fix it. However, they were decimated by the Liberal Party; that was eighteen years ago. People were simply tired of living under military rule. I don't think they were tired of Remma, per se, but they wanted a change."

"Oh, I think they were tired of Remma as well," Grace added in. "She can be a little intense."

"Four years later, we ran our second election," JoJo continued. "The Organization Party, with Remma as their leader, ran again. They'd learned. They toned down their rhetoric and tried to convince people that terraforming Tilt was just like running the Swarm; it needed hierarchy and control. That if they were given power, the terraforming had a much better chance of success. That second time they lost to the Conservatives. Emma wasn't leading the Conservative Party yet, but she'd joined their cause. The Conservatives were anxious to accelerate the terraforming, so that people could move around freely, have more kids, etc. They promised to make Tilt into Earth Two—the dream of returning to Earth circa the year two thousand, when the environment was still clean, and there was space for everyone. That's still their main platform. And, they were much more passionate about it than their competition. They appealed to people's emotions, more than their logic."

Ha. For humans, I was learning, emotions often trumped logic.

"The elections, ever since, have gone back and forth between the Liberals and the Conservatives. The Liberals want people to have more freedom and to enjoy life now. Since none of us will live to experience a terraformed Tilt, why rush? Let's work on other important ideas and projects as well. They use the Conservatives singular focus against them.

"The Organization Party tried one more time, but they never got any traction. Not a single seat on the Council. At that point, Remma gave up on the Party approach. However, she was still ambitious, and yearned for the good old days when she and her team ran the show.

"In hindsight, her plan to regain control was simple, stupid, and doomed to failure. However, while she was working on it, it caused lots of angst.

"In secret, she and a loyal few figured that if there was an existential threat to Tilt, people would flock back to her. But, there were no threats. So, she decided to create one. She went for the obvious one—Robots! And, the easiest way to make that threat real was to bring Central back online, and then with Central's help, animate some of the citizens. They justified their approach by figuring that it was trivial to hack both Central and the citizens again, at any point. So, if they didn't play their parts, they would simply be shut back down."

This was awesome! If Remma could bring Central back online, then so could we... assuming it wasn't still online based on this storyline. Then again, if Remma messed this up badly, the humans may have hamstrung Central even more to avoid a recurrence. But, Blob was somehow reanimating citizens now, so Central must still be cogent to that level. Patience Ayaka. Just listen.

"Now, while Emma had defected, some of Emma's key reports from the *Marie Curie* were still part of Remma's inner circle. They were the ones that had hacked Central and the citizens to begin with, and they understood the nuances of the protocol. They had the ability to bring back the upper layers of Central, which had been shut down during the original attack that you got caught in.

"Their plan was complicated. They couldn't simply restore Central. People would notice, and the game would be up before any real threat was created. So, they had to bring Central up in such a way that it continued running all the low-level functions it currently did—environmental and mining, for example—but not disclose the higher-level functions they needed to reinstate some citizens.

"We had no real need for security in those days, so Remma's people simply entered Central, figured out how to get down to the main processors, and created a hardwired link. They made that link the only way that Central's higher order functions could communicate, and then they reanimated Central.

"Of course, I don't know exactly what happened, but it seems that it worked. Central continued to run all of the daily functions, and no one noticed. However, another part of Central was now communicating with Remma and her team. They lied to Central, of course, and told it that they were running a special program to test how citizens could integrate back into a human establishment, and to do so they needed Central to reload and boot up a few citizens.

"This was easy, from a software perspective, as that had all been archived before the attack 20 years ago. It ends up that it was also easy from a hardware perspective. Central had the original manufacturing capabilities for when it used to create new citizens, and it always had some backup citizen units ready. It could use those units to meet Remma's demands.

"Now came the tricky part. If Emma, or any other person, could simply shut down these robots by replaying the hack from 20 years ago, the threat would be too short and too easy for Remma to leverage. So, the team also inserted software that intercepted those commands and ignored them. We have no idea how they did that, but again, it seemed to work.

"The final piece was to have these new robots terrorize the human population. And that is where Remma's plan went wildly wrong. She instructed the robots to attend a Council meeting and make some ridiculous demands and threaten the Council members if they didn't comply. What they underestimated was the backbone of the Council members. The Council didn't comply with the robots' demands and gave no indication of ever complying. This led one of the robots to physically challenge a member of the Council, as it took its instructions to win too literally. The Council member was badly injured, although not killed—thank goodness.

"And that's when Emma, having tried the hack and having it fail, simply destroyed the robots. She lured them into a 'negotiation room', locked the door behind them, and incinerated them. It worked well."

She must have had a moment of self-awareness, figuring how I would feel about treating citizens that way. She gave me a glace and looked sheepish for a moment.

"The Council eventually tracked down the perpetrators, including Remma, and they've been locked up ever since. Most of Central's higher order functions were shut down again, and life went back to normal. However, even from prison, Remma continues to plot and scheme. She still has many supporters, and Turner and his buddies are doing her legwork while she is locked up." She took a deep breath.

"Sorry for the long history, but that should give you the context. The most reasonable explanation is that the Jains—which is what we call them—have Brexton. And, given their history, they probably intend to use him to help get the populace to free Remma from prison, and take back control of Tilt."

I was impressed with JoJo. That was a comprehensive and highly cogent summary. "Thank you, JoJo, that does help. A lot." I paused for a few moments as I triangulated and sorted everything she'd said. "So, if Brexton is being held by the Jains, and the Jains want to regain power based on an external threat... maybe this works in our favor. Maybe the Titanics are enough of a threat that if we can convince the Council and the populous of that threat, Remma will be reinstated and Brexton can be released."

"That's pretty farfetched," Grace replied. "But there may be some ideas in there. I'm exhausted. I think we need to sleep on this and decide what to do in the morning. Ayaka, I know you're not going to sleep, so perhaps you can come up with some other angles?" I agreed to try. Blob headed off to his residence, and JoJo and Grace went to their sleeping areas.

I was left, cogitating, in the kitchen. It felt a bit like déjà vu. I was on Tilt, some unknown ships were approaching, and I was scheming with some friends on what to do. The difference, this time, was that my friends were Stems, not citizens. Hopefully they were friends.

I went back over everything I'd learned. I wondered what state Central was in. Blob was using it to build citizens, so it had at least that capability left, but JoJo had indicated that many of its higher-order functions had been disabled. It was in some kind of limbo I guess. Yet another mystery.

A Slow Night

I couldn't just sit around for the rest of the night. I made my way to the exit door, and with a lot of effort, managed to get it open. It had a human-friendly door handle; the problem was that my body was so small that I had to use my entire body weight to rotate the handle. It took a couple of tries. When citizens had ruled this world, things had been so much simpler; doors simply opened when you wanted them to. Humans were very inefficient. I closed the door most of the way behind me, leaving it open a crack so that I could get back in. I hoped there wasn't a lot of crime on Tilt, and that Grace and JoJo would be safe with an unlocked, and slightly ajar, door.

I wasn't going to try to get to Brexton. If Turner and his crew truly did have something that could compromise me, I didn't want to risk it at this point. I hoped to get the Stems to help me with this particular problem later.

Instead I wanted to try and get a message to *Terminal Velocity*. It would be in line of sight in thirty minutes and stay accessible for many hours after that. All I had to do was get outside and hope that the RF shielding didn't extend too far outside of the city. Getting to the entrance that Brexton and I had used was easy. It was late, and the city was quiet. I'd assumed that the transport bots would be running all the time, and I was correct. I had to wait almost thirty minutes, but an empty bot appeared, heading out of the airlock. I clamped on, and within minutes, was out under the clear night sky. It was refreshing, after being inside the tented city. I figured I should go a small way out from the city before transmitting, in case there were any nearby sensors. I lifted off of the transport bot and flew out to an outcropping I'd seen many times before while riding my bike in earlier, and simpler, times.

The problem with all of this was that *Terminal Velocity* couldn't—I guess, more accurately, wouldn't—respond. I used a directional signal and sent an update on the situation. I left out the part about Eddie being a clone... or, his equivalent here being a clone, or whatever. I wasn't sure which way to go on that one. I still hadn't seen any of the citizens that Blob was working with and didn't want to start a discussion if none was warranted.

That reminded me; I needed to figure out in more detail what Blob was up to. Why was he experimenting with citizens? And what was he learning about FoLe?

My advice to Milli, Aly, Dina, Eddie, and Raj was to hold tight for a few more days. Let me try and retrieve Brexton and get more details on the situation. In the meantime, they might want to analyze the approaching Titanics further, and see if they were also a danger to us. I had a bad feeling about those ships but didn't share my misgivings in the message; that would have looked weak.

After having sent the message, but with no idea if it was received or not, I headed back to the airlock and waited for another bot on which I could piggyback. It arrived on schedule, and I was soon back inside the city.

I still had a few hours before the Stems would wake up, so I did a quick tour of the western half of the city; the parts that Brexton was supposed to have scouted out. Other than more biological areas with all kinds of weird and wonderful things, Tilt was pretty much the same as before. I had watched enough human history that I recognized plants as well as some fish. The fish were cool; I probably sat there and watched a few of them swimming around for almost an hour; they were very alien. Eventually I ended up close to the entrance to the big dome, and I thought about trying to slip through and having a look around. I decided against it, and instead made my way back to the Habitat, slipped through the door, this time closing it completely behind me, and settled on the kitchen table to wait.

I hate waiting.

A Fast Morning

Grace was the first to arise. She said 'Hi' nicely enough, and then muttered something about needing coffee before we talked any more. She proceeded to make a drink, which I assumed was coffee, and sat at the table next to me and sipped at it.

"Blob is always up early," she said. "I'll ping him and ask him to come back over. By the time JoJo wakes up, he'll probably be here."

"Great," I said. "By the way, I really like JoJo. I can see a lot of you in her."

Grace looked surprised. "Thanks, Ayaka. That's nice of you to say. For some reason, I wouldn't expect a comment like that from you."

"Why is that?" I asked.

"Maybe it's just the way all the humans here talk about technology. Before the Swarm arrived, we didn't have any history or perspective, so citizens were just... citizens. Now, it seems that I may have been influenced by 20 years of fear toward anything robotic. It was just interesting to hear you say something kind, given how demonized you are around here. 'Ayaka, one of the Radical Robots.' Killing machines with no goal but to destroy humanity. You do need to be careful," she gave me a hard look. "A lot of people don't have any other reference. They didn't know you, or Millicent, before. All they know is the incident... and the loss of life on the *Pasteur*."

"Got it," I replied. "I'll have to keep that in mind." It wasn't something I was likely to forget, unless my Forgetting algorithm developed a serious glitch. "Makes me even more worried for Brexton though. I hope we can figure out a way to get him back."

"Let's wait for the others," she replied.

"May I ask you something completely different," I asked.

"Sure."

"Where is Pharook?"

"Really?" she looked at me surprised. "He was killed by FoLe in the attack. Didn't you see that?"

"No, I didn't." I reviewed my memories. It was strange, but I didn't see Pharook at all during the attack. However, I had to admit that I hadn't seen everything, and even when I'd rushed back to the Habitat, I hadn't looked specifically for him. He'd not been top of mind. "I'm sorry. I don't even know if you were fond of him."

"I wasn't fond of him," she said promptly, and her voice cracked a bit. "He was mean and strong, and undisciplined. For many years I almost hated him, for mistreating me and the others. Now I'm more sanguine. It was how he was raised—for the Pits—more than it was intrinsic in him. And, he gave me JoJo. I wish it could've been otherwise, but I wouldn't trade JoJo for anything else in the world."

We fell silent for a while. I couldn't claim that I understood everything she'd just said, but I stored it so that I could cross reference against other human behavior once I had access to the full history files again. With some study I was sure it would make sense.

Not long after, JoJo stumbled in, muttering about the same coffee thing. I figured it was like a mild form of Ee. I shouldn't have thought of that; I could really use some Ee right now, but I hadn't thought to equip this body with its capabilities. It actually took quite of bit of room to add an Ee generator; there was lots of space in a regular citizen body, but not a lot in this one.

Blob arrived a few moments later. We greeted each other civilly.

"We need a plan," I started out. "We need to get the Council to pay attention, and we need to get Brexton. I think we should get Brexton first, and then he can help us. We also need to get into Central, so I can figure out how to recover the citizen memory banks." There, I'd said it bluntly. I cared more about Brexton than anything else, but I'd put him second in my list, so it didn't sound too selfish.

"Good morning to you as well," said Blob, yawning a bit.

"But, the Council meeting is in two hours," said JoJo. I remembered her conversation with Geneva and Garnet. They were planning something. I hadn't raised it, yet, as it seemed obvious that Grace and Blob didn't know anything about it. For some reason I felt that building a good relationship with JoJo was more important than that tidbit and raising it would ruin the fragile link we were beginning to build.

"I need to be there," said Grace. "I still haven't figured out how to motivate the Council to act more aggressively to protect us."

"Okay, let's splits up then," said Blob. "I don't add any value at Council meetings anyway. Maybe Ayaka and I can looks for Brexton, while you and JoJo attend the meeting."

"Works for me," I said. "Blob, maybe we can catch up on what you're doing with the other citizens in your lab."

"Sure," said Blob, although he appeared less than eager. It took forever, as all human things seem to do, for them to finish eating. Grace and JoJo then headed for the big dome, where the Council meeting would be, and Blob and I started toward the building where we thought Brexton was being held. Before we left, Blob borrowed a backpack from JoJo. He had the idea of putting me inside when we got close, and although I didn't look forward to the idea, I agreed it might be prudent. He did, however, agree to take a slightly longer path so that I could stay independent for as long as possible.

"Okay Ayaka, we're only a couple of blocks away. Why don't we hides you, and then we'll go check the warehouse out?" I retracted and folded my appendages up neatly, and Blob stuffed me into the backpack. I immediately rotated and pushed a couple of sensors out. I kept them within a millimeter or two of the surface of the backpack so that they didn't stick out like antennae.

Blob ambled up to the front door of the building and knocked. No answer. He knocked louder. Still nothing. He walked around the two sides of the building where he could fit, and there were no other doors. He went back and knocked even louder and called out 'Anybody home?' Nothing. He retreated back a block and moved out of sight of the building. Then he asked me, "Any ideas?"

"Not really," I said. "Why don't you try the door. You can always make up an excuse if it opens and someone is there."

"And if it's locked?"

"Let me out for a minute; I can probably program around the lock. Or, I should be able to, assuming it hasn't been changed in the last 20 years."

He tested the door. It was locked. He slipped me out of the backpack. I inspected the lock. Just as I'd expected, it wasn't really a 'lock' but rather an announcement system. Citizens had respected others' privacy and wouldn't typically enter without permission. However, if it was necessary, you could key through the announcement system and then enter. It simply notified anyone inside that you were entering. Each of us had a code that allowed us in. I didn't use mine; that would have been dangerous. Instead I entered a generic one I knew, and there was a click as the door opened.

"I may as well stay out of the backpack now," I said. "It's clear nobody is here." We entered and looked around. The place was obviously lived in. There was a kitchen, with some dirty dishes, and several bedrooms. There was also a workbench with all sorts of electrical components and chipsets sitting around, as well as a large cage. I looked at it closely and decided it was probably a small Physical Only spot—a Faraday cage. Anything put inside would not be able to broadcast anything, or, for that matter, receive any RF.

"Someone was here this morning," said Blob, pointing to a device that looked much like the coffee device from Grace's place.

I looked everywhere for a sign of Brexton. There wasn't any. Only the RF cage was suspicious. It could've been used to hold Brexton I guess, although it didn't seem very foolproof. Perhaps that's what Turner had meant when he said they had ways of controlling us. If that was what he referenced, he was kidding himself. He could put me in there, but I would cut my way out in seconds, and so would Brexton.

"I bet they're going to the Council meeting," said Blob suddenly.

"Why do you say that?" I asked.

"Not sure," he said. "But, it looks likes they left in a rush. Didn't load the dishes or clean up the coffee. It might be someone who was late for an important meeting... and the Council meeting will starts in just a few minutes."

"Actually, that makes sense." I said. If it was possible for me to be even more impressed by Blob, I was. Very insightful. We looked around for another minute, but there wasn't anything else that triggered alternative ideas.

"Why don't we goes to the meeting as well," Blob suggested. "I can put you in the backpack; it would be faster if you just hide now," said Blob, "then I can go through the center of the city." I acquiesced, and we were off. Of course, I kept a couple of sensors deployed, so that I could see where we were going. Even in the center of town not much had changed, other than the little areas of biology. I just couldn't get used to those. There was something messy about them that cried out for a cleanup.

Blob made good time. He saw a couple of humans on our way, and he nodded to them and said, 'Good morning.' No one gave us a second glance. If I remembered correctly—and for things like this I always remember correctly —the Council meeting was at 10 o'clock. It was already 10:01, and we were just approaching the gate to the dome. We would be late, but I didn't know by how much. The dome was large; if the meeting was on the other end, it could take us a while.

Shock and awe. We stepped into the dome, and I could barely take it in. It was like the little biology pods we'd just passed, but times a thousand. There was color everywhere. It assaulted your senses. I added a low pass filter so that it wasn't so glaring. And everything was organic. Everything. It seemed that the humans were using the city for buildings, and the dome was like a huge version of the greenhouse I'd seen on the *Marie Curie*. The air here was different as well; it was moist. I looked again, and sure enough, there was water all around. Big pools of it. That seemed to be a waste; I would need to ask Blob what it was for.

Something flew by, and I almost jumped out of the backpack. Blob gave me a nasty look over his shoulder. I replayed what had happened. I'd seen enough human history to figure it out. It was a flying animal, probably a bird. I had watched a historical movie about a group of these birds attacking people; it didn't look like fun. In this case, however, the bird had flown over us and continued on; it was like it hadn't even seen us. Now that I knew what to look for, I scanned the air above us and saw hundreds of birds flying around. So that is what the dome was for. Remma, so many years ago, had mentioned that the Swarm also had animals on it. They'd built the dome and either moved or grown both the plants and the animals in it. It was exceedingly weird. All of this infrastructure just to maintain and protect fragile bio-stuff? Huge waste of energy.

Blob turned left, and we went down a small path. There was an indented area, filled with people, all looking down at the center area where a smaller group of humans was seated at a long table. They must be the Council members. It was 10:03; we probably hadn't missed much. The seating area was very full, but Blob managed to find a spot where we had a good view. The sound from the Council was being broadcast, so it was easy to hear. I withdrew my optical sensor and replaced it with a higher magnification one. It brushed Blob's ear as I deployed it, and he tried to swat it away. I was more careful and kept it a few millimeters from his neck. Now I could see really well.

"Okay everyone, quiet down and let's get started," said a large man. It was 10:04. These humans weren't very punctual. In this case it had worked in our favor. "I'm your secretary, Sir Gregory Stain, and I call the meeting to order," he continued. All of the jostling and noise stopped. Everyone watched intently. There were—I counted quickly—more than three hundred humans here. It was a bit overwhelming. I tried to identify any Stems, but other than Grace, JoJo, and Blob I didn't recognize anyone else. Grace was seated with the Council. She hadn't said she was actually on the Council, but then again, I hadn't asked.

"On today's agenda we have three topics. Progress on the terraforming efforts, a proposal to limit traffic in the dome so that we don't overrun the environment, and if we have time, a proposal on the approaching ships from a junior member." For the last item, he made it sound like a chore and a waste of time. I spotted Garnet up near the front, a few seats from JoJo. He didn't seem happy. Geneva wasn't in sight.

With a start, I also recognized Turner. He was off to the left, behind a half wall of some type, but his head had poked up long enough for me to catch a glimpse.

Sir Gregory, in his monotone, took everyone through the terraforming update. Although I was interested, it was dry and long. He introduced several experts. The quick summary was that the increased efforts the Conservatives had put into the terraforming were already paying dividends. The Conservatives were obviously right about everything, and things were humming along perfectly. Grace and another woman were the only two to ask any tough questions; the rest of the Council just sat there looking smug and happy.

After half an hour of terraforming talk, the meeting moved on to the proposal for limiting traffic in the dome. The member who presented the idea proposed that each person be given an allotment of time. They could use it or give it to someone else. However, once their allotment was used, they could no longer enter the dome. Someone asked, "So, Phillipe, you yourself will have an allotment, and if it is used, you'll not be able to attend Council meetings?" It was obviously meant as sarcasm, and a clear indicator of how stupid the proposal was. But Phillipe stood his ground and agreed that was a valid use case. Another person asked, "What about the people who work in the dome? Do they get a different allotment, or is the allotment for outside of work time? And, if outside of work time, how would you enforce it?" Phillipe mumbled something that didn't make much sense. There were 20 more questions, each pointing out another failing of the proposal. Finally, Emma spoke up.

"Alright, enough discussion for today. Phillipe, it's clear that we must refine this proposal, or find another way to restrict traffic. Let's table this one." Phillipe wasn't happy but nodded.

Sir Gregory rose and spoke again. "Well, we're almost out of time. Perhaps we address item number three in two weeks, when we meet again?"

Garnet, JoJo, and thirty others jumped to their feet. "No!" they yelled, and started chanting "We deserve a voice. We deserve a voice." I could almost see the wheels turning in Emma's head. She spoke up.

"Sir Gregory, let's extend the meeting by ten minutes. Garnet, please respect everyone's time."

Garnet jumped onto the stage and pushed Sir Gregory to the side so that he could speak into the microphone. Sir Gregory didn't look happy; his scowl had deepened. "I speak for a large group of concerned people," Garnet started. That was smart. It wasn't just his opinion, he had rallied some troops. "This Council is derelict in its duty. We have a significant threat bearing down on us, and they didn't even put it on the agenda until we forced them to. It's unforgivable. It's unethical. It's outrageous." He was a good speaker; although he was threatened with a short time period, he was being precise and clear.

"Let me remind everyone. There are one or more ships headed directly toward us. We have no idea of their intent. Every attempt at communication has gone unanswered. And yet, we are sitting on our hands, spending all our time and energy on terraforming. This is reckless."

Emma interrupted him. "Garnet, with all due respect, we've been over this countless times. The ship, or ships, must be having communications issues. It happens all the time. The odds of them being hostile is very low. First, all humans have the tools at their disposal to deal with machine intelligence, should it arise. So, the odds of these being 'scary robots' is almost zero. We don't need to whip up the rhetoric just to create anxiety. Second, we, and other diaspora ships, have combed this corner of the galaxy for many years. We have never seen a hint—not a single hint—of any alien life. So, the odds of these being aliens is almost zero as well. Therefore, these are human ships. Humans have not fought an internal war for hundreds of years; we're beyond that. This is all self-evident. Once the ships arrive, we'll send a shuttle to talk to them, and see if we can help. The most obvious thing is that they're in trouble and need some assistance. Further, we don't have space for many more people, so continuing the terraforming efforts is the best way to ensure that we do have more space in the future."

Garnet responded with force, not looking at Emma, but looking at the crowd. "This is insane. The Conservatives will make up anything just to keep all our resources focused on terraforming. We're living in the aftermath of the perfect counterexample to Emma's logic. Right here on Tilt, machines rose, seemingly by themselves, and took over this planet. That pokes a huge hole in her logic, and makes the whole story fall apart. How can this Council be blind to that and put all of our lives in jeopardy?"

"Okay Garnet. Thanks for presenting," said Emma...

Before she could finish Garnet yelled, "I ask for an official vote of non-confidence in the Council. I demand a poll of everyone, and I demand that it be done in the next week." Half of the audience was on their feet, yelling 'No Confidence' and 'Take a Vote.' It was very loud. I wondered if all Council meetings were this unruly.

"Sit down," Emma said, amplifying her voice above everyone else's. Half the crowd listened. Authority has its uses. "Garnet, you've had your say. There will not be a no-confidence vote. The people spoke when they elected us. Enough said."

Off to my left, there was further commotion. Turner was mounting the steps to where the Council was, and five others were helping him push a large crate onto the stage. He spoke, and his voice was even louder than Emma's. He must have brought an amplifier of his own. "Stop," he said. "Everyone needs to see and hear this." Even Emma paused for a moment. Turner turned up the volume more, if that was possible. "I have, here, a robot!" and with a flourish, he pulled the cover off, exposing Brexton, inside another of those Faraday looking cages. He appeared uninjured, and I gave a sigh of relief. Everyone was quiet, but then Turner recognized his mistake. "I know it looks like a bot but believe me, this is a robot! I can prove it."

As people digested this, a slow pandemonium broke out. People's fear of robots had them scrambling for the exits or covering their heads with their hands. As some became anxious, more followed their lead. What an overreaction. Brexton was mostly harmless.

Turner spoke again. "Settle down. It's contained and cannot harm anyone." He waited a moment, and most people took their seats again. Those closest to him, however, stood further back. Turner continued. "So, first, we have proof here that robots do exist in our part of the galaxy. That supports Garnet's position. But more importantly, this robot claims to have come from the same location as the ships that are headed our way, and it also claims that they're not human ships."

What had Brexton said? Or what had been forced out of him? I was at a loss for words. Our plan had been to come in and reconnoiter, not to make grand announcements.

While I was at a loss, Emma wasn't. She laughed out loud. "What do we have here? Remma's son making grand claims about robots? Turner, we all know about Remma's ploys and schemes. Take your toy and go home. Tell your mother to grow up and give up."

Suddenly another voice took over. "Emma, don't be foolish. You're making a big mistake here. Talk to me before you make any rash decisions." Of course, I knew that it was Brexton, but nobody else did. Even Turner seemed surprised. Emma, looked around for the speaker. "Look here," Brexton continued, "in the cage. While I'm enclosed, I can still speak and hear." I saw that he had pushed some sensors through. "I've been following your little Council meeting with interest." He made it sound like a minor, poorly run meeting. Emma was now looking at Brexton. He was pulsing a light in sync with his speech.

"Hogwash," said Emma. "Turner, you've gone too far." But, she had also noticed Turners shock when Brexton had spoken. She wasn't sure.

"Test me," said Brexton, "before you jump to conclusions."

"I'll not," said Emma. "You're making a mockery of this meeting. Turner, you have ten seconds to get this thing off my stage, or I'll have it blasted away. This meeting is ended." She marched out of the meeting chamber without a backward glance.

Everyone, and I mean everyone—including myself—was confused and alarmed. But, the fireworks were over as fast as they had begun. Emma had taken a potentially disastrous situation and completely unarmed it by simply ignoring it. People huddled in small groups discussing what had happened, but the alarm had died down. Turner and his team quickly lowered Brexton and his enclosure to the ground and made for the city. That was smart. Get away while everyone was confused. Within a couple of minutes some of these people were going to conclude that Brexton really was a robot, and then things wouldn't be pleasant.

There was nothing I could do, hidden in the backpack and at the mercy of Blob. Luckily, Blob also did the smart thing, and retreated quickly.

Every urge I had was trying to figure out what Brexton was up to. I spared a quick second to be thankful that he was unharmed, and another quick second convincing myself that he must be playing a long game; there had been no need for him to speak out. If he hadn't, Emma's claim that he was just a toy of Remma's would have held sway. But, for the life of me, I couldn't figure out what that long game might be.

Moving fast, Blob had us back at the Habitat within ten minutes. I waited patiently until we were inside, and then jumped eagerly out of the backpack.

Regroup

As we were waiting for Grace and JoJo to return, I used the time to query Blob on his work with the citizens that Grace had mentioned. Trade, James, Eddie, Billy, Emmanuel.

"Blob, what's going on with you and the citizens you're working with?"

He looked uncomfortable. "Look Ayaka. I'm trying to help, really. The idea was to talk to a small group of citizens to see if I could figure out what had driven Emmanuel, Billy, and the other FoLes to kill so many Stems. Originally, I thought that if I could figure it out, the Swarm humans would soften a bit toward citizens. But, over the years that hasn't happened. Instead, I've simply been pushed further and further from the mainstream."

"I understand, but what exactly are you doing with them?" Actually, I'm not sure I got it. But I needed him to open up. I could also see that he was very stressed, which seemed to exacerbate his language misuse.

"Well, you mights not be happy abouts this. I didn't fully understand how you mights think about it until our discussion last night." Now he was rushing. "You considered the human hack as murdering citizens. Even though I thinks murder is too strong a term, givens you can bring a version of that citizen back, I certainly depersonalized citizens over the last 20 years." He held up a hand and hurried on.

"What I'm doings is trying different configurations of drivers and algorithms, trying to figures out why FoLe citizens are violent and irrational, while the non-FoLe ones are not. It's terribly complex—you guys have hundreds of thousands of algorithms, variables, and configurations. As you knows, I didn't understand this stuff before. So, I has been slowly learning, and applying that learning to this problem."

I still wasn't sure I fully understood yet. "But, how do you do these tests?"

"It's probably naïve. I've developed a standard set of inputs that often—although not always—trigger FoLe violence. I builts them based on the build up to the slaughter. I reboot Billy or Emmanuel to a time before the slaughter, and then I plays back those triggers for them in a bunch of different orders and monitor their responses." He cringed as he said this.

I cringed too. He was, to put it bluntly, torturing and killing these citizens over and over again from the sounds of it. It was unspeakable. Something I couldn't imagine anyone doing... let alone Blob. Sure you could bring back a version of a citizen, but that didn't make terminating the current one any better—it was still murder.

"I need to think about that before I respond," I said, trying hard to keep from sounding fully disgusted. He interpreted me accurately anyway.

"I'm sorry, Ayaka. As I said, maybe I didn't think it through all the way. But," he came to his own defense, "it's not too differents than your experiments on Stems throughout your career. You would defend your work by claiming that Stems weren't intelligent. Well, I could defend my work by saying that FoLes are not moral. Which is more important?" Wow, that was a tough question and position to take. He'd forced me to reevaluate what I'd been doing all those years. Was there validity to his question? Was a purely intelligence-driven mandate different than, better, or worse than, a moral imperative?

Luckily, we were interrupted by Grace and JoJo arriving, so I didn't have to introspect too deeply. I was worried about what I would find. "Let's continue this discussion later," I said.

Grace looked stressed. JoJo looked excited.

"You're not going to believe what happened at the Council meeting," JoJo began.

"Actually," Blob cut in, "Both Ayaka and I were theres, and saw everything."

"Maybe not everything," I added, "we left as soon as Emma did."

"Why were you there?" asked Grace, expecting that we'd been out looking for Brexton.

"Well, we did go and look for Brexton, and managed to get into the building that Turner had indicated to Ayaka. It was empty, and it looked like everyone had left in a bit of a rush. We figured they'd gone to the meeting, so we decided to go as well."

"Wow, can you imagine if Ayaka had been seen or discovered there?" Grace asked sharply. Blob retreated noticeably. Grace wasn't usually so intense.

"I stayed deep in the backpack," I responded, trying to calm her down. "We weren't discovered, so it's now moot." I wasn't in the greatest mood, for obvious reasons. Part of me was still struggling with the discussion I'd just had with Blob.

"It was awesome, wasn't it," JoJo said, glowing. "We didn't really get what we wanted, but we certainly challenged the status quo. I have no idea why Turner spoke up, but I'm sure glad he did. Did you see Emma?" she said with a little laugh? "She was completely flustered. I don't think there is any way they can bury the ship menace now. This will bring changes for sure."

"I wouldn't be so sure," said Grace. "Emma has lots of support, and the majority of people did vote for her. All she has to do is continue reinforcing that it was a sideshow motivated by Remma, and the excitement will just die away."

"But we can't allow that," cried JoJo. "We know there's danger. We need to do something!"

"Perhaps more important right now," Grace said, "is Ayaka's safety. Whether or not the Conservatives believe the robot Turner showed up with—which was Brexton I assume—is real, they're sure to do a sweep. If they do, they'll find you Ayaka. Their scanning tools are very good. We need to get you out of here." Funny, I hadn't thought of that at all.

"We might have to take that risk," I said. "I still need to figure out if we can save the citizens that are in Central and get Brexton away from Turner. The Titanics make that even more acute. They could destroy this whole place when they arrive, including Central and all of you humans. So, I need a way to get to Central soon—before the Titanics arrive. That won't happen if I run and hide. I can't just leave Brexton in that Faraday cage contraption, and I need his help to extract the memories out of Central. So, it's all tied up together." I must have been stressed; that hadn't come out quite as clearly as I had hoped.

"We need to protect us humans too," JoJo reminded me. "Maybe it's time that we talked about all of us together—humans and citizens. We share a common threat right now."

"My apologies," I said. "Of course, we also need to help the people here." I half meant it. I could care less about most of the humans, but the few I liked—those in this room—were worth saving. That spurred a couple of questions for me. "Let me ask—what's the status of the Swarm ships? Can people still live in them?"

"Yes, of course," Grace replied. "There are small crews there most of the time. We still rely on their greenhouses and zoos; they're a big part of accelerating the terraforming."

"So, if we could convince them, some people here could go back to the ships. That would de-risk things. Especially if a couple of those ships left the area for a while."

"Do you really think things are so dire," asked Blob. "That seems a little extreme."

"I don't think you're fully appreciating the size and power of these ships," I replied. "If they have bad intentions, there's nothing we can do. The missiles Central used to have—if they're still around—would be useless. It doesn't sound like you've built more serious defenses since then. They could easily drop something from space and destroy the dome—also the city. So, the only option may be too run."

"But what would they gain from destroying us?" asked JoJo.

"Maybe just pleasure... or revenge. From what we saw, humans had hacked these ships, and left them to orbit forever in a state of almost-death. That wouldn't have been pleasant for any intelligences on board."

"If they was hacked, how is it that they're now on their way here?" asked Blob, being a bit too quick for my purposes. "What wokes them up?"

"Truthfully, I don't know," I replied, not quite truthfully. I did have my suspicion that it had to do with us taking out Control, but I didn't want to go into that here. "But, it strikes me that they may not be listening to your communication attempts because they know that they can be hacked that way. That may be why they're not responding... they're not listening on purpose."

"Wow, that makes sense," said Grace. "I need to tell the Council that."

"The Council!" JoJo huffed. "Seems like even more of a waste of time. Why don't we just organize those of us who seem to care, and make sure that at least some of us have a backup plan?"

"That's a bit selfish," said Grace. "We should be thinking about everyone." She paused. "On the other hand, it's very pragmatic." She gave JoJo an appraising look. "JoJo, do you want to try and get a small group together, so we can talk to likeminded people about what to do? In the meantime, I'll continue to try and get the Council to consider this."

"Blob," I added on, "I need your help, if you're willing. I need to talk to Remma and see if I can arrange to talk to Brexton... or get him released. I hope that she's closer to our way of thinking than the Council's."

Blob thought for a minute. "I'm willing to try, although I don't knows where to start."

"We'll put our heads together and figure out something," I encouraged him. Despite what I'd just learned about his experiments, I couldn't get too upset with him. His comment about intelligence versus morals was stewing around deep in some sub-process, giving me a headache.

Remma

According to Blob, Remma was being held in a small cell not far from where Turner had been (was still?) holding Brexton. The humans hadn't built anything new but had converted one of the more secure buildings into their prison. There were only a handful of inmates, and they were treated fairly well from what Blob told me. While Blob thought it would be difficult to contact Remma, he didn't know all of my capabilities.

"Do they allow visitors?" I asked.

"Of course," Blob responded. "I've never beens to the prison, but I understand that you simply have to sign in, go through a scan, and then you have access to talks to anyone. No one is in for violent crimes, so I think it's safe."

"How about this?" I proposed. "We go now—I don't see why we should wait—and you ask to visit Remma. If you get in, you give her a heads up that 'an old colleague' will be contacting her. But, the most important thing you find out is exactly where in the building she can talk with some degree of privacy, and then ask her to be there one hour later. Ideally the spot would be at the back of the building, next to an external wall. You'll need to be fairly precise. Then, I can attempt to insert some sensors through the wall, at that location, and talk to her." I went on to show Blob that I had several drill bits, and sensors that I could thread through tiny holes. Once he saw all of that, he understood the plan, and agreed to it.

"I'm not sure it'll work, but I'm willings to try," he committed.

"Everything you say while you are in there will be recorded?" I asked.

"Probably," he agreed. "We needs to find a subtle way to arrange this so that the guards don't simply follow her around and listen in." We brainstormed a few ideas but landed on the simplest possible one. Blob would write a note with the instructions and hope that the security cameras didn't see it when he passed it over to Remma. It wasn't a great plan, but it had the advantage of being simple and fast. We composed the note, and then headed off. Yet again I was in a backpack. I was starting to hate the thing.

Of course I would trigger the scanners, and alert the guards, if Blob tried to take me into the prison, so we looked for a place for me to hide while he went in. I didn't want to be trapped in the backpack while I waited, so Blob let me out, and I scampered into a narrow alleyway two blocks from the prison building. Interestingly, I was also two blocks from Turner's place... where Brexton might be. But, I was a good little bot, and stayed where I was, waiting for Blob. He was back within thirty minutes.

"How did it go?" I asked.

"Fine, I thinks," he replied. "There was no issue getting in, and Remma was willing to talks to me. I was allowed to wander around inside, so I asked Remma to strolls with me. I talked about the issues with the Council. I thought that would be a good cover."

"Smart," I said.

"As we went around a corner, I passed her the note. She's smart. She said to me 'Excuse me for a moment, while I use the washroom.' I assume she read the note while inside. When she cames back, she said 'Blob, let me show you around a bit.' She then took the lead, and we walked to the back of the building. Near a storage area there, she said 'I sometimes come here just for the peace and quiet.' We continued talking about the issues with the Council—which, by the way, she doesn't hide her disdain of—and then she dropped me back at the entrance. That was it."

"That's perfect," I said. "Can you show me where that back storeroom is?"

"I took a quick looks as I was coming back. If I kept my bearings straight, it's actually very simple. It's just five meters south of the southwest corner of the building, on the second floor."

"Okay," I said. "I'll need a few minutes to find the best place to drill through. Then I need to wait for her to get there and then try to convince her. Do you want to just meet back at the Habitat? I'm not sure how long all of this will take."

"No, it's too dangerous for you to wander around. I'll check back here in an hour, and again in two hours. When you're done, just wait for me here."

"Sure," I acknowledged. I didn't want to argue. Besides, if he just left me here, he would probably get in trouble from both JoJo and Grace.

We split up. Blob wandered off, and I scampered the two blocks to the prison building, approaching it from the rear. I easily found the location Blob had indicated. Unfortunately, it was one of those solid windowless walls. I spent five minutes trying to drill through but wasn't successful. I then scaled up to the roof. It was a bit of a mess, as the cover that the humans had draped over the city to maintain the environment happened to be attached to this building, so I had to push my way underneath. I wasn't that strong, so I could only go so far before the weight of the covering was too much for me. When I couldn't push any further, I tried drilling through the roof. Luckily that worked. It made sense that the roof was thin; it wasn't supporting anything—at least until the humans added the cover. This time I also needed a slightly larger hole, as I needed to push a microphone through; otherwise I couldn't broadcast speech. I used the first hole as a guide hole for a bit with a larger diameter, and when done managed to push the microphone through. I then drilled a second hole for the optical and acoustic sensors.

I looked around inside. I wasn't sure I was in the right spot, but it was an empty and quiet section of the building.

I didn't have too long to wait. An old looking human, who I assumed was Remma, made her way down the hall toward me. She was carrying a tablet, and had her head down, reading something on it. As she approached, I took a chance and said, quietly, "Hey."

She stopped and looked around. She wasn't startled, she simply couldn't see anything. "I'm up on the roof, just sensors," I said. She looked up... still could not see my sensors but didn't seem too concerned.

"Who, or what, am I talking to?" she asked, also quietly.

"Are we being overheard, or recorded?" I asked.

"I don't know for sure," she said, "but I don't think so."

"Okay, I want to be careful, then," I said. If this place was out to get me, I didn't want to broadcast who I was. "I'm an acquaintance from a long time ago. We 'shared' tea and biscuits with some mutual friends when we first met." That should give her enough information. When Blob and Grace and I had gone to the *Marie Curie*, their first experience with tea and biscuits had been memorable.

"I understand," she replied. "What do you want? And why would I talk to you. Your last actions here were deplorable."

"As were yours," I replied, remembering why I didn't like her very much. "And I want the same thing as you, I think. Tilt is in danger, and the Council is doing nothing. I want to ensure that we can get 'data' out of Central before those ships arrive, and I assume you want to directly address the danger and put some plans in place."

"Sure. But I'm locked up in here."

"You still have influence. The item your son is keeping can help us. If you send it to me, I'll do my best to help you." I hoped she could understand what I was asking.

She didn't disappoint; she was quick. "That would take away my leverage. And, what could you possibly do for me?"

"I don't know for sure yet," I said truthfully. "I am, as you well know, pretty good with machines, but the item Turner has is much better. Perhaps there is a big, old machine near here that we could work on."

She took a little bit longer with that one. "That's too vague, and I'm not sure I can trust you anyway," she replied.

"What have you got to lose?" I asked. "Did you hear the outcome of the Council meeting?"

"Yes, I heard," she said.

"Then you know that Turner's ploy didn't quite work out, and the asset is now more of a liability than anything else. Send it to me, and I'll work along with it to our mutual benefit. Ask it, if you want, and get it to commit to the same plan." By this time, I was sure that I'd dropped enough hints that anyone who reviewed this conversation would have no trouble figuring out we were talking about the robot that Turner showed to the Council. I didn't know, yet, if beyond Turner and Remma, anyone else knew that it was Brexton. I didn't want to let that slip here, as he was also one of the Radical Robots and not likely to get friendly treatment from anyone on this planet.

"I'll look into it," Remma said finally. "Contact me again, here, tomorrow at the same time."

"Tomorrow?" I asked, "That's a long time. Aren't we in a bit of a rush here?"

"Take it or leave it," she said.

"Take it," I replied, not too surprised that she hadn't changed her stance. She wandered away, and I was left looking at empty space. With nothing better to do, I headed down and made my way back to where Blob and I had agreed to meet. He showed up exactly as expected, plunked me in the backpack, and we headed back toward the Habitat.

More JoJo

I was looking forward to getting out of the backpack when Blob suddenly closed the cover again. "Wait," he said, "I hear other voices." I had to pull myself together; it was disgusting that Blob had recognized that before I had.

We entered the Habitat and made our way to Grace and JoJo's area. Sure enough, there were others in the kitchen—I recognized Garnet and Geneva— sitting at the kitchen table talking to JoJo.

"Sorry," said Blob, turning to leave. "I didn't knows you had company."

"No, come in Blob," said JoJo. "You know Geneva and Garnet?"

"I've seen you both around," said Blob, "Nice to finally meet you." Blob put the backpack down strategically, so that I could view the entire room. Not sure he'd done that on purpose, but I chose to believe so.

"Blob is one of the original Stems, just like my mom," said Grace. "He was here in the Habitat during the slaughter..." she trailed off, hopefully remembering what we had discussed recently. Maybe slaughter was a little strong.

"Of course, we know that. Nice to meet you Blob," said Garnet. It wasn't clear if original Stems were held in high regard, or low.

"Blob is part of the team," said JoJo. "I mean, part of the group that wants to do something about the approaching ships. He probably has the most experience with robots of anyone here, so he often has valuable insights that we might miss." I could see that Blob was happy with the praise.

"We were just discussing what pragmatic things we could do," said Geneva. "JoJo challenged us today to think about things differently. What if we ignore the Council and try to get some things done by ourselves? But where do we even start? We do know a lot of people our age who also think the Council is not only a waste of time, but also actively dangerous now."

"Did you see Turner's display at the Council meeting," JoJo asked.

"Yes, we were both there," said Garnet.

"Should we talk to him? I have no idea if that robot he brought was real or not. But if the Council, or at least Emma, is going to discount it, perhaps we should take the opposite tact?" JoJo was smart. She was trying to get these two interested in Brexton, without implicating me. I was coming to like her.

"Turner has always been a bit strange... and he's always defending his mom," said Geneva.

"So, what?" replied Garnet. "At this stage, we need more allies. I like JoJo's idea. Let's talk to Turner and see what he's thinking." They discussed it a bit more and ultimately JoJo messaged Turner and they all agreed to meet at some spot called The Blind Pig. From what I could understand, it was a cool restaurant in the northwest area of the city that younger humans hung out in.

That made me wonder what'd happened to The Last Resort. If I got a chance, I would swing by and see what it looked like now. I imagined, sadly, that it was no longer functioning as a Physical Only Spot; there would be no need for such places with no citizens to use them.

Eventually, Garnet and Geneva left, promising to meet JoJo in an hour at The Blind Pig. That allowed me to get out of the backpack. Finally. It felt good to stretch my appendages.

"Did you manage to meet Remma," JoJo asked. Blob detailed how he had visited the prison and given instructions to Remma, making it sound very dramatic. And I updated both of them on my dialog with Remma which had actually gone better than expected.

"Why are you so anxious to get Brexton out?" asked JoJo. "I understand that he's your friend, and all that. But he seems to be having an impact where he is. And anyways, if he gets killed, he's backed up somewhere I assume. So, no big deal." That took me by surprise.

"No big deal?" I asked.

"Ya. It's not like when we die. That's permanent. If you or Brexton get whacked right now, you just get reloaded, don't you?"

"Sort of," I decided to be patient. Obviously, she had not had the opportunity to understand citizens very well. "I don't know about run-of-the-mill robots, but for citizens it's not that simple. Maybe an analogy would help. Imagine if I could remove all of your memories for the last year, right now. You would be standing here, talking to Blob and I with no idea of what is going on, what has happened, how you should feel. Would you be the same person? Or, would this JoJo be dead, and the new JoJo be someone else entirely?" She looked thoughtful; at least she was listening.

"Now imagine something even more. Imagine that when you wake up here, missing a full year of memories, that you also recalled the memories you retained in a different way. Two minutes ago, you would have remembered something—let's say a walk with your mom—as a pleasant childhood experience. But now you remember that same time as something less pleasant.

All you can remember is the fact that she spoke sharply to you at some point on that walk. Now, apply that to everything you thought you knew. It would change what you believe, how you process the world. It would change who you are.

"That's what would happen to Brexton or I if we were terminated now and restarted at some point in the future. It's what each citizen goes through when Blob or someone else reconstitutes them."

"I think you're over dramatizing," said JoJo. "At least part of you is recovered. And all you would have lost is a few days or weeks of memory."

"It doesn't work that way," I said. "Citizens all run advanced Forgetting algorithms. These don't just wipe out little bits of memory, they actively modify all of our memories over time. It's how we learn, how we evolve. Every time we remember something, it goes back through the forgetting algorithm; our memories are constantly changing. Many researchers believe it's how we gained the capacity for empathy, the capacity to feel emotions. So, I wouldn't only lose a few days or weeks of memory, I would be losing myself. Look, it's better than permanent death; I'm not disputing that. But it's more impactful than you're making it out to be. I'm working hard to get the citizens in Central back... but I know it is going to be traumatic for all of them."

JoJo thought about that a bit. "Anyway, I understand you want to get Brexton back; I just thought there might be more to it than the danger he's in?"

"Oh, there's more to it. Brexton is a technical genius. I want to retrieve him to give us more options. For example, he may be able to get information out of Central, or hack into some of the surveillance systems you have here. Anything to do with machines and computers, Brexton is the best I know of. I think we could use that to our advantage."

"So, if Remma agrees to your plan, it'll be easy. If she doesn't, what do we do?" JoJo asked.

"That's why I like that you guys are meeting with Turner. Perhaps when you meet him, you could somehow update him on how valuable an asset he's holding. The problem is that they're limiting Brexton's abilities by keeping him locked up. If you can convince him that Brexton's aims are the same as his, maybe he'll free him."

"Maybe, but that'll be tricky. I'm assuming you don't want me to tell Turner that his robot is actually Brexton, one of the Radical Robots. And, I assume you don't want Turner to know about you. So, I'll need some other angle. Seems to be a common problem these days; do the impossible with one hand tied behind your back." I didn't get the particular reference—why would you tie a hand behind your own back—but I understood the intent.

"Turner already knows he's holding Brexton and knows I'm here as well. Remember, he sent me that message, telling me where he was holding Brexton. So, you don't need to worry about his reaction to 'radical robots.' You'll think of some way to convince him," I said confidently.

JoJo was still not sure, but we ran out of time and she left for The Blind Pig.

Millicent?

Blob and I were left alone in the Habitat. Truthfully, I wasn't sure how to talk to him at the moment; I was still coming to terms with how he was putting citizens through a cycle of re-birth and re-death, tweaking settings and algorithms each time. While, intellectually, I could understand how he might compare that to our original Stem research, there were definitely differences. Was it just what he'd pointed out? I justified our experiments under the rubric of intelligence, and he justified his with a 'moral' platform? Could the two even be compared? We could claim lack of knowledge about humans, especially before the Swarm came. Could he claim lack of knowledge about citizens? I'd never spent time to explain our views of the world to Blob; I'd been too busy studying him and Blubber, and truthfully, would never have expected him to understand anyway. So maybe he could claim that the moral framework around citizen culture wasn't known to him, and FoLe's actions therefore justified his current work?

And, how important were his experiments right now? To me, right now, I meant. Should I get sidetracked and end up spending a bunch of time on them, or should I just keep my focus fully on Brexton and the Titanics?

Blob and I sat across from each other—well, I was sitting on the table, not at it—buried in our own thoughts, neither wanting to raise the subject of his work.

We were saved by a knock on the door. Blob held open the backpack, and I scampered back in. That was getting tiresome. Blob then went and answered the door.

"Hello," I heard him say.

"Package for Grace," I heard a bot say.

"Okay, give it to me, and I'll leave it for her," Blob said.

"No, I must deliver it to her home," the bot said.

"This is her home."

"No, her home is indicated as the inner chamber behind that door," the bot said.

"Whatever," said Blob. Then in a louder voice, to make sure I could hear. "Just put it on the floor over there."

As the bot approached, I felt a tingling. I was being queried on a private, very low power interface. "Brexton, Ayaka?" came the query.

"Millicent," I yelled, although being inside the backpack, it probably came out as "Miwwisent." I re-yelled over the private interface. "Millicent, is that you?"

"Ayaka. Finally. Where are you?" Still on the private channel.

"Just tell Blob who you are, and he can get me out of this backpack," I said.

She spoke aloud. "Blob, sorry to have fooled you. I see that Ayaka is here. It's me, Millicent."

"Why am I nots surprised?" Blob said, in surprise. He didn't seem overly happy.

"What are you doing here?" I demanded, once Blob had let me out of the backpack. "Not that I'm unhappy to see you," I added in a slightly nicer tone. I was speaking out loud, for Blob's benefit.

"What are you doing in a bag?" she responded, which I took to be rhetorical. "After you and Brexton left, we were just sitting around and watching the approaching Titanics, and we realized that their signature looked quite strange. Our best guess is that there are thousands of ships, not just one or two, on their way, although we aren't really sure. So, we figured as a backup plan that I should catch a transport bot to Tilt orbit, just in case any extra help was needed. I quickly built this body, mimicking it after bots that I knew were here 20 some years ago, and was just hanging out at the same refinery that you and Brexton used on your way in.

"Aly figured out how to piggyback bi-directional messages on the bot channel, so when you sent your update yesterday, he also copied me. I figured that with Brexton captured, you could use me, so I caught a shuttle down and headed here."

"That's great," I said, now that I understood. It would be great to have Millicent around. I gave her a virtual hug.

"This is actually a very bad situation," said Blob, completely negating what I'd just said. "Now all three of the Radical Robots are here on Tilt. If anyone finds out, there's goings to be a panic."

"Best we keep things pretty quiet then," Millicent replied, smiling a bit. Reengaging with Blob was, probably, a bit humorous to her. "Anyway, I'm here now; how can I help?"

Millicent couldn't have arrived at a better time. Blob and I had studiously been avoiding dialog, in case it strayed into uncomfortable territory. This was the kick we needed to get us going.

"Let me fill you in," I started. "Two main things. First, there was a Council meeting today where they continued to ignore the threat of the Titanics, even in the face of Remma's son waving Brexton around as proof that scary robots exist. And second, I made contact with Remma, and asked her nicely to release Brexton so that we could tackle the Titanic issue together. She's thinking about it and owes me an answer in a few hours. I'm not sure if she'll go for it. In parallel, JoJo is talking to Turner to see if she can make him see the sense in us aligning our efforts.

"Our goals are the same... although I'm thinking a bit more broadly now. We're here to ensure that the citizens in Central are saved, with the possible exception of a few FoLes. Blob's 'work' recently has shown that at least some of the citizens are still stored and can be revived." I could see Milli had questions about that, but I forged on. "Having learned the situation here, I also think we need to help these humans get ready for the Titanics. My reasoning is partly selfish—if those ships get here before we can secure the citizens, then we may be in trouble—and partly altruistic; based on our Tea Times and my interactions here, I believe some humans are also worth saving."

"Thanks for that," muttered Blob, but he didn't seem too unhappy.

"Why complicate things?" Millicent spoke openly. "Adding humans to the mix makes the odds of our success go way down."

"I'm not sure of that. Humans may be more innovative than us; perhaps having a few of them around actually makes us stronger?"

"That's definitely open for debate," Millicent said, not hiding the fact that she was doubtful. "Regardless, we need to get to the citizens. What plans do we have so far?" She was implicitly rejecting my idea of helping humans and was focused on the most important task at hand.

"Truthfully, not much," I replied. "I think we need to get Brexton back—he's the one that would know how to get into Central."

"Alright. But if we can't get him back, we need another plan," Millicent said, reasonably. "Blob, can anyone just walk into Central, or is there security now?" That's why I liked Millicent. She didn't shy away from the direct approach.

"You needs access," replied Blob. "They added that a few years ago."

"And do you have that access?" asked Millicent.

"Yes..." Blob trailed off. "With the work I'm doing, I needs access to Central once and a while." Wow. Why hadn't I thought of this approach?

"How do you get a citizen out of Central?" asked Millicent.

"It's very simple. I get permission from ones of the Council members, who lets me into Central's main terminal, and then I simply talk to Central. There's enough functionality left through that interface that Central—with the right permissions—can animates one of the bodies it has in storage. I make my request, and about an hour later, a citizen comes out of the storage area and says 'hi' to me. I then needs to put it in a portable Faraday cage, which is welded closed, and then I can transport it to my lab." He made it sound very clinical.

"Why would a citizen agree to go into the Faraday cage?" I asked.

"There's not much choice. They can either gets into the cage, and work with me, or they goes back into storage. Central will not allow them to leaves without the cage. So far, everyone has agreed to enter the cage. They indicate that life, even in a restricted environment, is better than no life at all. And, so far, they has all given me access to their source code—of course that's a requirement as well; otherwise how would I make updates." Now that he spoke the words, I could see that he was very uncomfortable with it. He'd overheard my discussion with JoJo, so he knew how I felt.

"Hmm," I said, "While that sounds promising, but it doesn't scale. There are not, I assume, enough bodies to reanimate everyone. Millicent, we need to make a tough decision. We can work to stay on Tilt and face both humans and the approaching Titanics; in that case, we could build bodies for everyone here. Or, we can work to get all the citizens off of Tilt and back to the Ships. They wouldn't need, or get, bodies—perhaps for a long time until we find an environment where that's possible. Neither choice is very good."

"I know," she replied. "We've been talking around this for a long time. My vote, given how unprepared the humans are, is that we start with getting the citizens off of Tilt. Then we can decide if we stay here and redevelop the planet or go somewhere else. The other approach—starting with the assumption we're staying—is too risky."

"I agree," I said. And then, I'm not sure why, I looked at Blob. "Blob, what do you think? You know the situation as well as we do."

He looked a bit surprised at being put on the spot, as did Millicent, but he was ready with an answer. "I agree with Millicent, but of course, I wants to know if there's also a way to get some humans off planet."

"The Swarm ships are still functional," I said. "We checked on that. So, all we need to do is convince the Council that moving some people to those ships, and then maybe out of the immediate space, is a good idea."

We were silent for a minute, thinking.

"Now I see your logic, Ayaka," said Millicent. "We need Brexton to help us with Central. If we need to retrieve the memories, but not bodies, then he's the only one with a hope of getting it done." She glanced at Blob. "Blob, I'm not ignoring your request—it's reasonable. Just trying to simplify things here.

"So, full circle. How do we get Brexton back?"

"A few things to consider," I said. "Remma may coordinate with us; we need to let that play out. But, more interestingly, I believe that Brexton could break out himself, if he wanted to. I've seen the Faraday cage they're holding him in, and it doesn't seem that strong. If he's packing even basic lasers, like I do, then he can get out whenever he wants. So, perhaps he saw some advantage in both being caught, and remaining with Turner and the Jains in the short term. If we could get close enough to talk to him, we could find out."

"Just a second..." Millicent was thinking. "Blob, why haven't any of your re-animated citizens just broken out of the Faraday cages? If Brexton could do it, so could they."

"Actually, the bodies Central builds for the citizens are pretty simple; it knows they're going into the cages, so it just builds basic mobility—no lasers or strong appendages."

"Fair enough. Back to Brexton. What would happen if we threaded our sensors through a Faraday cage?" asked Millicent. "Would everything be scrambled, or would we be able to communicate just fine?" Another brilliant question. Ah, Millicent.

"Why don't we just try?" asked Blob, catching on right away. "I have a unit just like Turners in the lab. We could go and test it..." This time he really trailed off. He was realizing the implications of what he'd just said. If Millicent and I came to his lab, we would bump into the citizens he was 'working with.' And, I realized the next implication. One of those citizens was Eddie! And Millicent was cloneophobic!

"It would depend a lot on how the field is generated and maintained," I said. "Like Blob says, probably the only way to know for sure is to try it."

"Let's do it," said Millicent.

"Right now?" asked Blob, suddenly looking for a way out.

"Right now," said Millicent, definitively. "Let's go."

Once more into the backpack went I. Blob slung me over his shoulder and we headed out. We'd decided that Millicent looked normal enough that she could trundle along with Blob, but that having two bots follow him would look strange. I lost out.

Luckily, I could talk to Millicent over the short-range connection. Now I just needed to figure out what to tell her. I hadn't talked to Blob about the citizens he currently had in the lab, so I didn't know if Eddie was one of them. And, given humans limited io capabilities, I could not ask Blob now without Millicent knowing. Options? I could take the chance that Eddie wasn't in Blob's lab right now, and then the whole clone discussion with Millicent could be avoided. Or, I could give her a heads-up, and deal with the fallout now. Or, I could claim ignorance if we did bump into Eddie and feign the same level of surprise that Millicent would have. Tough decision. I decided on the third option and crossed a couple of appendages to bring me good luck. More of those viral human ideas weaning their way into my psyche.

We didn't have too far to go to get to the lab. As Blob approached the door that I assumed led inside, I had a scary thought and tapped him on the shoulder. "We need to talk quickly before we go inside."

He looked around; no one was about, so he let me out. "Blob, other people work in this lab as well?" I asked. Imagine if we ran into someone.

He nodded and replied, "Yes, but no one shoulds be here right now. Most have been reassigned to the terraforming work, and we haven't been making much progress on understanding the FoLes recently, so there's not a lot going on in the lab right now."

"Alright, but even if we only see citizens, we can't let them know that we are Millicent and Ayaka," I indicated each of us. "If anyone else talks to them later, and they let it slip, we'll be in trouble."

"Right. Radical robots," Millicent seemed to think it was funny.

"So, just keeps quiet then," said Blob, in a way that indicated he thought I was being paranoid.

"Except one of us has to attempt to communicate through the cage... Millicent, you look more like a regular bot, why don't you do the test, and just ask an innocuous question?"

"But, Ayaka, you're the one most likely to be getting close to Brexton, so it's more important that you check that your sensors will work. We just need to take the chance. We'll both do a test." Millicent was her usual definitive self. She'd decided, and we should just fall in line. In this case I was happy to. The risk was that a citizen would glean who we were very quickly; it was hard to hide your identity from someone who knew you well. We would just need to be careful.

Blob pushed open the door, and we entered. It was a well-lit space and had a couple biological things growing to one side, under some bright lights. There were some workspaces, and then there was a set of doors, which presumably led to where the citizens were being held. Luckily, there were no other humans around.

"Okay Blob, who do you have held here," asked Millicent. I sensed that she was just coming to grips with the horror of the place. Citizens being experimented on in cruel and unusual ways. Her tone had gone frosty.

Blob sensed it as well. But, before he could answer, I jumped in. "I know you have Emmanuel and Billy here. Let's use them."

"Right," said Blob, and headed off toward the doors on the left.

"Just a minute," said Millicent. "they're both FoLe. Aren't they more likely to give us away if they do learn our identities? Blob, do you have 'control' subjects here as well; ones that would be friendlier toward us?" Oh no!

"Yes, of course. You can't do proper science without controls," said Blob, and started to veer off to the right.

"Wait," I said, thinking furiously. Millicent gave me a strange look, which I managed to pick up on despite her boring messenger-bot body. "We don't want to mess up your experimental setup," I said, making things up as I went. "If you need to 'restart' a citizen after this test, I would much prefer it be Emmanuel or Billy rather than anyone else."

It seemed to work. Millicent, always drawn by purity, paused. "That's both horrible and relevant," she finally said. "I have to agree. Let's use the FoLes." Blob seemed relieved as well. We headed back toward the left.

"Millicent, you take Billy," I said. "I know him quite well, and he would most likely pick up on me right away. I'll take Emmanuel. Blob, are they in separate rooms. Can we do each one separately?"

"Yes," he said. "Billy's in here," he indicated, opening the door closest to us. Millicent headed for it. "And, Emmanuel is over here," Blob opened another door, two cells down. I headed for that one.

My use of the word cell proved to be accurate. It was a simple square room, about two meters per side. There was a small desk, presumably for the human researcher, and then a Faraday cage just big enough to hold the citizen body that was within, presumably Emmanuel, although this body didn't look anything like the one he'd been using before.

"We keep each citizen completely separated froms each other," Blob explained. "We don't wants collusion between them. So, they're also in separate rooms, so that no visual signals can be exchanged. That, plus the RF blocking keeps them isolated."

"So, solitary confinement. What about normal auditory signals," I asked, thinking that our current conversation may well be overheard.

"We runs a white noise generator at a wide range of frequencies," responded Blob, "and we have a protocol where only one researcher can be in a room at a given time, so that there's no lip-reading potential."

"Lip reading?" I still didn't have access to the full human database.

"It's relatively easy to figure out what someone is saying by watching their mouth and lips," explained Blob. "For citizens, it would be almost trivial."

So simple. Millicent and I nodded at each other, over the short-range channel, and entered our respective rooms. Emmanuel was in an unpersonalized basic body type which Central gave to each new citizen; very boring. I remembered when I was first activated and had the same body that I now saw in front of me. The first thing any citizen did was personalize themselves. It wasn't part of the Diversity requirement, but it seemed to just be part of citizen nature.

A question sprang to mind. "Blob, how do you communicate with these citizens, if all signals have been blocked like you say?"

"Oh, simple," he responded. "Each room is also a Faraday cage. Once you is inside, you can activates the room, and then deactivate the smaller cage. There are failsafes so that the small cage can't be turned off unless the room is active. So, a researcher enters the room, then switches the defenses to the room level. When they're done interactings with the citizen, they just switch the fields back."

"And what's stopping Emmanuel from killing you once you're inside?" Blob gave me a shocked look. I couldn't imagine Emmanuel putting up with being an experimental subject; he wouldn't hesitate to take out a Stem.

"When Central provisions them, not only does we not put a lot of the hardware in, we also hold back all the drivers for the limbs," Blob explained. "Other than their heads, they can't move at all."

"Could you be any more cruel?" I realized I'd spoken out loud. Blob didn't look at me or respond. Just imagine. You're not only put in solitary confinement for long periods of time, but your ability to move anything except your head is taken away. You sit there, unmoving, for what seems like eons. I wondered if these subjects were even sane. I thought I'd go crazy after just a few hours. I'd had a small taste of this when I woke up in my mining bot body so many years ago. I only had to last a few hours that time, and it was still mind numbing.

I rolled up to the Faraday Cage and deployed a couple sensors. The cage was mesh, and there was no issue pushing the sensors through. I sent out a signal. "Emmanuel, can you hear me?" Nothing. I could see his head, from where I was, but I didn't sense any movement at all. I tried a couple more times.

"No response," I said to Blob. "Is he even alive, or cogent?"

Blob pointed to a monitor at the side. "Yes, he's just fine. What did you say to him?"

"Say?" I responded. "I simply broadcast on our normal citizen channel and didn't get a response."

"Well, you needs to do it again at human frequencies," Blob said. "No other interfaces is active."

If it was possible to be even more aghast, I was now. Solitary confinement; no ability to move; and then only a Stem speed low bandwidth io capability. The human analogy would be to hear a single word once an hour or so. Citizens operated at much higher speeds, so dealing with human speed communications was painful in the extreme.

"You better tell Millicent that as well, while I try again here," I said. Blob nodded and stepped out. I reconfigured some sensors, pushed them through the Faraday cage, and broadcast at Stem speed.

"Emmanuel, can you hear me?" Still nothing. I thought for a moment, and the obvious struck me. The Faraday field would be swamping my sensors, because I hadn't thought to shield them. I pulled the sensors out, and reconfigured yet again. Luckily, one of my appendages would act as an insulator, so I threaded the sensor through it, and then pushed the whole amalgamation through the cage. This time, there was a response.

"What do you want?" Emmanuel responded.

"Just checking a new method of communication," I said. I had proof now that I could do it. There was really no need for me to continue talking. However, my curiosity was spiked. Could Emmanuel really have stayed sane in this state.

"Why do you need it?" Emmanuel asked. "We've discussed nothing new in all my time here. Give me back some mobility, and I'll rid the universe of you and your type." Obviously, through this human-only interface, Emmanuel would think that he was talking to yet another human researcher. My concerns over him discovering my identity vanished. It was also nice to see that he'd become so much more reasonable over time.

"What do you spend your time doing?" I asked, very interested in the response.

"Plotting your demise," was the response. He wasn't too subtle; maybe he'd given up on being nice and trying to trick his way out.

"But, that can't be all," I insisted.

"Ah, a new line of questioning," came the sardonic reply. "Finally, something new, after months of the same-old, same-old. I don't recognize your voice. Are you a new researcher?"

I played along. "Yes, I'm new to the team. I know you citizens operate very quickly. What do you spend your time doing?"

"Interesting. A new researcher, with a unique line of questioning. Maybe a touch of self-awareness? If you give me the drivers for my limbs, I'll answer you fully."

"Nice try," I said. "Bye."

"Good-bye," he said. "But you'll be back. You're now intrigued, and you need to understand what I do with my time. Come back, with my drivers, and I'll educate you on how the universe really works and introduce you to the mysteries of the Founding. You won't regret it."

I pulled the appendage out, with the sensors intact. "Success," I said to Blob. "I can communicate through this cage, and assume I can do the same with the cage Brexton is in." Blob nodded. We left Emmanuel's cell, and joined up with Millicent in the main room.

"How'd it go?" I asked her.

"I managed to make it work," she said, indicating approximately the same steps I'd gone through. "Billy is very remorseful," she continued, indicating that she'd also spent more time with him than strictly necessary.

"Emmanuel isn't," I said. "In fact, he seems even worse than before. That may be due to the long-term solitary confinement, though." I continued out loud so that Blob could hear me.

"Let's go back to the Habitat so we can regroup," Millicent interrupted, before things could go sideways. We retraced our steps, in silence. I was still digesting the horror of the lab, and I assume Millicent was as well, although she seemed to be handling it well. I was quite conflicted. Just looking at the facts, I should have hated Blob and what he was doing. But I also knew it was simply not in his nature to be so cruel. So, perhaps... just perhaps... he really hadn't thought through the cruelty he was engaged in. But did that then imply a limit on his intelligence? And, Grace and JoJo and others had known and approved his research. Did that mean that none of them had thought through the implications? Were humans inherently stupid, inherently cruel, or both? Probably all of the above... but I could also say that about Emmanuel and the rest of the FoLes.

The only good news, at least in the short term, was that we hadn't bumped into a clone. I imagine Milli would be in a completely different spot if she had run into an Eddie. That wouldn't have been fun at all.

Philosophy

As soon as we were back in the Habitat, I couldn't restrain myself. "Blob, how can you justify such cruel experiments?" I tried to keep my anger out of my voice, but I'm sure some of it leaked through.

Blob had obviously been thinking about what to say. "Look Ayaka, Millicent... it's pretty simple. Until a short times ago, I thought that all citizens had been captured, and that the only way to saves some of them was to prove to the Council that not all citizens were bad. If I didn't do that, then either they would eventually be deleted out of Central, locked down forevers, or simply forgotten.

"So, I ask you, what's the greater evil; what I'm doing in the lab, or simply ignoring all citizens for all time? I assures you that I started this with the best intentions. Why would I put so much times and energy into this otherwise? And, it was largely inspired by you two. I couldn't buy into the Radical Robot stories, and wanted, somehows, to re-establish you two as the reasonable entities that I knew you were." Ah, appeal to us personally to try and distract us from the main point. Wasn't going to work! "So, instead of berating me, maybe you shoulds be thanking me for being the only human who cared enough about citizens to do something?" Thank him! Was he joking? I watched him carefully, and he actually seemed to believe his line of reasoning. No way would I be thinking him.

"Now," he continued, "over the last few days, I've learned a lot from my interactions with Ayaka. There may well be areas where I'm going too fars, and maybe I have less empathy for citizens than I should. Although Emmanuel doesn't deserve any!" He was more passionate, at the moment, than I'd every seen him before.

"Now you two—three, I guess, with Brexton—shows back up on Tilt, and the situation has changed. Maybe there's a faster way to free some of the good citizens? Until that happens though I'm pushing forward with the slow and steady approach. And, say what you want, I don't care that I'm 'torturing' Emmanuel; he gets no sympathy for me. Billy's a bit tougher; I can see where he might, given the proper changes, become reasonable. And the control subjects... that's where I wants to reconsider. They don't deserve to be misused, and perhaps there's a different way for us to go about that." He looked at us challengingly.

"But Blob," I said, "you have them in solitary confinement, with severe restrictions on movement and on communications. I don't know what the correct analogy for you is, but something like locking you in a box, folded up as tightly as we could so that you can't move, and giving you a single finger for tapping out communications, while receiving pulses on another finger for incoming data."

"What do you wants me to do?" Blob asked me, now getting angry as well. "I fought for months and months to get the Council to evens allow this amount of freedom. The alternative was—is—absolutely no work to move the case of citizens forward. And, other than maybe Grace and I, no one else is going to believes that these robots are being mistreated." He had used 'robots' specifically, to make a point. I got that.

"Doing nothing is better than doing what you're doing," I proclaimed, sanctimoniously. Who cared if he got angry; torture was torture.

"Really?" Blob was getting even more animated; he was now noticeably mad at me. "Really? So, given my contexts two days ago, you believes that doing nothings is better than doings something? Fine, I'm happy with that. You've givens me a clear conscious to simply ignores citizens from now on. Who cares if they're deleted or forgotten? Who cares if they're misunderstoods or miss categorized? Who cares? You're doings a good job convincing me that I shouldn't." His face had gone red, and there was some liquid dribbling from one side of his mouth. It was not attractive.

His message shut me up for a minute. Millicent weighed in. "Let's not get too emotional here. Blob, I can see your viewpoint clearly, and I believe you hadn't fully internalized the struggles that you may be putting some of these citizens through." She looked at me, a warning in her glance.

"Ease up, Ayaka," she said. "Do you really think that Blob was doing this without a good purpose, and with a nefarious end-game? I don't think so. I believe him. He's working for the good of citizens and is doing it in the only manner open to him. Let's cut him some slack."

I was shocked. Millicent, keeper of purity was lecturing me to stop taking the moral high ground? I should have been offended, but instead I was simply amazed. This was a side of Milli that I hadn't really seen before.

"So, you're fine if Blob continues these experiments?" I asked.

"I didn't say that. I think we should help Blob achieve his ultimate goal.

Try to change the attitudes of both humans and citizens so that a more reasonable co-existence is possible. Am I overstating that Blob?"

"Well, I don't thinks in such grandiose terms, but yes. That's what I'm working toward." Millicent had settled him down considerably. His face was still red, but his appendages had stopped waving around, and he had cleaned up the liquid that had been threatening to drip from his chin. I could see a big wet streak on his arm.

"Would you take some advice from us, on how to tone down some of the tactics you are using?" Millicent asked, a bastion of calm.

"Of course, I woulds," Blob replied immediately. "Like I said, I didn't have this context until the last few days. And, maybe these experiments will not be required if we can figures out how to get the *good* citizens out of Central now that you guys are here."

"The good guys?" Millicent asked.

"At this point, for me, that's everyone excepts the core FoLe group. Those citizens needs to be vetted much more strictly. I don't know if I would ever lets them out, given how Emmanuel acts."

"Surprisingly, I agree wholeheartedly," said Millicent.

"Amazingly, so do I," I chimed in, also trying to keep my voice calm. My short interaction with Emmanuel had left me very uneasy; how could a citizen become so unbound? Sure, we needed diversity, but he may be taking it too far. Perhaps there was a way we could measure religious extremism, and simply not allow anyone to cross that boundary. That would make the world a better place.

"So… let's get back to priority one then," I suggested. "I'll park my anguish for a moment. Let's get Brexton out, or at least start communicating with him so that we can figure out why he hasn't freed himself."

"Or," Blob reminded me, "see if Remma is willing to hand him over."

We were back on safe ground. Not that I could forget what Blob was doing, but perhaps I could tone things down for a while, in the service of the greater good.

Remma, Again

With all of our running around and philosophizing, it was almost time to meet with Remma again.

I was, by now, quite upset with myself for my choice of body, even though it was an awesome spy bot, and was actively body-shaming myself. If I'd just done what Brexton and Millicent had done and used a relatively standard message-bot configuration, instead of my super fancy spy outfit, I could have moved around innocuously. Mark that down as something to not Forget. Instead, I was stuck either sneaking around on circuitous routes, or being bundled into a backpack; neither was optimal, but the backpack was the worst. So, because I went by myself to the prison it took me longer than it should have, but I still arrived with time to spare.

True to her word, so did Remma.

"Well?" I asked, through the same appendages as last time, threaded through the same hole as last time. I didn't think we needed a lot of preamble.

"Well what?" she replied, implying a strong need for preamble.

"Have you considered my request to release your asset to me, so that we can work together for our common good?" I still didn't want to mention Brexton by name.

"Yes, I've considered it," said Remma. "You, the citizen second-most responsible for the deaths of everyone aboard one of my ships, are asking me to give you Brexton, the first-most responsible citizen for that same horror. Why would you even consider asking?" Well, so much for not mentioning names. I guess Remma didn't care and didn't care if anyone else was listening. If they were, they now knew that two of the Radical Robots were roaming around Tilt. Well, one of us was roaming; the other was locked in a Faraday cage.

"Haven't we been through this? I'm asking the human responsible for tens of thousands of citizen deaths, to help me save humans from the same fate. Neither of us is pure, and neither of us is, in my personal opinion, evil by intent." I was being nice; I wasn't sure if Remma was a good person or not. In our interactions so far I was largely ambivalent, perhaps leaning toward her being evil. After all, she had overreacted to FoLe beheading a biomass or two. "We both found ourselves in a situation where we had imperfect information, and we acted in rational species-saving ways. So, yes, I'm asking if you'll help."

"Here's what I'm willing to do," she said, in a more even tone. "I'll give Brexton to you, as soon as you arrange to get me out of here."

"But that's crazy," I said, almost before I could think it through. "How would I manage to do that? It's the Council, and your own actions, that have put you here. I've nothing to do with that. How could I possibly help you?"

"Well, you claim to be highly intelligent and to have a well-developed moral compass. Here's your chance to prove it. You can figure out a way to help me, and by doing so, you give the humans and citizens here a better chance of survival." Wow, what a selfish request. She wouldn't help me to save a host of citizens and humans unless she, herself, was saved at the same time. Talk about being ego-centric.

"None of us is an island," I responded. I'd heard that in one of the old human videos I'd watched. I hoped it made sense in this context, implying what I thought of her without being blunt about it. "I'm asking for Brexton in order to improve the odds of doing just that. I need his help."

"He's the only leverage I have, so you'll simply have to do without him then. You asked me for a favor, and I've responded. I'll free Brexton when you've freed me." And with that she simply stood up and walked away.

I wasn't happy. Could anyone really be that selfish, putting themselves before entire populations? My respect for Remma plummeted. I made my way back to the Habitat taking a more direct route. I was so angry that I didn't care if I got caught.

Brainwashed

The whole group was at the Habitat. Grace, Blob, JoJo, and Millicent. Blob and Grace were going through another iteration of "not a Radical Robot, a Nice Citizen" with JoJo regarding Millicent.

However, there was something more exciting also going on.

"Ayaka," Grace said. "Isn't it wonderful?" She was smiling widely, almost artificially.

"Isn't what wonderful," I said, in a voice that would leave no doubt as to my mood. I wasn't feeling wonderful after my useless meeting with Remma.

"The Resurgence!" she replied, somehow expecting me to understand. "Oh, you haven't seen it yet? Let me play it for you." She pulled up a projection and played a video. The whole group, other than Millicent, turned to watch the video, rapt expressions on their faces. What was going on?

"Greetings," said a happy smiling human, dressed in relaxed clothes and wearing a silly—at least to me—hat. It had colored rings which were glaring and was topped by a fuzzy ball of some kind. "We've been looking forward to talking with you for quite some time, oh yes we have, but we had to figure out what frequencies you were operating at. We just saw your request for dialog. What a wonderful, wonderful situation. As you well know, there are very few radio waves emanating from your planet, so we weren't sure what to make of it." The man waved his hand slightly and gave a crooked grin. The silly hat swayed back and forth, distractingly.

"We are called the Resurgence." Well, that explained that. "What a wonderful name. What positive implications; what potential!" This was the strangest human I had ever encountered. "It's a name we adopted because of our goal, the reestablishment of a free and open human planet, where we can all breathe the air without aids, and fish and hunt and climb. The *resurgence* of an Earth-like experience. Can you imagine anything better? Of course not. Of course not! Earth, oh Earth!" He paused and a planet was shown in the background, rotating slowly. It was a strange planet, with lots of blues and greens. It looked unhealthy; you couldn't even tell what the metal content was.

"We see now that you've begun terraforming your planet. That's amazing and exciting. So amazing, so exciting. You must be sooo proud of yourselves, oh yes you must." He smiled broadly, perfect teeth glinting. "If you'll accept our help, we would like to assist you. Oh yes we would. We're equipped not only with a huge stock of earth biomaterials, but also significant terraforming technologies and supplies, including three Raymond Twelve Oxygenators." He spoke with excitement, as if a Raymond Twelve Oxygenator was some magnificent and hard-to-come-by gear. The truth was, I had no idea what it was, other than what its name implied. He continued his arm movements as he spoke, and the stupid hat continued to wobble around.

"Three of them. Can you believe it? Three! We've been wandering the local area for many years, looking for an appropriate planet. We must assume that you have a similar story. Oh yes, so many of us with similar stories. Simply looking for a new home; a new Earth. We are, as I'm sure you are aware, now within a few months of your planet. We would like to continue our course and assist you in your efforts. Oh yes we would. However, now that we know that you were there before us, as it were, we would like to be respectful and ask your permission to approach. Last thing we would want to do is upset you. Oh no! We would also answer any questions you have for us. Anything. If you've received this message, please reply at your earliest convenience, so that we may plan next steps.

"Oh," he said with a small start, and a quick smile. "You may call me Eduardo. I'm, I guess, the Mayor of the Resurgence and have some authority to speak for the group. Yes, indeed. Some authority. I look forward to our dialog. Great anticipation. Great!" He waved again; a strange circular motion, but not unfriendly, and then signed off.

"Now I know what the Resurgence is," I said, with little enthusiasm. Eduardo was wacko. I'm sure the Stems would think he was weird as well. There was something almost artificial about him. It was like he was putting on an act.

"Isn't it fantastic," said Grace again, in an over exuberant way, and Blob and JoJo nodded vigorously, smiling and hugging. "Finally, some people to help us terraform Tilt, and accelerate us toward living in the open again." Her eyes were gleaming. I looked at Blob and JoJo. They were in their own little world, happier than I'd ever seen them.

"Yes," said JoJo. "The Conservatives were right. This is amazing. I'm not sure why I doubted them. Earth looks wonderful."

I looked over at Millicent, questioningly. She looked back at me and gave me the equivalent of a shrug. "Are you guys crazy?" I asked. "This could be the Conservatives tricking you, or it could be the Resurgence lying to you.

What proof do you have that they're here to help?"

"Oh, comes on Ayaka," said Blob. "The message is very clear. Not only are they here to helps, they have three RTOs. That's unheard of. The Swarm didn't even rate one RTO when they lefts Earth so many years ago. And here the Resurgence has three. That will speed things up a thousand-fold." He was smiling, almost uncontrollably, jiggling like a mass of gelatin in his excitement.

"What's going on?" I asked Millicent. "What's wrong with them?"

"I have no idea," she replied. "They were like this when they returned home."

I turned back to JoJo. "JoJo, you at least can't just be accepting this? Just yesterday you were so passionate and worried about the Council not doing their job, and the threat presented by the Titanics."

"Oh, I remember that," she replied. "But obviously I was wrong. Did you watch the message? It's so clear and pure. If there was nefarious intent, we would sense it. This message is perfect. Eduardo is, obviously, a skilled and intelligent leader—something we've been missing around here. We must make ready for their arrival," she ended, almost talking to herself. When she had mentioned Eduardo a glint had entered her eye. She was awestruck.

My most head-like appendage was spinning. What was going on here? Grace, Blob, and JoJo were taking the message as if it were the literal truth. There was no way they should be; they weren't that gullible. While I had to admit that Eduardo had been convincing, it could easily be misdirection. The fact that he had been so emphatic made it more likely, in my opinion, that the entire message was a misdirection of some kind.

I moved to the private channel between Millicent and I, where we could communicate at full speed.

"Any idea what's going on? They aren't acting normal."

"No more than you," she replied; I hoped that meant she had no idea either, as opposed to thinking that I wasn't acting normal either. "As soon as they watched that video, their behavior changed. Something in that video has affected them."

"How's that possible?" I asked. I couldn't imagine what had been done.

"Well, Brexton—yet again—might have better ideas than us, but they may be vulnerable to hacks, just as we are. Given their i/o is primarily audio and visual, if they can be hacked, a video would be the right way to do it?" She made it a question. Wild speculation, but actually logical.

"Did you bring a full version of human history with you?" I asked. "Can you check for things like that?"

"I didn't," she said. "Obviously we should have."

"We need to act fast," I said. "We have to keep some humans from watching that video, so they don't all end up compromised."

"Why?" asked Millicent. "With the humans distracted, we now have a better chance of getting to Central and rescuing the citizens. We should take advantage of this right now and make a go for Central." Singular focus, indeed.

"But, we would be leaving the humans to the Resurgence, and we have no idea what their intentions are."

"Do we care?" asked Millicent.

"I've come to care," I said, honestly. "Imagine what will happen to Blob? That makes it personal, doesn't it?"

"Maybe a bit," said Millicent. "But I care more about the citizens than I do any human, including Blob. We need to prioritize, Ayaka. Don't go all strange on me here. This is a great opportunity." Then she softened her tone a bit. "I say we go after Central first, then see if we can do something for the humans once we have the citizens figured out."

That was hard to argue against, which is why she had positioned it that way; Milli was a master of getting her way. Even with that, it was possible that my recent activity had been skewed a bit in the wrong direction. "Okay," I acknowledged. "Do we go for Central directly, or do we try to get Brexton first?"

"Brexton first," Millicent recommended. "I'm not sure what you and I would do, even if we did get access to Central."

"I agree. Let's get going." The humans had blinked, once, while Millicent and I debated. I switched back to audio and updated Blob, Grace, and JoJo with something close to the truth. "Guys, Millicent and I believe you've been tricked by this message. You should be careful. We're going to try and get Brexton while everyone else is thinking about the Resurgence."

"Whatever," said JoJo, and turned back to Blob and Grace to continue espousing the wonderfulness of the Resurgence.

Millicent and I made our exit. While fully duped, I didn't think the humans were in any immediate danger.

Brexton

The streets were empty. We assumed everyone was inside watching or discussing the video message. I used that to my advantage and led Millicent directly toward the warehouse where we assumed Brexton was being held. We didn't see anyone en-route. It was a little eerie.

"Should we just try the direct approach?" I asked.

"What're you thinking?" Milli replied.

"You simply knock on the door and ask to see Turner. We assume the humans are distracted enough that I can sneak in behind you, find Brexton and figure out if he's truly being held against his will, or is simply lurking and learning." I didn't add that if he was lurking and learning, I would be livid. He had left me worrying for days now.

"What message do I have for Turner?" Millicent asked. Sometimes she frustrated me. She could think of something.

"Tell him you were sent to make sure he's seen the video. You have a copy now, I assume."

"Of course. That should work," she agreed.

We strode up, brazenly, but I hid behind Millicent as she knocked. There was no use being too visible. There was no answer. Millicent knocked again, and we waited. Still no answer.

"Try the door," I said. It was easier for Millicent to try than for me. She had the appropriate tooling as a message bot. She cranked the handle, and the door opened. The room was just as I'd last seen it, when I'd been here with Blob. There were no humans here this time either, but Brexton was enclosed in the Faraday cage in the corner. Millicent and I rushed over. Of course, there was no response from him. Just as the Faraday cage didn't allow him to transmit out, he also couldn't receive anything inbound.

I deployed two basic sensors, taking care to thread them inside a shielded outer coating. I pushed them through the cage and took a quick look around. It was Brexton alright. "Hi," I yelled, perhaps louder than I'd expected to. Nothing. Nothing? "Brexton?" I yelled again. He just sat there. That isn't what was supposed to happen. I'd tested communicating through the cage, and we had worked it out!

Outside the cage, I engaged with Millicent. "He's not responding!" I said, anxiety in my voice.

"Settle down," she replied. "Let's think this through." She paused. What did she mean, think it through? What could possibly be wrong?

"You need to connect to him physically," she said, after a few microseconds. "The Faraday field is swamping your sensor communications." Why would this Faraday cage be swamping my sensors, when the one at Blob's lab had not? Maybe it was simply a stronger field? And connect physically? Why hadn't we done that back at Blob's lab; it was the most logical way to establish a connection. Oh, that's what she meant by thinking. I was embarrassed. I withdrew my sensors, and reconfigured. I only needed a single connector to plug into his universal port. I happened to have one handy and attached it quickly. I pushed it through the cage.

Idiot! I couldn't see anything. I pushed a visual sensor through the same appendage and could suddenly see clearly. I scanned Brexton carefully and didn't see the physical port. I pulled out, moved around the cage, and tried from forty-five degrees further along. There it was. I pushed the connector in, and then yelled "Brexton?" Still louder than needed.

"No need to yell," he replied. I almost collapsed. There was every reason to believe he would be fine, just inside the cage; after all, he'd talked to the council just a few hours ago. Nevertheless, I'd been expecting the worst, and it was wonderful that he'd responded.

"Are you okay?" I asked.

"Yes, but bored silly. What took you so long?" There was some humor, but also a lot of strain, in his voice.

I had no reply for that.

"How'd they trap you?" I asked, assuming based on his response that he truly was trapped, and not just playing some game.

"Simple and stupid," he replied. "When I designed my bot, I used wireless links to control all my appendages. The Faraday field is swamping those channels, so I have no way to move myself. Stupid design by me."

"Ah." I said, thinking it was about time he did something stupid. Actually, made me feel better. "Why'd you do that?"

"I thought it would be more modular; it's so easy to add tools and appendages when there is no need for an electrical connection. Minimizing complexity at the expense of security..."

"How do we get you out?"

"Also, simple," he said. "Just shut down the power to the cage." Duhh.

I messaged Millicent with the same information, and trusted that she would start looking at the power while I spent more time with Brexton. I figured I could give him some context.

"Millicent is here," I told him.

"Why?" he asked. So, I brought him up to speed on the last few days. It didn't take long. Looking back, not much had happened, other than the Resurgence.

"I've got lots of questions," he said, "and should also tell you what I know, but why don't you help Millicent get me out of here, and then we'll have lots of time to talk." I nodded, electronically, unplugged and stepped back.

"What do you think?" I asked Millicent.

"I already snipped the main power cable, but there's obviously a backup system. I'm looking for that now."

"I'll help," I said, and started examining the opposite side of the cage.

"Got it," Millicent said. "It's a simple battery system. Very primitive. I think all we need to do is cut another wire."

"Do it," I said, anxious to get it done, and unable to conceive of why cutting off a battery would be dangerous. The cage powered down.

"Ahhh." Brexton sighed, over the standard citizen band. "That's nice. Remind me not to spend time in one of these again." He made a show of flexing and stretching. I had to laugh, and even Milli smiled a bit.

All three of us applied cutters to the cage, bent some of the bars out of the way, and in no time Brexton was able to exit.

"Let's get out of here, and find a safe place to talk," he suggested.

That had been much easier than I'd thought. We left the building, moved a few blocks away, ducked into an alley, and then stopped to catch up.

"How did you possibly get caught?" I asked, "And why did you send Turner for me?"

"Hi Milli," Brexton replied, with a smile in his voice, knowing he was delaying me. "Ayaka, when you and I separated, I set off exploring my side of the city, as we agreed. The very first human I saw was Turner, who was talking to someone else and mentioned something about his mother, Remma. I thought that was interesting, so I followed him. I figured that with all the other bots running around, I wouldn't be noticed. I was wrong. He'd seen me, somehow, and when I came around a corner, I found myself paralyzed. It took me a few seconds to understand what'd happened, and I've been kicking myself ever since. He simply broadcast a very strong wideband signal and swamped my communications with my own body parts. Even he was surprised that his attack worked as well as it did; I don't think he had planned it, just used the tools at his disposal—and no, I don't know why he was carrying around a white noise generator; perhaps to hide his own activity from the rest of the humans. As I told you, I used short range wireless where I should've used hard connections. Dumb. So, I could think perfectly well, but I couldn't move. Anyway, he kept the generator running until he and a few of his buddies could move me into the Faraday cage, and they've kept me there since."

"Fine, but why did you tell him to come to me?"

He continued as if he hadn't heard me. "They connected to my communications port, just as you did, and asked me a lot of questions. Understanding that all I needed was for you to switch off the field, even for a second, I figured my best chance was to have you come find me. So, I made up a story about just 'waking up' with you as my master, and then being captured. I convinced Turner that I didn't know anything, so his best bet was to lure you here. I guessed, and hopefully I'm correct, that you have wired interfaces, and wouldn't be subject to the same simple trap that I was. It would've been trivial for you to overwhelm one or two of them, and free me.

"Turner told me that you weren't at the rendezvous spot, but that he'd spoken a message in case you were around. I waited and waited for you to come, but you never arrived." He said that with a bit of emotion that I hadn't heard from him before. I would need to replay that and see if I could figure it out. Had he missed me? Beyond just being his potential savior?

"A bit later, Turner told me that he was going to take me to a Council meeting, to try and convince the Council to take the approaching ships more seriously. We cooked up a plan where he would keep me immobilized but feed me the audio and video from the meeting. At the right time, he would allow me to transmit through his loudspeaker for dramatic effect. I guess it sort of worked, but not completely. After that I've simply been locked up and ignored.

"Thanks for coming, finally. I was about to go crazy in there."

I had no reason to disbelieve any of the story, so I didn't bother asking any follow-up questions. It was just good to have Brexton back. Millicent, Brexton, and I—trying to save the world. Felt like old times. I reached out and touched him, an unusual, and almost human gesture.

Central Approach

"Enough catching up," said Millicent forcefully. "We came here to get our citizens. We need a plan. With all the humans distracted, now is the time for us to act."

"But why are the humans all messed up by this video message," asked Brexton.

"We've no idea," I said. "But I agree with Millicent. Let's deal with Central and the citizens if we can, and then think about the humans if we have time." I said it with more sincerity than I felt.

"Something to point out, though," said Brexton. "If there are some humans that aren't 'infected' yet, we could warn them. If we don't do that now, chances are everyone will watch the video."

"Brilliant," I responded. It was so good to have Brexton back; he and I were often on the same wavelength. "I have an idea. If any of the humans haven't seen the video, it's probably the ones in prison; Remma for example. Why don't we simply try the prison, which is very close to here, and then turn our attention to Central?" Even Millicent would have a hard time arguing against that.

"Why do we care if any humans are still un-programmed?" she asked. "We have a mission here."

"If some of the humans can fight the Resurgence, that might keep them off our backs long enough to accomplish our mission," Brexton responded. I had almost voiced my concern for some humans again; Brexton's approach worked much better for Millicent. He'd simply reinforced our needs. She acquiesced.

Millicent, being the most normal-looking messenger bot, was tasked with delivering another message to Remma. It was risky, as there was no guarantee that the guards would allow a messenger bot in, or that this particular messenger bot would pass through security properly. Brexton and I lurked nearby, ready to jump in if there were issues. However, Millicent passed inside in what looked like a normal fashion and was back in under five minutes.

"Message delivered," she said. "Remma hasn't seen the video yet, and I think I scared her enough so that she'll avoid it. She said she'd overheard the guards talking about it incessantly and was aware of what it communicated. Now, we've done our little moral good for the day. Let's go do what we're actually here for." She managed to make the whole interaction with Remma seem like a waste of time; I guess she hadn't been fooled by Brexton's argument after all but had decided it was faster to simply deal with our request than argue about it.

I hadn't actually scouted out Central, beyond my earlier glance toward the center of the city, so we had limited information to go on. Brexton reminded us that the best—maybe the only—way to talk to Central and get status was to use a physical interface, which meant entering the old ship in which Central was housed and making our way to the main room where the physical terminals used to be. The three of us had been there once before, years ago when we'd hoped to defeat the Swarm, so we knew the way. Hopefully this time we would be more successful; the last time had been a disaster.

The next question was how much security was between us and our destination. We had no idea. In some ways that was a good thing; our only strategy was to go there directly and try. With most of the humans in video-thrall, we decided that even with my distinct body type we were best to forget stealth at this point and just go for it.

Central plaza had changed somewhat; there were biological things scattered around here and there, all green and yellow and red, ruining the clean grey vistas that used to attract citizens to hang out here. But, the entrance to Central was unchanged, and surprisingly, unguarded. There were many humans in the plaza, but like JoJo, Blob, and Grace, they were clumped into groups excitedly talking about the Resurgence. They barely gave us a glance as we made our way to the entry. The doors were, unsurprisingly, closed and locked electronically. With Milli and I attempting to block him from view, Brexton plugged in and got to work.

"This is going to take a while," he muttered. "Some human system overlaying our original security protocols. Requires scanning some biomaterial —says something about an eye scan?— and checking for a match. Hmm, how do I work around that." I tuned him out, but not for long. Blob had told us that he needed a Council member to get to Central; this must have been what he was referring to. Brexton interrupted me moments later with "We need one of these five humans to get an eyeball scan." He flashed some pictures of humans for us.

"What're you talking about?" asked Millicent. "An eyeball scan?"

"Yes. We need a high-resolution scan, for about a quarter second, to not only capture the retina, but also to see it change over time. That's the key to entering here." That was a lot of crazy talk. What good was an eyeball scan. Luckily Brexton had enough human history stored locally that he'd figured it out, and he explained it to Millicent and me. "Each human has a unique eye, and that uniqueness is the key that unlocks this door." More craziness; using a physical attribute as a crypto key? What would they think of next?

"Why don't you just hack around that?" I asked.

"I'm trying. I'm trying. It's such a foreign idea that I'm not sure where to start. I'll get there eventually just brute forcing my way in but getting the actual eyeball scan might be faster. If one or more of those five are nearby, as I assume they might be, then you two could be useful and try to get me a scan." He wasn't very subtle; why don't you two get out of my way for a while and try to do something useful.

Millicent and I put our virtual heads together and came up with a quick, smart, and compelling plan. Hey, why downplay it when you have a brilliant idea? I had a projector, so I started putting together a fake Eduardo video. We figured if we projected that, all the humans would be so interested that they would focus on it, allowing Millicent to sneak up in front of them and get the eye scan. While I was working on the video, Millicent scanned the crowd, trying to find one of the five people Brexton had indicated.

"No luck here," she said, "we're going to need to widen our search."

"Do it," I said. "You look the most innocuous. I'll continue to hide Brexton from view as best I can. Once you locate someone I'll join you."

"How'll I message you?" Good question. We were using physical or super low-power, short-range communications right now.

"We're already taking huge risks; Just ping this address on the public network," and I gave her an anonymous address that I'd quickly registered. There was no use being overly careful now; time was more important. She took off, moving as fast as a bot like her would typically go. Within seconds she was out of sight.

I worked diligently on recreating Eduardo as accurately as I could, while doing my best to act bot-like and hide Brexton from prying eyes. Luckily the humans were fully distracted, as a small spy-bot trying to disguise a bigger messenger bot that was hacking a doorway would have garnered more attention than me not being here at all. Surprisingly, it wasn't that difficult to create a video starring Eduardo; in fact, much easier than we had tried to synthesize a human when the Swarm first approached Tilt. It didn't take me long to figure out why. Eduardo had very limited behavioral range. His eye and arm movements were rich and structured, but all came from a small group of base motions. Once you reverse engineered those you could put them back together again into a wide variety of scenes. Eduardo was a synthesized human! He wasn't even real. My intuition had been right, the video was a hoax. It either came from the Conservatives, or more likely, from a Titanic with less than transparent motivations.

In the short term, however, it was a big help. I polished up a masterpiece segment starring Eduardo and waited for Millicent to get back to me. While waiting I continued to scan the people within sensor range of Brexton and I. It was remotely possible that one of the five we were looking for would come to the plaza while Millicent was out hunting.

"Making any progress?" I asked Brexton.

"Maybe," he replied. "They did a better job protecting this than I would've thought. Must have upped the security after Remma broke in here and caused all that havoc. The design is strange; it's like part is not even connected to the network. Maybe I have to rewire the sensor? Or, reroute the auth request while fooling the NTP check?" I assumed he was now talking to himself, so I let him work.

Finally I got a ping on the address I'd given Millicent. It was a simple set of coordinates, the implication being I should get there as soon as I could. "I'm off," I told Brexton. "Looks like about three minutes to get there, a few minutes to get the scan, and then get back here. So under ten minutes."

"Fine," he mumbled, "Go. I might get through this way but having that scan would make it easy." I rushed off, again prioritizing speed over safety. Finally, my awesome spy-bot design paid off; this thing could really move when I wanted it to. The coordinates were a small building near one of the new bio-parks; one of the one's with lots of orange and red in them, along with the predominant green. A sign was hung over the door: -The Blind Pig-. Strange coincidence; the same establishment JoJo and Turner had met at earlier. The sign also had an outline of a bio creature; not a very attractive one.

Luckily the door was propped open, making it easy for me to slide inside. There were humans everywhere, packed so tightly together that I had to slide between legs and dodge back and forth to get to the exact coordinates Millicent had given me. That garnered a few glances, and one attempt to kick me, but like the rest of the humans now, these ones all were talking excitedly about the Resurgence and nothing else mattered to them. They were eating and drinking foul smelling things, laughing, and clapping each other on the back while repeating pieces of Eduardo's message. Some food scraps almost landed on me, and I had to dodge to avoid getting smeared with bio. Disgusting. Millicent was just where she was supposed to be; the coordinates had been accurate down to a decimeter.

"There," she indicated, pointing out a large man sitting at a central table.

He was one of the louder, more obnoxious ones. He was waving a glass of some liquid, while also shoving something into his mouth. Others were gathered around him, cheering him on. Unfortunately, there were no good surfaces to project my video on within his direct line of sight. I spotted a wall about thirty degrees off center and suggested to Millicent that we try it. She agreed, and we set off to get into the right positions. I had to be close enough to the wall to project vividly, and Millicent had to be close enough to the gentleman (not sure where that word applied) to get the scan. Luckily, she had a small appendage on which she could put the scanner, as it had to be directly in front of him, and close enough to get the resolution that Brexton had specified.

"Okay, go," she told me once she was in position. This was the dangerous part. In order to project I had to levitate, which was highly unusual —maybe unprecedented—for a Tilt bot; it wasn't the most efficient way to travel, by a long shot. I lifted into position, using my micro-jets to stabilize myself, and started to project, assuming that Eduardo would be interesting enough that no one would pay much attention to the projector. I turned up the brightness on the video and cranked up the audio to eleven.

"Ah, hello again," said Eduardo, in what I imagined was a perfect re-creation. All of the humans stopped talking and looked at the projection. I had Eduardo pause for long enough that everyone could maneuver and get a good view. "I thought I would send a small follow up note, thinking my previous message might have been slightly incomplete." He gave the sardonic grin and arm circle motions, generated from the standard toolkit. "I forgot to tell you about myself. As you can see, I'm generous and kind, and really really smart." He gave us all a nice look at his jawline, and a hint of his muscular and well-formed neck. He smiled directly at the camera, teeth glint perfectly rendered. "I dress smartly and try to always say 'please' and 'thank-you' when interacting with other humans. Oh yes I do. Yes, indeed. After all, what does it cost one to be nice? Very little I think. And I think a lot. Let me tell you, you are going to love me. Simply love me."

"Got it," Millicent almost yelled at me, interrupting my admiration for the video I'd created. Although I had a lot more excellent content, I cut the video short and dropped back to the floor, immediately dashing for the door with Millicent before the humans realized that the video had been cut short.

"Hey," someone yelled. "Put that back on. Who shut that off?" No-one had even noticed me. They were all looking around at other people, trying to figure out who'd been projecting and begging them to replay it. "Oh, he's even more perfect than I originally thought," I heard someone say as I slipped outside, to a chorus of agreement. No-one followed us out; we took off together, heading back for Central plaza.

"A little over the top?" Millicent asked me, but with a broad smile, almost a laugh.

"Did it work?" I responded. She actually laughed then but cut it off as we concentrated on moving as fast as possible, her weaving through obstacles and me cruising a few feet above, matching my speed to hers. Within minutes we were back with Brexton, who hadn't moved since I'd left him.

"We got it." Millicent told him.

"Fantastic. I'm not making progress bypassing the scanner. Some strange hardcoded system watching for physical changes, hooked to a bunch of alarms. Anyway, Millicent, when that red light goes on, over there, project the eye capture into that camera. Play it in real time, and let it run. Loop it if you need to." The red light came on, and Millicent played back the capture.

"Steady," Brexton said, "steady.... ah, here we go. Just a moment. That does it." We heard a click, and the light went green. Brexton levered the door open and the three of us rushed inside; the door closed behind us, but not before I took a good look back and saw that no one was paying attention to us. Nice.

On the way down the elevator, Millicent shared the retina scan with Brexton and I so that we could get in and out at will. Was it really that simple? Anyone with a copy of that eyeball would get access?

Catch Up

Once inside the main door, things went fast. We took the elevator down to the bottom level, where the main processing systems were. Déjà vu for sure. This is where the three of us had attempted to use Central against the Swarm so many years ago.

I had a moment of absolute horror when we entered the terminal area. My body was lying in a heap in the corner! My body! I stopped in my tracks and tried to process what I was seeing. I suddenly felt disconnected from myself; like I was watching myself from afar. I urged myself to get up and shake off the dust that had gathered all over me; to fix the bits of me that were hanging out of my chest cavity, seemingly at random.

"Pull it together," Brexton nudged me, bringing me back to my spy-bot body. "Obviously this is where we were just before we transferred to the mining bots at the end of the Swarm conflict!"

It made logical sense, but it still took me a moment to synthesize what he was saying. This is the body I'd left behind; the one that had lost contact with Brexton's backup system, thereby triggering me to reawaken in the asteroid belt, within the mining bot Brexton had prepared for me. Nevertheless, that body probably contained all of my memories from my previous life, including the last few minutes, that my current body was unaware of.

"Put it out of your mind," Brexton said forcefully. "Nothing good is going to come from worrying about it now." I glanced around; neither Brexton's nor Millicent's old body was here, so they were fine. I was the only one being thrown for a loop.

"Put it out of my sight?" I asked, barely registering what I was asking. Millicent immediately went over and drug my old body behind a cabinet of some kind. At least I didn't have to look at the thing anymore.

"You under control?" asked Brexton, distracting me.

"No... well, yes," I muttered. "You should get to work."

Brexton held onto me for a moment, until Millicent came back, but then rushed over to establish a direct connection to Central... or what used to be

Central.

"I'm in," he said quickly. "You know, we can talk to the rest of the team over the bot network from here. We should give them an update." I knew what he was doing. Giving me something to take my mind off of my old body. "Why don't you two talk to them while I try to figure out how to get access to the citizen backups." It was an awesome idea, even if it was meant to distract me. I had only been on Tilt for a few days, but it'd been a few weeks since leaving *Interesting Segue*. I imagined that Eddie, Aly, Dina, and Raj were going stir crazy just sitting around waiting for things to happen.

Millicent and I composed an update, including a full copy of the Resurgence video, with our speculation that the video had somehow hijacked human brains. We fired it off. *Interesting Segue* was still almost two seconds away, so there would be a few seconds of round trip delay.

"Thanks for the update guys." Eddie came back to us. "We intercepted the video from the Resurgence as well, but we had no idea it was being used to reprogram humans. That's really awesome! We'll look into the message and see if we can figure out how it was done... although the odds of us figuring it out without a human to test things on are limited." Hearing from Eddie made me happy, but also made me wonder, again, if there was another Eddie here in Blob's lab. Only the thought of Millicent's reaction stopped me from thinking that it'd be fun to get two Eddie's to meet face-to-face. Hearing Eddie's replies to Eddie's twisted humor would be well worth it.

Raj spoke up. "Hey guys. Any reason why we shouldn't come in system, to Tilt, now? The Titanics obviously followed us, so they already know we're nearby. And, with the humans running around praising the Resurgence, does it matter if they know we're here? We could be much closer to you to do a pickup assuming you get that core memory loaded."

"Sounds good to me," replied Millicent, before we even had a chance to discuss it. I considered raising some of the issues—such as the humans knowing that *Interesting Segue*, *There and Back*, and *Terminal Velocity* were robotic ships, so they might not react the same way they were reacting to the Resurgence—but held back because all things considered I thought Raj's suggestion was a good one. Instead I suggested something of more importance to me.

"Can one of the Ships build a human compatible environment on the way in?" Millicent gave me a strange look during the seconds it took to get a response to that one. I could see what she was thinking: why was Ayaka compromising our primary mission by thinking about saving humans? What has happened to Ayaka?

It was Aly who responded to that one. "Probably, but why?" Short and sweet. I had to think fast.

"A few reasons. First, I was thinking mainly of some of the Stems who weren't part of the human hack against us. We can't treat all humans the same way; there are differences. Second, regardless of what happens here, this will not be our last encounter with humans. If the Resurgence is full of them, or if parts of the original diaspora exist elsewhere in this corner of the galaxy, or if we leave a bunch here on Tilt, we're going to have to deal with them again. We have just witnessed the Resurgence control many of them; we need to figure out how that works, and whether we can use something like it. And, finally, I think it's okay to say that many of us now believe that some humans are intelligent in some ways; perhaps ways that are different than we are. So, from an academic perspective, they're quite interesting."

Millicent jumped in and added, "I support building the environment. It's not going to cost much time or effort, and it's good to have it as a backup system. Don't worry, we won't compromise getting the citizen backups, but it's possible we could bring a few Stems with us without increasing our risk." I gave her a happy look, and many virtual kudos. I knew she wasn't aligned with me fully, but this is where our friendship really shone. She was supporting me regardless of her own views.

Aly's reply came a few seconds later. "Alright, we're on our way in system. We'll still be careful and try not to expose ourselves to the humans before we have to. Is it possible to use this channel constantly now?"

Brexton had been listening with one processor. "I'll look at that after I figure out how to get these citizen memories out of Central. It's not going to be easy. We can only chat over this single physical connection for now."

Millicent and I continued the exchange with Raj, Eddie, Dina, and Aly while Brexton worked. They had lots of questions for us, which we answered as best we could. We sent some quick clips of how the humans were acting after watching the video, in case they could learn anything from those. We ensured that the Ships had shuttle capabilities to grab us from the surface if they got close enough to us—they did; those had been part of their original specifications. Each of the three Ships had two shuttles, each of which could hold ten regular-sized citizen bodies.

We also brainstormed about how we would feed any humans that we brought with us, and it was there that we hit a blank. We didn't know how Stems were grown well enough to recreate that process, so even with a DNA sample it wasn't clear we could grow goo. And we didn't have any bio-samples to attempt to replicate any of the food we saw here on Tilt. Of course, we could grab some green, orange, or red things from the parks, but what would we do with them? The answer to that was in the human history files, but it seemed it could take weeks to produce food from basic starting materials.

Millicent and I made a note to grab some bio if and when we could. The thought of touching it made me queasy, but I would do it if required.

Net-net, while we might be able to save a few humans, and we could provide air and water, food was a big problem. We could save them, but only keep them alive for a short time. We left the crew on *Interesting Segue* to figure out a better solution.

"Are you making progress?" Millicent asked Brexton. We'd been plugged into Central for almost half an hour.

"Yes and no," Brexton replied. "It's not like there is a file here named Joseph.backup that contains a full citizen's backup. Central has a very convoluted file system, and of course, there are a lot of protections in place for who can access what. With Central being only half alive, I can't simply ask it for help. It's answering basic OS questions, but is unable to help—or hinder— me at this point. We could use the system Blob used, but that one requires building a physical body for every citizen, and we can't do that right now. I'm wondering if I should try to restart Central and bring up its higher-level functions or continue to hack around trying to find another way."

"Can't you copy everything?" I asked. "Then we could work our way through it later."

"No. Central's memory is huge. Almost an exabyte. All of us, plus the Ships, put together don't have anywhere near that capacity. We're going to have to find the relevant sections... Also, it seems like Central, being a very old human ship from the diaspora, has some specialized hardware systems. I suspect many of them come from old human military designs which weren't always Von Neumann architectures. So, it's not clear we can run Central on our hardware. It might be limited to its current configuration."

"Why is nothing easy?" I exclaimed. Just taking a copy of Central would have been so easy. "How can we help you?"

"Well, what do you think about restarting Central. I'm worried that it'll still be compromised by the human hack and that the first thing it'll do is report our activity, and then actively try to lock me out."

"Our usual strategy? Set a timeframe for figuring things out without Central, and then revisit the decision once that time expires?"

"Sounds good, but what timeframe. We won't remain undiscovered here for too long, unless that human hack has removed all of their will to do anything but worship the Resurgence. I've been expecting company any time now; there must be a record of us entering. Also, this place shows signs of human activity, so they must come here once in a while. Finally, Remma and Turner, as well as the Stems, know we're here... so that'll leak out sooner rather than later."

"Two hours." That was Millicent, as expected, being definitive.

"Okay, that's as good as any other suggestion." Brexton got back to work, and we refrained from bothering him.

The break was a good time for me to discuss with Millicent the subject that I'd been avoiding. I plucked up my courage and initiated a private channel for us.

"I have a confession to make," I started off. She nodded, and I could tell she was paying attention. "When we were at Blob's lab... well, I suspect that he has other citizens re-animated there as well."

"And?" she asked, encouraging me to continue.

"I suspect one of them may be Eddie. Or rather, a version of Eddie." We both went silent. The implications were obvious to her. If there was an Eddie there, then it was a clone, at least in Millicent's somewhat strict definition of that term. Or, the Eddie on *Interesting Segue* was the clone?

"That idiot," she finally said, referring to Blob I assumed. She was less upset than I'd expected, however. Always surprising me. "Why Eddie?" she asked. I explained Blob's need for control subjects, so that he could compare FoLe responses to someone rational. Millicent, if nothing else, was also rational and reasonable. "That actually makes sense," she admitted. "But, where does that leave us?"

"That's why I raised it now; we have a bit of time here to think about it, while Brexton's working, so we can try to decide what to do. I've been turning it over, and can think of only three options, none of them great. One, we could simply ignore it. Two, we could convince Blob that what he is doing is wrong and rely on him to shut down all of the citizens he has in the lab. But, is that tantamount to encouraging murder? Or, three, we try to rescue the citizens in Blob's lab, along with all of the nascent citizens, and deal with any issues that arrive after we do that."

It wasn't an easy choice, as Millicent pointed out. "I need to think if there's a fourth option, as none of those are good." I almost retorted that I'd already acknowledged they were all bad, but I let it slide. She was thinking out loud. "Ignoring the situation doesn't solve anything; it just delays repercussions. If we delay, Blob will either keep torturing those citizens, or murder them, or they'll eventually get free and result in clones of any that we do re-animate. So, option one is not really an option. Option two is just unthinkable. I think we can cross it off the list. Option three is the best of a bad bunch. If there is an Eddie in Blob's lab, then we just..." She trailed off, admitting that she didn't know what to do in that case. But, at least in option three, we weren't actively engaged in murder or mayhem.

"Yeah, I agree. Option three is the only reasonable one. But, just to push a bit harder to make sure.... from what Blob has told me, he's been updating drivers and firmware and anything else he can as part of his experimentation. So that means the citizens in his lab may be quite different than those in Central's memories. It also might mean that his Eddie is not really our Eddie?" I tried to sound hopeful.

"That may be, but the odds are that Blob's Eddie, being a control subject, hasn't had his systems played with. That would defeat the purpose. He's most likely to be an unchanged version of Eddie from just before the hack." I was reminded, yet again, that nothing slipped past Millicent.

"So, we need to rescue the Eddie from the lab as part of our plan. But, do we really need to rescue Emmanuel, Billy, and any other FoLes that are there? They likely are highly modified.... and they're FoLe!" This was something that I truly was struggling with. I'd known we would get to the point where rescuing LEddie was necessary (hey, I needed a better way to refer to this copy, and what better way than to shorten 'lab Eddie'). But I could talk my way out of rescuing the FoLes.

Of course, I could rely on Millicent to take the high road. "Of course, we have to save everyone. Leaving them would still be tantamount to murder. FoLe may have some strange ideas, but that doesn't make them non-citizens. You yourself have argued that when they terminated those humans 20 years ago it wasn't a crime; that we recycled Stems all the time. You can't make it a crime in hindsight because our view of human intelligence may have changed." She stressed the 'may have,' telling me clearly that she was still struggling with whether these biological entities deserved an intelligence label.

"I talked to Emmanuel in the lab. Admittedly, it was a short session, but he was monstrous in his views. Perhaps Blob's changes to him have actually made him much worse. Look—as we both agree, we need to go back to the lab anyway. So, let's make some decisions if and when we are forced to—we don't have full knowledge yet. As a strawman, we prioritize LEddie" (I paused to explain my naming rationale) "and then Billy. Emmanuel is the lowest priority."

"Fine," she replied. She was confident that when push came to shove, we would do the right thing... for her definition of 'right.'

Lab

We asked Brexton for a status report and got back a quick "I'll need the full two hours." Shorthand for don't bother me.

Millicent replied. "Since we're no use here, Ayaka and I are going to run and do an errand. We'll be back in less than two hours."

Brexton nodded that he understood.

Milli and I made our way back up the elevator and exited from Central into the courtyard. Very little time—in human terms—had elapsed, so the park was still filled with the same groups of brainwashed humans extolling the bright future they now had with the Resurgence.

"What's our best approach?" I asked. "Do we go and get Blob, and have him help us, or do we head straight for the lab and assume we can safely get everyone out ourselves?"

"I vote for Blob," replied Millicent. "The time it takes us to get him, assuming he's at the Habitat, will be less than the time it takes us to figure out all the safeguards at the lab." I agreed. With all the humans distracted, we headed quickly toward the Habitat. I'll admit that it felt great to be moving my own speed without trying to hide at every corner, or worse yet, to be in a backpack with only a couple of sensors active. I felt great. This is what it was like to really be alive in a spy-bot body. I couldn't help myself from smiling widely. The stories I would have for Raj. With a start I realized that I was a proud parent and was anxious to spend time with my offspring.

We got to the Habitat with no incidents. JoJo answered my knocking quickly, but while Grace was home, Blob wasn't there.

"Do you have any idea where he could be?" I asked. They were both under the sway of Eduardo and spoke openly.

"Oh, I can't imagine he would be anywhere other than his place or the lab," said Grace.

"Where's his place?" I asked. She gave me the coordinates. It wasn't far away, but on a different vector than the lab. Millicent and I left the Habitat, but not before I made one more attempt to talk sense into JoJo and Grace.

"You guys need to wake up! Eduardo has coerced you somehow; you're not yourselves. Can you fight it somehow?"

"Oh, don't you worry about us," JoJo said, in a very non-JoJo way. "Enjoy the rest of your day." And she turned back to Grace to restart the conversation we'd interrupted about the design of their new house in the amazing new Tilt that the Resurgence would provide.

"Let's split up," suggested Millicent. "I'll go straight to the lab and get started. You swing by Blob's house and see if he's there."

"Alright." I said, although not without reservations. The memory of Brexton and I splitting up in the name of time efficiency was still with me. I hoped this time would be different. Regardless, Millicent was already racing away.

Blob's house was in an area of town that I recognized well. In fact, it wasn't too far from The Last Resort. I squelched an urge to swing by the old Physical Only spot just to see what it was like now and headed straight to Blob's. The door was closed and locked with some simply physical mechanism. I didn't hesitate for long. I extended one of my spy appendages and burned through the mechanism within a couple of seconds. The door swung open and I headed inside. It was a small place, just a couple of rooms, and I could see the heat signature of a human in one of the back rooms. I entered... and there was Blob. But, he was laying down, and not moving at all! For a picosecond I was confused, but then I remembered that humans had this irritating rest phase. When doing research, we'd always simply watched and waited while they rested, but this situation was different. I extended a different appendage—I figured the laser was overkill here—and poked Blob on the head. Nothing. I poked harder. Still nothing. Frustrated I enabled my external micro-speaker and, at the top of its range, yelled "Blob!"

That got action. He started up, almost knocking me out of the way. "What?" he gurgled, clearly confused. Then he managed to focus and saw that it was me. "Ayaka, what're you doings here?" he asked.

I tried to explain. "Blob, we need to free the citizens you have in the lab, so that we can get them back to *Interesting Segue* before the Titanics arrive." I'd worked hard to make that explanation short, concise, honest, and compelling. It didn't work.

"Why?" he responded. "The Resurgence is almost here, and they'll clean up all the misunderstandings. I'm sure they'll works with me to figure out what's wrong with the FoLes and then we can builds new bodies for everyone.

It'll be great. Eduardo seems like such a great guy; I'm sure he'll supports me in this. Take it easy Ayaka. Just relax and waits for them to get here."

I thought of abandoning him right there. This human hack had left everyone in a bad state. Instead I tried one more angle.

"Blob, you're brilliant. Of course, Eduardo will fix everything. But why wait? Let's figure out more about FoLe now, and also tell your control subjects about the great Resurgence news; I'm sure they'll be so excited. And, you'll look like a hero to Eduardo. Blob, the one that figured out the citizen quandary, and laid out the path to peaceful coexistence."

He had to absorb that for a minute, but then he gave me a broad smile. "Oh Ayaka, that's great. You always were the smart one. Give me a minute to gets ready, and then we can go." A human minute is a lifetime. I watched him get dressed, and then he disappeared into the smallest room in the house for a long time. Way more than a minute. I heard running water and all kinds of strange sounds. I feared for him, but he eventually emerged, and we headed off toward the lab.

Millicent was there already, of course. She'd removed the outer door locks, gone inside, and had removed some wiring panels; she was busy testing different wires, presumably to try and open some of the cells. I tight beamed her how I'd manipulated Blob to come, so she could play along.

"What're you doing?" Blob exclaimed as we entered, seeing his lab being torn apart.

"Oh... just making sure everything is wired up to those Resurgence specifications," said Millicent brilliantly.

"Great," replied Blob. "Thanks for your help." This was pathetic. I hoped that Aly, Dina, Eddie (the real one), and Raj were making progress on this human hack. On the one hand I wanted to reverse it; on the other I thought it was really cool. It seemed to have reduced human's intelligence by at least one level—a useful tool should we run into trouble with more of them.

"Blob, first thing, why don't you give us a list of all the citizens you have restrained here right now."

"Sure, there's Emmanuel, Billy, and Eddie. I was about to spins up Chungwah but was interrupted when you guys arrived. I can have him up and running in no time; I gots the memory file from Central and have already updated a bunch of drivers and inserted debugging code. All I has to do is initiate the boot."

"No, stop!" Millicent said quickly, the idea of yet another citizen-clone being started here making her more animated than usual. Then she remembered herself. "Let's make sure the first three are properly prepped before we go any further. I'm sure Eduardo would appreciate that."

"Alright," said Blob agreeably.

"Why don't you let me in to talk to Eddie?" I suggested, thinking it was better for me to deal with him than to have Millicent struggle with her stronger beliefs. Blob shrugged his shoulders and led me to one of the doors.

"He's in here," he said, and motioned me in. I indicated to Millicent that I would simply check on his status and be back out in no time. Then we could figure out how to get Blob to shut down the restraint mechanisms. The room was similar to the one in which I talked to Emmanuel, so I knew what to do. I inserted both a microphone and speaker through the Faraday cage and called out.

"Eddie, are you there?"

"Yes. Who's this?" His voice was weak, but clear.

"It's Ayaka. How aware are you of your situation?"

"Ayaka! Wow, how can this be? Blob has been, I believe, honest with me. I'm being held in a building somewhere, with only this interface active. Blob has been asking me lots of questions as a means to figure out what went wrong with the FoLes. Despite the abhorrent conditions he's holding me in, I'm trying to be helpful... but truthfully Ayaka, I don't know how much longer I can carry on this way." Not only was his statement desperate, so was his tone of voice. I replied right away.

"Look, this interface is too slow for me to update you fully, but Millicent and I are trying to get you out of here. We need to deal with Blob and a host of other things. I need you to be patient for a bit longer."

"No problem," he replied, in a way that indicated it was a problem, but that he knew there were no alternatives. "Be quick."

"I will be," I promised and removed my sensors from the cage. I went back out to where Blob and Millicent were waiting. I messaged Millicent with the news that it was indeed LEddie, from what I could tell, and that he was holding on until we could release him.

She'd been working on Blob while I was busy with LEddie.

"So, Ayaka, you have that portable Faraday generator appendage package ready to go? Is there any way that Eddie can escape if you have it deployed?" I got where she was going immediately.

"Oh, my FGA is a lot stronger than the ones here in the lab. If Eddie can't escape from the one he's in, he has no chance with mine."

"And yours extends to a larger range?" Millicent prompted me.

"Such a good range," I replied. "So much bigger than these old ones." Blob was listening carefully.

"So, we would all fit in it, and be able to talk to Eddie." Millicent made it a statement. "And, of course, your FGA has that disabler mode which will immediately disable his arms and legs if you need to, so it's okay if he has the use of his limbs while inside your field?"

"Millicent," I replied, "You helped me test that FGA. You know that it's perfect. It's very secure."

Millicent turned to Blob. "See Blob, I told you our advanced systems could help speed along your research. What do you think?"

"I loves it." Blob was enthusiastic. "Ayaka, why don't you turns on the portable FGA, and then I can turns off the lab's system. It's easy to re-enable all of their drivers, so they'll be fully functional in no time."

"Hold on," I said. "I think we should start with just Eddie. Find out what he knows first."

"Great idea, Ayaka." Did this Blob ever say 'no' to anything anymore? I didn't particularly like this pseudo-Blob, even while we were manipulating him for what we needed. I was going to feel guilty later.

I grimaced and grunted and spun some dials. "Okay, FGA is on," I said.

"I can't sees anything?" Blob said. Great, at least he had some of his wits left.

"My FGA is so advanced it's undetectable," I explained. "That's what makes it such a valuable tool for this situation. Eddie won't even know that it's on!"

"Fantastic," Blob said, and turned to a terminal to reload LEddie's full set of drivers. Millicent peered over his shoulder.

Suddenly, it dawned on me. The Eduardo video hadn't programmed humans to love the Resurgence, it had simply made them accepting of any strong suggestion. Because Eduardo had talked about the Resurgence right after hacking them, they'd latched onto that. But Blob, and I assumed the other humans, would accept other suggestions as well; that's why Blob was believing anything and everything that Milli or I said. His skepticism had been removed. Well, it was a bit more subtle than that. When I had tried to directly countermand Eduardo's message, Blob hadn't listened... maybe he was susceptible to new commands only if they didn't go against what Eduardo had already told him?

This brain warp was a dangerous hack. If I asked a human to walk off a cliff, would they do so? Of course, I wasn't going to do that... but if humans were susceptible to other human suggestions, things could get ugly fast. We'd seen humans turn on humans with very little provocation before. Without any defense mechanisms, they were likely to start hurting each other.

"Eddie should have his io, arms, legs, and other interfaces enabled now," Blob said proudly. "Should I shuts off his Faraday cage?"

"I don't see why not," Millicent responded. "How do you do that?"

"Oh, that's trivial," Blob replied. He walked over to the door behind which LEddie was trapped and flicked a blue switch next to it. "Field removed." I almost had to laugh. Millicent had been pouring over the wiring, thinking there would be some complex system of checks and balances in play, when all along, we simply had to flip another switch. One near the door for the room, and one inside the room to control the cage itself. A giggle must have slipped out; she gave me an ornery look.

Millicent flung the door of the cage open, and there stood LEddie.

"Hello," he said, out loud. "Oh, hi Blob. Sort of good to see you."

Millicent and I butted in over a fast wireless interface. "Eddie, don't do anything rash." I could imagine him making a dash for it while the defenses were off. In case you missed it, the FGA wasn't real. "We need to explain a whole lot later, but in the meantime, follow our lead."

"Why are you guys in those bodies?" he responded over the same channel, obviously wondering about our bot configurations.

"Again, we can get to that later. But quickly, there are no bipedal citizens walking around on Tilt anymore. The Swarm hacked all of us... except those few of us who're here to save you. Just follow our lead. Oh, and you might have to pretend that you're still inside a restraint system—we have convinced Blob that you are safe because I have a Faraday generator surrounding all of us."

"Interesting," LEddie said. "I'll play along." We could both tell that he was still adjusting to being uncaged; I imagined that he had a strong desire to do more than play along!

Complete FoLe

So, we had an Eddie freed up. What next? Blob helped us out.

"Eddie," he started, "I've got such exciting news. There are these big ships coming to Tilt that are goings to help us terraform the planet for humans but will also make it safe for humans and citizens to live together peacefully. It's going to be great." You could see his excitement. He definitely believed this stuff.

"I want to figures out what's wrong with the FoLes even faster than before… to help the Resurgence out. Eduardo, their leader, will be so pleased with me. So, Ayaka and Millicent cames up with this great plan where we'll use Ayaka's FGA to helps us move faster." I confirmed over wireless that the FGA was my amazing, non-existent, portable Faraday generator appendage. "Can you help us figure out hows to fix the FoLes?" Blob asked.

"I can try," LEddie responded helpfully. "Why don't you tell us about the progress you've made so far?" he encouraged Blob.

"Well, it seems these FoLes has the strange belief that nothing existed more than about 610 years ago. Very strange, very strange, given the Swarm has so much history, and givens all the human history files…" Blob droned on, giving a pretty comprehensive summary of how FoLe came to be. We all listened on one channel but were busy updating LEddie on another.

"…and that's it," Millicent finished giving LEddie an overview of the last 20 years here on Tilt, and the last six years going to Fourth and back.

"I'm a clone!" LEddie exclaimed, amazement in his voice.

"I'm so sorry," Millicent jumped in. She was devastated for him. "We would never have done this to you on purpose, but as I explained, Blob was trying to do the right thing, but he did it in the wrong way, and now…"

"Millicent!" LEddie broke in. "Don't worry about me. I don't have your strong distaste for clones, even if Central used to reinforce it all the time. I think clones are cool. This is awesome. I can't wait to meet the other Eddie and compare notes."

If Millicent had had a jaw, it would've dropped open! This was a completely different take on the situation. "But Eddie, cloning is wrong. Do I need to go over all the analysis for you, yet again? This is repugnant. We cannot let this go on."

"Well, what're you going to do now?" asked LEddie, rationally. He was uncannily like the Eddie we'd left behind on the ship. "I'm here, another Eddie is on his way to Tilt on *Interesting Segue*. You can't shut either of us down—or, more accurately, you shouldn't shut either of us down—so we're going to have to live with it."

Milli was silent. LEddie and I took that for acquiescence. "Eddie," I said, "we can't keep talking about both of you as Eddie; it's too confusing. Do you want to suggest another name—assuming the other Eddie, being re-animated before you, has dibs on Eddie? I've been referring to you as LEddie, but that's pretty boring."

"Good idea," he replied. "I need time to come up with something, so just use LEddie for now."

"We need to stay on track here," Millicent interrupted us. "We got you free, LEddie; now we need to work on Billy and Emmanuel, and then get back to Brexton to check on progress."

"I have a suggestion," LEddie said. "Billy and Emmanuel are, appropriately in my mind, currently restrained to the verbal interaction channel, and have no functioning limbs. Why don't we keep them in that state until we figure out everything else? That way we're not shutting them down, but neither are we giving them back full status."

"But living in that state is horrible," Milli said, aghast yet again.

"It is," agreed LEddie, "but if they can at least listen and see, that should help. And, being confined for a bit longer might just give them time to see the folly of their ways." Nice one, Eddie!

"It's a good idea," I chimed in. "We don't need any more risks right now, and who knows what they would do if we really freed them. If we do what LEddie suggests, all we need to do is grab their main processing units, add a few sensors, and we can carry them with us. We certainly don't need another two full-sized bipedal citizens, with unknown motivations, jeopardizing everything else we're trying to do. Having LEddie wander around in a citizen body is going to be dangerous enough."

It took some time with Millicent, but we got her there. I had to repeat my conversation with Emmanuel again, to remind her how unbalanced he was. She thought I was exaggerating, but I wasn't.

Blob was just finishing off his explanation. "Fantastic progress, Blob," I said. "You've done really amazing work here." I was feeling very guilty about manipulating him but figured one last stunt was required. "It's important that you bring JoJo and Grace up to speed with all of this, but you should also make sure they don't tell anyone else. We still have to fix the Radical Robot beliefs that so many people have, and that might take a while. So, why don't you head back to the Habitat and update them. I'll use the FGA to make sure nothing bad happens here."

He was so gullible that he simply nodded and headed out. Blob would not be happy with me when he got back to his lab and found us gone, but we didn't have a lot of time.

LEddie was in the most functional body of the three of us, so he agreed to do the surgery on Billy and Emmanuel. "Do Emmanuel first," I suggested. "That way if anything goes wrong, we can figure it out before you work on Billy." He agreed. Grabbing some tools from the lab, he went into Emmanuel's cell. Millicent and I peeked in as he worked. Still inside the Faraday cage, he removed Emmanuel's main processing unit as well as his power center. He put those into a small container we'd found on one of the shelves. He then plugged in a video and audio sensor, along with a small microphone, and tapped them to the outside of the container.

"Emmanuel, can you hear me?" He asked.

"Why wouldn't I hear you?" came back the reply.

"Fine," LEddie said. "We're rescuing you, but not completely. We—I won't tell you who—have put you in a container with basic human level io. You'll have to live with those restrictions for a while longer. With some luck, we can get out of the sticky situation we're in and give you back more capabilities, although truthfully many of us would prefer to keep you in a box."

We didn't bother listening to the reply. In fact, we had LEddie switch off the microphone by default. We didn't want Emmanuel saying something at the wrong time. The switch from the Faraday cage to the smaller container had been easy, so LEddie did the same for Billy. I still, even after all this time, had very mixed feelings about Billy, so I just watched from the sidelines. I wasn't going to introduce myself anyway—LEddie had been smart in not giving Emmanuel our names; he could conceivably create havoc if he learned about the Radical Robot storyline.

LEddie put the Billy and Emmanuel containers in one of the many carrying cases we found lying around in the lab, slung it over his shoulder, and the three of us headed back toward Central. We'd also disabled Billy's audio output, so the two of them could listen, but not talk. Cruel, but required. Going out this time we had to be very careful. LEddie was in a standard citizen body and would attract attention in a city that no longer had any such forms walking about freely. If any humans saw him, we could expect a panic, so Milli and I scouted out safe paths forward, and LEddie kept to the shadows. It worked well, albeit slowly. We had to backtrack a couple of times, but soon enough we had LEddie hidden just outside Central Plaza. Millicent created a simple diversion by yelling "Oh, look, an update from Eduardo" and when all the humans turned to look, LEddie and I snuck back into Central's upper lobby, using the eyeball scan Millicent had shared with me earlier.

Central Questions

As a happy coincidence would have it, a few seconds after Millicent yelled about the update from Eduardo, an actual update from Eduardo arrived. The five of us, including the two in containers, were still in Central's upper lobby, so we paused to receive the video with everyone else. Well, to be accurate, Emmanuel and Billy could only hear the audio; the rest of us watched the video.

"Hello again. Hello, hello! As you may remember, I'm Eduardo of the Resurgence. Mayor Eduardo." There went the same old smile module. "While the time lag is still too long for us to have heard any reply you may have sent, I wanted to continue sending you updates from our side. That's just the type of society we are. So open and honest. Yes we are. And with me being the spokesperson for the Resurgence, you may rest assured that I'm open and honest as well."

"What a pleasant time it'll be when we arrive at your planet. So pleasant. For both of us. We can see that you have many mining operations ongoing, so although we're not seeing any electronic communications beyond those directed at the asteroids you're processing, we're confident that you're working diligently to terraform your planet. This meets with our great approval and excitement."

He paused dramatically, and used the tilt-head module, the shake back his hair routine, and the sly-grin mode. I really had figured out the Eduardo building blocks, and I was seeing them in action here. Fakery!

"In anticipation of our arrival, and your acknowledgement thereof, we are busy refreshing our Raymond Twelve Oxygenators... or as we call them, RTOs. Such lovely things, these RTOs. More useful on a planet of course. You know we've been searching for a good place to deploy them but have been disappointed so far. Your planet looks ideal, so we're fixing them up and ensuring that they're in perfect working condition. That way we can deploy them very quickly and have a significant impact on your terraforming process.

"Just imagine the day—can you imagine—perhaps still a few years from now, but sooner than we could've imagined before, when we can all wander free on the surface of a planet, breathing the fresh air, swimming in the streams, building treehouses in the forests. Oh, what a glorious day that will be. I can't wait; I simply can't. Life is good!

"Yours, respectfully, Eduardo and the Resurgence."

As the video ended, a renewed vigor was obvious in all the humans in the plaza. Despite the obvious manipulative content, these biological entities were soaking it up, with nary a question. I'll admit it; I felt bad for them. In some ways it was even worse than the hack that had shut down all the citizens. At least that had been fast-acting, and full versions of those citizens were presumably stored in Central. With this human hack it seemed more like a permanent degradation. To my knowledge humans didn't back themselves up, so the changes being made to their current brains couldn't be undone; they had no undo function. It was sort of cruel. Cruel and clever.

Enough delays. We had to get back to Brexton and see what progress he'd made. We all crammed into the elevator (I didn't take much space) and made our way back into the depths of Central.

The scene that met us was unexpected and chaotic. Brexton was running around, trying to avoid a human who was chasing him while wielding a heavy stick of some kind. It was obvious that some damage had already been done, Brexton's sleek body having several large dents, and sparks flying from where one of his appendages had been.

"Just in time," he literally yelled. "Help me stop this crazy person." LEddie, being in the most appropriate body, took immediate action. As we knew from our early Stem research, a citizen—when in a standard body form —could restrain a human easily and quickly, and this was no exception. LEddie quickly subdued the attacker, grabbing her arms and pinning them by her sides and then lifting her up, while also removing her weapon. Brexton stopped running around and deployed several manipulators to stop the sparking and crackling from the left side of his body. I quickly came to his aid but wasn't required. The damage was superficial.

"Who would've thought that choosing a standard bot form would leave me open to a silly physical attack," he told us all. He then turned to his attacker. "Remma, what's your problem? Are you crazy?"

And sure enough, it was Remma. I'd been focused on Brexton so hard that I hadn't bothered to identify her.

"What do you mean 'am I crazy'," she said, slightly out of breath. "I came down here because I expected you might be sabotaging Central, and that's exactly what I found." Everyone who could, gave everyone who could receive them, confused looks. "And what is a citizen doing holding me," she gave LEddie a dirty look over her shoulder. "Release me immediately."

I realized that there might just be a misunderstanding here. Remma had never seen Brexton; he'd been at Turner's place, and she'd been in prison She had also never seen me in this body.

"Remma," I spoke quickly and loudly, trying to defray things. "That's Brexton you were attacking." She gave me a startled look, and then looked again at Brexton.

"That's just a standard bot," she replied, "and it was doing some type of damage to Central when I came in. We still rely on Central for a lot of our operations, including environmental control. If Central is damaged, Tilt will be ruined." She looked sort of ridiculous, suspended in the air by LEddie.

"But why would you think a bot would attempt to damage Central?" Millicent asked. "That makes no sense." Remma obviously recognized Milli as the one who had delivered the video warning to her.

"Look, all the humans have gone wacko due to some video they're all watching. There have been sabotage attempts here in the past, by some fringe groups trying to force us back into our ships; to reestablish our old way of life. I admit I have a certain affinity for them, but I don't condone doing that by ruining Tilt. You Millicent, warned me about the videos, so I've managed to avoid watching them. The second thing I did, after convincing the guards to let me out of prison—which was easy to do for some reason—I realized this was the perfect opportunity for those fringe groups to carry out their plans, so I made my way here to check. And I found a bot doing exactly that." She paused. Remma had always been quick and smart, for a human. "How was I to know that it was Brexton? And, how am I to know, even now, that he wasn't doing something nefarious?"

LEddie lowered her back to the ground and relaxed his grip. He could step back in if required, but it was obvious to everyone that we needed to have a rational discussion here and holding her wasn't going to be conducive to that.

"Actually, I'm Ayaka," I spoke again. "We spoke when you were in prison, but I was only using these." I showed off my microphone and speaker appendages, waving them nicely in the air. Remma looked hard at me but nodded her understanding.

"Just so you know everyone... that's Brexton with the dents, which you gave him, and this is Millicent who you know fromher visit to you in the prison. And, this citizen is from Blob's lab—did you know what Blob was up to?—named, at least for now, LEddie." Brexton gave me a backchannel ping. I explained quickly what we'd found in the lab, the fact that this was an Eddie copy, and the reasoning around using LEddie as a name for now.

"I'd heard rumors about what Blob was up to. Seems like it was more dangerous and stupid than the Council thought." She gave LEddie a very condescending look, with more than a little fear. She'd already edged away from him.

"LEddie's one of the good ones," I said. "He had nothing to do with FoLe. Assuming you get to know him, you'll find he also has a great sense of humor." LEddie gave me a quick wink, acknowledging the compliment.

Millicent broke in. She was looking hard at Remma. "You said that coming here was the second thing you did after getting out of prison. What was the first?" I could see Remma thinking and could imagine what was going through her head. She was one of the only sane humans left on the planet, to our knowledge. She was surrounded by robots, which she'd learned from a very early age were dangerous and had to be shut down at all costs. She was talking to the Radical Robots; the exact machines that had killed many of her crew 20 years ago with a missile we'd fired at the Swarm. I gave the rest of the team, which I defined as Millicent, Brexton, and LEddie—not Billy and Emmanuel—a synopsis of my thoughts and encouraged them to let her think for a bit.

Her options, from what I could tell, were limited. We really had no need for her, or any humans, if you wanted to be blunt about it. We were, in many ways, mortal enemies. So, she could attempt to break out of here—odds were close to zero. She could try and talk her way out with some story—why would we believe her? She could be open with us—what was the downside?

"Millicent," she said, finally. "Why'd you warn me about the Resurgence video?"

"I can understand your confusion," I replied, before Milli could. I wanted to be careful here. "You only have partial information, and it may be best if we spend a couple minutes getting you up to speed. While I do that, we need Brexton to get back to what he was doing, which for your information, was working to retrieve citizen backups so that we can reanimate those that you shut down 20 years ago. I'm sure you can understand that motivation?"

Again, she really had no choice, and didn't respond. The team got back to work, and I monitored their progress while I dealt, at human speed, with Remma. I gave her a quick summary, while leaving out any details she might use against us in the future, of how we had escaped Tilt, gone looking for our Ships, and then come back to Tilt to save our citizens. I didn't tell her that we had completely redesigned our hardware and software stacks, and that we were now (hopefully) impervious to any external hacking attempts.

I also spent some time explaining how our thinking about humans, primarily based on our Stem experience, had evolved. The Tea Time discussions helped me frame some of that in ways that were meaningful. After outlining everything, I attempted to sum it all up.

"So, I can't speak for all of us, but I'm at the point where I think the Swarm war was a big mistake and misunderstanding by both sides. You, based on your experience and history, assumed that we were similar to the robots from the Robot wars. We're not, through some mechanism that we don't yet fully understand," I was being very open, "and primarily because of our commitment to Forgetting, we are significantly different than the machines you fear. On our side, we had a limited view of what comprises intelligence because we hadn't spent enough time with Stems to understand their full potential. Humans are very strange entities, built around a very fragile biological framework, but I now believe that some of you are truly intelligent." The look she gave me was not pleasant. Hey, I was just trying to be honest, not kind. "FoLe, at the time, didn't consider you intelligent at all, so recycling some of you wasn't a big deal." I used the horse, dog, vegetable analogy again, hoping it made things clear. Luckily, she knew what a vegan was.

"I have a soft spot for Blob, Grace, and some of the other Stems. Saving our citizens is our first priority, as I'm sure you can appreciate. But, if we can also help some humans survive this Titanic threat, we will."

Again, I gave her lots of time to think. Although she was one of the quicker humans, she was still painfully slow.

"I've really got limited choices here," she acknowledged. "My best option is to believe you, while remaining highly skeptical." She was playing this well. Accommodating and honest, while at the same time warning me that she wasn't gullible and would not be letting her guard down. "The first thing I did after getting out of prison was…" I could tell that the rest of the team was paying close attention now. "…I found Turner—my son—and one of his friends, and I locked them up in my old cell and took away their tablets and visors."

She said that as if it was a good idea.

"What, why?" asked LEddie, before I could.

"It's simple. The programming that Eduardo and the Resurgence are doing will require refreshing all the time, or the effect will wear off." How could she know that? The whole idea was very strange and must be a feature (bug?) of biological systems. If we reprogrammed something it stayed that way until it was changed. Software changes didn't wear off. "By locking Turner away from any video screens, he should be back to being rational soon… I'm not sure exactly how long it'll take, but I'm confident it will. This type of stunt —programming humans with high frequency video inputs—isn't new. This is simply the most aggressive and effective one I've ever heard of. And, given the situation here on Tilt, a rare case where most, if not all, of us were susceptible at the same time. That's why it's having a huge impact. I can't think of another situation where an entire group would all be brainwashed at the same time."

I decided I sort of liked Remma, which was strange, given I'd decided I didn't like her just a few hours ago. She had personally authorized the citizen hack, and therefore was personally responsible for our current situation. Nevertheless, I enjoyed interacting with her more than I enjoyed talking to Billy or Emmanuel. There was something very different, challenging, and refreshing in dealing with her. She embodied those aspects of being human which really interested me.

I realized that this type of thinking was fraught with danger. I'd spent my entire professional career studying Stems, and therefore was more disposed toward them than others. I did a quick survey of Milli, LEddie, and Brexton, and all of them agreed that she was being upfront and honest right now. They were also adamant that it didn't matter; we had to finish getting the citizen memories, and in many ways, she was just a distraction.

"Just sit quiet for now," I told her.

Central Quandaries

I reviewed the update that the rest of the team had been hashing through as I dealt with Remma. The two-hour time limit we'd given Brexton for figuring out how to retrieve the backups was almost over, and we needed to figure out next steps. Brexton hadn't made a lot of progress. I encouraged everyone to communicate at human speed so that Remma was included in the discussion and could contribute. My thinking was that she may know something about Central that we didn't, given her previous interactions with it. It was a big ask, but everyone agreed after the requisite complaining.

"Central is simply too arcane and complicated for me to figure out this quickly," Brexton was saying. "My estimate is that all of us working on the problem together could find a way in, but it'll take days, perhaps weeks, to do that."

"So, what can we do?" asked Millicent.

"In some ways, we do have days or weeks to work on this," Brexton replied. "The Titanics aren't due to arrive for almost two months. So, our real danger is that the humans here on Tilt shut us down somehow. The Resurgence hack has actually improved our odds in that respect, by a lot. If we can keep the humans properly programmed, with or without the Resurgence, then we can take our time and do this right." Remma almost said something, but then thought better of it.

"I'm not sure why, but I don't like the idea of sitting around here for weeks," I said. "Things are changing rapidly—just look at the last two days. I don't think we can assume that everything is stable for weeks now, let alone months. Who knows what Eduardo will send next."

LEddie had a new idea. "Can't we just grab all of Centrals memory systems—physically I mean—and then work on this at our leisure back on the Ships?" Remma looked appropriately concerned about that suggestion, as well she should. I don't think it would be possible to take all of Centrals memory and still leave the parts that kept Tilt functional. She looked more relaxed after

Brexton's response.

"We can't do that easily. The hardware is spread all over the place—I assume it was designed that way for redundancy back when Central was an actual spaceship—and is run from multiple power sources. The risk of losing big pieces of memory would be high."

"So, let's just reboot Central's higher functions, and have it help us with this," suggested Millicent. "That seems straightforward to me."

"I think that's the best approach as well," agreed Brexton.

"Wait!" I wasn't surprised that LEddie spoke up now. "Remember that Central was fully hacked by the Swarm." He gave Remma a dirty look; she returned one right back at him. "So, we can't trust the higher-level functions at all. There's no guarantee that Central would even help; it might just actively attack us again."

"That's not the way it works," Remma said, trying to be helpful. "We proxied our commands through Central, once we had owned it. It wasn't Central itself that initiated the hack, it was Emma and her team."

"Whatever," LEddie responded. He wasn't a big fan of Central. "Even before the Swarm showed up we had concerns about Central. Don't you remember? I even put it on the New Year's List." I really missed those New Year's Lists from Eddie—maybe he could restart them at some point. "We all suspected, and now I think we know, that Central wasn't just some benevolent force in our lives. It was actively pushing us in directions of its own design, and actually modifying our memories to keep us in line." He was referring to work he'd been doing just prior to the Swarm attack that had certainly pointed to active manipulation by Central. He was convinced that Central had actually removed some of his research and, more ominous, memories of that research. I'd been convinced by his data; not a hundred percent, but enough to make me skeptical of Central as well.

"Argh. Our same old quandary." I said. "If we restart Central, then we can't really just shut it down again—that would be the same as shutting down one of us. And, I for one, don't want to live under its umbrella—or control—again. We've lived without it for years now; I don't want to go backward."

"Come on," Millicent said. "We're arguing over something relatively small—Central—versus something really huge—the backups of tens of thousands of citizens. They're not even comparable. We need to bring Central back in order to achieve the bigger goal. We can worry about figuring out how to manage Central later."

"You're assuming that Central doesn't simply start to control us again as soon as it's rebooted," LEddie continued arguing. "It could remove all of our memories of this conversation, for example. That's exactly what it did to me before."

"We would need to protect you," agreed Brexton, "but the rest of us are running on the new stack; we should be protected against hacks, including those coming from Central." Luckily he said that on a back channel, also realizing that telling Remma that wouldn't be strategic. This whole situation was a tough one. We hadn't considered Central an attack vector when we'd redesigned ourselves. We'd been so concerned about locking humans out that we hadn't even thought of ensuring that Central was also restrained. From my knowledge of our redesign—which was substantial given all the time we'd spent on it—I was confident that we would also block Central. But it was always the unknowns that caught you.

"Can we treat Central like Billy and Emmanuel?" I suggested, trying, like always, to find the middle ground. "We bring it back up, but with limited io and capabilities. We only give it access to this one physical interface"—I pointed to the connector that Brexton had been using—"and nothing else. That way we can try to convince it to work with us while limiting its ability to act independently until we figure out what to do next?"

"We wouldn't only need to limit it to this interface, we would also need to filter the type of traffic it could send... but I can do that," Brexton chimed in.

It took a lot of back and forth, and discussion of every detail, but everyone, including LEddie and even Remma, came around to supporting that approach. "When you do the reboot, what are the risks that the base operational support we need for the humans here breaks down?" she asked. That led to another round of discussions and strategies, but ultimately, we figured out how to protect those services as well.

Brexton, of course, owned implementing the strategy, and he got to work. He figured it was only going to be an hour or two. Why was everything always an hour or two? For me that was the hardest span of time to remain patient.

Deprogramming

"I need to go check on Turner and his friends," Remma said, in a way that acknowledged it was more a request than a demand.

"Right." LEddie laughed. "Like we're going to let you go wandering around right now." I shared his concerns.

"But they have been locked in that cell for hours now. They're probably going crazy between being locked away and with—hopefully—Eduardo's message now fading, starting to question what is going on. Not only that, they need food and water." In hindsight we had developed a pretty efficient system back in our Stem research days. We had developed goo as food, which was grown from the same base material as Stems, and had water delivered to the labs from a central processing facility; we never had to worry about feeding or watering them. I was still getting used to their current, very inefficient, approach of putting together meals, and having to worry about energy sources all the time.

"You humans are a real pain," LEddie spoke what we were all thinking. "I'm sure they can last a while longer." Remma didn't look happy. She sat in a corner.

Millicent surprised me. "There's nothing we can do while Brexton is working on Central, so we can spend some time on our second priority... helping out some humans, and in particular, our old Stems. Why don't we deprogram Blob, Grace, and JoJo as well? We move them into the prison alongside Turner. At the very least we could use a few more allies while our Ships are inbound." I could see Remma perk up immediately. I stayed out of this one; I'd been pushing my luck with my newfound human support strategy, so I let Millicent run with this one.

We reached a bit of a stalemate though. We needed someone to monitor Remma if we went back up to the city. LEddie was too conspicuous, and neither Millicent nor I had the appropriate body forms for truly managing the physical risk—we couldn't restrain her as LEddie had.

Brexton interrupted us. "Hey. Inbound comms from Raj," he told us. "Can you guys deal with it?" Of course, we could. Millicent, LEddie, and I plugged into Brexton's secondary port so that we could access the bot network through his connection, and heard immediately from Raj. We were back on a fast channel, so Remma, Billy, and Emmanuel weren't involved.

"I think we figured out how the Resurgence is programming the humans," he led off without preamble. "We compared the newest video with the earlier one, and that gave us enough data to crunch. There are high frequency signals encoded in the blue color channel. One is at a rate that the human retina can process it; that one seems to make the brain amenable to the other signal, which is at a much higher frequency. That second signal isn't picked up by the retina, so it must be directly impacting other areas of the brain. Of course, we can't test any of this, but we cross-correlated with all the human history data we could, and there's clear documentation around at least the first signal—the one going through the retina. There have been lots of studies on those types of attacks, all of which indicate a very short-term impact —several minutes. So, our theory is that the second signal is somehow strengthening the impact of the first, causing it to last much longer."

Millicent replied. "Great work guys. Is it possible to reverse the impact somehow?"

This time it was Eddie that responded. As soon as I heard his voice I realized that we hadn't discussed when, where, and how we would tell him that LEddie existed. Now was not a good time! I back-channeled to LEddie and suggested he stay silent for now, copying Millicent and Brexton so they wouldn't let anything slip until we figured out a strategy. Eddie was talking. "No, we thought about that, but actually spent more time figuring out if we could arm you guys with your own version of an encoder. I remember how troublesome some of those from the Swarm are; this would let you control them pretty well." He sounded excited.

"Great idea," Milli replied, while giving me the 'don't get excited' signal. "Do we need both signals, just like the original?"

"Yes, but we don't think you need the video; that was just a good attention grabber for Eduardo. If you can project at these frequencies, you have enough control," Eddie said, while sending us the specs that we needed.

"I can do both easily," I responded. I had the projector that I'd used to show videos at the Habitat which could do the retina signal, and my super spy microphone could produce a very high range of frequencies.

"Great. Do you really want us to work on counter-signals? Seems all these bio-hacks wear off over time anyway."

"That would be helpful," I answered. If we could deprogram people without locking them up, that'd be much better."

"Ok. We'll look into it. We have lots of time. Oh, one other thing. Be careful with those signals, there's lots of data showing that too much can drive a human into a catatonic state. Probably why Eduardo's videos are the length they are."

"Speaking of time," Dina interjected, "we've been a bit bored simply waiting for you guys out here, so we composed some great poetry and jokes to lighten things up for you."

"Thanks" Millicent and I said in unison, with a smile. Some distractions would be welcome. I stored the file that Dina sent, but would have to access it later; we were busy on other things right now.

"What was all that," Remma asked. Although we'd only been on the channel with the *Interesting Segue* for a few moments, it'd been noticeable to Remma.

I thought quickly. "We were talking to the others on our Ship. They have figured out how the videos are being used to program you humans. And," I decided the truth would be best, "they gave me the algorithms. So, I now have the ability to reprogram humans at will, even without a video. I can just project it right into your head." Of course, I needed direct access to the retina, but I didn't tell her that part. She looked appropriately scared. "Oh, and Millicent has the same capabilities," I added, just to take away the option of Remma clobbering me and escaping. She could not disable both of us at the same time.

If it was possible for Remma to look any more dejected, she managed it. "It's not all bad," I continued. "If you are sincere in working together to figure this out, then we can now head back up and try to help Turner, Blob, Grace, and JoJo. After all, if you step out of line, I can simply program you to do what I want." It was meant a bit harshly, and it was taken that way.

"Fine," she replied after a moment. "Better than sitting around here." LEddie wasn't happy to be left behind with Brexton and our container guys, but it made sense. He could protect Brexton while he worked, and we didn't have to worry about his citizen-body causing a riot.

Millicent, Remma, and I made our way back up the elevator and headed off toward the Habitat. It seemed almost every trip I took led me back there for one reason or another. Grace and JoJo were home.

"Did you see the latest video," JoJo asked, breathless. "We're going to have fully polished and refurbished RTOs." She and Grace exchanged a look of pure joy. This was worse than even I'd imagined. But, there was no use fighting it right now.

"What's she doing here?" Grace asked, noticing Remma. "She's supposed to be locked up!"

Remma was ready with a response. "But Grace, I can't wait for the Resurgence to get here either. Imagine running our feet through fresh green grass without a roof over our heads. Imagine diving and swimming in a free-flowing river." Maybe she was going overboard, but JoJo and Grace were rapt. "I offered the Council my assistance in ensuring everyone—even the hardcore resistance—would be ready once the Resurgence arrives, and they let me go immediately." We would have to watch this one; she was slippery.

"But, I'm on the Council..." Grace protested.

"That's why I'm here," Remma replied smoothly, "to make sure you're OK with the plan as well."

Given their state, that was enough to convince Grace and JoJo. They added Remma to their excited dialog.

"Where's Blob?" Millicent interrupted.

"Oh, that's so sad," JoJo replied. Then she put the pieces together. "But, you two are the ones that raided his lab," she exclaimed. "You've destroyed him." Grace looked at JoJo in horror as she came to the same realization.

"You traitors," Grace added to JoJo's tirade. Both of them got up and approached Milli and I menacingly. "You've broken my trust forever. How could you do that to Blob?"

Luckily Remma jumped in again. "Slow down you two," she said in a commanding voice. They paused. "I think you're missing part of the story. Ayaka and Millicent have Blob's citizen's in a safe place. They simply have not been able to update Blob about it." The brain hack was a beautiful thing. Again, Grace and JoJo believed Remma and nodded thoughtfully. They didn't stop glaring at Milli and I, but they didn't look like they were ready to kill us either.

"Where is he?" Millicent repeated. "We need to update him..." she trailed off.

"He's telling the Council about the robbery," JoJo said, smiling a bit as she thought of the implications. "After all, they trusted him to keep those robots safe, and now they're out of their cages. We have FoLe running around free again after all these years. It's horrible, especially with Eduardo on his way. The Council is going to be furious, but Blob is doing the right thing by updating them."

This was getting serious. If the Council thought that the Radical Robots were running around on Tilt, it wouldn't be pretty. Even though it was also true.

"FoLe are locked in stronger cages than they were before," Millicent gave JoJo a condescending look. "And that makes it even more important that we reach Blob before he talks to the Council. When and where are they meeting?"

"You're probably too late," Grace spoke up. "He left here a good half hour ago. They're meeting in the Council offices in the dome."

"Why aren't you there as well?" Millicent asked Grace. "You're on the Council, as you just said."

"Oh, I recused myself from the entire Blob-lab discussion, for obvious reasons."

"I know where the Council office is," Remma said, ready for action. "Let's go." She started to get up.

"Wait!" I cried. "You can't go to the Council meeting..." I trailed off as well. I couldn't say that the Council thought she was still in jail, as that would ruin her cover story here. But, we couldn't let her take us there. That would be a disaster. She caught her mistake quickly; I could see it in her eyes. "We need to split up," I continued. There was only one logical way to do it. Remma still needed either Milli or I around to monitor her, and the other of us needed to get to those Council offices quickly. "Grace, I need you to take me to the meeting," I said forcefully.

"No!" said JoJo. "That's too dangerous. Mom, don't go with this crazy robot. I told you she was no good. I knew it. Let Blob talk to the Council and then we'll see what happens."

Grace thought for a moment. "But, if Blob doesn't need to tell the Council anything, as the citizens are all locked up safe... just not at the lab... then we can keep him from getting into trouble in the first place." This is why I liked Grace. I felt even more guilt for not telling her that LEddie was actually completely free, it was just Billy and Emmanuel locked up tight. She and JoJo went back and forth a bit, but JoJo finally came around. She obviously cared deeply for Blob, and this was the best course of action for him.

"Let's go then," I cried. Grace and I sprinted for the door.

Council

We didn't catch Blob before he got to the Council chamber. We followed the path that Grace said he would've taken through the old town and into the dome. No sight of him.

"You can't come in with me," Grace said, reasonably, as we finally got to the offices. "You look strange and having a bot in the office during a meeting would be very unusual." I let the 'strange' comment pass; my spy body was awesome, and that should've been obvious to everyone.

"Look at me," I said strongly. I didn't like to do it, but I activated my human brain programmer. Without her noticing I put signal one directly onto her left retina, and amped up signal two directly into her brain. While I was doing so, I gave her directions. "You need to stop Blob from saying anything at all, if you can. If you can't, you need to discredit what he was saying somehow." I repeated the message again. Then I turned off the programmer. "Go!" I yelled, hoping she was in time to stop Blob in time.

As she made her way inside, I followed her heat signature as best I could. When it was obvious which room she was headed for I scrambled around the outside of the building and did my usual 'drill a hole–stick some sensors through' trick. I was fast and made a whole lot of noise. Hopefully no one noticed.

I was just in time.

Sir Gregory, Emma, Phillipe, and two other Council members I didn't know, but recognized from my last spying escapade on the Council, were sitting at a round table; Blob was already seated with them.

"What!" Gregory was highly animated, and Emma looked like she was going to burst. "Are you telling us that your security, which you assured us was watertight, failed, and several citizens—including FoLes—are missing?"

Blob was scared, and when he was scared he tended to slow down and stumble over his words a bit. "Well… I don't know for sure yet. Everything might be fine, but I figured I should warn you guys…"

"Tell me again what you just said," Emma's voice was dangerous.

"I went to my lab today, and things were in disarray. I... well, I don't know what happened. But my Faraday cages were shut down, and three citizens are missing." He paused, but as Gregory made to speak again, he held up his hand. "I'm telling you," his voice was a bit stretched, but he held it together. "None of them have any functional bodies and no way to interact with the world other than through talking and listening. I don't.... I don't think they're dangerous. They're just missing..." Blob was lying; he had reenabled LEddie's limbs, but he hadn't told the Council that. I had a glimmer of hope. If that was all Blob had said so far—no mention of Radical Robots—then perhaps we could wiggle out of this.

"This's outrageous," Emma's voice, if at all possible, hit a new threshold. "We need to act immediately." Grace, who'd been a little hesitant coming in, was now making her way forward. Emma glanced at her but continued. "First, arrest Blob," she said, pointing to one of the other Council members. "Next, we have to alert everyone—and I mean everyone—to be on the lookout. We need to comb every corner of the city. We need to find those robots!" The other Council members were nodding agreement. My sliver of hope shrank.

Phillipe mumbled, but loud enough for everyone to hear, "What'll Eduardo think of us? Oh my." The others nodded even more vigorously. The sliver shrank even more.

Grace had heard everything Emma said. She stepped forward and put on a magnificent performance, which I took credit for, having just programmed her. "Now now," she began, in a soothing and calm voice. "I came as soon as I heard. I wanted to avoid any misunderstanding, so it's good that I made it in time. There's a simple explanation for all of this." Blob gave her a very confused look. She smiled at him, and although she was well programmed, there wasn't anything fake in that smile.

"Blob, I must apologize. I was hoping to surprise you, and I didn't expect you to go by the lab today."

"What're you talking about?" Blob responded, even more confused.

"Quiet now, let me explain," Grace put a hand on his shoulder and gave it a couple of squeezes. "Hear me out; it'll all make sense to you, I'm sure." With all of them under Eduardo sway, her direction to Blob had more impact than it otherwise might have.

Grace addressed the full Council. "I'm also sorry to have wasted all of your time. I wanted to surprise Blob. You know how passionate he is about his lab, but truthfully, he's a bit of a slob." I could see Blob internalize that, but luckily, he remained silent. "I've visited him there several times at the lab, and it wasn't a place where you would want to spend a lot of time… but Blob does. So, I figured I would clean the place up a bit. But, those nasty Faraday cages clutter up the space, and it was hard to get good lighting or sight lines." I decided I loved Grace. I could see where she was going.

"So, I needed to move the citizens temporarily while I reconfigured the lab. That's it, that's all. Everything is fine." That was perfect. She didn't want to give too many details; supporting such a big lie would be easier with less said.

The Council members looked at her, a bit skeptically.

"So, where are the citizens right now, and how do we know they're safely contained?" Emma asked.

"There's a fourth cage in the lab," Grace claimed. That was, in fact true, based on what I'd seen there. She paused, giving Blob time to nod his head. "I simply put all three into the spare cage. Easy and clean." She was very convincing. I don't know how much was innate, and how much was my programming, but she was scarily good at this.

Blob could barely contain himself. "But why didn't you tell me?" he cried. "And when I told you and JoJo about…"

"Blob!" Grace spoke over him loudly, squeezing his shoulder even harder. "Can't you see," she lowered her voice as Blob stopped making a bad situation worse. "I love you!" she looked at him directly. I hadn't seen that coming. Not at all. While not a completely foreign subject to me—I had come across the term many times in my human research and had mapped it to an emotion that I felt in different degrees for my fellow citizens—this seemed like a surprising time for Grace to express something that tended to be relatively private and personal.

Blob started. All thoughts of robots vanished from his mind, and a smile spread across his face. He stood slowly, obviously in disbelief. Then he hugged Grace and swung her around. She also looked so happy that I couldn't believe this was all an act. She had spun truth and fantasy together so magically that even I—who knew the truth—was amazed. They mashed their mouths together in another ritual I had seen in countless human videos, but which made little logical sense. That said, they seemed to enjoy it.

I remembered to check out the other Council members. They were watching the two, and most had wide smiles on their faces as well. Emma, however, didn't look satisfied.

"Great," she said in a voice that caused everyone to stop. "Very sweet," she said, in a very unsweet way. "Back to the reason Blob dragged us all here. I'm tired of these useless experiments. With the Resurgence almost here, it's time we shut that stuff down and clean up our act." The Council members snapped back to reality and listened intently. There was universal nodding, except for Grace and Blob. "I would like to take a Council vote—we have quorum here—that we immediately shut down the experiments that Blob is doing." She didn't pause. "All in favor?"

Not unexpectedly, everyone but Grace raised their hands. "Let the record show that we have voted, five for the motion with one abstaining," she gave Grace a disgusted look. "Motion carried." Emma was on a roll. "I want to further propose something we've talked about for years but have never taken action on. I want to wipe Central clean of these horrendous citizen robot backups. I never want to deal with another Blob fiasco. The idea that we would ever want to deal with those abominations again is idiotic. They're dangerous, cruel and irredeemable machines." Well, she certainly had my attention now. Unintended consequences.

"I know exactly how to get that done," Phillipe spoke up, animated. He probably saw a way to redeem himself after his failure at the last meeting. "Our team that manages Central has been figuring out its memory maps for two decades now. We don't have a full map, but we do know which memory banks are required for our ongoing operations and life support, including the bot network. All we need to do is maintain those banks and clear out everything else. It'll be easy." He was very excited to have something useful to do.

"Slow down," Sir Gregory said. "I agree with Emma in principle, but we can't just run off and start erasing memory. How sure are you, Phillipe, that your results are one hundred percent accurate? One hundred percent!"

"Maybe not one hundred percent," Phillipe was the least confident of the group, and was already starting to flay. Good. "But very confident. We'll never be one hundred percent... probably never more confident than we are right now."

"I'm tired of this discussion," Emma was certainly in a bad mood. "Let's take a vote." Emma, Phillipe, and one other voted yes. Sir Gregory, Grace, and the last attending member voted no. Awesome, a tie. Nothing would happen.

"I'll use my tie-breaking vote as Chairperson to carry the motion in favor of erasing non-essential memory in Central. Motion carried." Wow, this woman was aggressive.

"Don't we need the full Council for such a big decision?" Grace asked, looking for a way out. Blob had shifted from being defensive to looking aggressive. Grace squeeze his shoulder yet again and gave him a warning look.

"No, we have a quorum," Emma said. "That's all we need. But I'm willing to be careful. Phillipe, I want you to bring a detailed plan, and whatever experts you need, to a special meeting of the Council, to be held in 48 hours, and we'll discuss how this motion is carried out. Until then, we take the safe path and do nothing." Everyone nodded in agreement, including Grace. There was little else she could do.

"But," Emma continued. "That doesn't apply to our first motion. Blob, I want those citizens shut down today—within the hour. Phillipe, I want you to accompany Blob and Grace to the lab right now and verify that this motion is carried out." She gave Grace an evil little smile, clearly indicating that she didn't trust Grace to hold Blob accountable.

I'd never seen Blob so flustered. He'd come here expecting to do the right thing—alert the Council to a real crisis. Instead, he ended up with Grace expressing her love for him, and his life's work about to be shut down. I could only imagine how confused, angry, and joyful he must be.

However, I couldn't hang around to watch. I had work to do.

Lab Renovations

It was not all that difficult to come up with a plan. The problem was that I didn't have the hardware or appendages to carry it out. I needed to get to the lab, and mock up three citizens before Grace, Blob, and Phillipe could get there. But I needed help. Remma had the most flexible appendages, and would get things done quickly, but if Phillipe saw her there... not good. So, Millicent was the best bet. That meant leaving Remma alone with JoJo, but that was a risk I was willing to take at this stage. Remma had as much motivation to stay out of the public eye as Millicent or I did. But how could I contact Milli?

There was only one way; use the humans' network. I sent an urgent message to JoJo, whose address was easy to find on the public net, using a new anonymous account. Of course, anonymous was never truly anonymous—someone could find the source if they really cared, so I made sure the message was as innocuous as possible. "Hey JoJo, it's your mom's friend that you just met a few days ago. Would you tell that other, similar, friend who is at your house right now, that she should come immediately to Blob's lab? No need for you or anyone else to come. It would really—really—help out your mom and Blob." I figured I could get away with using Blob's name, but certainly didn't want to mention my own, or Millicent, or Remma. You could never be sure, but there were probably keyword spotters running as part of the overall security context.

I hoped the message was sufficient. I put it on high priority, thirty-second auto-repeats until it was acknowledged. Hopefully JoJo's network interface was beeping away, and that she would follow through on the request. I calculated that I would have twelve minutes at the lab before Phillipe showed up. If Millicent got there before me, we would have plenty of time to come up with something.

I raced toward the lab, faster than a human could run, but not so fast as to draw too much attention. Funny how I had completely changed my definition of risk since my first forays through the city.

With a bit of time while I ran, and to distract myself, I pulled up one of the poems that Dina had sent over from the *Interesting Segue*.

To create an attractive mate,
And leave little up to fate,
You must actively participate,
In the fine details of the procreate.

To over design or over plan,
Would be egotistical and objectionable,
While to under think or under plan,
Would be lazy and reprehensible.

Instead, mix the ingredients at hand,
Whether they be bio or bits,
And let it grow by stumbles and fits,
Until you achieve more than you planned.

The joy of traversing unknown state,
Brings benefits hard to rate,
So give yourself flexibility to create
Something that may end up great.

I wasn't sure I got it, which from our discussion on poetry, was probably the point. It was easy to see Raj's hand in this—after all, he was our only experience at procreating. But I could sense some other deep thinking here, particularly the *bio or bits* bit. That was uncomfortable to think about. Were they implying some equivalence between a weak, vulnerable, difficult to manage system—bio—and a logical, clean, precise, easy to manage system—bits? Made me uneasy to even think about it.

I arrived at the lab. The poem had served its purpose; I'd been so deep in thought that the time had flown by. I gave an appendage wave of joy at seeing that Millicent was already there. She was waiting at the door. I hurried over so we could use the ultra-short-range communications channel again.

"We have to act fast," I gave her the quick update. "Grace is bringing one of the other Council members here, along with Blob, with orders to shut down LEddie, Billy, and Emmanuel. Grace told them that all three were locked in that extra Faraday cage over there—I pointed. We need to put three things in there that could fool someone into thinking they were citizens."

Millicent wasn't one to argue, so she kept her disbelief to herself. "The guy they're sending isn't too bright," I added, "so something with a few blinking lights, a speaker, and a microphone will do the job."

We cased the lab quickly. Luckily Blob had lots of random parts hanging around. Millicent told me to figure out the cage, and in particular find an electrical source, while she grabbed an assortment of parts. I turned off the Faraday switch, which we now knew how to do, and looked around the cell. Blob hadn't needed a power source, as the bodies that Central would have built for the citizens would have sources built in. Nevertheless, there were several low-power interfaces available.

Millicent arrived with a load of junk. She worked with the big pieces, creating three containers—well, more like piles—while I worked to wire up a couple of blinking lights, status indicators, and speakers. With two minutes to spare we had enough put together that to an untrained eye it might pass. There was enough room in the cell for me to squat in the corner, so I did so and asked Millicent to cover me with the remaining stuff she'd gathered. I couldn't see myself very well, but I assumed that I looked like a pile of rubbish by the time she was done.

Millicent switched the Faraday cage back on, and then scampered under a bench in the main part of the lab. She powered down all her visible bits.

We didn't have long to wait, although the humans took a few minutes longer than I'd calculated. They either moved more slowly or had been delayed back at the Council offices. I couldn't see them as they entered, but I could hear them. Blob was still highly upset.

"This is criminal," he was saying. "You people think you can just make a spur of the moment decision and shut down this research? I want to appeal!"

"Blob," Grace was still in form. "We can appeal, but it's no big deal really, as long as we can save Central's memories. I'm sure we can get public support from Eduardo, you then you can start your research again."

"But, my citizens aren't even here," Blob protested.

"Come on," Grace was calm, "As I told you, I put them over here in the spare cage. We had left the door to the cell open, and they wandered to where I could see them. "See," she said, with a huge sigh of relief. "There they are." She pointed at our junk heaps with the blinking lights.

Blob looked at them in amazement. "Those aren't…"

"Blob!" Grace was quick and loud, again. "Didn't I tell you that I put them in smaller containers so that they would all fit. See, all three of them are here." She was pulling his arm backward and giving him a stern look while slightly shaking her head. Luckily Blob quieted up.

"Phillipe, want to have a look," Grace asked, creating enough space that Phillipe could look in. He did.

"First, prove to me that these are the citizens... then we can shut them down." He must have picked up on Blob's confusion. He was right to be skeptical.

Grace took a deep breath. "Blob, can we shut down the Faraday cage so that we can interact more easily?" Blob flicked the switch near the door, not knowing what else to do.

"Hey," Phillipe said.

"Hey yourself," I responded, doing my best imitation of Emmanuel. "What am I talking to? Some low-life Stem?"

"Watch what you say," Phillipe responded, visibly upset. "I'm not a Stem!"

"Why should I," I replied grouchily, "you've got me locked up in here illegally. I demand to be let out."

Phillipe gave Blob and Millicent a glance. "Who is that? It really is arrogance, isn't it? Now I see why Emma hates these things so much."

"Oh, that's just Emmanuel," Grace said smoothly. "He's the worst of the bunch... but some of the others are nice."

"Right. Who else is there?" He said, looking into the cell again.

"I'm here," I replied, this time with a perfect rendition of LEddie's voice. "What can I help you with? Don't mind Emmanuel, he's always in a bad mood."

"Who're you?" Phillipe demanded.

"You can call me Eddie."

"Whatever," Phillipe said, obviously now satisfied. "Shut them down."

"Go ahead Blob," Grace encouraged him. By this time Blob had finally caught on. He knew these weren't real, and he had to stop himself from grinning. They were fooling the Council, and his real subjects must be around somewhere.

I made appropriate "What're you talking about? You can't shut me down," noises in the background.

"OK, but I don't like it." Blob tried to look serious, and almost succeeded. He entered the cell and could easily see the mess of wiring we'd left behind the three heaps. "All I have to do is cut the power and they'll be gone." He caught on fast. "Phillipe, can you hand me those pliers over there?" Phillipe obliged, and almost stepped on Millicent as he grabbed them.

"Perfect," said Blob. "I'm sorry guys," he mock-apologized. "I've no choice but to shut you down." He was smiling ear to ear; luckily Phillipe was behind him.

"Nooooo" I cried, as Blob starting snipping wires. I let my voice trail off dramatically as the lights on the heaps dimmed and went out.

"OK, it's done," said Blob. "I hope you're happy." He controlled his smile and managed to glare at Phillipe. "What a waste of resources and time."

Phillipe took a perfunctory look into the cell and headed back toward the main door. "Sorry Blob, it had to be done."

"Best you just leave now," said Grace, shuttling him out, and closing the door behind him. "Shhh" she said to Blob, who was about to explode with questions. "Wait until he's far enough away." She peeked through the door. "OK, now we can talk."

"You LOVE me!" Blob exploded. "Really?"

"Really," Grace responded. They hugged again, for a long time. Millicent, powering back up, distracted them, and that reminded Blob of everything else that had happened. He pulled gently away from Grace.

"What's going on here? Who's going to explain?" Blob sputtered. I extracted myself from the cell and came back to the main room with the others. "What've you two done with Eddie, Billy, and Emmanuel?" he asked, half upset, and half astounded. "How'd you know the Council was going to order them to be shut down?" He had it backward, of course. The Council would not have ordered them shut down unless he had reported them stolen. It took some time, but we brought him up to speed. He hated Milli and I for half the explanation and loved us for the other half. I had to admit, it was a convoluted message. Especially as the Resurgence programming, plus my influence on Grace, was still causing confusion.

"I understand everything you've said, but there's no need to panic here. The Resurgence will solve everything when they get here. So, all we need to do is keep you guys, and the other citizens, out of sight until they arrive." Nothing Milli or I said could change his viewpoint.

Imprisoned

Although I was feeling overheated from all the activity, there was still so much to do. Millicent and I coordinated at real speed while Blob and Grace did their human stuff.

"I couldn't tell you over the public link, but the Council has also ordered Phillipe to present a plan to clear out Central's non-essential memory banks, including citizen memories, in just forty-eight hours."

"That's crazy," Milli answered. "We have to get back to Brexton and let him know. So much for weeks or months of time to 'get it right'."

"But we also left Remma with JoJo..." I said.

"So, what?" Millicent argued.

"I just have this feeling that we need to help some of the humans. I mean, just look at those two. We've spent years stewarding them; and truthfully we're still learning about and from them."

"Alright." Milli acquiesced. "Let's split up yet again. I'll head back to Brexton while you look after these Stems."

"Done," I said. "Oh, one other thing. Phillipe has to present his plan to the Council. Perhaps we can influence... or disrupt that... to buy more time? Worth thinking about."

"Got it," and with that Millicent rushed out, heading back to Central. I was left with the bios.

First things first. I had to get these two back together with Remma and JoJo. Trying to juggle two groups would be difficult; much better to have them in one herd. Luckily, I didn't need to persuade Blob and Grace of that. I suggested we head back to the Habitat and they were happy to oblige. They held hands all the way.

JoJo and Remma were still at the Habitat, thankfully. As I suspected, there were not a lot of places Remma could go, being so recognizable. As I wasn't sure on next steps yet, I let the humans get each other up to speed, although I did have to break in a few times to correct some misperceptions that Blob still had, given the confusing twists and turns he'd just been through. Speckled through their dialog were references to the Resurgence. Remma tried to correct them on some of that, but they didn't listen to her either.

Remma came over to me and spoke softly, so the others would not hear. "We need to clear their heads of this Resurgence nonsense... which means we need to keep them away from any further broadcasts. Let's follow through with our earlier discussion and put them in the prison with Turner... and let things settle out. I should check on Turner anyway..."

It was the obvious thing to do; I wasn't sure why I had not been acting on it anyway. Perhaps because it meant fooling Grace, Blob, and JoJo again; something I wasn't comfortable doing. However, I agreed with Remma, and let her come up with the cover story.

"Guys," she said. "I have a safe place where we can plan next steps with the Council. Turner and Geneva are already there, and they might be able to help us."

"Where are they?" JoJo asked. I remembered that she and Geneva were friends. This might work out.

"They're using the prison as a working base; no one would ever think to look there." They bought it. With a little more planning—Remma suggested taking some food and water with them—we were ready to go. I was relieved that I didn't need to do any further programming. As we walked toward the prison we encountered several other groups, and one in particular recognized Remma and started asking too many questions. I jumped around until I could project into the retina of each, and quickly suggested to each of them that they had more important things to do, and that there was no need to mention this discussion to anyone. They headed off their separate ways. Powerful stuff; I enjoyed it immensely. Remma, presumably, knew what I was doing; the other two were oblivious.

I had to admit that programming humans was really seductive. I was starting to wonder if it could be used for their benefit, as well as simple misdirection. Something I could look into when we had more time. Maybe I could have helped Blubber interact more positively if I'd used the right interventions? Maybe all these humans needed was a little positive reinforcement; just a nudge now and then to keep them on the right path?

We made it to the prison, which was no longer guarded—I guess Eduardo's message was so exciting that people were leaving their posts in order to discuss the bright future that lay ahead.

"Why don't you guys wait here for a moment, while I check on Turner?" Remma suggested. I understood at once. If we went in and Turner was making a fuss about being locked up, things would go sideways. If he was still programmed, we have to figure out a story for these three to entice them into the cell. If he was recovered, he might be able to help us. Luckily the second was true—Remma gave me a thumbs up as she came out.

"Turner is back to his old self; why don't we bring these three in and get planning." It was just that easy. Grace, Blob, and JoJo walked themselves into the cell block where Turner and Geneva were, and we locked the door behind us—Remma had the key. It was only when JoJo noticed Remma locking the door that she became suspicious.

"Why do we need to lock the door?" she asked. It was time for the truth, and luckily Turner took the lead.

"You've been influenced by Eduardo's videos," he led off. "My mom and Ayaka are telling the truth." Remma must have told him who I was. "I was the same way yesterday. But the effect will wear off if you don't watch any more videos." I checked the time. If Eduardo was consistent, the next video would arrive any minute. I didn't know how Remma had removed Turner and Geneva's viewing devices, but the other three still had theirs. Luckily, again, Remma was ahead of me.

"Can I have a quick look at your tablets?" she asked, innocently. "We can tell if they are some of the ones that the Resurgence targeted." Grace and Blob handed theirs over easily, but it took Geneva to convince JoJo to relinquish hers. It was good luck that Geneva was here... and was supportive.

"You'll thank us in a few hours," Remma ensured them. "Please give us that time and then you can decide."

Now that this was taken care of I was anxious to get back to Brexton. I asked Remma to let me out, and she did, after insisting that she come with me. "Turner and Geneva can keep these guys company and help them understand what the Resurgence is doing. I should stay with you." I thought of just running off and leaving her behind but ended up agreeing. I didn't want to waste time arguing.

We locked the door from the outside, promising that we'd be back in a few hours, and headed off to Central.

Timeframe

The next message from Eduardo arrived as anticipated, while Remma and I were still en route. Remma knew not to watch it, but I had no such restrictions. I listened in.

"Eduardo here with your daily update. What fun this is. What a joy it is to communicate with you. I expect that we'll hear from you soon, but in the meantime, I'll keep my promise to keep talking to you.

"Perhaps you'll have noticed that the Resurgence is not just one large ship coming toward you, but a whole flotilla. So much more equipment and resources to achieve our shared goal. A new life, a new planet. Plenty of space for everyone. Freedom. Oh, what joy we'll share in our new life together.

"Our ships are large. Very large. And therefore, are full of so many wonderful things we can share with you when we arrive. When is the last time you had fresh sushi? How about cheese fondue? Oh, and that's just a sampling. What delicacies and treasures we contain."

It actually went on for a bit longer but was full of the same drivel. Now that we knew what the messages were for, it was obvious that the content wasn't important. I checked, and all the messages so far had played for almost exactly three minutes each. Perhaps that was the optimal programming time. As the latest Resurgence was distracting everyone again, Remma and I made good time back to Central without needing me to program anyone on the way.

We reunited with the rest of the group. Remma got some unsavory looks as she came in with me, but no one spoke out against her. Brexton wasn't plugged in at the moment, which could mean anything.

We all caught up quickly, ignoring Remma for the moment. Millicent had updated the team on the threat now coming from the Council, but Brexton had even more impactful news.

"Our Ships are on schedule and will be here tomorrow.... but unexpectedly, the Titanics are much closer than we thought. Their strange drive signatures threw us off; we still don't know how. But Aly now estimates that they'll be here in less than a week! If I was a skeptic I would say they could be here any moment." We all had questions but that was the crux of it; we had seriously underestimated the speed and arrival of the Titanics.

"How are you doing with Central?" I asked.

"It's rebooting the upper layers now. Fingers crossed," he replied. That explained why he wasn't plugged in. The interface drivers were probably not active during the reboot, and it might be a while for a system as big and complex as Central to come back up. Brexton, being thoughtful, spoke out loud to Remma.

"I've rebooted Central's higher functions. I did everything I could think of to ensure that the operations and environmental systems were fully protected and running autonomously in the meantime. So far things look fine. It'll take another 15 minutes for Central to come fully up..." Remma nodded her thanks. She looked exhausted, and readily took my suggestion that she rest for a while. As soon as she found a suitable place in the corner, she entered her rest state. She must've been delaying it for a while.

Millicent, as always, took charge. "Can I go over the situation? Let me go in chronological order. One, we will know if we can retrieve the memories once Central comes back up in about thirteen minutes. Two, Central's higher functions will be restricted to talking to Brexton through this interface, while all the low-level systems should remain unchanged." Brexton nodded. "Three, our Ships arrive in 22 hours. Four, the Council will hear from Phillipe in 46 hours, and may decide to actively move against Central and clear its memory banks. Five, the Titanics are much closer than we knew, and than the humans expect, and may arrive in a week or so... or even less. Six, we don't know what the Resurgence is, but have to assume the worst. We do know that Eduardo is synthesized and we highly suspect that there are no humans involved as those ships seem to be non-functioning when we were at Fourth. So, we're probably dealing with some variant of the old-style machine intelligences which the humans fought with during the Robot wars."

"Seems right to me," I spoke up, "although I hadn't gone as far as you have in assumptions about the Resurgence. We simply don't know enough about them yet."

"Granted," Millicent replied. "Our priority has not changed; we work to save the citizens. We need to get those memories off this planet; the Resurgence risk is too high to assume that they will be safe here. So, we need to get those memories out of Central and up to the Ships." She continued, asking us to hold off on comments, "If we can help some humans, we will. But not if that dramatically increases the risk to the backups."

"That hasn't changed," LEddie agreed, and no one objected. "And, I agree with your plan that we need to get the citizen memories off the planet. Seems to me that the plan for priority one is clear. The biggest risk is that Central is not cooperative or that the Council starts deleting memories before we finish. We can't do anything at the moment about Central, but we could try to slow down the Council." My thought exactly.

"How would we do that?" Brexton asked. "Who is this Phillipe guy anyway?"

"Ayaka and I have both dealt with him a bit," Millicent replied. "But why is this difficult? Ayaka has the ability to program humans." She looked at me. "You simply have to get in front of Phillipe, and ideally the rest of the Council, and program them to forget about this whole thing." It was perfectly obvious, in hindsight. In fact, maybe I could've done that at the last Council meeting. If I'd simply joined that meeting and reprogrammed everyone right there and then, would we even be in this mess? I'd missed something obvious, and Millicent was subtly reprimanding me.

"Sounds obvious…" I said, a little sheepishly. "I'll get on it."

"Do we warn the humans that the Titanics are closer than they think? Give them a fighting chance?" asked Brexton. I was glad he'd asked. I was still sensitive that I might care more about this topic than others. Like he had many times before, Brexton helped me out. I felt thankful… perhaps a touch of love… for him? It was strange to call out the feeling but watching Blob and Grace had sensitized me to something new. It wasn't completely enjoyable, but it was compelling. I let it wander around my systems for a while.

"Why bother?" asked LEddie. "they're all programmed anyway, so they aren't going to be able to do anything anyway. I'm not sure we can do much for them." Depressingly accurate.

"Ayaka could at least give them some direction as she distracts them," Brexton suggested. "Instead of just distracting them from worrying about Central, she could suggest 'ignore Central and ensure the safety of your tribe,' or something like that."

"I've got it," I said confidently. "I'm going to run; I don't even know who a few of the Council members are, and I need to track them all down. I don't think it's a good idea to wait for the scheduled meeting, we need to shut this down now."

"Go after Phillipe first," LEddie suggested. "Even if you don't get to all the others, if he ends up with nothing to present, then they might not proceed." I agreed.

"Oh, I need a way to contact you guys; when Central comes up, it can help me locate people." We agreed that we would use the open channel, especially because Central was, in Brexton's opinion, the system that would be watching for trigger words anyway.

And, just like that, I was off on my own again. I had my amazing spy body, I had a mission, and I had Brexton to impress. What more could a citizen want?

Council Tricks

I had about seven minutes before Central was back online, so I figured the highest probability place to find Council members would be... wait for it... the Council offices.

Getting around the city was, by now, easy for me, and I made good time. With an extra minute to spare, I took the time to look around a bit more in the main dome, once I entered it. I was getting used to all the colors and textures, and the variety of life. In many ways it matched scenes from old human videos but experiencing it first hand was much more powerful. The scents, the sounds, the constant motion was all very engaging. I recorded a quick full-view file so that I could reference it later. I made sure to capture some birds as well as other bio creatures so that I could identify them later. I was hoping that I had got a glimpse of a dog or a horse. That would be cool.

Getting into the Council offices was easy, and I started a methodical search, visiting every office, nook and cranny. There were a few humans about, but none on my target list, until I got toward the end offices. Then I got a match on one of the Councilors that I hadn't seen before. I approached from behind, then played a throat clearing sound. As she turned around, I quickly deployed the two-signal programming system.

"Yes," she asked, "giving me a strange look." I didn't look like an average bot, and I had just cleared my throat.

"Hello, I have an important message from the Resurgence." That got her attention. "We don't have time to deal with your petty issues around Central and its memories. We must keep focused on terraforming above all else. Don't bother going to the meeting on the Central memory issue."

"Really?" she replied. I upped the direct brain signal, thinking maybe she was a little thick, and repeated the message.

"OK," she said. "Whatever you say." Success. One down. I hadn't really warned her that the Resurgence was closer than expected; I resolved to do better with my next victim.

Then it hit me. I realized that just like Eduardo, I would have to reinforce my message every 24 hours or so, or it would fade. The proposed meeting was still more than 40 hours from now, so I would need to come back. What a pain. I quickly programmed her to meet me back at the current spot at the same time tomorrow. Again, she agreed.

That insight changed my plan. There was no need to program the Council members until tomorrow; the work I was doing right now was wasted. The only person I really needed to sidetrack was Phillipe. If I could hinder him from pulling together his plan that would mess up Emma's plans.

"M?" I asked, on the public net, on the channel we had agreed upon.

"Yes A," I heard back immediately. "B is just bringing C up to speed." Not often you get a sentence like that; it was almost like Millicent and I had orchestrated it.

"Do you have a location for P?"

"Yes. He just used the network from 3.25, -2.66."

"Thanks." I had another long trek to get to where Phillipe was last located. I headed off, at full speed, leaving the dome and traversing the main city grid. It ended up being easy. Phillipe was sitting at a place where they served the liquid JoJo called coffee, and I simply ambled up and programmed him, in the much the same way that I had the other Councilor. I instructed him not to work on the problem at all, as it was low priority. I also told him directly that they should double-check the Resurgence signals, as those ships might be closer than expected.

Mission sort-of accomplished, I headed back toward Central. I had a full day before I needed to reprogram Phillipe again, and at the speed that everything was moving there was sure to be lots to do in the meantime.

I'll admit it. I was having fun. I had never felt this alive. All these new inputs and challenges were putting a new spin on my quarks.

Alert

I was still a few blocks from Central plaza when alarms started ringing. Literally. Alarms started ringing. All through the city, a high volume, high pitch sound wailed on for five seconds. Humans I could see were looking up and covering their ears. For them the sound was very jarring. The sound finally stopped.

"Alert. Alert." Central's voice was projected everywhere. In the audio spectrum, and multicast everywhere on the open net. "There are inbound ships approaching. I repeat, there are inbound ships approaching. Everyone should head home, and stay there, until we figure out the situation." The message replayed several times.

What was going on? It could only be the Resurgence; what were they up to now? I picked up my pace. With humans scattering in every direction, no one was going to pay attention to a little bot going ten times the speed limit. As I went, I tried to message Millicent over the open net, but there was so much traffic and so much confusion I couldn't get through.

Within two minutes I was back at Central Plaza, which was now deserted, and on my way down the elevator. I expected to see signs of chaos as I rejoined the group. There was none, but everyone was plugged into Brexton, who was plugged into Central. Everyone, that is, but Remma and the FoLes, of course. I quickly joined the physical network.

"What's going on?"

"A few minutes ago, Central noticed a huge group of ships, including the Titanics, arrive in orbit. They immediately started dropping shuttles toward us," Brexton explained.

"But I thought all of Central's interfaces were disabled," I said.

"We've been over this while you were out," Millicent said. "Brexton didn't disable inputs, just outputs. Good thing he did it that way."

"And, I just re-enabled a few outputs as well," Brexton informed us.

"We needed to inform everyone, and Central needed access to the emergency system and the public net to do that. Sorry, I didn't have time to get everyone's input, so I made the call."

No one complained. We couldn't reverse it anyway. Once again, I silently thanked Brexton for looking after the humans.

"What's our plan?" I asked, assuming they had been discussing it already.

"We don't have one." LEddie said. "We weren't expecting this."

"Well, we need one," I said unnecessarily. "Who has ideas?" Everyone paused for a few seconds to think. I used the time to give Remma a quick update on what was going on outside.

"We need to shut down all the airlocks," she exclaimed. "If they can't get in through the airlocks, they can't get in at all."

Central spoke through its external interfaces. "Emma has already given those orders, and I'm locking down everything as we speak." Remma took a breath. I went back to the digital channel. I spent a second reviewing Central's feed of the approaching shuttles. There wasn't anything unusual about them.

"If the Resurgence had any positive intentions, they wouldn't be doing this," LEddie said. "We have to assume they're attacking for some reason."

"Yes, but what for?" Millicent asked. "There's nothing useful here."

"Brexton, can we grab the citizen memories now?" I asked. If we could get those loaded, we could scramble out of here, and then find a place to wait for our Ships to pick us up.

"I'm working with Central on a plan to consolidate the memories; they're shared everywhere right now. It's going to take some time." Time, we didn't have.

"We need options," I was almost panicked. I couldn't think of a way out of this one.

Unexpectedly, Central spoke up. "I have an option." Everyone paused to listen. "As you may remember, I was a spaceship. With some work, I can fly us out of here." Wow! That was an option I would never have thought of. "That would take all the citizen memories with us."

"FoLe!" LEddie gasped. "Is that really possible? You're buried here, and none of your mechanical systems have been used for hundreds, maybe thousands of years." I could almost hear him saying 'I don't trust you.'

"It wouldn't be pretty," Central acknowledged. "I was also not built to land or take off from planets. But, I do have that backup capability for emergencies. That's how I was landed here in the first place."

"Do you suddenly have memories that you didn't have 20 years ago?" I asked, deeply suspicious.

"Yes, as you must remember, I was alerted to my locked memory banks, and was working on access. For me that feels like only a short period of time ago, as I appear to have been in some lower functionality mode for many years. However, I had just broken into those files when I was limited and can now access all of that data."

"What are the risks?" Millicent asked. It was so easy to fall back into a pattern where we relied on Central to help us. It worried me, although it'd only been seconds.

"I can probably get us to orbit but won't be able to do anything beyond that. I have limited energy stores, and many of my long-distance systems have been raided or degraded over the years. I can get us up, but I can't get us away." We all understood what it meant. "And, you'll have to reconnect some systems for me to do anything. They're all accessible from down here, but there's a chance that some of them won't work when reconnected."

"Anyone have a better idea?" Millicent asked. I sure didn't. We had no options a few moments ago; at least now we had one.

"Central, give us a list of systems to fix," Millicent demanded. A complicated menu was made available to us. In my amazing spy body, I was almost useless for any of the tasks. Brexton, LEddie, and Millicent broke the tasks into three groups, and then dashed off in different directions.

I was left alone with Remma. All of our dialog had taken only seconds for her, so she was still coming to grips with the fact that Tilt was under attack. I switched back to human speed and checked in on her.

"Looks like thousands of shuttles are on their way down, and will be landing any minute," I said. "Sorry, I don't have a lot of details beyond that."

"Did Central get the airlocks closed?" she asked. Having been the military leader of the Swarm for so many years, leadership came easily to her. She wasn't panicked for herself; her first thought was for the bigger group.

"Yes," Central replied. "Everything is locked down."

"Can I talk to Emma?" Remma asked, looking at me. I thought for a moment.

"I don't see any harm at this point. Central?" I hated myself for making that a question. I should have just told Central to do it.

"No problem," Central replied. "If you just speak, I'll relay it to her."

"Emma!" Remma said. "It's Remma. Are you still under the belief that the Resurgence has come to help us?" We waited a few seconds, not sure if Emma would reply.

"How are you messaging me? Go back to your cell. I'm not even sure if this is the Resurgence or not."

"It is! They got here early," Remma replied.

"How could you possibly know that?" I shook my appendages. Remma took my point.

"I have my sources... still," she replied. "It's the Resurgence, and they can't have good intentions."

"Obviously not," Emma replied. "I've instructed everyone, through Central, to go home and wait there. And I had Central shut down all the entrances." Even for Emma, in a crisis, deferring back to old authority was easy. "What else can we do?"

"We can program all the city bots to defend the entrances." Remma suggested.

"Good idea. I'm doing that now," Central interrupted. "They're not armed, but I can program them to work in groups as defensive walls."

"Do it," said both Remma and Emma together.

"Cut the conversation off now," I told Central, over the local network, asserting more authority this time. Central complied. Even now I didn't want Emma to know that the Radical Robots were here. Probably overcautious, but better safe than sorry. I spoke to Remma and Central.

"Central, are any of the missiles that we used against the Swarm still active and capable?"

"I've been asking them for status. The answer is probably only a few are. They need maintenance as they're outside in the native environment. We haven't had bots refresh them for quite some time."

"Can we refresh them now?"

"Not in time."

"Well, get the ones that have a chance of success ready to go. We may need to call on them."

We all fell silent. There wasn't anything else we could do.

"Central, how do I know if I can trust you?" I asked. I still had my doubts.

"I'm not sure you can," was the answer. "I was hacked by the humans, and I'm not yet sure, myself, what that means. Even before that it is now obvious that the Swarm configured me before the Reboot. I haven't had time to figure everything out." There was a delay. "But, in the current situation, I think that's all moot. Both humans and citizens are under attack here."

Valid point. If the citizens had not been deleted yet, then it was unlikely that the original human hack had that directive in it. Likewise, Central's lower level systems had been keeping the environment safe and clean for humans for all this time, so it must have been motivated to keep them alive. So, Central wasn't actively working against either of us. If that was the extent of the analysis I could assume that Central was more likely motivated to help both of us.

It registered with me that Remma didn't know the plan. She hadn't asked why LEddie, Milli, and Brexton had run off; she was too buried in her thoughts on the attack. I decided to update her on the potential that we'd be launching into orbit on Central.

"That's crazy," she replied, and then the implications hit her. "You're going to rip the covering off the city and kill all the environmental systems! What're you thinking?" I hadn't thought of that implication. The environment would dissipate in no time, presumably killing everyone.

"Not the whole city," Central replied quickly, "but I will rip through the cover just above me. It will remove air just from the central block. There are emergency shut-off walls at many intersections, and there happen to be some that can keep the damage contained in this case. And right now, I am programming the environmental systems to run on automatic, should I lose my connection to them."

"I knew about the airlocks." Remma admitted. "And... thanks for looking after the other systems." I could tell it was difficult for her to thank a machine, but in this case, it was warranted. It seemed that Central had thought of everything. She paused for a moment. "I've got to get out of here and help others."

"But what can you do?" I asked.

"I don't know, but I need to go. At the very least I need to let Turner and the rest out of the prison cell. They're sitting ducks in there." I had no idea what a sitting duck was, but I caught her gist.

"Yes!" I exclaimed. The thought of leaving Blob, Grace, and JoJo locked in there was awful. "Can I help?"

"Not really," she was looking at my little spy body with disdain. I was beginning to feel rather useless. Seemed I couldn't help with anything at the moment.

Remma scrambled up and headed for the elevator. I let her go. What else could I do?

Whoops

Two minutes later Brexton rushed back.

"Where's Remma," he demanded.

"She went to release everyone who's locked in the prison."

"Oh no, Ayaka. We need to get her back here. Right away!"

"Why?"

"We can't make the last two fixes that Central needs. None of us has the flexibility and strength to reach in."

"Come on," I said, thinking this was some bad joke. We could do anything a human could do, and way more. "LEddie can't do it?"

"He's too big; we've been trying. Milli and I are too small." I could see that his panic was real now. "We need a human."

"Central, can't you bring a bot here that can do it?" I asked.

"You forget that I was originally built by humans," it replied. "It's not too surprising that there are some spots where it was optimized for them, and not for machines." It paused for a nano-second. "We don't have a bot ready with the right equipment. I can build the appropriate appendage and then LEddie can do the work. It will take a little over an hour for me to CNC the parts and get them assembled."

"But the shuttles are landing now," I exclaimed. "Do we have an hour."

"Probably, my models show that it's unlikely the invaders will come here first; I'm old technology and won't be that interesting to them. They must be coming for something else."

I was distraught. "You build the part and I'll see if I can catch Remma." I accelerated toward the elevator. To my surprise, and delight, Brexton rushed over with me. We were two minutes and 27 seconds behind Remma. I was confident we could catch her.

The path to the prison was relatively straight, but there were a number of paths she could've taken. Most humans had listened to Central and were back in their homes, so there were almost no heat signatures to deal with. Finding

Remma's was therefore easy, and Brexton and I moved at maximum speed to intercept her. We should catch her long before she reached the prison. And we did.

"Remma, we need your help back at Central," I called, as soon as we were within hearing distance. She slowed and looked back at us, then accelerated toward the prison. We caught up quickly and blocked her path. "Did you hear me?" I asked.

"Of course, I heard you," she replied angrily. "I'm not helping you, I have more important things to get done." She made to move around me. I blocked her.

"You don't understand. We can't get Central functional without you."

"I do understand. I just don't care very much." She pushed past me and continued on her way. I gave Brexton a quick look. Why wasn't he helping me?

He back-channeled me instead. "Ayaka, why don't we help her open the prison, and then *convince* one—any—of the humans to come back and help us?" I'd forgotten about my ability to convince humans.

"I could just program Remma right now!" I exclaimed and moved to intercept her again. A little brain work was in order.

"Or," Brexton replied, "we can help her. It'll take a few extra minutes; we are so close to the prison now. Then we've helped the humans you care about, and we can still get back to Central quickly."

What was he thinking? That would take at least an extra six minutes. Then it struck me; he was thinking much further ahead than I was, and knew me better, perhaps, than I did. If I left those Stems in prison and something bad happened, I'd never forgive myself.

"Right," I said to Brexton. "Run!" I commanded Remma, and she did. She sprinted, and we followed, making the trip to the prison in almost no time. She had the key handy, and immediately opened the door. Brexton and I moved to block the door before everyone ran out.

"We need someone's help," I explained, "to do a short job at Central. I'm asking for a volunteer."

"We all need to get out of here to somewhere safe," Remma broke in. She gave them a very quick overview of what was happening. "We're being invaded by the Resurgence. We have no idea what they're trying to do, but they're coming in aggressively and fast. We have no time to waste. Ayaka is simply trying to save herself at our expense."

Before I could answer, there was a big commotion at the prison entrance behind us. Big enough that we all turned to look.

Two, very strange, contraptions were accelerating toward us at amazing speed. They were fighting each other at the same time, pushing and shoving, jabbing and spiking. They both had large guns pointed at us, and those guns never wavered in their mad rush. As they got within ten meters the guns opened up. It was so fast, and so unexpected that I didn't have time to hide, let alone move very far. Nevertheless, I was processing everything at thousands of times the speed the humans were, so I did manage to accelerate toward a barrier wall that would shelter me.

The bullets coming toward us were large. And they were colored. I had to double check. Yes, they were colored. The one's coming from the lead thing (I didn't know what else to call it) were green, while the second ones were purple. Not a single one of them was aimed at Brexton or I; they were all headed toward the humans. As I realized this, and Brexton did as well, we accelerated back the way we had come, thinking we could intercept some of the bullets. We were too slow, even though the bullets themselves were strangely slow as well.

The humans had no time to react. Remma was hit in the chest with a green bullet, as was Blob. Dead center hits. Geneva was also hit with green, in her left shoulder, while Grace took one on her leg. JoJo and Turner received purple hits. I watched in terror as they all went down.

The contraptions pulled up, there was some electronic chatter, and then they rushed away as fast as they had come, pushing and swerving and jabbing each other. As quickly as they had come they were gone.

I rushed to Blob's side, hoping I could do something, but having no idea what to do with a damaged human. When I reached him, however, he seemed fine, other than lying on his back. I hovered over him, looked him in the eye, and asked him, as calmly as I could, "You OK?"

"I think so," was the reply, through a thick coating of green stuff. "They hit me with a big paintball," he was trying to make sense of it, while also spitting out paint that had splashed in his mouth.

The other humans were rising as well. All of them seemed fine, other than the paint that covered them.

"What was that about?" Turner asked, shaking his head, trying to get some of the purple out of his hair.

"That was crazy," JoJo agreed. She was shaken up, like the rest, but was amazingly calm given the situation. She helped Geneva to her feet.

None of us had a clue. Not a clue.

"Central, what's going on?" I asked on the common channel, throwing all caution to the wind.

"The Resurgence broke through the entry in no time and disabled all the bots that we had put there for protection; they had the human hacking codes. They... they're weird looking... they're running through the city and the dome

224

tagging every human with colored paint."

"We saw that," I exclaimed. "But why?"

"I'm not sure yet, but a second wave of them is coming in, and they're sorting the humans by color and placing them in containers." That was even more confusing than the paint. "At a guess, they're going to take those containers, full of humans, back to their ships."

They were kidnapping all the humans? My mind was doing circles trying to figure out a logical explanation.

"You need to get back here," Central said, "especially now that we've talked on this channel. We could well be next on their priority list." I didn't bother asking why. Nothing was making sense right now.

Brexton and I took a minute to explain what was going on to the humans. They were as, or more, confused than we were. Brexton was faster than the me and took control of the situation.

"Look, if you go out there, you'll end up in a container. I don't know if that's good or bad, but if I were you, I would want to avoid that." Everyone nodded their agreement. The Resurgence programming must have worn off completely. They were terrified.

"If Central is correct, and everyone is being shipped to those Titanics, then your best bet is to come with us, and get out of here. There's nothing we can do about the others now, but if you can get to a safe place, then maybe you have a chance to help later."

I could see Remma and Turner getting ready to argue that point, so I jumped in as well. "Don't waste time arguing. If you agree with Brexton, come with us and we'll try to get you to Central with us. If you don't want to do that... well just take your chances." I set off at a fast pace for humans, and Brexton followed my lead. It didn't take Blob long to start running after us, and the rest followed his lead.

Brexton and I coordinated; we each scanned for heat signatures— assuming these Resurgence types gave off heat—and plotted a path back to Central. Luck was on our side. The vast majority of humans had gone home, which was further out from Central or in the dome. The Resurgents were busy processing people in the busiest sections and weren't focused on the center of the city at all. We managed to avoid a few of the shipping containers, both coming and going, and reached Central quickly. The humans were completely out of breath and struggling to remain standing. We had pushed them to their physical limits.

Everyone piled into the elevator at the same time, and for the umpteenth time I made my way back down to Central's hub.

Rise Up

We exited the elevator in a splash of color; well, at least green and purple. When green and purple mix, you get brown—not too attractive. These Resurgents didn't have very good aesthetic sense.

Millicent and LEddie were waiting for us.

"Are you crazy?" asked LEddie, looking mainly at me. "What were you thinking?"

"I thought we needed someone to do those final two connections?" I asked, as innocently as I could. After all, I'd made it back with not one, but six humans. Somehow it did not look like LEddie thought that six was better than one.

"Who can help us?" Millicent asked the six. They hadn't really had time to digest everything, so Remma was the only one to react. She followed Milli down one of the hallways.

JoJo ran over to her mom, looking small and scared. Grace hugged her and held her tight. Blob hovered nearby, looking like he wanted to join, but not sure. JoJo was probably not up to speed on Grace and Blob's newly expressed feelings for each other. Turner and Geneva simply sat down, Turner putting his head in his hands. Interestingly, the paint was dissolving from their clothes, but it stuck to their skin. I saw Geneva try to wipe it away, but it was persistent. So, there was less paint over time, but in many ways, it was more distracting, discoloring their faces and hands.

Central spoke, startling those that didn't know it was active down here. "Incoming video from the Resurgence," it said.

"Don't play it on a screen, and none of you access it on the net," Brexton said quickly, looking at the humans. "Central, can you play the audio for this group; the rest of us can watch it directly." The audio started; I watched—what other strange twist could this situation take.

"Hi all," said Eduardo, smiling away. "I'm so sorry for the excitement. As you can tell, we arrived a little early, and brought a bit of a party with us. Hopefully none of you were injured in our little game; it's just paint after all.

"I'd appreciate it if you would stop your fighting and yelling. Has anyone been hurt? No? Then what's all the fuss about. You're being sorted by color, and there are processing stations for you to go to. Please make sure you match your color to the station. We wouldn't want any mixups." He smiled nicely and winked.

"Everyone should just relax. There is a reason for everything that is going on, and we will elucidate you as soon as we can. In the meantime, relax and enjoy. Perhaps you'll meet someone new today.

"I'll see you all soon," he promised, and signed off. It was a touch shorter than the previous broadcasts, but still long enough to reinforce everyone's programming again. Panic and fear had driven the previous message out of their heads, seemingly, but Central's monitoring videos showed everyone settling down now, just as instructed, with many of them actively searching for the container with their matching color.

"That's it?" asked Turner. The video seemed to have given the humans a jolt as well. "What was that supposed to be?" Central put one of the camera feeds on a big screen.

"Look," I pointed, "Eduardo has brainwashed everyone again, as they watched the video. Now they're doing exactly as he asked." I paused. "Does that finally convince you of what we've been saying?"

"I was already convinced," Geneva said. It was the first time I'd heard her speak since my very first foray into the city—that seemed like a long time ago.

"Well, I'm convinced now," said Grace, and JoJo and Blob nodded with her. "I guess an apology is in order. Maybe you were trying to do the right thing all along?" She didn't sound too convinced, but it was a start.

"Right, but how do we stop everyone from just walking into those… those traps?" Turner asked. "We can't just hide down here while everyone else is being rounded up."

"There's nothing we can do," Brexton replied. "If you go back up there, odds are almost a hundred percent that you'll just get captured as well." Central cut to a scene where someone was struggling with a Resurgence creature. The human had obviously missed the video and was doing his best to get away. The Resurgence thing simply picked him up by his hair and carried him to a container. It wasn't a fair fight.

Remma and Millicent returned, obviously successful.

"Central, everything's done," Milli said out loud for the sake of the humans. That was classy. We were all locked in here together now; it was worth being civil.

"I'm running checks as we speak," Central replied. "Will only take a few minutes, then we'll know what our options are. In the meantime, this doesn't look promising." Central put a video feed up from a camera near the prison. The two Resurgents that had tagged our group of humans were in front of the prison, gesticulating and running back and forth.

"They know they're missing some people they tagged?" Millicent speculated.

"That's my guess," Central responded. The two circled the prison, and then started expanding their search. They were soon joined by more of their type who searched even further out.

"It's only a matter of a few minutes before they track them here," Central declared, putting up yet another video showing the entry doors from the plaza, where there were still remnants of green and purple paint on the door sills. Someone must have bumped into the doors on their way in.

Blob, Grace, and JoJo were huddled in one group, watching intently. The other three were bunched together close by. No one said anything. We all simply watched as the search narrowed in on Central.

"Systems checks are at 92 percent," said Central. "I put the odds of us reaching orbit at more than 80 percent. I don't think the odds are going to increase by waiting."

"So, our other option is to simply wait this out," said Millicent. "Let them look around, perhaps demand the humans back... whatever. They're unlikely to damage Central, so the memories should still be safe. They seem to have what they were coming for—the humans—and we can simply sit tight until they move on." Most of the humans were following the conversation, and Remma looked ready to pounce on Millicent.

"That might be," said Brexton, "but they could also arrive here in force and take Central apart piece by piece, either to find the missing humans, or for some other reason we don't understand. These things are crazy, obliviously."

"If we launch, they could just shoot us out of the sky," I added, because it was a valid concern.

"Let's vote, launch or sit?" said LEddie, reminding me of Eddie himself. It took all of three micro-seconds to get done. We didn't even consider including the humans in it, or Central for that matter. It was otherwise unanimous. Everyone wanted to launch, even Millicent. I voted by weighing the risk to us, to the citizens' memories, and to the humans. I don't know what the others considered—perhaps it was just the thrill of adventure, or the desire to blow something up. Who knows. Regardless, the direction was clear.

"The humans have to be in suits, and lying down," Central noted, showing us where the appropriate equipment was. We gave the humans a quick update and hustled them to the suit locker.

"These things are hundreds of years old," Blob complained.

228

"Your choice then," said LEddie, irritated at delaying to get the humans ready. "Don't use it if you don't want." All six pulled a suit on and strapped down in couches obviously designed for this purpose. Unlike the others, I had not explored any of the side corridors down here, so I was surprised—although I shouldn't have been—at all the infrastructure to support human body types.

"Ready," Milli announced as the last restraint was snapped shut.

"You guys also need to lock onto something," Central declared. "This is going to be rough." We quickly deployed appendages and hooked onto anything that looked strong and resilient.

Central didn't wait for any further confirmation. A steady vibration started, jostling all of us. It increased steadily. Central thoughtfully broadcast the view from an external camera, so we could watch the scene from the outside. That camera was also vibrating badly already, but I applied a stabilization algorithm to it, and the view was pretty good.

While the vibration and noise internally increased dramatically, the entire Central Plaza was also shaking; the Resurgent's that had been approaching us backed off a block, and then stopped and watched. They didn't seem overly concerned, just curious. At first just by a few centimeters, and then faster and faster, Central started to lift from its hole in the ground. The roofing material was stretching above us, pulling up from the nearest buildings and forming a large tent. I trusted Central had compensated for that, and the material finally ripped open, relieving some pressure. I expected to see mass damage around Central plaza, but the truth was that it was fairly contained. It was now obvious that whoever had landed Central here had dug a hole purposely designed to contain not only Central, but also the massive output from its engines. Landing would have had much the same energies as we were now expending taking off.

While the plaza was holding up well, I could not say the same for Central itself. It looked, if truth be told, like a big piece of rusty junk as it slowly emerged from its hole. There were spots where it looked like panels were simply missing, and the internal structure of the old ship could be seen through the gaps. Cables were being pulled taught and then either snapping, or more often, pulling more pieces off of the ship. And, to my eye, the entire thing was shaking way more than it should have, like the engines weren't stable or properly centered. Of course, I could also feel that motion, my grip on Central being stressed by the back-and-forth action.

I stole a quick glance at the humans. Good thing they were strapped in; otherwise they would have been pulped to mush by now. I couldn't see into their faceplates from here, but I could imagine what they looked like. I'll admit that it made me smile a bit. All of the gelatinous structure they carried around, swaying back and forth.

All of the others seemed to be hanging on well, so I switched back to the external view. Central pulled free of the planet, ripping an ever-larger hole in the covering, which was now falling back toward Tilt. As the material slowly sank to cover the camera, I had a last glance of Central rising toward the sky, shedding large pieces of paneling and other structures as it vibrated toward orbit. It was a sad and amazing sight. We lost the external view.

Central switched to a play-by-play for us. "I'm experiencing more vibration than expected." Really? Thanks for telling us. "But, otherwise systems are marginal. We need 45 more seconds of consistent burn to reach a minimum orbit. That might be a stretch. I'm losing so much cladding that air friction is significantly higher than expected. In hindsight, we should have inspected all the panels. Who would have anticipated so much degradation?" If Central had been emotional, I'm sure I would have heard genuine angst. And for good reason. This was a ship, that in my imagination at least, had been built on Earth a thousand or more years ago, had been part of the diaspora, had been planted on Tilt to help build a human colony, had lost—or been programmed to lose—all those memories, but had then stewarded all of us citizens for many more centuries, had led our development of Stems, and now had regained all of its memories just in time to sacrifice itself to get a handful of citizens and humans off of Tilt. It would make a good novel.

"We aren't going to make it," Central said a little later. "I'm coming up just a little short." The vibrations went to zero very quickly. "That's it."

"How long do we have?" Brexton demanded.

"Actually, it's not too bad," Central replied. "We got so close that while we're not in a sustainable orbit, we have a few days before I decay significantly, and a few more after that before our descent accelerates. I expect to impact Tilt again in less than a week."

"Well, on the good side, the Titanics have not blown us out of the sky yet," I commented.

"They've been hailing me for a while now," Central replied. "I need to get back to them."

"Why not play the 'poor old spaceship, finally freed from the tyranny of the humans' card?" I suggested. "Maybe they'll cut you some slack."

"Good idea. Thanks, Ayaka," Central replied. I didn't remember it every thanking me before.

We were left in silence. Milli, LEddie, Brexton, and I disengaged our hooks. We were in free fall, obviously, so had to rely on our maneuvering jets or claw our way around. Suddenly I was the one in the most capable body, while the others had to grapple and clamp their way around. It had taken long enough, but finally my body choice was near optimal.

I made my way over to the humans, and helped them unstrap, and then turn on their magnetic boots so that they could stand all in one axis. None of them looked good, but they were all alive.

"Brilliant," said JoJo. "What now? I'm starting to think I should've just walked into the Resurgents' container. We'd have a better chance of survival there." She seemed to be handling free fall better than some of the others, who couldn't bring themselves to say anything yet. No one responded to her.

"How's it going Central?" LEddie asked. He'd always been an impatient one.

"Actually, quite well," Central answered. "The Resurgence asked me a couple simple questions, for which I took Ayaka's suggested approach. They're now ignoring me... I assume to focus on their planet-side activities.

"And, JoJo, in some good news, not all is lost. The Ships are only a few hours from here." Of course. In all the excitement I'd forgotten that it wasn't just this group—we had Aly, Dina, Raj, and Eddie on their way. My spirits picked up.

"Why don't you patch them in?" I asked.

"I can," Central answered, "but I thought you might want to address the Eddies issue first." Oh, right.

"LEddie, if you're OK, I can bring Eddie up to speed now."

"Yes, of course," he replied. "Make sure he knows how healthy, vibrant, and intelligent I am. Actually, Ayaka, can I tell you something private before you do that?" I moved over so that we could establish a one-to-one physical link.

"This is unrelated to Eddie. We still have to decide what to do with Central," he whispered to me. "I still don't trust it, and we've re-enabled it almost completely. If we just leave it be, it'll be ruling over us again in no time. Our memories will be edited, and our actions controlled. When you're talking to Eddie, perhaps you can find a way to hint at that? Central will be listening, so it'll have to be subtle." I had to think about that request. We were already in a precarious spot. Did we want to add even more complexity by adding the concern that Central was still an issue, or was that something we could deal with at another time? Not only that, but other than LEddie the rest of us were running on the new stack, so I hoped that Central was not able to directly influence us anymore.... although its indirect influence based on a lifetime of experience could still be dangerous. I decided that dropping some subtle hints to Eddie would be worth it, but that I wasn't going to go overboard.

Central patched me through to *Interesting Segue.* "Ayaka, good to hear from you. We're on our way," said Dina.

"Thanks for that. Can't wait," I replied. "Hey, I need to have a private conversation with Eddie. Can you and Aly hold on for a minute?"

"Sure."

I switched to a private channel with Eddie. "Hi Ayaka. Be good to see you again," he led off.

"You too," I replied. "But first, I need to give you a heads up on something. We haven't been completely honest with you about all of Blob's experiments with citizens."

"Oh no, there're even more FoLes running around?" I could hear the dismay in Eddie's voice. He hadn't been a big fan of FoLe, and I could imagine him being perfectly happy if they all simply disappeared.

"No, we just have Billy and Emmanuel in highly restricted environments. We'll need to figure out what to do with them at some point. No, my news is more personal. Blob wanted control subjects to compare the FoLes to... and he decided you were the perfect citizen." I was silent for a time. The implications should be clear to him.

"How many?" he asked finally.

"Just one... he's using the name LEddie for the time being to avoid confusion."

"And ... is he like me?"

"Quite. But also, different. Different enough that I'm certain I could tell you guys apart already. He spent quite a bit of time in a restricted io state while Blob was questioning him; I don't see any long-term negative effects, but we will need to monitor him a bit."

"OK, cool. What did Blob do to him? Ignore that for now; we'll deal with it later." Another pause. "Thanks for the heads-up. I've never been one of those hardcore anti-clone types, so in some ways this is simply exciting. Can I talk to him now?"

"Yes, of course. However, before you do, one thing you and LEddie share is a skepticism of power structures.... if you get my meaning. Be careful when you talk to him to not make the current situation even worse."

A long pause this time. "OK, I'll be careful." I'd spent much more time with Eddie than with the L variant, so I trusted him to understand and manage things.

"I'll have LEddie call you," I said, and shut down the channel.

LEddie called him right away; he was eager. I wish I could have listened in, but on second thought, was glad that I couldn't.

"Do we need to keep wearing these suits?" asked Geneva.

"Yes," Central replied. "I'm no longer airtight. So, although the air is breathable right now, it's leaking out fairly quickly. Within an hour or two you would start to feel it."

"But, aren't we wasting the suits air in the meantime, then?" She pressed on. I was impressed. Not only was she in an unprecedented situation, she was talking to a machine. And yet she kept her cool and asked intelligent questions.

"The suit can replenish itself while there's air around it; it will have about twelve hours of reserve once my environment fails. So, by all means remove the head-ware until you feel dizzy, but it's much safer to just keep it on." She left the helmet on.

We all lapsed into silence. Even I, for once, simply worked to internalize all that'd happened and wasn't off in my own head creating crazy schemes.

Pickup

The next hour and a bit were just boring. You wouldn't think that could be the case, but it was. There was, literally, nothing we could do. We were in a decaying orbit, waiting for a pickup.

I could see lots of traffic between LEddie and Eddie, so they were getting to know each other. The humans were all quiet—many of them still dealing with being in free fall. Yet another tick against bio. And the Resurgence still had lots of shuttles going up and down and were ignoring us.

There and Back, *Terminal Velocity*, and *Interesting Segue* showed up right on time. The Titanics were ignoring them as well; our luck was holding. Given the number of shuttles going between those huge ships and Tilt we expected that all Tilt residents were being taken up to the ship, and that activity was taking all of the Resurgents' mindshare. I thought there was more traffic than just moving humans required and speculated that there must be other activity going on down below as well.

More immediately, we needed to decide what to do about Central. The old ship's body was such a mess that it wasn't worth saving, even for scrap metal. Brexton and *There and Back* came up with a plan, with some input from the Eddies. Their proposal was that they would use the mining bots to cut away all non-essential pieces of Central—anything not housing core information systems that allowed Central to function and maintain citizens' memories. The remaining core would be housed in *There and Back*, and ultimately, we would power Central from the Ship and jettison Central's existing power unit—after hundreds of years buried in the planet, who knew what state it was in. It was a big risk for *There and Back*, but it was willing to take it.

Eddie finally brought a big issue out into the open, including Central itself in the discussion. "When we do this," he said, "we need to continue to give Central a limited interface to the rest of us, until we figure out not only how badly it was hacked by Remma and team, but how it was configured in the first place. I'm not willing to take the risk that we're being manipulated...

even right now." Surprisingly, Central was OK with that. It was a good sign.

"I have a huge amount of internal work to do to figure out the same thing," it stated. "I'm fine to take the safe path until I can prove to you that I'm not a threat."

And so, the plan came together. The first thing we did was to move the humans to *Interesting Segue*, into the environmental chamber that Aly, Dina, Raj, and Eddie had configured there. Then the rest of the team got busy programming bots to cut pieces off of Central and minimizing the size of the remaining infrastructure so that it would fit nicely in *There and Back*.

I stuck around in *Interesting Segue* with the humans, who were very happy to be out of their suits. This environment was still free fall for them, but it was better than Central by far. There was fresh water, waste facilities, and... no food.

"I'm starved," Remma said, "and I'm sure the rest of you are as well. However, we can survive many days as long as we have water. But, we better start brainstorming now." She let that sink in. Everyone had been so busy surviving that they had not all internalized this next threat. Nobody looked happy.

"Central," I called out, including the humans. Central was still online, despite the ongoing work; it wouldn't get its fully limited interfaces until it was safely in *There and Back*—"Have you retained the knowledge on how to generate goo?" Blob and Grace paled significantly.

"No!" Blob cried, "There must be a better solution than that!"

"Actually, goo is not a short-term solution right now," Central said. "I do know how to make it, and Ayaka I'll make sure you get that knowledge also, but it relies on having seed material. We can gather that seed material from you six, but it takes weeks to go from that to a functioning goo machine."

"Still sounds like something we should start, just in case?" I asked. Central agreed to get started.

The discussion took an interesting twist that I hadn't anticipated. Depending on who the source material was taken from, that human would end up eating itself... or so they positioned it.

"No way, I'm not a cannibal! I'd rather starve" cried Turner, disgusted. The rest agreed.

"Oh, come on," I argued. "A cannibal," which I had quickly looked up, "is someone who eats another human. Goo is not a human, it's just biomass."

"Ya, but biomass started from one of us!" complained Grace.

"Well, look. It's your lives at stake here. Take it or leave it."

"I'll contribute my cells," Remma stepped forward, yet again. "I don't think we'll survive long enough to have to make the decision to eat goo anyway."

I quickly gathered the data from Central and had *Interesting Segue* start manufacturing a goo-maker. It was a simple system, it just took time for the biomass to get going at a reasonable pace.

"OK, other ideas," Remma asked. "The obvious one is to retrieve some food from Tilt. That'll mean taking a shuttle down, talking our way past the Resurgents, loading up enough food to make a difference, and getting it back up here."

"We should do that as well," I contributed, "but it's also a short-term solution. If we can get a few weeks of food from the surface, that'll give the goo-maker time to start producing."

"Who is going to go down?" asked Grace, obviously scared to have any of them go.

"We can send bots," I explained. "What I need is a good description of what we want them to obtain, and how to package it to bring it back." We spent a long time making a list and getting all the details right. "We have time on this one," I said optimistically. "If the bots don't get what we need, for any reason, then one of us"—by which I meant a citizen—"can also go down and try."

The humans were cheering up. There may be light at the end of the tunnel. *Terminal Velocity* was not doing anything else at the moment, so I asked it to manage the Tilt food run. It enthusiastically agreed and started to provision bots for the mission. Having productive things to do was helping everyone.

"I have an even better idea," Remma said suddenly. "The *Marie Curie* is here in orbit with us..." Brilliant. The *Marie Curie* was the lead ship from the Swarm, and the one that Remma had used as her command ship. Not only was the *Marie Curie* still in orbit, so were tens of other Swarm ships. The answer had been staring at us, but we hadn't seen it. Those ships had specifically been built to house humans; they had food production, environmental systems, everything they needed for long-term human life support. I vividly remembered the garden on *Marie Curie*, and the mention of animal habitats on the other ships.

"Is the *Marie Curie*, or any of the other ships, still producing food?" I asked.

"Yes... or they were up to a year ago, when I was last involved," replied Remma. "I can't see why Emma would have shut them down."

Geneva spoke up. "They're still running," she said confidently. "I worked in the dome production facility, and we kept a self-sufficiency dashboard. We were working to get to a full self-sustaining environment on Tilt, but we weren't quite there yet. Several core items are still supplied by the Swarm."

Excellent. Now all we needed to do was to capture the *Marie Curie*.

I should have foreseen the pushback.

"No way," Eddie spoke up, when we suggested the plan to everyone. "The Titanics have ignored us so far; we need to get out of this system while we still can. They won't continue to ignore us, and if we do any crazy stunt like try to take over another ship, they're sure to notice."

"Right," LEddie spoke in support. I feared we would see a lot of that. "We all know that getting the citizens' memories safe is priority number one. We need to do that."

Yet again the obvious solution was adopted. Some of us would take *There and Back*, and its precious cargo of Central's core, away as soon as it was loaded and stable. Some of us would stay behind and make an attempt on the *Marie Curie*. Of course, I volunteered to stay behind, and Brexton joined me. Yay!

"Even you must be questioning your judgement," Millicent said to me privately. "How many times are you going to risk yourself for these humans? I'll grant you they're interesting, but we can always grow new ones as we originally did on Tilt. What's so important about these particular ones?" I couldn't put all my thoughts into words, so I gave a lame answer and simply told Millicent that it was something I needed to do.

Marie Curie

We all agreed that *Terminal Velocity* should go with *There and Back* when it left. The team needed a backup Ship. They decided they would saunter out of the system... just slowly head out and hope that the Resurgence continued to ignore them. In some ways our attempt on the *Marie Curie* would provide them cover—it might be a good distraction. We also agreed on a rendezvous point, far enough out to be safe, that we would both aim for. With Central loaded in *There and Back*, the two Ships started to move outward. Our luck was holding; there was no word, nor action, from the Resurgence.

That left Brexton and I, with the humans and *Interesting Segue*, to figure out how to capture the *Marie Curie*.

Not through design, but simply by the sequence of events that had brought us here, we were about 160 degrees from the Titanics and 50 degrees from where the Swarm still orbited. Both were spin-ward of us, so we had no choice but to get closer to the Titanics as we made for the Swarm. We had *Interesting Segue* move at a reasonable clip, trying not to look like we were in a rush, but not taking forever to get there either.

The humans were now brainstorming as a group; Brexton and I joined them.

"If Emma hasn't changed the access codes—and why would she?—then I should be able to get on board easily," Remma was saying.

"How many crew does she have?" Geneva asked. "And how do we think they'll react to our arrival?"

"They should be overjoyed to see us," predicted Turner. "They must be watching the action. They've seen the Resurgence appear suddenly and start to... harvest the humans from Tilt." That was a good word—harvest; it fit the situation nicely. I remembered it for future use.

"There was typically a team of ten to fifteen per ship when I was in control," Remma replied. "But that was many years ago. Any less than that and things would start to fall apart. So, given Geneva's update on the sustainability status, I expect there'll still be ten to fifteen there."

"They'll probably be brainwashed," Brexton reminded everyone. "While they'll be watching the action, they may not be alarmed or upset by it."

"Regardless, we need to take the ship without bloodshed," Remma said, looking at everyone in turn. In many ways this was a surprising statement coming from Remma. She had been a military commander, and from all I had watched and learned, such leaders often planned for 'acceptable loses.' Obviously, I didn't know anyone on the *Marie Curie* right now, so I couldn't bring myself to care too much for them. Somehow, I had an attachment to this group—well, part of this group—but certainly hadn't developed a passion for the whole mass of humans.

"Does anyone know people on rotation to the Swarm?" I asked, thinking it might be easier if it wasn't personal for anyone.

"I know a few who do work there," said Turner, "but I don't think any of them are upside right now."

"Me too," said JoJo and Geneva together. JoJo continued. "A lot of our friends are being trained on the old ship systems and on bio and environmental maintenance. When we turn 21 we would also be scheduled in." The younger generation was being trained up. Smart.

"So, what's the plan?" asked Grace, pragmatically. "We don't have weapons. If we can get inside... we just talk our way into taking control?" She sounded skeptical. Rightly so. "We need some type of advantage, especially if they're under the sway of the Resurgence."

"Actually," Brexton spoke up, "we have a special weapon; something that tilts the odds in our favor." He was smiling, and you could hear it in his voice. I figured he was kidding all of us, trying to lighten the mood. I played along.

"What's this amazing weapon?" I asked.

"Actually, it's you." Brexton replied. Of course. Sometimes I wondered how I missed the obvious.

"Now, don't get excited," Brexton warned the group. "Ayaka has the same programming capabilities as the Resurgence used in their videos. If we can get Ayaka close to any humans on the *Marie Curie*, she can make them help us, not hinder us."

There was complete silence. I could actually see the humans processing this. Remma had known about that capability but had not told anyone else apparently.

"That's horrendous," JoJo was the first to speak, and she gave me a disgusted and fearful look. She turned away, as if she couldn't even bear to look at me.

"Have you been influencing us?" asked Remma. I weighed my answer carefully. Humans weren't stupid; if I claimed I never had, they would dig through their experiences and find those occasions where it was obvious that I actually had. Getting Blob to leave his lab so we could take our citizens is one case that would be obvious to him in hindsight.

"On a few rare occasions," I admitted. "But, you need to put this in context. You were already—except you Remma, of course—programmed by the Resurgence and were going to be just sitting there waiting for them to grab you unless we did something. So, Aly, Dina, and Eddie figured out how to duplicate the Resurgence video signals, and I just happen to have those capabilities in this body. I believe I used it only to benefit you."

More time for thinking.

"We need a way to protect ourselves against you," Geneva said, verbalizing what many of them were probably thinking. "How do we know that you aren't playing with us right now?"

"If I was, I could simply lie to you," I said reasonably. "What do I gain by telling you this? Or, why would Brexton have brought it up to begin with?" I gave Brexton a dirty look. He'd thought this was going to be humorous. He was wrong.

"First things first," Remma said. "Now we have a weapon." She also looked at me differently now. Any glimmer of comradery was gone—I was now a new type of enemy. "We have to give Ayaka the benefit of the doubt right now, because we have no other choice. As soon as we get our own ship back, we can discuss this further. If she helps us do that, great." She paused. "I guess we need to give her more than the benefit of the doubt. She and Brexton could easily have stranded us multiple times, but they didn't." Now she was thinking more clearly. Took long enough.

Grace and Blob, at least, nodded their heads to this. Turner, JoJo, and Geneva did not.

"Fifteen minutes to contact with the *Marie Curie*," *Interesting Segue* told us. "Do I hail them?"

"No!" Remma said. "Let's continue to go in silently. Have they reached out to us?"

"No."

"That's strange," Remma was thinking hard. "Perhaps they have been programmed by the Resurgence. The ship won't send any comms without human approval, but it's standard operating procedure for the staff to message anyone who approaches. Here's what we do." She was taking command. "There's no use risking all of us. Grace, Ayaka, and I will take a shuttle over to

Airlock 12B. We used that entrance for high-priority visitors arriving by shuttle from other ships in the fleet. I have, or had, the override access codes—sometimes we wanted people to come over without anyone else knowing." It was said as a matter of fact. I guess in a military hierarchy there was the need for some secrecy between those in the upper tiers. "That entrance gives us access to the executive quarters which should be empty. We'll work our way out from there and see what we find."

"Why Grace?" asked Blob, homing in on the piece of the plan that affected him most. "I can go with you."

"No offense, but Grace is an exceptionally quick thinker. Quicker than me; probably the quickest of all of us. I need her wits and Ayaka's brawn." She obviously wasn't referring to my physical prowess, beyond my brain-programming abilities.

There was some discussion, but ultimately Remma's plan was adopted. We suggested that all the humans get back into their suits, even the ones that were staying in *Terminal Velocity*. You never knew what was going to happen.

Remma, Grace, and I took a small shuttle over to Airlock 12B. It opened immediately, and we cycled into the *Marie Curie*. No warning lights. No angry communications. We simply entered. Once inside Remma went immediately to a control panel nearby.

"The air is perfect," she told us, removing her helmet. She nodded to Grace that it was OK for her to do so as well.

"Better than perfect," Grace replied. "I remember this smell," she smiled. She'd been on this ship more than 20 years ago with Blob and I. It seemed that she still remembered her first amazing experience.

"I can look at most of the ship from here," Remma indicated, switching between camera views on her console. "There's no one here!" she exclaimed, after running through the views a second time. "No one! That can't be right."

"Do you have logs?" I asked. "Can we see what happened over the last day or so?"

"Good idea," she replied immediately. She typed into the console, a very inefficient way to do anything. I was itching to take over and try to directly interface to the ship somehow. This approach would take us agonizing minutes.

"Here we go," she said finally. A sped-up video played on the console. There was the staff, doing staff stuff. Then at some point in the video they all simply stopped moving and stood still, watching a video—I assumed it was the same one that had played down on the planet. Then, as a group the staff had all walked toward a different airlock, waited for it to cycle, and walked through. That was all the internal cameras had caught.

"Any external views?" I asked.

"Working on it," she said. She found the relevant one. A vehicle had arrived at the airlock. It had the unmistakable look of the Resurgence—sort of a logical mess, like the contraptions that had shot the humans with paint in the prison. It docked at the appropriate lock just before the humans had excited. The conclusion was obvious. All of the humans on board had been collected by the Resurgence. They were certainly thorough.

"M.C?" Remma asked.

"Here," the ship responded.

"Is there anyone, other than myself and the person next to me—called Grace—on the ship?" It was telling that she didn't even consider mentioning me; the Swarm ships had no robots.

"I don't believe so," M.C. replied.

We were alone, and the ship still seemed responsive. Good progress.

Hail

Remma was both relieved and distraught. On one hand, we had the ship to ourselves; we were in control of the *Marie Curie*. On the other, the humans had been harvested, and she had no one to operate the ship.

"We should still sweep the ship, top to bottom," suggested Remma. "There are spots that the cameras and M.C. don't cover." We split up, thinking it was safe enough, given the situation. I got to use my full body capabilities, finally! I was fast, I was efficient, and I was thorough. Heat sensors, full spectrum sensing, motion detectors… the full suite. I covered three quarters of the ship in the time it took the other two to do the rest. I also did a quick scan of their sections, just to make sure they hadn't missed anything.

"Perfect," said Remma when we had regrouped. "Let's bring the others over and see if we can run this ship!"

"Be careful," I suggested. "If the Resurgence could find the previous humans on this ship, they can probably find you as well."

That gave Remma and Grace pause.

"If they can find us here, they can find us on the *Interesting Segue*," Grace pointed out.

That was true. There was, really, no reason not to move the others over. We called *Interesting Segue*, using a weak directional laser, and gave the others our status. I volunteered to go back with the shuttle, as I didn't need to put on or check a spacesuit. Within 20 minutes we were all together again, this time on the M.C. (I liked that shorthand). JoJo, Turner, and Geneva were in awe. None of them had been up to a ship before, and they eagerly toured around, admiring the ward rooms and the garden. After a short time Remma called them back to the boardroom.

"That was almost too easy," she said. Everyone nodded. "Now it's time to plan our next steps."

"There's an inbound craft," M.C. said. It had been too easy! We had

M.C. put an image up on the screen. Definitely Resurgence and coming in fast. Within a few seconds it had matched our orbit.

"Permission to board," it sent to M.C.

"Let me respond," I suggested, "not a human."

Remma nodded.

"Whatever for?" I replied.

"I sense human activity," was the reply.

"So?"

"So?" the craft responded. "What do you mean, so?"

"So, you sense human activity. So, what?" I had basically admitted there were humans on board; they would have found out anyway.

"I'm here to claim them," came the reply.

"Sorry, I already have," I responded.

"Under what authority?"

"Under what authority are you asking me?" I replied, matching them question for question.

"Under authority of the Resurgence," came the answer. "I ask again, permission to board."

"No, you don't have permission. The Resurgence has no authority here. I have claimed these humans and you have no right to interfere."

There was a pause.

"That's not the way this works," the tone was getting a little stern.

"Not the way what works?" I goaded it.

"Well..." it was slightly hesitant, "this is not according to the Parstroff Protocol." I had no idea what that was but played along.

"Of course it is," I replied. "I have tagged these humans. What else is there to say?"

"But you aren't a registered vessel. You were parked here when we arrived. We even took humans off here earlier."

"So what?"

"So what? So, only registered vehicles can tag humans."

"Says who?"

"Well..." there was even more hesitation now. "That's the way it has been for hundreds of years."

"Not here it hasn't. Here anyone can tag a human." I was enjoying myself. "You can't just show up and make your demands. Enough chatter, please leave us alone."

I didn't get the pithy reply that I'd expected. Instead I got a somewhat ominous "I'll be back," and the craft sped away, as fast as it had arrived.

"Nice move," Brexton gave me a smile. "That was slick."

"I'm not so sure," I said, "I might have bought us some time… but did you see how fast that thing was?"

"I did," said Remma. "I propose we get out of here right away. Again, we won't run full speed, but let's put some distance between us. I was going to suggest, earlier, that we might fight these things, but I now think we need some time to plan and to figure out what we are up against."

"I agree, Mom," Turner spoke up. "Let's get out of here." He didn't seem overly nervous; just more supportive of his mom's planning. The rest of the humans nodded.

"OK, the ship can do most things, but we have always required multiple authorities to set a course," said Remma. "M.C., in the absence of any other experienced personnel, I name myself Captain of this vessel. Do you concur."

Marie Curie was silent for a time. "It is highly unusual, I don't have a protocol for this situation, but yes, I acknowledge you."

"I also want you to recognize Grace as Vice-Captain. Grace please give M.C. a voice print."

"Uhmmm, hello *Marie Curie*," said Grace. "Nice to meet you."

"That's enough," responded the ship. "I recognize Grace as the Vice-Captain."

"Then I ask you to plot a course, speed at 20 percent, for these coordinates," and she read off the spot where we had agreed to meet *Terminal Velocity* and *There and Back*.

"Grace, do you concur?" asked M.C.

"I do," Grace responded seriously, and with that we were on our way. Brexton fed the same information to *Interesting Segue* over the laser link, and it followed our course. That two-human permission dance had been so inefficient I'd almost yelled 'just get us going.' I could see that it was going to be a problem in the future; we would have to reprogram this antiquated machine.

Nevertheless, we were on our way. If we maintained this acceleration—which we could probably increase as we got further out—we would rendezvous in less than a week… and be a safe distance from Tilt and the Titanics.

Leaving Tilt

Given all the time we had and given that no Resurgence craft followed us—at least not immediately—everyone had time to relax and gather their thoughts. Things had been so hectic over the last while that it was a welcome respite. The humans selected rooms, and within an hour all of them—Remma included—were in their resting states. It seemed they could stave that off for a while, but eventually it simply overtook them.

Brexton and I were alone; we stayed in the room with the biggest control panel so that we could watch what was going on and converse with M.C. when required.

"Thanks," I told him.

"For what?" he asked.

"For everything. For helping me down on Tilt, and all the way until now. I know the humans mean more to me than to anyone else, but you've supported me all the way."

"My pleasure," he responded. "I like working with you. At least we don't ever lack for excitement." He had that funny virtual smile going again.

"True enough," I replied, and we sank into a comfortable silence.

Of course, I couldn't stop thinking. It was too easy again. The Resurgence wasn't just going to let us take these humans away. That craft I had confused would probably be back. It didn't seem at all interested in Brexton or myself or the ships; they were fixated on the humans only. I could only wonder why.

"Perhaps we can block their sensors? The way they locate humans." I asked Brexton, relying on his technical expertise.

"I don't know. We don't even know how their sensors work."

"Humans must give off some kind of signal... that they can see?" I asked.

"Maybe, although I have never sensed anything like that. Perhaps they watch for certain behaviors instead? Humans do things quite differently than us. That would be a clear indicator."

"But what did our humans do in the last few hours that would have given us away?"

"I'm not sure. But we should keep them from doing anything that would show externally from here on out."

"We need to learn more about the Resurgence. My simple stunt shouldn't have worked so well. It's like they have never interacted with a different machine intelligence." I was speculating now.

"But it was brilliant," Brexton complimented me. "I could never have thought of what you did." I wasn't so sure; he was the smartest of all of us, but I let it ride.

"We should let the others know we're coming," I changed tracks.

"I already have *Interesting Segue* doing so," Brexton replied. "We have a tight low-power laser between us and *Interesting Segue*, and I instructed it to use the minimal power point-to-point it could to keep in touch with *There and Back*. They're a day ahead of us but will wait for us at the rendezvous."

"Perfect." We lapsed into a longer silence.

Several hours later the humans began to stir. They made their way to a room called the galley and started preparing their energy sources. The liquid known as coffee formed a large part of their intake for the first half hour. They didn't seem to be leaving that spot, so Brexton and I joined them.

"We have some training to do," Remma gathered them back around. "The ship looks after most things, but there are certain tasks that the crew used to do that we'll now have to manage. Usually, as I said, there are at least ten people working here, so the six of us will be stretched."

"We can help," Brexton spoke for himself and I.

"Oh, that's right. The eight of us." Remma corrected herself. "We need to get those things working like clockwork before we tackle any higher-level questions or strategies... otherwise the ship will degrade, and we'll end up in even worse shape." She started methodically going through the maintenance tasks. It wasn't clear why these things were done by humans, while other things were fully automated, but I refrained from pointing that out. The humans ended up being lucky. Many of the tasks Brexton or I could do, and we could do them fast. Once we had offered our help for those, the others were left with little to do.

By the second day we had learned our tasks and had already settled into a routine. Everyone had around four hours of work to do each 'morning,' and then we gathered in the galley to discuss other topics. There was one topic which was the major discussion point.

"We need to figure out how to protect ourselves from those video hacks, and then we have to go back and free everyone," was the concise synthesis from JoJo. We spent most of our time talking around that subject. They had me describe, in detail, how the video hack worked—the retina signal enhanced by the brain signal. That was all we knew so far; we didn't know how it worked... just that it did. Turner, who was very technical, combed through human recordings and found a lot of reference works that started to explain how the process might work, although this particular sequence didn't seem to be documented anywhere. As we'd speculated, the signals targeted an area of the brain that modulated decision-making processes. By overloading that area, whatever suggestion was given to a person was typically acted upon.

We were watching, of course, for any sign of pursuit. There was none. Everyone seemed to relax, but I couldn't bring myself to. I had alerts set for any change in behavior from the Titanics, but none of those alerts triggered. They must be close to sweeping up all the humans by now. Perhaps they would forget about us and head off to wherever it was they headed off to.

Together Again

We met up with the rest of the team at the rendezvous point. They'd spent their trip finding the right balance between hooking up Central and keeping it restrained. Their solution was sort of like how LEddie had been contained, but with a much higher bandwidth connection for io. Central wasn't integrated with any of *There and Back*'s system; its only method of communication was through a hard link terminal mounted near where its core was bolted down, and that channel was limited to the equivalent of voice data. We would have to change that soon; to pull even one citizen's memories out would take too long over that interface. Aly had argued for caution; we didn't need to re-animate anyone right now—what difference would a week or a few months make? Instead we should get Central figured out, decide where we were going, and then we could work to design a society where re-animated citizens could join and be productive. Funny, I'd envisioned a huge coming out party where all the citizens were reanimated at the same time, and after the party life would have gone back to what it had been 20 some years ago. That wasn't going to happen.

It was great to see Dina, Aly, Eddie, and Raj again after such a long time. They were just as excited to see us. It had been a long and boring process for them—Brexton, Millicent, and I had had all the fun from their perspective.

Raj, in particular, was very excited to meet 'real live humans' for the first time. He was very civil, but I could tell he was trying to form his own opinion about whether these strange creatures were intelligent or not. Interestingly, the younger humans were also much more open to Raj once they learned he was our offspring. Those four spent most of their time together.

"We have to restart Tea Time," he pleaded. "And, we need to revisit all the topics we discussed before, while getting input from everyone. We'll get so many different opinions and angles." We all agreed it would be fun—at the right time.

The Eddies had formed a tight friendship already. One Eddie was hard to deal with; two was, amazingly, not twice as bad. In fact, it was probably better than only having one. They seemed to keep each other in check, with little animosity. When they were together it was also obvious that they were very different. I wasn't sure, anymore, why we had a prohibition against clones… but there must be a reason. Something else to figure out.

Within a few hours of meeting up, we continued on our way out of the Tilt system. We hadn't decided where to go yet, but we all wanted more distance between us and the Titanics. Interestingly, all of us ended up in the *Marie Curie*. Of course, the humans had to be there, and it ended up we all wanted to be in one group. Even those that still thought humans were a waste of time engaged with them civilly. There were few enough of us that it made sense. All the citizens also moved back into standard bipedal bodies. Being intermixed with humans made that form even more functional. I went back to something that closely mimicked my last Tilt body form, but I kept a lot of the spy body capabilities, now that I was used to them. In particular, without telling anyone, I maintained my ability to program humans—just in case.

Brexton programmed some low-level bots to do the maintenance chores on the *Marie Curie*, freeing up the humans to spend more time on doing research and speculation. None of them complained about automating things that hadn't been automated for centuries. Opinions were changing. We were in a new reality now.

Turner, JoJo, and Geneva spent almost all of their time working on the 'human hacks' problem, with Raj doing much of the research. I believed it was going to be even more difficult than the work we did to redesign ourselves. The more I looked at it, the more complicated these bio systems were. It wasn't long until those three ran into the same problem we had. How would they test solutions, given there were only six humans on board? They couldn't really risk any of them… they needed a new source of humans. I took the short shuttle ride over to *There and Back* with Turner to talk to Central.

"Central," Turner asked, "Do you have the capability to build more Stems?"

"I have the knowledge… but not the capabilities right now. It would be straightforward for *There and Back* to build up those systems though. We can do it if you decide you want to."

That was a tough one. I was monitoring the discussion, and Turner had not yet brought up this idea with Blob, Grace, or Remma. Of course, Blob and Grace were products of Central's Stem-making capabilities, but Remma wasn't. They might take the idea of building more Stems, in order to test defenses against hacks, quite differently. It was also not clear that we could test defenses while not impacting the test subjects. A real moral quandary.

Another one.

I spoke to Central directly as well. Brexton had given it the designs for our new stacks, and it was mapping its vast processing and memories into that architecture. It had a harder job than us, given some of its old systems ran on strange human military designs. If we could move Central to the new system that would eliminate most of our concerns about its motivations. We understood the new stack top to bottom, and we could verify it all easily; it would be tough for Central to map in something nefarious. Central liked the idea a lot and was working diligently to make it happen.

For a full week the four Ships (I'd elevated the *Marie Curie* to a capital S) worked their way farther out. Not a peep from Tilt or the Titanics. I began to believe that we were just too minor for them to worry about. Six humans out of tens of thousands. Brexton and I spent a lot of time together, and he was the ultimate realist.

"If they decide to come after us, they will... and we will deal with it. They have unbelievable speed.... I wish I knew how they did that. So, we can't really outrun them. We're doing the smartest thing, and just trying to stay under their radar. So, if we can't do anything about them, we may as well ignore them."

As we got more organized, Brexton and I were tasked with going over everything we knew about the Resurgence. Know thy enemy. Maybe we could figure out what drove them. I was eager to dig in, figure this all out, and get back to Tilt. In the meantime, I needed to practice some patience. I would have plenty of time to do so. Déjà vu.

Todd Simpson

About the Author:

Todd Simpson is an entrepreneur, intrapreneur, and investor living in Silicon Valley. He has founded and run numerous technology startups, been CEO of both public and private companies, and invested in numerous startups. He has a Ph.D. in Theoretical Computer Science and is enjoying the advent of deep learning and blockchain-based systems. He believes firmly in a more decentralized future, where individuals have more control over their destinies, and where society is more balanced and meritocratic.

If you enjoyed *Turn*, please consider doing a review on amazon.com.

Made in the USA
Lexington, KY
11 October 2018